K
E
N

S
I
B
A
N
D
A

THE RETURN TO GIBRALTAR   i

PB

Proteus Books, a Division of Proteus Films.

ALSO BY KEN SIBANDA

BOOKS

If God Was a Poet

The Songs of Soweto: Poems from a Post Apartheid South Africa

SCREENPLAYS

Hannibal the Great
Vindicator
Species Venus
The Triangle

THE RETURN TO GIBRALTAR

KEN
SIBANDA

The Return to Gibraltar

A Novel

Return to Gibraltar is a work of fiction. Names, characters, places, and incidents are the products of the author's imagination or are used fictitiously. Any resemblance to actual events, locales, or persons, living or dead, is entirely coincidental.

.

Proteus Books, A Division of Proteus Films
P.O. Box 32, Creswell, North Carolina

Copyright © 2011 by Estate of Kissinger Nkosinathi Sibanda

All rights reserved

Published in United States by Proteus Books, A division of Proteus Films

Grateful acknowledgement is made to the following for
allowing to reprint previously published material

THE MACMILLIAN COMPANY:
Except from "The Mind of Primitive Man" by Franz Boas,
copyright © 1911 by Franz Boas. Copyright Renewed.
All Rights reserved. Printed with permission of The Macmillan Company.

1. Science – Fiction.   2. Historical–Fiction.   3.Spain Moors – Fiction.
4. Race Relations – Fiction.   5. US Military-Fiction.   I. Title.

PB

Proteus Books, a Division of Proteus Films.

Library of Congress Control Number: 2011920826

ISBN 13: ISBN 9780615438979
ISBN 10: 0-615-43897-0

Printed in the United Stated

Second Edition

Book designed by Charles Lowder
charleslowder@verizon.net

Contact Publisher: publisher@proteusfilm.com

Book title code 8

I hope the discussions outlined in these pages have shown that the data of anthropology teach us a greater tolerance of forms of civilizations different from our own, that we should learn to look on foreign races with greater sympathy and with conviction that, as all races have contributed in the past to cultural progress in one way or anther, so they will be capable of advancing the interest of mankind if we are only willing to give them fair opportunity..

- *Franz Boas*
The Mind of Primitive Man

Special Theory of Relativity:

All the phenomena of nature, all the laws of nature, are the same for all systems that move uniformly relative to one another.

General theory of Relativity:

The Laws of nature are the same for all systems regardless of their state of motion.

- *Dr. Albert Einstein*

Love is the highest form of truth.

Ken Sibanda
New Jersey, 2011

K
E
N

S
I
B
A
N
D
A

For Ethan

Acknowledgement

A book is in many ways a work of art that's never complete. The many people who contributed to its finality is almost immeasurable.

To Charmaine my wife, who played the role of a motivational speaker and whose kitchen doubled up as a study - thank you for the sincere and thoughtful contribution. To Luis F. Diaz, who seemed to always understand the gridlock unfolding in the novel and gave a needed encouragement when motivation was low.

On the technical side, my editor Mary Nagler, the book designer Charles Lowder and the printer, Black Classic Press, who all seemed to derive more joy in this project than I initially expected; and conducted themselves professionally even when dealing with a writer unaware of the publishing side to a book's finality.

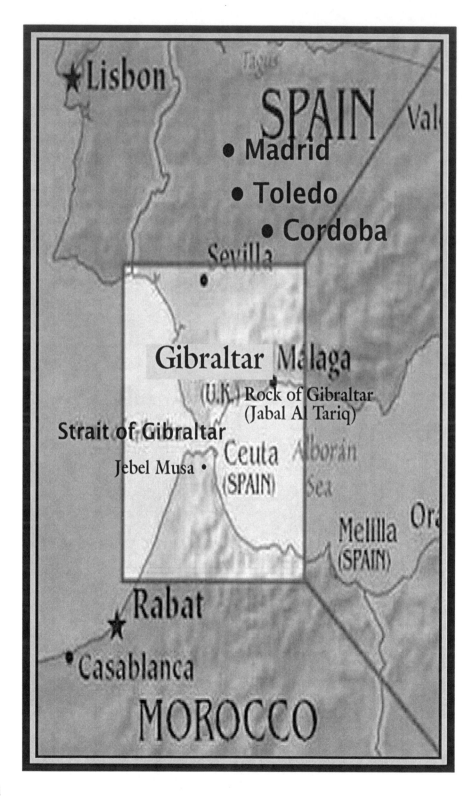

KEN SIBANDA

PROLOGUE
The law is the life.

Sometimes life acts according to outcomes. The thought arose as Horace Bates began to speak. For now he assumed the full caricature of Mustafa Al Mutaseed, the man he was impersonating.

"Your learned magistrate, we submit respectfully that the defendant has not committed treason. And that all this is a big mistake," said Horace.

The magistrate, Thomas Sanchez, sat staring at Horace, unamused by the denial. He had the contempt of a man who has seen it before - the sully, dry eyed look of disengagement.

He interjected, "Mr. Mutaseed, it is my contention that your denial has been noted - please continue." He did not want to offend the counselor-at-law but he did not want to encourage him either.

"The evidence…" at that moment Horace was interrupted by the magistrate knocking his wooden hammer on the top desk.

"Today is just pleading, no evidence please, just plead: guilty or not guilty. You know, in our civil system we have already presumed he is guilty and your client must prove he is innocent?"

"Yes."

"So enter your pleading senore," said the judge.

After contemplating whether he should ask the judge to throw the case out for lack of evidence or merely enter a pleading Horace said, "At this moment sir…your honor… we would like to have the case dismissed."

"Senore, you do know the rules of our Spanish courts don't you? We cannot dismiss a charge merely because you want it dismissed. The defendant must give us evidence of his innocence during trial. This is Spain 1491 and we do not dismiss cases here. That is the English common law system. I am tempted to ask…may I see your practice certificate please?"

Horace stepped forward and handed over the pocket sized book. The rest of the book had dated stamps and official notary. It read:

Mustafa Al Mutaseed

Abogado

Admitted 1491, A.C.E.

Horace handed the judge an impressive forgery. The judge looked at the perfectly torn piece of paper and looked on its back.

"Good," the judge said, "but how come you seem lost senore?"

"Because this man is innocent judge. He did not commit the treason he is being charged with."

"Maybe that's because you think he is innocent," protested the judge.

The judge perused the certificate of practice for a second time, this time slower. "You got this certificate only recently senore, I can tell – that's why you are asking these questions. You are supposed to be a court appointed counselor and not a court appointed mistake senore."

Horace's embarrassment at his lack of legal skills made him hesitant, given the idea that in another world, in real time, he is a Harvard law graduate.

The magistrate continued, "Adjourned until next week Tuesday for evidence. The court notes an innocent entry." The judge looked at Horace from head to toe while shaking his grey mash of hair. "Who is this clown,?" he thought.

The air in court stiffened as everyone stood up to give the magistrate his ceremonial and ritualistic exit. The defendant, Rashid Muhammad, the Moorish general who until recently was the top most commander, stood up wondering who is this court-appointed attorney who now holds the keys to whether he lives or dies. He had never heard of a Moorish abogado named Mustafa Al Mutaseed.

Horace needed fresh air. The court's stifling sophistication made him feel small and victimized. Troy was also in his mind. Was Troy well hidden? Did he leave Troy in a high place?

As the court attendants started to disperse, Horace approached Rashid. The Moors were so called because of their dark skin, a skin color similar to the goat-herders of Sudan, that color associated with the enchanting midnight.

Rashid had not moved since the judge left. So at ease with himself that the mundane surroundings became somewhat majestic. He stood six feet two inches and was dressed in traditional Muslim garb. Red stitched with beautiful colored embroidery, Rashid's overcoat did not betray the courage of a general now captured. He had what is known as grace under fire.

*

Rashid is much the warrior when pressured. His gaze is never fixed on one thing for too long, always moving. This suggests a man who understands that a moving target is the most difficult, thought Horace. He nodded his head at Rashid.

The two men shook hands and still Horace continued thinking, "Got to get back to Troy. What if Troy is compromised? Will I get back?" The smell of Spanish flowers and the sweet aroma of a well cooked banquet wafted in through the windows. "Assallum Allakum," Horace greeted Rashid, in pitch-perfect Arabic.

Patio de los Arrayanes. Jan Zeschky. 2006

BOOK I

K
E
N

S
I
B
A
N
D
A

CHAPTER ONE

Two days ago, and indeed two years ago, Horace had been a man on the up, a Harvard law student. That was before Troy the heavy lift jet, before The Program and before Spain. Under the sun's collegial warmth, and the umbrella of Harvard's intellect, Horace had maintained a daily dose of legal reading. It had been evening - some two years ago when it all began.

Soft, moonlit beams enter the gothic buildings known affectionately as Harvard square. It is here that America's intellect and elite begin to study seriously. While the moonlight does not separate the common man from the Harvard educated, it seems to illuminate the ever present, peculiar Horace Bates: a third year law student at Harvard School of Law. Horace reflected on the evening's measure of beauty with a hint of trepidation, beneath the brow of confidence lay a hesitant and soon to be attorney-at-law.

Ray, as he liked to be called, had been the first in his family to enter law school. He hailed from the small town of Carthage, North Carolina. The kind of place William Faulkner, the famous American scribe, would visit and never leave.

Those first two years of law school had passed by like water going through a morning faucet - starting off cold, but soon becoming room temperature. Horace initially spent his time admiring the pompous architecture The buildings suggested an attainment of a novena, intellectual Buddhism, "Know thy self." In those two years, he had gone from a C+ student to moderately B. As one of a few black students, the college had assumed that he somehow is a representative of African Americans and that his presence liberated the race. Horace reflected on this. In his hand he held the International Law book by Professor Stephen Hicks.

International Law - a subject some legal minds do not believe should be taught - would be one of the elective classes Horace took in the fall of 2008; when third year kicks in. Horace entered the library feeling the weight of the moment. The third year dropout rate was something Horace had to contend with.

"Hey Ray, how was the summer?" Jason Hemmer, the pot-head librarian asked.

"Ray" was short for Horace - the affectionate nickname people had given Horace for always being mellow. In high school his posse of friends coined a song for him: his friends sang for him while Ray did some bebop moves modestly executed.

"That's it Ray," said one girl who was eyeing Horace as a prospective

KEN SIBANDA

boyfriend.

"That's the man, right there," said Dixon, his cousin. All the time the others clapped like a church choir as they shouted:

Ray jammin', never moved by the bammin'…

Ray never puts in a jam

Ray always Ray –

"I was in the Hamptons – seriously," said Horace.

"Did you really go to the Hamptons?" inquired Jason.

"No, only in my dreams buddy boy. Jus' messing Jason; that's what Harvard's for – right? So that we can afford Hamptons one day," said Horace.

"That's the spirit," replied Jason.

Horace continued into the library, all the while present and alert. He wanted to know which other law students made it to third year and had not been kicked out or as it was called, 'ko-d.' Horace took a seat at the rear of the library where the evening sunlight still warmed the place. School had not officially started and so he was ahead of the game; preparing for classes by early reading gave him the taste of accomplishment.

Just then Jonathan came his way. Jonathan was the rumor mill, always updating people on what other people were doing. Horace had forgotten that Jonathan liked this section of the library. He kind of owned it.

"Hey Ray, what's up?"

"I'm good, and you?" said Horace, trying to hide his shock at seeing him. "Really good to see you man."

"Same here son. Hey, did you hear that Tammy was ko-d? Her dad was really mad."

The rumor mill was starting to grind and Horace wanted out ASAP.

"I heard, a shame…," Horace replied, getting up. He put some books in his bag to act like he was already leaving.

Tammy was the university president's daughter who had entered the law school through the back door. They called it "BD." She concentrated more on dating than academics. The agreed narrative on Tammy was that she thought not just some black men wanted her, but all black men wanted her; from Kunta Kinte to Denzel Washington.

"She's the one who BD-d," said Jonathan.

"That's what they say, I gotta' go Jonathan. Nice seeing you." And like that Horace got up. He did not like rumors and tried to minimize his interaction with people who did.

He found a desk and chair about twenty yards away. "I lost him," said Horace to himself, putting his law books on the desk. "This cat has issues." His newest seat was still warm from the afternoon's sun shine. Horace felt like it was a good find.

Horace took a seat at the desk and started reading. He turned his head again to see if he could see Jonathan. Nothing – he turned his head the opposite direction and could see Harvard's emblazoned lawns through the window. "This college is a testament to the affluence of society's best. It stands upright and confident," he thought. "No other college in human history seems to have such a perfunctory feeling, almost a punctuation mark concluding the terms of progress and wealth." It was time to hit the books and Horace took the International Law text book.

International Law invoked a happy thought in Horace's mind of an easy law subject. He was merely taking the subject to improve his GPA. It did not bother him that students regarded International Law a subject for cabbage heads and law philosophers. Horace turned to page 429 and began reading the assigned case. This case was the first case reading for Professor Stephen Hicks, who apparently also wrote the text book he had so gregariously recommended. "This book is a leader in the area," said Professor Hicks at a student "meet" the previous semester.

The case title read: *The Monarchy of Spain v. Rashid Abu Muhammad, 1492 ACE - (Old Law Reports). Horace quickly flipped through the book. The case was only two pages long. He noted treason and violation of state secrets as key issues. "Interesting," thought Horace, as he started reading. Like most law students in their final year, he only read half of the prescribed reading so, two pages was not that bad. Two pages were a good start for third year...*

The Monarchy of Spain case of 1492 revolved around the trial of the Moorish general Rashid Abu Muhammad, a decedent of the Amazigh (free men) or Berber tribe from the sands of Morocco's dusty war-path. Horace had only heard about Morocco in movies. He had never read a case on Morocco or Spain for that matter. He looked over the case and noted the limited use of past cases cited and something else. "This appeared to be a test case," thought Horace.

Horace read through the case header and syllabus to establish what the case is about. He read slowly. It's not the speed of one's reading, but the retention of legal ideas and concepts that separates a brilliant law student from one just winging it. His eyes slowly moved across the words, absorbing the finer print of the case.

"The court having heard all evidence does find that the defendant Rashid Abu Muhammad, a Moor in this Monarchy, guilty of treason. The evidence received by the court from the prosecution and given by defense of Mr. Muhammad, represented by Mustafa Al Mutaseed is that it is more likely than not the crime of treason has been committed."

Horace concluded in passing, "This is such a low threshold for guilt in a treason trial." He continued on to the verdict. At page 430 it read:
And her majesty having addressed the defender directly and applying our beloved civil law, do hereby find the defendant guilty of treason and sentence him to death by gallows.

Attached to the case note was the charging criminal complaint, which read:

<u>In The Civil Code of Spain:</u>

Spanish Monarchy:

The King of Spain
V.
Rashid Abu Muhammad

<u>Complaint Number 1233</u>

December 1, 1491, Kingdom of Grenada, Al Andalusia

Senore Rashid Muhammad, a Moor, you are hereby charged with plotting against the King of Spain, Ferdinand I and Isabella I for the purposes of treason. It is charged that on June 12, 1491, you purchased a musket 0.55 from Javier Mendoza. You conspired with others, still unindicted and solicited the musket for the murder of King Ferdinand I and Isabella I. Further it is proved by charge that the musket was intended for assassination of the King and Queen while both were holding court on December 15th in preparation for Christmas. This was supposed to inspire a de-colonization of Spain and an end to the successful reconquesta by Christianity: And to reassert a Moorish governance on Spain as a government in Madrid. You senore, are charged.

The Magistrate,
Grenada seat,
Signed

Thomas Sanchez

Horace finished reading the case and was mildly surprised. He wondered whether this was manna from the heavens or whether it was providence - so short a case. The other explanation could be that Professor Hicks was playing a trick on the students trying to see how much self motivation the students had. On occasion, professors would create a parallel diversion to the law. In Constitutional Law for example, the professor offered a news article as a case brief. Later on in class, the same professor then drilled the students for not looking up the case. Horace sadly recalled the incident.

"You are all Harvard material, now get this, this is the last time you will hear it. While graduates from other law schools merely see the world as presented on the map, the Harvard graduate sees the nature of the world without a map…you have to dig in class, read and research," said the professor, his heavy frame casting him in a memorable moment. "The law is the life; you are in this to see what limits human freedom and not merely to practice law. If you want to be a practitioner, go to a public interest school." At Harvard we are not practitioners, we are legal minds…without law, life would not be what it is!" That always struck Horace as somewhat accurate if not common sense. Now, is this the same lesson, dig deeper into the case? Minor diversions can be created in order to introduce core legal theory, he concluded. The case read like a set-up, he could smell something beneath the benign surface; it was like removing the lid on a can of bad tomato sauce.

Horace put the puzzle together. This is supposed to be a case for treason against Muhammad. It reads like a case for bad legal administration and a miscarriage of justice. Horace considered the evidence against Rashid Muhammad: a gun and a witness by the name of Javier Mendoza. His mind was stimulated like the two halves of a magnet finally centered into the right direction. His mind started going into over drive…

"Who was Abu Muhammad, who was Javier Mendoza, who were the Moors, who was the magistrate and why was the evidence so minuscule, almost as if to tease the defense or scare them. Perhaps, it was all a political case? These questions entered the back of his mind and his subconscious felt as incoherent as his conscious. There were no answers.

Horace checked his twenty dollar Casio watch and got up to get a cup of coffee at the canteen. His watch read 8:30 P.M.

Harvard had started to have its quintessential symbiotic moon: a shared commune, a safe haven for incubating minds, the feeling everyone is on the same page. So Horace felt safe taking a stroll through the many dark corridors towards the canteen. He called it a canteen but in actuality it was a four star restaurant next to the Kennedy School of Government; this is where foreign leaders and future leaders were hosted. Many leaders of Asia and Africa had dined here…"Black coffee this late reminds me of deep woods North Carolina…" thought Horace, juxtaposing high life with his roots. "Everyone seems to drink coffee more than water in Carthage, North Carolina…" He smiled; "Being away from home gave it value or half its value," Horace concluded. "Instead of home is where the heart is, they should have said home is where the mind is…"

KENSIBANDA

THE RETURN TO GIBRALTAR   23

At the restaurant, the maître d' stepped forward and greeted Horace. "Good evening sir."
This reminded Horace of the respect the name Harvard carries with it.
"Good evening," Horace said.
And then Horace heard a familiar voice calling his name.
"Ray…Ray." The voice beeped. "First day of school and someone is already drinking coffee and hitting them books," she inquired. It was Maria, one of the workers at the restaurant.
"Kinda, how are yah," said Horace, "only making sure that I look the part."
"You are almost done, your parents must be proud of you."
"Very proud, I am hoping to move up from Casio to Breitling when I graduate," said Horace, as he poured in three quarters coffee with some milk and a little splenda. He did not like sugar. "Raw sugar is like an illegal high: the crack of the common man," Horace agreed with himself. When he first started drinking coffee he coined the phrase, 'I like my coffee the same way I like my women: black and thick.' Now two years at Harvard, he could no longer say that and maintain a serious face and so he decided some milk might do the trick. Black coffee rusted his insides and gave him the kind of mild indigestion pointing to intolerance of raw coffee beans.

Months ago, the family doctor, Dr Gamal, had been blunt: "Maybe you should take your women mixed, Mr. Bates. Some milk never hurt anyone."

In the restaurant, Maria Espinoza was impressed with the young man before her. Maria's face was exquisite and betrayed that she was an actress. She had the kind of eyes associated with women from Asiatic countries, deep seated black eyes.
"When you become big time, with the Breitling watch, don't forget us little people," said Maria, her face animated but relaxed.
"I won't forget you, not with this kind of coffee…," said Horace. "For now - I must do these remaining two semesters and at the end of the tunnel there's the Breitling." Everyone in close proximity laughed while others had the discomforted look often associated with people who do not like to see two grown ups flirting.
"Do you want anything with that coffee?" asked Maria, her eyes fixed on Horace. This made Horace feel like the only person in the room. The Man –
"I like Maria." Horace almost said it aloud. An affair with a Harvard staff member would lead to too much gossip; people won't see it for what it is, especially in a place like Harvard. She is cute though.

Horace dashed back to the library and on his way back he ran into the librarian Jason.
"Closing in three Ray," said Jason running for the elevator. He had started closing the library floor-by-floor.
"No problem."

Horace went back to his study area on the second floor. Back to thinking - the case of Rashid Muhammad in Spain 1492. He was getting tired and his eyes started to get heavy. He closed the text book and headed for his apartment three blocks away from the law school. He walked to his apartment.

A big black man walking confidently in the streets of Cambridge, Massachusetts; serious with no hint of tepidness, enjoying the late evening's breeze and the forlorn night. He headed eastwards. As he walked, his mind intermitted the idea of the Spanish court case against Rashid Muhammad, somehow his mind could not switch off from the case. It was hooked.

"In the case, a brother decked out, or did the Spaniards know something that's not in the book?" Horace questioned. He unrolled his Native Tobacco cigarette and inhaled the sweet smell of flu cured tobacco; this took him back to Spain again. It had become a fixation. He soon would understand why.

CHAPTER TWO

Horace arrived at his room close to 10:00 P.M., content that his lodgings' complimented the meager earnings of a third year law student. Already 120 thousand in debt, he felt like he was buying a law degree. His apartment was neither extravagant nor miserly: the correct measure of modernity and affordability. Horace rested for a moment on his green sofa, still taking in the case of the Spanish Moor. Outside, the noise of Boston's traffic belted the window's metallic frame. It all made for an intense climatic episode in which he felt heavy headed. It was the hunger. He hadn't eaten dinner. Through the open window he could see the poor man's Harvard, as it is known - Suffolk School of Law. During the day the copper roof tops of Suffolk shined through in sparkles because of the cheap copper metal used during its construction.

Horace poured a glass of ice water. His fridge, empty and desperate looking, only had quick-fix-college-food; nothing seemed edible let alone qualified as good food. It was like the servings of an explorer navigating his way up Mount Everest. Water, frozen fruit, peanut butter, bread, some Romaine lettuce and humus are littered in the fridge like loose change. Horace drank the water and went back to resume his relaxation. Even though he was hungry, he was too lazy to cook. On his way to the bedroom he had pushed the play button on John Coltrane's Love Supreme. "Now, that's what I'm talking about," thought Horace, stretching his legs and yawning. His 210 pound frame bounced on the bed and he felt the weight from all the studying. Over the past two years, he had gone from 250 pounds to 210 pounds on a 6' 2" frame.

The phone rang and he contemplated answering it. He walked towards the phone and looked at the caller ID. It was Roger. He did not want to talk to Roger, especially this late in the evening. It would ruin his night and usually conversations with Roger went into the early morning hours. He needed the time to prepare for tomorrow's class: the first day of fall semester. Horace silently counted the number of rings before it finally died out. "Dude, it's the day before class – I will get to you tomorrow." Horace shook his head letting the thought go. "Cheap phones, are the most annoying."

The question remained unanswered in the back of his mind: who were these Moors he had been reading about? Horace stretched his hand out and touched the Business Law text book. He opened the book to the case of Ortiz v. Walt Disney 2006, a case known for the business judgment rule. After reading the case for a good thirty minutes he changed clothes for bed. His eyes got heavier and the gnawing hunger was soon overtaken by fatigue. He tucked himself in for the night like a lazy lion in the African jungle.

*

The next day was Monday – the first day of class. Horace started his day with the usual shot of cheap coffee; Not organic - strictly of the .99 cents per pound type. He took in some cereal and that was all. When he arrived at law school he was happy to see that the school was giving free breakfast. "Good, I really need this," he thought, lifting a cream cheese bagel off the table. Free meals meant more pocket change.

From the corner of his eye he saw Roger approaching.

"Hey Ray," said Roger. Upbeat as always.

"Hey Rog," replied Horace.

Roger's full government issued name was Roger Hickman, a lanky kid off the Midwest with a protruding jaw line. "At some point the hormones peaked during adolescence," concluded Horace. Roger's frame resembled a giddy high school quarterback and he descended from a long line of Harvard educated lawyers. Legacy, they called them.

"First day of class. The classes are starting. You feeling good about this year? After this we're done." Roger said.

"I feel like the third year is really a waste of time to be honest, we already have the core for the bar exam. What will International Law and all that other garbage do for ya?" Horace replied.

"That's what a law journal said a while back, after two years we have enough information to take the bar they say," replied Roger. The two friends were starting to draw a crowd with their high voices.

"It's all about the money – the third year money in the final year to pay for tenured professor's vacations," said Horace.

"While you at it don't forget the yacht," interjected Roger.

"And the big Jacuzzi with the play-boy pin-ups -"

"Funny, you got jokes. Look at us, just two minutes and already we giving the economic biography of the place. How was your summer though?" laughed Roger.

"What can I say Carthage, North Carolina is what it is."

Third year law students gathered in the foyer of the law school entrance like a pack of penguins. "It seemed that Harvard was simultaneously giving education in return for anonymity," thought Horace. He held that thought while his facial sneer betrayed a feeling of discomfort by the second. They were all waiting for the magical 8:45 A.M. when classes start. Just then Horace spotted a new student in the third year class. He looked at the new student and turned to Roger.

"Roger look, fresh meat. Seems like we have a virgin in our final year," said Horace.

"Virgin alert!" Roger said. "What are you talking about dude?"

"Look there," said Horace, moving his eyes in a pointed stare.

"Why does someone change to Harvard in the third year, I don't get it," said

Roger, his face serious.

"It's Harvard, get in by the back door. Get in any way possible if you can! The rewards are tenfold." Roger found the observation a bit of a stretch.

"You and your histrionics, maybe he never even tried. Harvard came knocking on his door."

"Do they do that?" Horace asked.

"Sometimes," said Roger, "sometimes."

"Is that right, you learn something new every time you come to campus," said Horace.

"Let me save the analysis for a more appropriate time," said Roger, turning his face at the new student.

The two finished their breakfast at about 8:40 A.M. At 8:45 A.M. the first order of business would be class. Roger's classes for the third year consisted of a varied assortment of the easiest picked classes. He had chosen; Advanced Evidence, Business Law, Business Organization, and Conflict of Laws – all these considered doable and if the grapevine held true, required minimum homework. It was common knowledge that in the third year of law school, most law students considered it a time to sample more exotic beer and a time to seal the deal on a prospective husband.

Now, Roger and Horace arrived at their Business Organization class ready for a seat through – this technically meant hearing what others learned and learning through observation.

At room 56 of the law school, the students sat like an audience awaiting the start of a tragic Italian opera, anticipating the fluctuations and low points, reading, sanitizing the moment, all eyes looking at the blank board. "It was somewhat of an irony," thought Horace, "that the next generation of leaders can be made to sit and stare at a blank chalk board."

The class waited to see what the professor looks and sounds like "is he sexy," – "is she hot," – is usually met with disappointment given that book smarts are seldom reinforced by outward appearances.

Horace let Roger take a seat and he did a three hundred sixty degree turn absorbing the room's parameters. "Impressive," he said, "The class has some of the cutest girls yet."

It was unlike Horace to make a quick decision based on a few facts. The name Horace seemed to imbue him with a balanced outlook on things, even his walk resembled that of an English man cleaning his tobacco pipe while his guests waited impatiently for his return. He had the patience of the panther and the patience of the hunter.

The song that played when he was a kid had made a lasting imprint on his future conduct...

"Ray, Ray always jammin' never bammin'"

But today he was not feeling easy. He wanted to get back to International Law and for this class to end. "Tuesday – tomorrow, is the day we discuss this *King of Spain v. Abu Muhammad* business," he thought to himself, trying not to look ahead at a black chalk board. Horace's third year risked being the year of obsession with just one case. He had read of men who obsess about one thing until they are certified mentally incompetent. Perhaps this is what happened to Jim Morrison, also known as the "Naked Lizard." At every concert Morrison would wait patiently to show himself to the world. Such an obsession is usually dangerous. Man is more than one thing viewed from different angles.

Horace had still not sat down and he made a mental note to read more about the "Moors." Maybe there was a clue in their history that could unlock his obsession. Or it could have been empathy: one black person identifying with another black person. In high school Horace had read very little on black history. The only thing he really could converse about was Dr. King, and that was mainly on the, I Have a Dream speech. He felt embarrassed that a Harvard educated black man knew nothing about black history and that probably the white students knew a sizeable amount more than he did on Africa in general.

In high school Horace's curriculum primarily consisted of European history; it begun with Christopher Columbus and went right up to George Washington: it then concluded abruptly with the civil war. These three subjects in American history provided a seminal afterword. Nothing was mentioned about the Native Americans and the Africans who disappeared from history pages to make way for 'Manifest destiny,' which Horace nicknamed, "Manifesto destiny."

Nothing was ever said about the response to manifesto destiny - the anti-colonial struggles around the world, and definitely not the Moors. Horace found this to be crippling. It cemented in his mind a burning impassioned fire to educate himself in the affairs of the colored man for the past seven centuries. "Only the high points" he rethought the previous statement, "I don't have the time for Africa's blood wrenched past, jus' high points."
Students in the classroom were starting to stare at Horace who finally took his seat. Unbeknownst to him, his interest in the history of Moors was beginning to open a Pandora's Box and his own set of (manifesto) manifest destiny.

*

Horace scanned the classroom for a final time trying to see just who might be holding…"One or two," he concluded, "But nothing was really happening…"

And like that Horace decided he did not want to do Business Organization and would select a different elective. "Anything but this," he thought.

Horace left the room, and Roger was surprised. Horace accidentally ran into the Business Organization professor; Professor Rolf Smith. "Mr. Bates, will you be joining us?" asked the professor.
"Oh, good morning professor – no – I need a different elective to even out my curriculum."
"Be patient. Just edit this class for today," said Professor Smith.
"Okay," said Horace, not wanting to sound testy.

Before sitting, Horace scanned the girls, this time he had a better view and because of this he managed to spy some interesting "stuff." This time Horace spotted a few white girls, a couple of black girls and one or two Asian girls....EUREKA, this is the right class after all. How did the professor know, thought Horace - smiling.

Horace did not care much about the skin color of a girl: he judged women by the content of character ---- or so he imagined. It did not matter that the girl is white, black or Asian, "As long as she is holding..." Harvard had failed dismally to knockout this part of his heritage; he was descendent from a long line of illustrious ass lovers. His dad, his dad's dad: all the Bates men - united in the love of ass. And they all considered appreciation of the derriere a bit of an art-form; the way the Chinese would consider Kung Fu, or the Native Indians - hunting of the bison.

And because of this overbearing love for the ass or big behind - as it is known in the suburbs – he remained in the Business Organization class. "In the future," thought Horace, "I will make sure I go for the business courses, this is where one finds attractive women." Horace pretended he had not seen what he just saw and finally sat down, ready for the class to begin.
Roger raised his hands surprised, and whispered "What are you doing?"

*

The class was over at noon. Horace, without saying a word to anyone, headed for the Harvard college library. For his research into Moorish history, he decided to go to Widener at Harvard yard; certain that he would find something there in the colossus collection.

Horace knew what he needed and how he would get the information. His approach was to look for unpublished material like dissertations that offer fresh insight to their subjects. "The greatest mistake in research," pondered Horace, "is use of secondary material as the source of information. Usually unpublished material holds the keys to new understanding."

He entered a keyword search under, 'MOORS.' And that returned over a thousand entries. "Not quite what I was looking for," Horace said.

Just then he turned away and his eye caught the dark silhouette figure of the new student, starring at him. Twice today his eyes had locked with the new comer – first at the foyer and now at the library. Horace turned away. He did not want to come across like a paranoid character in some horror sketch whose impressions are strange enough because of ongoing exhaustion and stress. "Such exhaustion makes you imagine things," thought Horace, "and then it becomes like a dream within a dream."

"Who is this new student?" Horace wondered. He shifted the search engine, thereby making it only search between 1350 and 1450 Spain. He tried the search button again and this time the result was a little bit more encouraging, "Like the first rains preceding a drought" he agreed with himself.

Horace carefully wrote down the names of two historians, a James McQueen and a Susan Thatcher. "All high sounding names," he concluded, jotting the names hurriedly on a legal pad. The two researchers had received PhD's in Spanish History from Harvard in the '60s.

He meticulously searched for names. Determined that the only thing he would consider would be anything with Moors in the title, nothing about the history of the inquisition and the history of Spain in general. Horace wanted the meat and bones of the matter --- who were the Moors; who was Abu Muhammad, how did he get there and what happened to him after the guilty verdict? His search would be for an informed study on the Moors, not a diversion confounded in history, and definitely not intrigue. Two years at Harvard, Horace found himself liking research; the way a writer enjoys the feel of pen's ink mating with good quality paper. "Art comes in different colors to us humans Ray," said Horace Bates Sr., making the then five-year-old Ray's favorite cream-of-wheat. "When ever your heart finds beauty then art can happen!" His father's words slipped across his mind as he opened James McQueen's dissertation aptly entitled, *The Moors of Spain: Power in Andalusia*.

Horace knew to avoid dissertations with high-flying titles like - *The Sexual History of Africans in Spain at the turn of the 15th Century; The Sexual Appetite of Post Menopausal Moorish Women in the 15th Century and The Black Male in Spain in the 15th Century* - all of which seemed rather gratuitous and shallow.

It took Horace about two hours to read both dissertations. By the time he finished, it was close to dinner time. Horace then left Widner library in the direction of his apartment. He mentally regurgitated his new found intelligence about *Abu Muhammad and Spain* during the walk home. "The Moors were black Muslims who inhabited Spain from 711 - their conquest - until 1492, January 2 - their defeat. Under Moorish rule their empire was termed affectingly Andalusia. In stock the Moors were comprised of members of the Berber tribe in Morocco, black Africans mainly from Senegal and Arabs."

The term Andalusia derived from Vanda-lusia, the land of the Vandals, an East Germanic tribe that invaded the Roman Empire in the 5th Century. The vandals are known primarily for sacking Rome in 455. Now he felt like he could argue Spain v. Muhammad confidently. "The basis of law practice is to be informed of the history of the problem, say nothing about it and argue the mitigating facts. One cannot argue facts if they do not know where those facts originated from," concluded Horace.

Now, Horace could argue the case with his eyes closed. The die had been cast and he was ready. Exiting the building he saw the new student and again the two exchanged familiar looks. "Am I being stalked," thought Horace, "I have to tell this kid to stop, who ever he is." It was not the way the strange student looked at Horace but the timing of it. Every time he locked eyes with the student it was as if he had met him before and yet the two had never met. The new student had an airy-headed look about him, the look of a lone nut casing its target. He gave off the discomforting body language of an unknown suitor from the fringes of a village. Horace felt like a cowboy watched from a distance in the bushes by an unknown posse. He was unimpressed and irritated...

Horace turned away from the new student and took out his cell phone. He looked up again and the student was going through the exit library magnets. From a distance he saw the guy turn around and look at him again...

Horace felt the hair on his arms standing and the room seemed to get smaller. "Maybe I am imagining things, the kid is new in town," he decided. This diffused the moment. It was Roger calling on the cell phone.

"Roger, do you want to meet up…it's Ray."

"Hey Ray, where have you been, we were looking for you," said Roger.

"…doing research on the Muhammad case, I told you about."

"Is that the Moor?" Roger asked.

"No, the general who happens to be Moor!"

"Okay."

"Seriously that's the truth," said Horace.

"Okay, I get it Jessie Jackson. He is a general who happens to be also black. Don't pout; black is incidental. White people ride a thin line I tell you. We can't say things that black people get paid to sing about?"

"Se amigo," said Horace, "comprehende." Horace did not want to start debating the pros and cons of black and white interaction; he was too tired for that.

"What else is going on. I heard that Maria at the restaurant was asking a lot of questions about you --- deep background shit. Does he have a woman; what kind of women does he like; the whole nine yards. Mr. Frankie Hot Pants," laughed Roger.

"I am not really interested Rog," said Horace. He left the library and was on the Boston metro bus. "I have a lot on my plate."

There was some thinking on the other side and Roger said:

"What ever happened to that job offer from the law firm last semester - Ray, what's it called – *Zimmermann and Brightman and Associates?*"

Roger had just reminded Horace of the strange job offer he had received last semester in the mail from a law firm he never even applied to. A downtown law firm in Boston's legal district. For a moment he was ashamed of forgetting that and said: "Roger I will call you back later, gotta bogey down oon." The friendship between Roger and Ray almost seemed seamless. Listening to the two one could not guess that Roger was a white suburban kid with a thousand disc collection of rap music who only dated black women.

He got on the bus. Thoughts about the Moors, and the job offer all seemed to collide into a potent confusion: water and oil. There was a likelihood that two distant worlds were slowly coming into contact.

CHAPTER THREE

The next day Horace woke up on the wrong side of the bed. The previous night had been warmer than usual and now dry sweat was caked on his forehead, giving him a prematurely aging face for a 24-year-old.

Horace noticed the sweet smell of bacon from the neighbor's kitchen. "When was the last time I had breakfast?" thought Horace. "Last week, but seems longer." Horace found the absence of food key to his balancing act.

His calendar read – 8:45 A.M., International Law. "Good, I can't wait to show off what I read about our dear friends the Moors. This is a political case."

*

The International Law class was composed of the most articulate and far reaching law students possible. The most ambitious, those who would one day become the next Supreme Court judges, Assistant US Attorneys and ambassadors. Horace recalled what Kennedy had said in his campaign speech of 1960, 'We want ambassadors who can speak the language....' That always struck him as simplistic but true, what purpose does it serve for an ambassador to merely know English and be trapped in some Pacific village.

In the classroom, Roger was present, as well as the new comer. Again Horace locked eyes with the new student, sending chills down his spine. A measure of discomfort nestled a gnawing feeling in his stomach.

"I have to introduce myself to this cat." He got up and approached the new student. There was a static feeling in the air.

"Hi, I'm Horace --- people call me Ray," he said making sure that his voice was confident. Perhaps a habit of the endangered Alpha male...

"I am Abdullah Salem," replied the newcomer. His voice accented to a pitch suggesting English as a second language, with the hint of the Arabic as primary.

"So you transferred..."

"Yes," said Abdullah, his eyes darted out in each response. Almost robotic -

"From where?" Horace asked in an inquisitorial manner.

"Seton Hall in New Jersey," said Abdullah. A slight smile did not betray the realization that this would be quite an accomplishment for many ---- from Seton Hall to Harvard. From Seton Hall law school to Harvard is like going to the moon from New Jersey, essentially you have arrived, observed Horace. "What is your opinion about professor Stephen Hicks, our International Law guru here?" Horace asked.

Then came the didactic answer. Abdullah said:

"From what I know and have read about him, he is a brilliant man. He wrote an article in Foreign Policy Magazine on the need for one International Criminal Code. He argued well actually. It talked about a common human ethics and accountability."

It all sounded like bullshit to Horace. He said, "Pretty impressive, you have been at Harvard for a week and you already have specs on Hicks. I got to tell Roger about this."

"Who is Roger?" Abdullah asked.

"I am getting a little ahead of myself but I will introduce you to Roger during recess." Horace then extended his arm and it went a little bit too far to the left.

"By the way, are you Muslim?" asked Horace.

'Yes, originally from Egypt," came the reply.

"I have always wanted to visit Egypt," snapped Horace, his face lit up.

"It's a beautiful country, we call it Kermit..."

"Interesting, I never knew that Kermit is the original name, what do you know? Welcome to America Abdullah."

Horace did not say a word about how strange he always found it that people migrating to the United States were leaving behind these 'beautiful countries.' He let sleeping dogs rest. Maybe another day...

The welcome to Harvard – had a condescending ring similar to when a person wishes another person good luck when good luck is unnecessary. The mood between the two suddenly became confrontational.

"I am an American, naturalized – and have been for the past five years."

"Hmmh," said Horace, the words caught him off guard. "I apologize; one should never judge others by outward appearances." Horace did not like being cowed by this newcomer, why was he being so feely touchy like that...

At that moment Professor Hicks walked in. His well-fed body, pot-belly dangling, thumped right through the middle door.

"Quiet. Unless you are 3L, International Law, now is as good a time as any to leave," said Professor Hicks, walking like a Roman general inspecting prisoners at a coliseum. Left, right, left, right...the impeding march of the constantly present soldier. Naturally this interrupted Abdullah and Horace who each took their respective seats. Both men had failed to make a good impression on the other. Horace spotted Abdullah making an entry in a note book. This was somewhat awkward...

Professor Hicks took the auditorium and said, "The Moorish case as it is known - who can give us the facts, anyone?" Once at the pulpit Professor Hicks appeared to grow in statute, magnified by the position he held as an official teacher at Harvard. When the question finally registered several hands went up and Horace was one of them. Professor Hicks looked at his seating chart, he raised his head – this resembled a hippopotamus rising behind a river raft. "Okay, let's see here...Horace Arthur Bates please."

Horace shot up and looked ahead. "The case of the Monarch of Spain v. Muhammad is seminal in the study of international law," said Horace, his confidence made him appear more articulate, "In 1492."

Professor Hicks interrupted, "Please no historic commentary just the facts and the holding Mr. Bates. Essentially what is the holding between Spain and Muhammad? I want facts Mr. Bates. Save the commentary for country club conversations which by the way, are better told while wearing an expensive watch, like a Rolex submariner." The students burst out in a collective gut.

This made Horace contemplate whether the students were laughing at what the professor had just said or whether they were laughing at him. It was impossible to conclude, especially when you are standing at the chopping block...

And what a chopping block, conceded Horace, here at Harvard, you are heated then hammered into shape until you assume a suitable chaste. Professor Hicks was an indulgent blacksmith.

The class finished laughing in varied spasms with the last concluding in a sort of overreached guff. A deep silence then permeated the class and you could hear a pin drop. Horace had lost track of his train of thought. He struggled to regain his composure.

Slowly he said, "the facts of the case, are that a Berber, also known as a Moor named Rashid Muhammad," – Horace dared say Rashid Muhammad was a general of the Moorish army – he continued, "Purchased a musket from Javier Mendoza in Toledo, on June 1491. The dealer reports that during the purchase the Moor, Abu Muhammad made a slip of the tongue and said, 'The gun is being purchased to finish off King Ferdinand and Isabella, those two children.' And based on this evidence Muhammad is tried for treason and found guilty of conspiracy to commit high treason. Ultimately this leads to the defeat of the Moors on January 2nd, 1492 and clears the path for Christopher Columbus."

Again Professor Hicks shot in, this time less abrasive than before. "So based on hearsay evidence a man is sentenced to the gallows, Mr. Bates! This is solely the testimony given by Javier Mendoza in the court, the owner of the gun store in Toledo. I ask you now Mr. Bates – why do you think we should begin the study of international law with this case, in other words, why is this case so important?"

Horace was ready for that question and said, "I think the case is important because it tells us that treason only required one witness in the international system, however our constitution; *Article 3, section 3*, now says clearly that treason should be proven by a minimum of two witnesses." Horace paused feeling he nailed it.

"You are so wrong, Mr. Bates," said Professor Hicks, there was a mutinous uproar of hissing because the class felt Horace had done a good job. "Does anyone know why this case is important?" No hand was raised and the writing on the wall could be read a mile away – we don't know why.

"The case is important, and do write this nonsense down," said Professor Hicks in chevalier style, he always referred to important exam notes as nonsense. He continued saying, "The case established the need for a. personal jurisdiction b. domestic security c. custom ---- thank you Mr. Bates, everyone

Mr. Bates did a good job, it's hard to see how we as an international system have inherited certain customs from domestic practices."

The class's attention was now firmly in place and Professor Hicks had succeeded in laying the cornerstone for a challenging and engaging International Law class for the semester.

"Mr. Bates alluded rather loosely, that our Constitution, and that International law is not a single document. It is the accumulation of historic customs transplanted from the constitutions of many countries and then projected as international expectation at the United Nations for example. Unless we can find a custom or a practice in a historic nationality, like 1492 Spain, we do not have the basis for international customary law. In other words what the English did in their country, what the Germans did and what the South Africans did - you have seen the classical case of what the Spanish did, creates a legal basis for a joint law," said Professor Hicks thumping his potentate frame in animation. On occasion he raised his hands like the ring leader of a medium sized gang. The class took down the 'nonsense' as the information seemed to roll off the Professor's lips effortlessly. The information then diffused from the mouth of Hicks and to the ears of the students creating a sort of story teller's suspense.

For the rest of the class Mr. Hicks proceeded to give an informative lecture based on the above premise ad expanding from the mere two pages of Spain v. Muhammad, to a full two hours.

After class Horace snuck out unseen and headed towards the campus restaurant for a coffee. Maria Espinoza met him at the door.

"Hey Ray," said Maria, careful not to appear too happy or else she would betray her deepest desires. After all, she was five years older than Horace.

"Hanging in there and you?" asked Horace.

He went up to the counter and ordered a cup of coffee.

He took the coffee and his hands tightly lifted the cup from the counter. Beneath the cup a piece of paper remained- a wet piece of paper. He almost threw the paper into the trash can but something told him he should look at the writing on it.

It read: Maria - 213-435-9887.

Horace's eyes looked at Maria and it seemed like a primal bond had begun, like two Celtics dancing, only time could tell where their dance would take them; the dance of two would-be-lovers.

CHAPTER FOUR

Wasted –

That's how Horace felt coming out of it... The hangover hung over his head giving him insomnia. It was only the first week of law school but he felt wasted. The night before, he had stopped at the Irish pub on Wendell Street and asked for a pint; Guinness Stout. And then another pint... When finally the pints reached five he felt light headed.

Within the first week Horace was starting to fall for the first girl willing to part with her number voluntarily; he was being stalked by Abdullah and already he was somewhat behind in his homework. Horace owed Professor Hicks 50 pages in International Law and Professor Smith, another 25 pages in Business Organization.

Wasted in the first week was just how his head seemed to evaluate the whole affair. Maria Espinoza, on the other hand lying nakedly next to him on that cheap college mattress had a certain glow on her face. She left that Wednesday morning early before Horace woke up. In what appeared to be left handed writing, she left a note that read:

Ray
See you at school,
- M

The note suggestive of Maria's happiness came as a surprise to Horace. He wanted this to be a one night stand, and not a union. "Forever, until ever" he thought, "Is not in the works right now." Horace did not want to pay the note a passing look. Many students at the last league of Harvard had flunked out in third year. One thing for sure he thought, I need to slow down. Horace recalled his mother in their sully home in Carthage, North Carolina...

"Don't bring me no women who can't cook – you hear me," said Pauline Bates, as she made her son an afternoon snack, what is termed in the south – loosely as – 'something.' Mrs. Bates in front of a stove was almost animated to the point of resembling a picture from the Renaissance era. Uncorrected by censorship, the light rays entered her kitchen window and then dimmed through the back door. In the light her bright colored dress seemed electrified. Mrs. Bates stirred the grits, adding an exact amount of butter making sure it was flush and not lumpy. Southerners don't like lumpy grits...

"Don't do it," says Mrs. Bates, still beating the grits with a whisk. "I might be old, but age does bring with it its share of wisdom."

The thought of his mom and the grits and Maria's note gave for an untimely predicament. Later that day, Horace stopped and obliged Maria's request. It was brief, but as new lovers often indulge themselves, it's not quantity that matters but quality... Horace agreed with himself. He left hurriedly and headed for the law library.

On Wednesday, towards the middle of the afternoon, Horace ran into Abdullah, the mysterious Egyptian, whom Horace was certain also doubled up as a stalker in his spare time. Abdullah approached Horace with a smile on his face, a smile that appears on the genial looks of newly migrated Africans. Something that Americans lost during the American Revolution, a quest for life with abundance, thought Horace.

"Good to see you Ray."

"Good to see you too, sir."

"See you in class."

"Yes, see you in class."

The conversation progressed unassuming and plain.

"So how is everything?' asked Abduallah.

"Every thing is pretty good and how is everything on your end."

"Everything is good."

"And since everything is good for both of us, see you later," said Horace.

Horace was having fun with the idea that Abdullah did not seem to understand American culture in general. "We don't say get lost here," he thought as he walked away, "instead we say, good luck and smell ya' later. And if you are dumb enough to think the good luck actually wishes you well then sorry my dear friend. It's a polite way of saying you need it, sonnofagun."

"Good luck Abdullah," said Horace.

"Thank you Ray, you're so kind."

From the corner of his eye, Horace saw Abdullah putting an entry into his note book. "Gotta be kidding me with this cat man," Horace said to himself.

The memory of last night was something Horace had not yet attended to. Last night with Maria in his arms seemed like nothing in the world mattered. In the middle of the night he had opened his eyes and looked at her in admiration.

Maria Espinoza had the quintessential Latin look one finds on Telemundo – the Spanish television station. The right kind of beauty mixed in to give one a sort of Cuban flare within a Spanish flame- effortlessly poetic. A descendent of Venezuelan immigrants, she was two generations American and wanted desperately to be an actress. From what he gathered last night, Maria worked in the restaurant while also auditioning and taking acting classes. On days when she was not at the restaurant, which were few, she imitated life on plays such as Lopez de Vega's, *Dog in the Manger*, and William Congreve's, *The Way of the World*.

"What are you looking at," Maria had said.

"At you," said Horace.

"Do you regret?" asked Maria.

"Not really," said Horace, his voice sounding regretful.

The air in the room loosened like the buckles on the boots of a swashbuckling lieutenant in the high seas; lies seldom sound correct, thought Maria, letting it go.

In class, a seminar on the foundations of Constitutional Law, Horace continued thinking about his beloved Maria. He had started something that he could not finish. He listened to the dull and uninspiring lecture.

Professor Jackson said: "The foundations of the constitution were not really law but the accumulation of history or the garbage that did not belong in other law subjects. The garbage is then recycled back to us as constitutional law."

To which Horace opined, "Why in the heavens, does every goddamn law professor seem to speak in such riddles," he continued to listen, his attention divided between the cerebral lecture and the warmth of last night's evening with Maria.

Later that afternoon, Horace met Roger at the fountain stand next to the law library, the usual meeting spot for students who still considered tobacco useful in unlocking legal studies. "I tried calling you," said Roger, immediately upon seeing Horace, "what was up with you? The whole night..."

"I was busy."

"Busy doing what Ray? It's just the first week. Only if Maria accidentally made it to your room." Roger's voice had a bite of sarcasm, he was playing half deck, and already the rumors of Horace and Maria were starting to make the rounds and Roger wanting to make sure he had an inside scoop.

"Now where would you hear such a dumbass thing like that, plus you know how I take my coffee?"

"Black and thick..." said Roger.

"So amigo."

Roger took the reply for – yes I am seeing Maria, but I am hiding it.

"You don't have to worry about me sharing your little secret with the world, Maria is fine dude," said Roger, energetic like a rapper on M.T.V.

"Rog, let it go. Me and Maria are not going."

Roger took that as yes but I will kill you if you tell anyone. He winked – gotcha'.

"No problem amigo. Listen, a couple of us are going to this new pub, The Honeymooners off your place. It's actually on Wendell Street. You wanna' come? The Sox won. It's at 6:30 P.M."

"Count me in Rog," said Horace parting ways with Roger. He headed for the library.

On his way there, he could not help but concede that law students spend a lot of time in the library, on average six yours a day. Horace read for three hours and then at 5 P.M., he took a break. His cell phone, whose ringer was set on vibrate, indicated a missed call from Maria.

Horace left the library on his way to the campus restaurant. He saw Jason, the librarian who high fived him. This reminded him that he better be

KENSIBANDA

careful not to mess this up and forget where his bread is buttered --- he had to get that piece of paper, the law degree. On the other hand Maria was a catch. No one could deny this...

At the cafeteria the maître d was setting up some menus on the front tables.

"Hi, is Maria here?" asked Horace, I have a book she wanted." The maître d had that look of a seasoned manager who has learned to read people by merely asking the right set of questions.

"She actually left for the day and you are?"

"Horace Bates."

"That sounds like the name of a great man."

"I was named after my dad, who was named after the poet Quintus Horatius Flaccus."

"Oh, how nice, the Roman poet from Augustan Rome, very impressive Mr. Horace, and so one day you will seize the day, won't you? Carpe Diem."

Horace did not know what the maître d was talking about, but he found that certain people aged above fifty seemed to talk in gibberish after learning that his name was Horace.

Months later Horace would realize that, Carpe Diem - "Seize the day" in Latin, is one of Horatius' most famous poems, but for now he was blind like a staggering drunk on New Year's night.

*

Horace entered the pub and he could not help himself because the place seemed to demand an immediate write-up...

Honeymooners: the new pub was one of those places Steinbeck would have termed as a reflection of a frozen America. Its walls plastered with bras, a size too large, and its doors with signs like, 'Uncle Sam Wants You.' The Stars and Stripes hung predominately everywhere, and on the walls were proud soldiers at Iwo Jima. The main part of the bar had a scent that digs into ones lungs like peach cobbler at your granny's table. As soon as Horace spotted the bar he proceeded to the table adjacent to the painting of Hemmingway holding a shark off the port of some Spanish adventure. It is what the French term – *le petite life* – the small life, to engage a shark like this, thought Horace. However, the painting provided both the curtains and the drapes for the gentlemen seated behind it. Horace moved his head sideways and saw the first law student – Abdullah. The others were Roger, The Greek and Tommy. The posse had started with their beers and Roger offered to buy Horace a drink.

"Call it Ray."

"The usual Guinness..."

The Guinness came delivered by the waitress who seemed to enjoy the attention of the pub's half drunk married men, strutting proudly like some high strung geese in heat. It did not hurt that she had, as it is known in Boston: 'The goods.' For the others, their beers were Pilsner for Roger, Blue Moon for the Greek, and iced tea for Abdullah. Horace found the idea of a Muslim drinking iced tea in a pub in Boston commendable.

There was something about Abdullah that still bothered Horace, whether it was the confidence of his gaze or the idea that a Muslim could even go to a pub, all seemed not to add up. "Horace needs to stop with psychoanalysis. He is not qualified," he agreed with himself, adjusting a three legged-stool.

Horace sat directly facing Abdullah. He ordered another Guinness, and then changed his mind as the waitress returned. "Hold off on that," said Horace, with the usual high flung sincerity, enough to get a mortgage approved with no additional spot check. Horace had 'that' about him; that slow moving effect of General Stonewall Jackson on the Romney Expedition. The others could feel this - even Abdullah.

As the waitress was heading back Horace said to her, "You look new. Are you new here?"

"Yes, first week," said the waitress.

"This is also our first week of school at Harvard law," Horace said, making sure that HARVARD LAW carried in the pub.

"Is there something else I can help you with?" She asked, somewhat unimpressed. The word Harvard had failed in its humble insistence...

As the waitress left Horace she said to herself, "Not another one of those Harvard types: the type that seems unable to take no from women." The previous week she had been stalked by several Harvard boys who all insisted they were the next great thing since the invention of white bread. And all of them tried to play it down saying, 'It's nothing really.'

Horace remained mesmerized by the girl. "Someone is in some sort of daze, Horace, Ray..." said Roger, trying to snap Horace out of what was starting to be an uncomfortable stare.

"Horace, you cool dude," said Tommy, the tubby looking straight "A" student. Tommy played peacemaker to the process, a sort of low-level United Nations.

"The girl definitely is not a believer," said Tommy, the irony sieved through the beer. The whole group burst out laughing. What was real in the bar was the effect the annunciation, 'Harvard' had on the attendees. Since 1636 that prodigious name carried with it the liquid that holds things together, observed Horace.

The conversation between the four students focused mainly on girls and booze. Occasionally, Abdullah interrupted to remind the gentlemen that the conversation was becoming crude.

"Ice cubes on..." said Roger, at which Abdullah interrupted.

"No, no gentleman..."

"See the new dean Ms..." said Tommy.

"No gentlemen that's..." said Abdullah waving his arms in the air like a referee in a boxing ring.

All in all, Horace felt like the night was a good one and one which Sinatra would have been proud. Moments later the foursome departed in separate directions. An explosive fissure of shrapnel seemed to be the after taste of the evening and Horace started towards his apartment on Wendell Street. The Greek, the richest of the students, headed to a more affluent neighborhood

K
E
N
S
I
B
A
N
D
A

while the rest seemed to return to quarters the kind where you have to lock every door six times over.

The only thing on Horace's mind was Maria. As Horace got around to the steps of his apartment, Maria was waiting for him, her silhouette shadow under the burning evening lights seem to raise the stakes. She has definitely chosen the right profession, concluded Horace.

Maria wore a J. Crew trench coat and under it, a red garter belt. The only thing missing was a director to yell, "Roll camera, speed, and action."

CHAPTER FIVE

Horace respected Africans. "Flamingoes, that can't fly…" From the last he heard from Abdullah, Egypt's real name is Kermit, thought Horace, but I need to independently verify that; and what would be the real name of America he poked? Always the provocateur…

He said his parting words to Maria and was heading for class, continuing with what always made him feel like a muckraking law student; the search for the truth behind law education.

He saw Abdullah as he entered the International Law class, and tried to avoid him but was unlucky.

"Yesterday was a fun day," said Abdullah trying to sound like a suburban American kid.

"Yes Abdullah very much so," said Horace, raising his eye brows like an English choir instructor. "Abdullah just what kind of Islam are you practicing, you go to pubs now?"

"Sometimes we are not perfect," – came the over baked answer.

"I can imagine," said Horace, "maybe if the whole world had more accommodating Muslims like you this cold war would not be happening?"

"I agree," said Abdullah, "but remember, cold war has its moments of thaw."

"… and that I will," said Horace.

Abdullah continued, now he seemed to be livened and eager to have a soap box moment. He said, "A bar is jus' a bar, its not political, the issue dividing us is politics and not religion, and as you, of all people know Ray, politics belongs to the winner," piped Abdullah, with enough Americanisms to break any presidential china. Abdullah tended to communicate in the manner in which non-Americans seem to first learn American English: heavy on the sitcoms.

"I hear that," said Horace, playing the role of the ignorant American in Burma, "and so, would you say that Islam is the natural dissent to Christian ideology?"

Horace asked, testing the muddy waters of Abdullah's reasoning.

"All I am saying is that Christianity and Islam disagree mostly on political policy --- excuse me, foreign policy and how foreign policy is to be implemented"

To Horace, the words sounded tightly wound and prepared.

"Interesting," said Horace, trying to change the subject. Horace knew that Africans in general, this includes Egyptians and Algerians, have an acquired taste for higher learning. It is said in Nigeria one can throw a rock and hit any assortment of high-end professionals: a nuclear physicist; an obstetrician; a chemical engineer or a law professor.

"How has your first week been?" asked Horace.

"So far so good," said Abdullah. "Do you have time to meet someone and have lunch tomorrow? You know you are African American and I am African ----very close."

Is he suggesting that Africans and African Americans are brothers, Horace contemplated asking, but instead said, "But we really are not culturally the same, you know."

"No really, we are brothers," insisted Abdullah.

Horace did not know how to treat the invitation; normally he stayed away from being too close to other law students. Envy at the law school was worse than poison. But this time he felt an obligation to help another "African" as Abdullah had insisted. Harvard admitted only a handful of black students of which Abdullah was one. He did not want to brush-off a future ally or future president. One never knows with these things. Who would have imagined that the skirt wearing Macedonian Alexander-the-Great would end up all the way in India...

For Horace the matter was fairly simple - allies were the sort of stuff one needs when attending Harvard law; someone to argue your case and advocate on your behalf and to remove the daggers from your back. Abdullah would make a good ally. One needs to be part of a band of brothers to arrive at the summit as one...

"Okay, Abdullah, tomorrow - since you are so insistent. You are my brother, we will have lunch tomorrow. There's a place called Zoë's across the street, not gourmet but good food."

The two men shook hands again and in the background under the guise of Harvard's towering solitude - a bond was formed. A bond that seemed Calvinistic in its nobility; Abdullah the African and Horace the African- American.

CHAPTER SIX

Friday, with its dose of lethargic hues, came soon enough. And Horace, waiting in the Northern entrance, resembled a lone gun for hire. This was yesterday's designated meeting spot, outside the eatery Zoë's. This time Horace hoped to start afresh and to start a new friendship based on a new found set of African - 'Ness.' Horace's closest friends were the women who he was currently dating. Then there was the pack; Roger, The Greek and Tommy. Maybe this friend is what he needed, he agreed with himself.

Horace entered the cinnamon scented eatery and waited for Abdullah. He did not like waiting because it gave him the bug in his stomach. "A quarter full," he said to the waitress pouring his cup of coffee. Moments later, the Great Abdullah walked in.

"Good to see ya," Abdullah said.

"The day is good and how is your day?" asked Horace. Before Abdullah could take a seat, Horace bit in. "So Abdullah, tell me, why do I always seem to run into you in the most private of places?"

The question was unexpected and Abdullah's facial expression became serious. Between the brows were the signs that Abdullah will age prematurely given the ease with which the frown came to his face.

"I really don't know brother. What are you drinking today, coffee?" he said, trying to get away from the subject.

"I am drinking your answer," said Horace zeroing in on the tension. It felt like a sauna in the middle of a desert. Horace was good at this kind of debate; getting your subject to talk. In High School he had made his history teacher answer her own question:

Ms. Evans had scanned the room for the most unprepared student.

"Horace, who was President Reagan married to?" asked Miss Evans.

"That's easy mam…president Reagan was married to Mrs. Reagan." The class went hilarious as the laughter went through the cheap ceiling at Charlton High School.

"Seriously Horace, we all know that when Nancy married Reagan she became Mrs. Reagan but…"

At this point Horace yelled, "Her name is Nancy Reagan." Another collective outburst -

Miss Evans, the teacher was the least bit impressed. She said, "One day you will make a good lawyer. You have the knack of making people answer their own questions, and correctly." She did not know that she was making a million dollar prediction and betting the odds.

Back at Zoë's, Abdullah wondered how best he could avoid the question just asked --- still hanging. Horace scanned the room and said, "Why are you following me?"

Abdullah's eyes shifted and his neck elongated like a spinster bitten by an unexpected bed bug. He said, "Well, I know that we are the only black men in class, that's why. Maybe, I am trying to reach out to you."

"Have you ever heard of criminal harassment here in the US?" Horace asked. His voice lined with sarcasm.

"Come on Ray." Abdullah said in automatic rebuttal.

"Jus' joking man, but for a moment, I thought your ass was psycho - stop doing that. I get it. We are all black. We need to stick together, even when we have nothing in common. I get that."

"That's putting it mildly."

"No, that's the political correct way Abdullah - remember something," said Horace. He leaned forward and lowered his voice. "Sometimes, the black person in the room, is the one you have to watch out for. We blacks here in the states know this my friend. When all the whites have disappeared into their tin shacks in the suburbs, it's the black person who will screw you over, then blame it on white people. Do you know that a lot of drugs are pushed by blacks onto other blacks? People are people. Maybe you have more in common with the other white students?"

"But who makes the drugs?" Abdullah asked.

"...still you don't destroy your own people - that is a fine line man. We blacks sometimes treat each other like garbage here in the States. All I am saying 'Brother' is that people are people; color does not change what's in the heart! Who makes the drug --- who gives a damn, not the arresting officers or the jurors sitting in the jury box."

The conversation had a bitter aftertaste and the two men now sat looking at each other not knowing how to proceed.

"If it helps you Ray, I was not following you."

Horace decided to roll with the punches again. "Is that right?"

"Yes, that's right..."

"Then tell me something, as they say, humor me -- why do you seem jumpy around me Abdullah? Do I intimidate you?"

"No, this ...is a new city for me. I am settling down."

Horace could see that Abdullah was playing the race card. Why didn't he just come out and say ---- 'Lets be friends,' and that would be it. Horace continued drinking his coffee while staring at the Muslim-American-African ---- he did not know what to make of him.

There was a long awkward moment of silence and Horace asked. "What do you really want from me Abdullah?"

This again took Abdullah by surprise. He thought the subject was over. There was no letting go. It was true what the rumors said about Horace. Even though he had a low GPA, he probably was the smartest and most likely to succeed from their law class...

"I want to introduce you to someone, a physics professor at Harvard; he is working on a project," said Abdullah confidently.

"I am not interested in physics. Remember, I am in law school."

"Give me one minute," Abdullah interrupted.

"No way," Horace said.

The catty exchange started to annoy Horace and he decided it would be for the best if he walked out.

Maybe then Abdullah would get the message.

Horace hoped to ignore Abdullah for the rest of the semester. Then he said, "Good bye Abdullah and good luck, I have work to do!"

He walked out of Zoë's. On his way out he ran into what he concluded must be the physics professor. The man, wearing a traditional Muslim garb and turban, seemed familiar with Abdullah as he strolled into the cafeteria. He wore the attire one normally expects to find either in Jordan or Saudi Arabia, a clean blue wrap-a-round - the kind of heavy blue Boutros Boutros Ghali, the former United Nations secretary general, was known for, sky blue with a sedated dullness.

Horace walked out of Zoë's, not wanting anything to do with Abdullah or the professor he was supposed to meet. He spied the professor from the corner of his eye and he could see that he was carrying a plate, a jet plate covered by a piece of cloth. The plate had the letters, T-R, sticking out and the rest of the plate was hidden - the way a child hides sugar in their mouth forgetting to wipe their lips clean. To Horace the whole affair seemed a torrid and scandalous affair; the beginning whimpers of an infantile game.

For the rest of the academic calendar Horace made a promise to himself, he would avoid Abdullah like the plague in winter. He stretched out into the evening and met the cold wind in his face with much composure. "I never want to see that cat again…"

CHAPTER SEVEN

orace sitting on his sofa cut a lean figure against the silhouette. He breathed in as he started talking... Four hundred and fifty miles South of the New Jersey Turnpike, taking route thirteen, one arrives at the state of North Carolina. Take another fifty miles east of Elizabeth City, then another fifty miles south and you arrive at Carthage, North Carolina. This is the birth place of Horace Arthur Bates, Jr.

Here in the backwoods of the south, Horace entered the precarious world on November 23, 1984. He prematurely arrived with that characteristic smile on his face, that was neither planned or in need of an explanation. The "Ray-Ray smile," as it became known. His mother, Pauline, welcomed the new born to their abiding family of four.

"Premature is a sign of greatness," she said, making a place for the baby in one section of the master bedroom.

"Make sure he is in the warmest part of the house," said Bates Sr.

"Honey look, he is so handsome, what will we name him?"

And since Horace was the first born male to a family that had for now two girls, Denise and Cleopatra, his father said, "That's easy, we will name him Horace Arthur Bates, Jr." As soon as the name came out, Junior started smiling from ear to ear.

"Look, he already responds to his name. Something I tell ya," said Bates Sr.

Horace Arthur Bates, Sr., the father, was a formidable individual. He served in World War II and his own father, Clifford Bates, had shot a man for speaking the wrong way to him. It was common knowledge in Carthage that the Bates don't take shit from no one. Crossing a Bates was like crossing a fire and praying in vain that you don't get burnt.

Just how Grandpa Clifford Bates shot a man would depend on whose version of history gets printed or copy written first. Some say, "The man said... he is a good for nothing trigger happy boy", others said, "the man said...it was self-defense protecting his family." The most truthful explanation could perhaps be found in Grandpa Bates' own words:

"I saw three men riding a horse enter my home..."

During those days, the way things were, it did not matter if someone had a mental illness, nor whether someone was schizophrenic or not. What mattered was that he had returned to some atavistic state and had to be punished. Because of the many hours of long labor since the age of fourteen Grandpa Bates had developed schizophrenia and imagined things: men on horses...

The judge at the county courthouse in Carthage did not seem impressed by any of the evidence offered on Mr. Bate's mental health. In modern terms the judge's behavior would be termed the malpractice of law, Horace observed.

"And how do you plead sir?" said the judge addressing Mr. Clifford Bates.

"Not guilty by reason of self-defense," replied Joseph Goldberg, Grandpa Bate's retained lawyer. Even in those days the Bates were fairly middle class and almost on the wealthy side. Black families from around came to the family when they were in need of a quick loan.

And so Clifford Bates could afford for himself the best lawyer money could buy. And he got good ole Joseph Goldberg, the civil rights man. If preceding reputations held true then Mr. Goldberg was worth every dollar – a sharp shooter, a hired gun, ready to strike for justice and human rights.

Mr. Joseph Goldberg, dressed in an anti-climatic grey suit, stood up on that early September morning of 1947 and approached the jury for his patented closing. Years later Horace would pull up the closing from the legal search engine Lexus-Nexus under the tab – *State of North Carolina v. Clifford Arthur Bates (1947) Superior Court Records (NC)*.

Mr. Joseph Goldberg said, "Your honor and members of the jury, this is a simple self-defense case. This man here, a loving father had the right to defend himself in his own home. This is what makes America a great country, you can protect yourself. In other countries this is not the case. Should I remind you [Attorney removed handkerchief and wipes forehead, says something to himself] Mr. Bates is an American just like any one in this room and is entitled to the same rights regardless of color. On January 12th, 1947 the deceased walked into the home of Mr. Bates while he was having dinner with his family and said, 'I'm gonna teach your black ass a lesson son.' Now unless I am in Russia or in the jungles of Africa, you just don't walk into a man's home and tell him you are the new law in town and make threats. The word is provocation ladies and gentlemen of the jury. You don't make threats in another man's home, that's not how it's done here, not at all."

It took the jury a matter of hours to find Mr. Clifford Arthur Bates not guilty. Even a not guilty verdict could not save Grandpa Bates from being socially ostracized. Grandpa Bates could no longer work or do any of the things he previously could. A year later in 1948 he moved to the Bronx in New York. The next they heard of him he was married to a Cuban lady and working as a used car salesman for Ford Motor Company.

Every time Horace Bates heard this story told by his father again and again like the anticipation of a hurricane, it left a chill on his spine. He did not know where to place grandpa in the illustrious family tree; other Bates men were lawyers and doctors, and seemed to have been something from out of the ordinary, pioneers or statesman; who refused the criminality of the day, thought Horace.

From Horace's arrival home, Bates Sr. had insisted on a new baby crib. "It's good luck."

Superstition ran somewhat deep in the South and yet the Bates were also considered outwardly to be more in tune with science than superstition. Bates Sr. always joked about the scientific needs of blacks. "Blacks need, both here and in Africa, to take science seriously" he said, moved by what he perceived as short comings in black communities. "Instead of buying a pipe line, invent one." It almost seemed that all the science in Bates Sr. had passed down to junior who read anything science related.

The Bates lived in Carthage, a low lying town of less than 40,000 North Carolinians. Carthage is one of those towns where everyone appears to know who your granddad is and what he did in the eighth grade. Its deep creek meadows, roads meandering out into the fields; dirt-packed easements and esapements communicated an old America once best lived in the countryside. An America back when bread cost twenty five cents. But like a puzzle it appeared that this was also where the old agricultural America had met the new industrializing America, and a fist fight broke out. From the '50s onwards the town had in its background the agricultural side and in the foreground the factories and paper mills.

A couple of factories were scattered in and about Carthage, together with acres of farmland growing corn and sugar. This was not the heartland of America but it cut pretty close. So close that Horace often dreamed of America's heartland.

Carthage was an experiment on the molding of the old America with the new America. Horace often saw in it the old ways blended to the new. But, there was a peculiarity and a specialness about Carthage that could not be verbalized but merely learned from those who visited it. Carthage was known to produce high caliber individuals. With a population of forty thousand under the most recent census, it had the highest per capita of doctors, lawyers and scientists. Folks liked to joke about it and say, "Genius is in the water." All Carthagians had an inside joke --- 'It's in the water,' and they would burst out laughing. It's in the water meant many things. one of which was = it's right in front of you and you can't see it and the other was that, it's formless, and ever changing.

From this southern Appalachian background fueled by America's ever changing demography sprung Horace Bates Jr., and in 2007 he entered Harvard School of Law. One of four black students capable enough to win a position in the class, and so was born his patented remark, "Luck is not necessary, only God."

This surprised most Carthagians, because Horace became the first from the town to go to Harvard. Other lawyers in the town had gone to Yale, Stanford, Columbia and New York University's law school but not Harvard. That was, 'Ray's thing.' James the blacksmith had said, "...th' water dat kid did drink.." While the other Carthagians looked on and wished Horace well, they said, "That Bates boy is going to be president one day. Maybe even the first black president." Horace found himself in the typical predicament of being the first black person entering something. The first thing on people's minds is when are you going to cash in and what are you 'Gonna get from this,' Horace concluded, packing his luggage and heading for the Harvard orientation week.

From time to time, Horace reflected on his humble origins and a nomadic smile sojourned to his face. Carthage became a mantra…Go Horace Go… every time Horace thought about Carthage his dreams lit up beautifully like a light bulb; he could see all the colors and inanimate objects; Such was his history and only time would unwind it.

Maria absorbed the tale of Horace's origins seated in what looked like the cheapest sofa south of Boston. The two watched a classic from the Turner channel. It was befitting and appropriate, Maria said to herself.

"An American classic for a classic man…" She was falling for him.

CHAPTER EIGHT

The weekend looked dull. The first weekend back at Harvard should have been better than this, Horace thought. He shuffled in for a Friday night at his apartment. He had to do some house keeping, the kind of things one does when most of their time is already taken up by the Sisyphus rhythm of reading. The first weekend had arrived but the spirit was not moved.

Horace's room looked like it had already taken more than a week of Harvard law. The bed smelled like two lovers had tumbled through...that's the ticket. The white sheets still crumpled and the pillow flattened like a pancake. Maria was spending the weekend with her family in the Red section of Boston. The Red District, the Hispanic neighborhood, where many were greeted with the proverbial, 'What happened?' Horace did not consider the relationship as interracial or birracial. "This is one race," he joked to Roger, after Roger questioned and questioned him on the repeated smell of ladylike cologne he was picking up. "There is only one human race and many cultures of hatred in the world..."

So on that Friday night, Horace buried himself and attended to his room's ever meticulous look. Later that evening he pulled out Professor Hick's case book. "Still can't believe that's the end of Abu Muhammad: the Moor," Horace concluded. He wanted to go to the bar for a drink. He enjoyed sampling foreign beer and had heard about a new "Mill" beer from Belgium. A beer strictly brewed on an ale that's one hundred percent wheat. "Fascinating," Horace agreed. He always felt that somehow the person who invented beer had gone unnoticed by the Nobel Prize Academy.

This time the pub was an obscure low lit pub going by the name, *Heavyland*. Horace always thought the name *Heavyland* likely a last minute suggestion by a corporate attorney running out of business names to suggest to his client. Horace put the week's events together. "Perhaps, I have been too hard on Abdullah, the Muslim. Maybe I need sensitivity classes. Should I give him a second chance? No, my sixth sense tells me I did the right thing."

The bartender's presence interrupted his thoughts and Horace said, "Hit me with a Mill will you."
"Mill, coming up. Hey, don't think too much," said the bartender walking towards the foreign beer cellar. He unlocked the cellar with a six pin combination as if to imply that there was hidden treasure to be found.

The bartender resembled an old man from the old prohibition era. He looked as if he had jolted from the badlands of Atlantic City, New Jersey and found a new home in Boston. The sulky look of a man you leave alone, combined with the deep seated eyes of a former criminal all made for a tick-tape acquaintance. Horace made a mental note to minimize his conservation with the bartender in case his words come back meaning the exact opposite to what he intended.

In every city he had been, Horace noticed that on occasion one finds residents that would seemingly do better in another city. "Not everyone is Boston," Horace agreed with himself, looking at the bartender, still struggling with the combination to the cellar.

Horace thought back to the time he seriously started sampling beer. It was the Guinness that did it he thought. His mind took him back to Professor Norman Law, the English law professor he had in first year.

Professor Law, an England-born Professor of Criminal Law, had been visiting professor at Harvard during Horace's first year. The Englishman who found every nonconsensual touch needed to be punctuated with, 'Excuse me please.' The first Guinness Horace ever drank was courtesy of Norman Law. At the end of year Professor Law took the class for a drink. Seated in the center of the bar and appearing very much the accomplished teacher of law, one would had mistaken him for Socrates if one was not aware that most of what he said was either written by someone else or misquoted. That fateless night at *Heavyland*, the lights were shimmering and the music folksy.

In between the thundering drop of the Guinness and the intellectual ideas, Professor Law said, "The Guinness mate, is an acquired taste mate...." Professor Law sipped the draught beer, letting the bubbles give him a white top mustache. "He is a pro, in Guinness," thought Horace. Professor Law also taught Horace that the English by common practice, while mild-mannered, were eager to prove that they were superior to anyone who doubted it, whether it was George Washington or the African rebel.

"Yeah, the sun never set on us for a while," said Professor Law, alluding to British Imperial dominion. "We are the only nation, we the English, who have really done a good job with this colonization thing; we have taught the world the difference between savagery and civility..."

The students were silent; they did not want to castigate the Professor, - as Thomas Jefferson did in 1776 - and accuse the English of violating every human right known to mankind. None could capture the sentiments of Jefferson, thought Horace...

To prove this, let facts be submitted to a candid world...wrote Jefferson; his pen flowing with the poetic. Horace loved it, every word of it, contrasted with Professor Law's self serving monologue:

"We English have contributed rather tremendously, splendidly actually," the diatribe continued. Professor Law had conveniently forgotten to mention the many groups that rebelled against the English, including Washington's - from Burma to Kenya, India to South Africa, Hong Kong to Malawi; an unfaltering list. No, Professor Law had redacted these facts and was supplying the class with emotional Guinness. All these rebel groups had rejected British morality. Professor Law lifted the pint of beer like someone raising the Union Jack in some obscure outpost with a loaded name like British

South Central Asia, "Cherio mates, good job getting into Harvard."

Professor Law enjoyed congratulating people and wishing them good luck, even when luck was not necessary.

"Good luck at Harvard…" he said, uninvited, to the surprise of the students including Horace who seemed to wonder whether luck was really necessary here.

"Good luck at Harvard," he said again, this time with laughter ending it all like a punch drunk boxer.

Horace started to wonder whether luck would be necessary or whether it was now a question of sustained hard work, belief in God, in God we trust, and networking. He decided to answer back.

"I doubt that luck will be necessary sir," said Horace having taken enough of the man the students called Union Jack behind his back.

To which Professor Law having taken a second to contemplate replied, "Horace, my dear friend, I agree with you entirely, but good luck mate, anyways."

Yes, the Guinness reminded Horace of the English man, and so he took it with a measure of hesitation while waiting to sample the other Mill beer. Friday would be a mellowing time for reflection, he concluded and as soon as he was done, he would get back to his apartment. Hopefully, the bartender can figure out how to open the cellar…There at his apartment Horace was bent on calling Maria, Roger, and his mom. He would not call Abdullah, the mystery man.

CHAPTER NINE

On Tuesday after the International Law class, Horace geared up to begin work at the law firm of *Zimmerman, Brighton, and Associates*, a downtown boutique specializing in both criminal and corporate law. Here, as a part-time associate, he would learn the ropes and start off observing, doing clerical work and then progress to motion writing and brief writing and finally to the highest mode of law practice – litigation. After litigation there is nothing left but an appeal, noted Horace, dashing off into the subway train. That dreaded appeal ---- and how many men have really reversed their judgments?

The progress from student to full fledged attorney had come somewhat effortlessly and Horace began to feel that the part time job at *Zimmermann et al*, was a blessing in disguise. His belief in that God was methodological: for him God's law is the highest and that a man can never rise above what God has dictated for him.

When Horace arrived at *Zimmermann et al*, he was met by Timmy, a brooding attorney with the look of a man watching every detail.
"Horace Arthur Bates," said Timmy pronouncing the name the way a judge does the name of an outstanding felon.

Horace wore the traditional Victorian colors for attorneys, the dreaded grey. On any given day, imagined Horace, the greyest suits are to be found in the jaded corridors of America's superior courts. The grayness of business suites normally implies neutrality or the innocence of profundity but in reality is nothing but trial strategy, he agreed with himself. He smiled - the idea innocuously relevant...

"How was your trip?" Timmy continued, playing the role fully. He adjusted the white suspenders to his pants, effortlessly, as if to suggest a heritage in wealth.

"Good...I will get used to the train ride," said Horace. The Boston train ride was not like New York's or Washington's, it was not even comparable to European mechanical superiority, thought Horace. The Boston trains were bigger, faster and more modern than New York's. And that simply meant one thing — he could not lie about the train being the cause of his lateness. The last time he checked, the Massachusetts Train Authority operated with a fanfare of punctuality.

Timmy took Horace around the first set of law offices close to the entrance. In the words of the Rastafarian Bob Marley, to see what - 'Carries the feeling me youth...'

K
E
N

S
I
B
A
N
D
A

"This is Jack Givens. He handles the mail," said Timmy stretching his hand out towards Jack the mailman.

The two went round a bend into a spacious set of law offices. "Having fun," Timmy said. "This is Jennifer, she is an associate in the commercial practice…this is Alfred…energy…this is Albert…litigation…" He carried on like a family uncle. By now, Horace had forgotten the first names of the attorneys he had been introduced to. He could only remember the few, the sexy ones…like Jennifer. It helped that Timmy made an abrupt stop.

"That's it for now; let me show you where your office is located." Timmy took Horace to the back room of the first set of law offices; this looked like the anteroom of a building adjacent to the entrance of the firm. Something reserved for a big shot, Horace was impressed. "Not bad," he said to himself. "Here we go Horace," said Timmy.

"Call me Ray."

"Ray it is," said Timmy stretching his hands, a welcome gesture aimed at symbolically entreating Horace. "Do you have any questions? If so, ask me directly now, no pussy footing around here, my extension is 2055. I will take you out for lunch, a late lunch really, I know you law students eat mostly peanut butter sandwiches. What's the new dean, Dean Sandra…ahh."

"Washington," Horace interjected.

"Yes, Sandra Washington… What's she feeding you?" Timmy asked.

"The usual…"

Timmy ignored the monotone answer and said: "I like late lunches. They allow you to refuel and keep chomping at the bit."

At that Timmy disappeared into the molten shadows of the expensive law offices, the law offices were befitting of the King of Brahma.

Lunch came soon enough and Horace left with Timmy for a high end restaurant a couple of blocks from the law firm. The two men sat in the limousine and Timmy made sure the message was being communicated fully and silently…this is big.

For lunch Horace ordered a steak. No steak in his entire life had ever tasted so good — certainly not the steaks in Carthage. No boy, this steak must have been FDA approved ---- grass fed. Horace dug into it while Timmy spoke. Timmy struck Horace as the kind of man who enjoyed the sound of his voice - soap-box man.

"Yeah…you will do well here, just don't rush. Take your time."

"Thank you." Horace said, making sure he did not appear Harvard-headed as they call it.

"We will start you off in criminal litigation."

Horace shot off, almost losing a piece of meat in his mouth. "Criminal practice, you guys actually do criminal law, is this international criminal law?" Horace asked.

"You are surprised, once in a while we want to help out those who need help the most, you feel me, and criminal law is really the basis of all law."

"A law firm that practices criminal law, wow. I have heard of very few law firms that do criminal law."

"Again, we do what we can, and keep moving, criminal law is the stuff that determines society Ray, who is up and who is down. If you want to find the geniuses in society who never made it, go to the state maximum penitentiary. That's where you will find the best criminal defense lawyers."

"Indeed." Horace replied, trying to take the lesson in stride, this was definitely not the criminal law he had just taken at Harvard. But again he had read somewhere that law school is different from law practice; you have to learn things all over again.

Horace then remembered that his cousin, Dixon Bates, is doing time in North Carolina, Plymouth County, for bank robbery. Timmy adjusted his chair, pulling sideways, and then lifted a Chardonnay, a cheap looking Chardonnay, and a dessert type---certainly not from the plains of Burgundy France, something that makes you look inexpensive.

Things like that Horace noticed - the incongruous elements as he called it. Things like an expensively dressed man with no watch and cheap shoes, an expensively dressed women wearing twenty dollar cologne. As a teenager Bates Sr. had warned Horace not to do that. "You don't wear a suit with no watch," said Bates Sr., adjusting Horace's moccasins. Bates Sr. had spent his last penny to pay for them.

Back at the dinner table and Timmy still in his element leaned backwards as if in a rocking chair. "Yep, criminal law is the ticket...did Eric Seligman Fromm the philosopher not say that a successful revolutionary is a statesman and an unsuccessful one a criminal."

Horace did not want to appear like he was on a different wavelength and he said, "Existential – a man is as great as the conditions he finds himself."

"Or he can rise, Ray. Rise above them." Horace was never interested in rising above shit, all he really wanted was some change in his pocket, and he looked away at the shiny crimson floor with the square Jackson Pollock design.

"For tomorrow we want you to observe some cases, we also want you to shadow Jack Beaver, your mentor," said Timmy. "Jack is the best Ray. He recently defended the Dunlop case...you remember the case don't you."

"Yes, I remember, the one about the company's CEO accused of stealing employee's pensions. Who could have missed that in greater Boston, it was all over the place."

"Allegedly," Timmy said.

Horace was still amiss. Why would such a prestigious firm bother with criminal defense? He did not particularly like criminal law. It left a bad taste in his mouth. Horace imagined that it was part of the game that on occasion some guilty people go free and some innocent people end up behind bars. Criminal law says you can't do this and you can do that. It is bound to find man and woman who just do what they feel like doing, he concluded to himself. Horace looked up at Timmy who was beginning to sense boredom in the young man.

Horace was grateful; after all he had entered the law firm from what appears to be the backdoor. His 2.3 GPA was something of an unspoken truth that everyone seemed to be ignoring. Back at the office a huge set of files awaited him with the inscription *State v. Stephen Ridges.*

Horace read the file slowly. Steven Ridges was a thief who had robbed the downtown National Bank by pretending to be the computer technician fixing the electronic teller system. The statement of facts said that Steven had walked from the heist with three million. Bank robbers seem to want anything but just one million in our days, said Horace to himself, flipping through the file. Sometimes they would rather have nothing to one million…

At 4 P.M. the associate named Jennifer entered Horace's office, dressed in colorful patterns that associates normally wear when trying to make an impression on the senior partners, not too chic but bright and professional. "Horace is it, you can go home now. Timmy told me to tell you that you can leave at 4 P.M. today, courtesy of the law firm."

Jennifer struck Horace as a good fit for the law firm. She had been there three years when Horace met her and carried herself with knee-jerk professionalism. Jennifer appeared to belong in a fashion magazine and not in the cut throat dungeons of Boston's elbow punted law practice.

Horace left and headed for his apartment. At his apartment, a phone message from Maria was waiting for him. He played the message.

"…Ray…I am stopping by; I hope you had a good day. Love you, Maria…"

The message ended with a lingering silence complements of a cheap answering machine. This heightened last phrase, 'I love you.' …cut through the room like a knife going through warm butter. 'This is going too fast, far faster than I expected,' said Horace to himself. Someone is going to get hurt. Horace never returned the phone call choosing instead to let his silence speak for him.

At 7 P.M., a knock on the door reminded Horace of Maria's self-made appointment. The wooden door sounded off into the late evening, a bird's flapping wings. The atmosphere was operatic but intimate.

"Come in," yelled Horace as soon as the knocking ceased. He then opened the door and there in front of him stood Maria Espinoza, as beautiful as ever. The only thing different was that this time she had a back pack, for the rest of the evening.

Horace led Maria into the apartment. He made sure that his face did not let loose any sort of negativity.

"…and so, how is your new job," said Maria, moving her eyes like a seductress on legal sedatives. Damn she is good, thought Horace. Maria stood close to the evening window and the light hitting her from behind was like the limestone entering a man's eyes without his consent. The beauty and the statuesque figure, were all mellow. She definitely has a future in acting thought Horace.

Maria turned around and caught Horace staring. "Are you looking at me?" she asked, blushing. She moved away from the window.

"Yes, I am staring, no reason to lie," said Horace.

She smiled. She was used to all sorts of compliments. When she walked along on her way home from work, the local boys would start whistling in jungle frenzy. She accepted beauty as a moment of total surrender…

"And how was the firm?" asked Maria, repeating herself.

"It was good. I still can't believe this happened to me. I got a job without even applying, you believe that, and it's a real job."

Maria's face lit up as she turned on the TV.

The next morning before leaving his apartment Horace received a phone call from Timmy.

"Horace…sorry Ray, can you work today? I know we originally talked about two days but can you come after school, the Ridges case needs some work." When affluent men ask - you listen, Horace agreed with himself.

"I can do that," Horace said.

Maria turned around and heard the whole conversation. She started unpacking her clothes and as she prepared to take a shower Horace looked delicately at her. 'She is more precious than rubies,' he said to himself. "So you never talk about the acting. How is that going?"

"I might be doing *Hamlet*, Ophelia soon," she said.

"*Hamlet*, ain't that something," said Horace. He always associated the British play with high class trust-fund American life: a son in the Hamptons perhaps trying to prove his father's assassination. This is definitely not the blue collar solution to who killed daddy…

"Hamlet might just be the one you get noticed," uttered Horace. Remembering that all it takes is only one piece of work to enter the public's eye to be taken as a serious contender. It appeared that almost all performers were one performance away from being discovered. Horace imagined Brando doing a monologue, 'I am one performance away,' in deep baritone. He got back to reality and said, "Nice, very nice."

The next day at the office.

A noise wrestled throughout the law offices, soft and gently; he spotted a commotion from a distance.

"Is everything okay?" asked Horace, not wanting to appear too nosey. Later on Horace heard that the two most senior partners were involved in a clandestine affair and this resulted in an alteration.

The version Horace heard was not reliable. It came from Jennifer and was said speedily as she dashed off, not wanting to appear like the unpaid police informer doing freelance work Horace had inquired discretly. Jennifer's version was that the two partners are as power hungry as two foxes forced to share the same hole and that each accused the other of social climbing. Now, apparently one of the partners, John Brightman, the son of the founder Timothy Brightman, had had enough and was done. Sarah, the other partner, was not, and she wasn't having it.

Sarah ramped into John's office, wielding a nameless authority and said, "You will be done, when I am done with you. You hear me John." That declaration was heard throughout the office building.

Horace let sleeping dogs lie and began looking at the discovery documents in the Ridges case file. He thought about the whole incident between the two partners John and Sarah. Looking up at the placard that read - *Zimmermann & Brightman and Associates*, he thought, 'Surely, the higher you go the crappier it gets.'

*

At the end of the fall semester Horace decided he would volunteer for Ruben Howard's presidential bid. If Reuben won, he would be the first black president of the United States. Horace's grades were still the occasional C+, but out of the blue he pulled an A+ in International Law. It was providence knocking on his door.

Horace was entitled to a vacation from *Zimmermann & Brightman and Associates'* given the part-time hours he worked and so for the fall break; he would help good ole Reuben Howard, the totting black governor of California, run for president.

CHAPTER TEN

As the close of semester neared Horace found himself at his apartment seated on his sofa. In only a matter of days he would be done with the first semester of third year.

The unflinching teeth of the shark in mid-waters, the stick in the fire burning, the determined volcano pouring; all these disjointed images reminded Horace about the persistent man on his trail, Abdullah.

Later that night, Horace nestled in his green sofa, a generous gift from a departing former German exchange student going by the flamboyant name of Harold Grass. It had been a delectable gift. "You can have this if you want it," said Harold, putting his Lufthansa air ticket in his back pack. The sofa was still in pretty good condition and Horace sat on it watching the evening news on a late Sunday night. Then came the call...somehow thought Horace, people seem to know it when you are at home. It's the dammed schedule, I tell you... The phone ringing was like a bell ringing through an ocean of calm.

"Yes, Horace here. Who is this?"

"Horace, it's Maria ...how are you babe?"

"Good Maria, and how are you?" said Horace.

"...I miss ya..."

"I miss you too."

"...and how was your weekend?" asked Maria.

"Good and yours?" asked Horace, trying desperately to deepen his voice. And since women can smell desperation, Maria felt it...she concluded to herself that desperation is similar to wet turpentine on a neighbor's fence – very hard to miss. The conversation was progressing superbly, the usual talk between lovers before they say what's really on their mind.

"I want to ask you something," Maria said. Her voice trembled with delicacy; a flight pilot engaging a rocky weather storm.

"Yes, anything," Horace said automatically.

Then the dreaded question every man has no answer for since Adam in Genesis.

"Where is all this going?" asked Maria.

The question hit Horace, throwing him to the floor like a heavy wind. He did not fall but his thoughts stumbled, and he struggled to gather his thoughts. He pretended not to understand the question.

She repeated the question, this time clearer than before. "Where is all this going? Us Ray? Are we dating? What's going on here?"

"Yes Maria, we are now officially girlfriend and boyfriend."

The answer was uttered with a high note intonation: a premise to being funny. "That's good. Then you will have no problem introducing me to your friends as your girlfriend."

Horace's heart sank and he asked, "What friends, what are you talking about now?"

"The ones I see you talking to at the law school, you know."

"Ohh, those friends, I have no problem with that." That was a lie and Horace's voice had the hint of the melodramatic iambics to it.

"My girlfriend is the 'Help' at Harvard and why does she now want introductions for crying out loud. Sleeping with the help - how does that make me look?" Horace said to himself.

"Right," Maria insisted. Breaking what appeared to be an eternal silence she ended with, "See you manyana, papi."

"Okay Mamie, esta manyana esta mucho." The Spanish was an alliteration of common Schwarzenegger catch phrases. Horace dropped the phone and said to himself, "What a mess, I tell you." Horace continued his thought as far-fetched as the second coming of Genghis Khan.

Monday would be his final day at the law firm; his heart was heavy anticipating the end of the semester. This was mixed in with the confusion of the present. Horace knew a change of pace was necessary.

On Monday after class, Horace went to the law office for his last day of work. Timmy Teague met him at the door. "Hey Ray, I want you to meet some people," he stretched out his hand. It appeared like they had been waiting for him.

"This is Sandra Macintosh, a partner here, and this is Lionel Ironside." Lionel was African American. Horace wondered to himself, "Where did they get this soul brother from?"

Lionel wore a tailor made suit which complimented his conservative hairstyle, something that you would expect Barry Goldwater to wear on Election Day. The whole man seemed to be one sepia spin after another, a walking tailgate.

He leaned forward entering the revolving door, as the two big shots stood back. The two were taking a closer look at their investment.

"I am Lionel Ironside, good to meet you Ray, and I can tell you that the pleasure is wholly ours here. I have heard great things about you," said Lionel, dotting his eyes as if to minimize the room's sunlight.

Timmy continued moving around, a choral master painting sound from nothing, "And this is Michael Christopher, all partners here, like you some day."

Sandra McIntosh then seized the moment and said, "We have heard great things about you."

"I don't know what you heard," said Horace quite amazed at the red carpet treatment.

Timmy motioned in the direction of the conference room, "This way today Mr. Horace Arthur Bates, please." Horace often wondered why powerful people often went an extra mile to create theatrical melodrama – like crying during interviews- 'Seems a bit off-pitch.'

The conference room was well decorated - almost gaudy. It had the usual Japanese Samurai sword, a picture of Lincoln the lawyer and the law firm founders; he still did not know their first names after a semester of receiving a generous salary from the law firm. 'Seems like the last name is good enough,' thought Horace.

"This is a beautiful room." Horace said to Timmy. He had never quite seen anything like it; it resembled the melting pot of an epoch and the discernments of an era gone. The picture of Abraham Lincoln struck him as not the best choice. "They could have done better," he said to himself. Horace considered himself a Washington man, by which he meant George Washington – He then turned his head away from the picture. "They should have put Washington up there." But again if it was up to Horace, George Washington would be everywhere, the one dollar bill was not enough…

"We did not invite you here to comment on the conference room Ray. Take a seat. We want to talk to you about something sir," said Lionel, splicing the intense effrontery with a soft touch. The Greek hero Midas would have been impressed — Midas being the Greek hero known in Greek mythology for turning everything he touched into gold.

"Ray, so that we are on the same page, your grades were good, but not the best as you know, since you earned those grades." Horace nodded his head in agreement.

"In all fairness we thought we should have this conversation with you do you know after close to four months why we hired you?" Timmy asked, in an editorial sounding voice. Horace nodded a 'no' and the others adjusted their water bottles. "We hired you because of what your law professors said in these reference letters, right here." Timmy opened a manila folder with several letters

"But I never asked any of these law professors to write a letter on my behalf," said Horace in amazement. He was learning the truth, that in the real America letters of reference and insults are written all the time without anyone requesting them. Horace accepted the new found thought and his face relaxed.

"We are the ones who asked for letters of reference on your behalf. Here's one from your Criminal Law professor, a Norman Law, actually from the United Kingdom, '…most potential I have yet seen but is yet to realize it.' Here is another one from your Constitutional Law professor, '…will make an excellent constitutional law man.' Now Horace I could go on. I do have a couple more, but our point is not to inflate your ego."

Timmy stopped abruptly and looked at the others, the pause suggested some tribal quorum had taken place and an agreement had been reached merely by the punctuation through silence.

Timmy then said, "You know Ray, I was once your age. I am Harvard '66, Sandra is '74 and Iron here is recent, class of '84… I never understood that success requires hard work even if you are talented. We are willing to give

K
E
N

S
I
B
A
N
D
A

you a chance because we believe your personality is the right fit for us. You know some of the greatest men…and woman were C+ students; Winston Churchill, the Kennedy brothers Jack and Bob, John Major and Nelson Mandela, all straight C+, on a good day maybe D+ students. We believe and I need to start using the word - believe here, that you have the potential. You speak well; you get along well with others and understand the law. This is what we want; we are not looking for a straight 'A' Cracker Jack who does not get along with anyone, but for people who make brilliant lawyers like you Ray." This was uttered in the usual kiss-your-ass high talk of corporate America.

Timmy's heels, beneath the table, tapped on the wooden floor making his presentation slightly musical; think Billy Elliot performed off-tune. He waited for a response from Horace. None came. Timmy reached out his fatty looking right hand, a hand that resembled a boxer's.

"Welcome aboard, your position is now permanent here."
Horace did not know what to say, "Wow, thanks Timmy, Sandra, Lionel…"
This cemented the beginning law practice of a C+ student as a junior associate at *Zimmermann & Brightman and Associates*. A combination of the right references, timing and what Union Jack might have termed - good luck.

CHAPTER ELEVEN

The end of fall semester arrived and Horace began feeling much like the accomplished law student: a part-time job at a prestigious law firm --- and that involved getting the guilty off on a technicality, he thought. While the course work was not difficult, on Horace's mind the most was Maria and what to do in such a predicament, a love predicament.

"Write to me when you get to Carthage. That name actually sounds like another country, I can't recall- interesting," said Maria, standing on the side of the train sipping an organic Acai berry drink. The organic market had sky rocketed in Boston: organic fruits, organic milk and even organic baby diapers.

"I will make sure to write," said Horace, not sounding very confident in his answer, almost like a school child unsure seven multiplied by seven is forty nine and not seventy seven. Maria looked at him, her brown eyes accentuated by the station's Victorian architecture made for a complementary match.

"Okay, now," said Horace, giving Maria a kiss. He entered the train and sat mid-way on the train, and next to a window.

He looked out of the window and saw Maria looking at him; her eyes fixed at the train arcade were starting to tear up like the clouds attesting to a drought. For a moment the train moved slower than usual; the curling whistles, smokey puffs and the metallic synergy.

The wind blew past the train. It tugged the under plates and smoldered underneath the train. The wind then continued upwards, fluttering the windows, casing Horace's face like a delicate make-up brush. The train pulled out of the station, accelerated and gained speed. Within a minute the previously romantic couple was now merely a thought. Their union seemed to stretch as the train pulled away. As such, their parting mirrored that of the train's forward motion. It produced in Horace, a loneliness; the kind of lonesomeness shared by two people who were intimate the night before, the letting go of the ego as the soul is encapsulated, a dangerous giving of the self, imagined Horace.

Fourteen hours later, the Boston Rider, arrived in Carthage, North Carolina breathing out the fumes of a journey that, except for the occasional ticketless homeless traveler, was uneventful. In the fourteen hours Horace had read a book about the democratic front runner Reuben Howard, the first black governor of California. Horace liked to use his down time as a chance to catch up with popular non-fiction. His father had warned him about the vagaries of wasted time.

Bates Sr. leaned forward, and said, "Time wasted can never be found…" He constantly did some of the many chores around their two bedroom house on Creswell Road. Whether he was mending the broken fences or fixing the stove that refused to light up, once the malfeasance had been spotted, old man Bates would dig in like a vulture.

True to his father's lesson, Horace had not wasted time. The time he spent on the train had informed him about the man known as Reuben Howard. Reuben Howard was 43 years old, had the kind of complexion that approximated Muhammad Ali on a day when Ali had not been sparring, a clearly mulatto color. Like most presidential hopefuls, he stood above 6 feet; specifically 6 foot 4. This made him quite the American male archetype; the hunter and not the hunted, the cowboy and not the Native Indian.

Americans, thought Horace, seem to believe that with height must follow respect and greatness; maybe that's why John Adams was reduced to being Thomas Jefferson's side kick, thought Horace.
Height had its rewards in American society; Horace continued thinking – himself at 6 foot 2 inches. He had enjoyed being tall first hand. People always expected more from him like a water hose letting out water to put out a fire, every drop seemed to matter.

Reuben Howard went to Harvard and graduated in 1968. This made him a revolutionary kid, Horace thought. The children of the revolutionary period were more in tune to the rebel in America. He was married to another lawyer, Barbara Richards.
She was in private practice and had practiced law for close to ten years. They were both class of 1968, and so it appeared to Horace, that the ivy towers were good mating grounds for the intellectually gifted. Barbara now worked at *Smith, Baker and Richards*, an international law firm, and was a full fledged partner. One of a few women to be given that opportunity to perambulate with the boys!

Barbara Richards still used her maiden name, and was always seen on the campaign trail, as the loyal wife at her man's side. She was the kind of woman you take on a safari trip to a remote village in Kenya and Botswana and know that she will shoot any wild animal that dares test its claws on the expedition; the kind of lady that can finish writing your political speech and you wouldn't even notice the changes - or notice that just a few minutes ago the speech was half-done if not half-baked; the kind of lady who is feminine and yet also a partner. Reuben had taken advantage of that, showing Barbara at every public event he could. The press liked her, some even said, 'The only reason Barbara was not running for president was that America was not ready for a woman president, especially a black woman president.' But Barbara's supporters were adamant. 'Look at Oprah,' they said, '…Barbara is more popular than Oprah.' These utterances were heard in many bus rides and in the streets of California's melting pot.

But for now, all the lights were on good ole Reuben Howard, as he was known by his persistent democratic supporters. Then there was the possibility of Barbara failing as a presidential candidate as had happened to Susan Pellegrino.

It was the dirty campaign of '78 that 'Done it for Susan Pellegrino'...
Susan had worked so hard to appear as a, 'Man's Woman,' that she had
decided to go quail hunting with 'The boys.' On the hunting trip two things
happened that were not penned by any of her advisers. The first was that the
gun choice had been replaced with a Winchester Model 70 Super Shadow.
Now, this gun has been discontinued and is very difficult to handle, especially
if you don't grip the rear handle. In addition, a difficult terrain; the darkened
potholes on the rockery, the thickened forest and the meandering dust lands,
can outdo the gunner.

In the summer of 1978 Susan was hunting and a squirrel parried its
perky head over a shrubbery. All the men on the hunting expedition knew that
this was a squirrel and not a quail. Susan was having nothing of it, she insisted,
"It's a quail...goddamit Charlie..." and rounded her segment of the hunting
troop for what turned out to be a forty minute chase. The 'Quail,' forty minutes later after taking a shot to the midsection, was discovered to indeed be a
squirrel and very much alive.

The next day Susan had a press conference at which point it was too
late. She even tried to serve the press corps with homemade cookies and milk
but to no avail. The pinch of the mommy was in play. When the misogynists
got a hold of the story, Susan was in trouble: "How can you trust a woman
who can't even be honest about whether they know how to shoot or not? She
is a liar...liar, liar panties on fire." The animal rights groups were more unfor-
giving – "She left a squirrel dying you know; she is heartless; completely
un-presidential." The speaker of the house majority Isaac Petty proclaimed,
"She is unfit to command and I really honestly doubt that she is fit for anything." And with those words the speaker had sealed the epitaph on Susan
Pellegrino, ending what appeared as a promising career in politics.

When Horace read about the Susan story in the book about Reuben
Howard he concluded, that the saying, "A day is a long time in politics" might
actually be true. Susan had gone from front runner, to 'don't call us, we will
call you.'

All women in America knew that should they ever seriously run for
the White House, they would be subjected to 'The Pellegrino test.' Or according to Shakespeare's alluringly impartial *Hamlet*---- 'To be or not to be' --- we
are subjects of unfair examination...

For now, Ms. Pellegrino and the quails were not a factor for Reuben
Howard. Reuben's only Achilles heel was that he was black. America had never
had a black president before and people wanted to know - are we really as
racist as the liberal press says? - Or, is grandpa the only racist relic from the
past, frozen in South Korea?

*

The train wheeled into Carthage National Rail Station; the only train
station in town. It was built in the early 1880s and had an ingrained look of
pre-reconstruction, from before Abraham Lincoln freed the slaves; before the
west was tame and before General Custer locked heads with Crazy Horse at
Big Horn. The train pulled in the country and the folk continued as if the train

entering was an unseen entity in Carthage. Mrs. Bates was waiting for him in front of the train station. She did that even though Horace was now almost 28. She still treated him like he just arrived from the hospital. "Some things never change," said Horace looking out of the train at his mother's broad shouldered, astute presence in the station.

Horace entered the family home knowing what to expect. The warm smell of cinnamon bread, the scrambled eggs blistering with cheese on top and the sweet aroma of coffee brewed fresh from the coffee pot and poured over local heavy cream – unpasteurized. After Horace settled in, it was his mother who interrupted the silence.

"How was your trip?" Mrs. Bates said. She then noted that her son had lost some weight.

"Good mom, how have you and dad been?" Horace answered, putting his luggage onto the kitchen counter. His two elder sisters had already moved out of the house and were now married off; one, Denise, to a doctor and the other, Cleopatra, to an engineer.

The kitchen had been redecorated and looked far more modern than the rest of the house; stainless steel tops, shiny hinges on the cupboard and a two door fridge. Either the tax return was hefty or dad hit the lottery, thought Horace to himself.

"Where is dad, it's Saturday?"

"He is still asleep….R, we are so proud of you, look at where you came from. You are an associate at a law firm and you haven't even finished the degree. *Zimmm...and Associates…* Zimmermann, I remember. I thought that you were adding the man just for emphasis. You kids, are always - man this, man that, but this is someone's name?" Mrs. Bates asked hesitantly.

Horace almost burst out laughing. His mother was funny like that. He said: "Yes ma, it's Jewish. A lot of Jewish names have '-man' at the end."

His mother thought about what her son had said for a minute and said, "How is everything otherwise?"

In the South, that was another way of repeating the first question and hoping for a more truthful response; at least that's how it was done in the Bates household.

"I'm fine ma."

"Good Ray…don't start lawyering me…hurry off to your room and Horace, your cousin …he wrote to you."

"My cousin…" sighed Horace.

Horace knew who his mother was talking about. She was talking about Dixon Bates, his uncle's first born currently incarcerated and serving ten years for armed robbery. Dixon and a couple of his friends inspired by what appears to be the ghost of Jessie James saw it fitting to withdraw money from where no deposit was ever made and to do so using an armed gun pointed at the bank teller.

The story was that on the day of the robbery, Dixon and his friends were overheard saying, "Give…me..tha..money bitch," to an older lady in her fifties, a highly respected church goer. Horace imagined Dixon's slurred delivery and his mountain head playing the part. Dixon had a huge head and a neck that seemed even bigger.

Needless to say, thirty minutes later, the policemen found Dixon and his friends counting the money at a traffic stop and eating fried chicken.

Horace knew what the letter was about, and as his mother handed him the letter. He dreaded what was inside. "Cat's probably a 'Mrs.' by now," said Horace to himself. Prisons were notorious for their sexual appetites… maybe that's where the phrase, 'Keeping it real' comes from.

Horace looked hesitantly at the letter. He had an inkling what the letter would reveal. For starters, he had grown up with Dixon. He used to jump rope with Dixon after Sunday school, with the other kids singing, 'Ray never bamming always jamming.' He remembered it like it was yesterday. The two also hunted birds, shooting them with homemade catapults. Horace had gone to white man's Harvard while Dixon had progressed to the black man's Harvard.

In his bedroom he opened the letter:

Ray,

Mr. Big time lawyer. Please visit me in college. I need to talk to you. Someone tell me about a defense I might have and when you graduate I want out, me and you brothers. Brother Ray please!

The letter continued half colloquial and the other half grammatical errors. The sort of stuff that would make Hemmingway go bull watching and shiver with goose bumps in his sleep. Substitution of a verb for noun is never acceptable for those facing incarceration, thought Horace looking at the letter. Now holding the letter in his hand he did not know whether he should laugh it off or to take it seriously. The writing was certainly bad English, but the emotions were definitely real. He remembered the face behind the pen and the man behind the misspelled verbiage - all real. As real as the ground we walk, Horace agreed with himself. He looked downwards at his expensive Harvard issued Nike sneakers and he concluded that he would help Dixon, just like that. It did not take a lecture from a professor about the benefits of volunteerism or a grand quotation from Eleanor Roosevelt, no – Horace was informed plainly by what the Frenchman Marcel Proust would term 'Remembrance of Things Past.'

"There is something about friendships that produce a synaptic response when you realize years later that someone you once called friend or cousin is now inhibited from full expression; the infirmity of the mind; arthritic swelling and stiffness; slow gaiety; all symptoms and not the real person you once knew," Horace said to himself.

Later that evening, as his father reminded him of his full name - Horace Arthur Bates, Jr., Horace contemplated two things; the first was to help Dixon Bates and the second was to help Reuben; both black cats, on different sides of the fence. Outside the darkness of the evening and the spacious lands surrounding made for good meditation. The Bate's home was the only home within a twenty mile radius and its lone light shown out into the unintimidating wilderness. Even the wolves stayed their hunger.

CHAPTER TWELVE

The winds of political change were blowing towards California's presidential candidate Reuben Howard: graceful and future US president. They appeared to affect him entirely. From a distance, many Californians were starting to say, they saw a man approaching a summit and a pinnacle; an invisible mount Everest. Throughout the country the spirited impulses could be felt; the rural folk were giddy while the urban folk were as opportunistic as a foot soldier.

In California the first black governor wanted in, to become the first black president of the United States. There is a saying that goes like this: the oval office is the height of progress for any American sub group whether it is Irish, African American or Hispanic, thought Horace. This was the thinking in 2008, when Harvard educated lawyer Reuben Howard eyed the prize, beckoning with confidence he readied himself for war - politics as war.

Horace arrived in California on the usual Boeing 747, self-financed, half starved and eager to put in volunteer work.

The Los Angeles Air Port glistened with the political on the day of Horace's arrival. Checking in at the main entrance Horace observed that each political party had some kind of placard or campaign poster. The republicans had the elephant, that indomitable and indispensable asset; demanding as much grass as any political herbivore. The independents had their man; a skier who wanted alternative energy, observed Horace. The former astronaut Alan Shepherd beaming with his campaign...*Lets Tap into Space Energy*...Horace thought the point through - 'How about gestational energy; or human waste as energy.' The whole evening started to have the aftertaste of seeing a bad bikini at the beach. What's worse - the bikini itself, its lack of fit or an overweight body forcibly-stuffed into the bikini burlesque style, Horace contemplated.

The village campaign headquarters served as the place for the volunteers. It was a self funded bread and breakfast commune just for Reuben Howard. Here, ambitious campaigners and Horace himself were managing the interpersonal side to the campaign. The campaigners, most of them naïve kids, were so ambitious that you had to make sure that anything said was favorable to Reuben Howard.

Many Californians were beginning to find the Reuben presidential campaign a bit over the top and found ways to dodge them; 'I have to feed the cat,' 'I have to get an oil change,' and the best still – 'I have to renew my gym membership.' It did not help that the thunderous storming of the campaigners was causing a stir in the locals. The campaigners seemed to believe

K
E
N

S
I
B
A
N
D
A

that their man is 'The one.'

At the campaign village, Horace unpacked with the unsteady ease generated by being watched. It would appear that within the last three weeks he had unpacked and packed a total of four times; each time more succinct. It was becoming a habit.

The village was run by Jamie Austin who assumed the role of the leader-in-chief. A political whizz kid, he had the inner scoop on America's varied political campaigns. A middle sized man, he had the appearance of what an actor termed 'Washed out' looks like. And he played the part to a perfect tee; year-old sneakers, a goatee and a white T-shirt with sweat stains suggesting his life as witness to a higher calling, almost a testament. The arrogance could be smelled a mile away, especially once he opened his mouth.

Jamie approached Horace and there were thumping noises made from his sneakers. "My name is Jamie Austin; you will be working closely with me, you really at Harvard son?" Jamie asked. Jamie's face livened up with the kind of expression a good detective riding shot-gun gets when he spots a most-wanted suspect.

"Yes, third year law school." Horace replied agitated.

"Are you really sure you at Harvard?" Jamie asked yet again.

Often times Horace would get the usual doubting Thomas' who would assume that for some reason he was lying.

"Yes, I am sure that I am at Harvard."

"Very well then…" Jamie said disappearing into the sea of bedding lined up in the dormitory. The volunteer headquarters looked liked a college dormitory; imagine Wesleyan in the '60s. His departure left a sense of sourness in Horace's mind…two minutes have gone and someone is already suspecting that I am lying…

Moments later the threatening shadow of Jamie reentered the dormitory storming like a bull in Palermo.

"Sorry man…you really are at Harvard, isn't that something…welcome."

What Horace did not know was that within three minutes of the silence Jamie had double checked Horace's Harvard status. Calling Harvard's Rector directly and reaching his private estate in Virginia; all this done so that he could make sure Horace deserves the Harvard first class treatment and that he is not lying.

Then as if in total regret, Jamie said, "Tomorrow you will accompany me to the convention after the primary results come in; we have to find a way to use that Harvard law degree."

*

Back in Carthage, North Carolina, Mrs. Pauline Bates worked her house and thought about how many conversations she had with her son concerning his future. She recalled talking to him just before he left for California.

"R, you know what they say about money," she quibbled. "It's only as good as the spender!"

"And I have no idea what that means ma," said Horace raising his hands up in the air.

"It means money can come but it's up to the hands receiving the money."

"Simple enough, they need to put that in the Harvard syllabus," said Horace.

Mrs. Pauline Bates was well into her seventies, and had been married to her high school sweet heart for over fifty years. In her eyes one could see the times past and in her son's eyes one saw the times to come. Mother and son had a bond that only another woman would be able to break. Mrs. Bates, found the thought frightening, a field mouse haunted by the spectacle of the overfed aristocratic cat.

Sometimes Pauline could be overprotective and at other times under protective, but her intensions were well made; 'Mother knows best R.'
Horace reflected again on tomorrow; at the prospects of meeting Reuben Howard; and at the Boston he left behind...

....Boston looks beautiful in the fall Horace recalled. The blowing breeze uncovers the velveteen grey buildings creating a romantic ambiance. Horace had adjusted to Boston. Three years ago he was like a country dandy looking for pumpkins in a haystack. Boston was just too much for him, the haze of roads truncating back and forth created confusion that only a map unwinds.

Some days Horace would take a scenic route back home. Those were the days when Boston felt like a comfortable glove on the hands of a professional boxer.

...He would walk it off, normally taking thirty minutes and getting his heart rate up to a slight palpitation. Walking became the only form of exercise he did, especially after Bates Sr, told him that, 'Pumping iron will make you look more bull than intellectual. A lawyer has to be lean and mean.' Those words from Bates Sr were uttered while Senior balanced a brandy on the rocks in one hand.

And so Horace remembered the days gone at Harvard when he would walk it off, one foot at a time; the sun almost about to set – but now, he came back to the reality that California, with Jamie as the quarterback, would be somewhat different. No walking here. He took a deep breath and inhaled the area's polluted air into his lungs, almost choked on it, and a sense of discontent covered him like a blanket covering cold weather.
Horace looked at the single bed that would be his apartment for the coming weeks. He was now bombarded by memories of Harvard. Those walks to Wendell Street...

And as he walked often untouched by the snares and dirty looks held at a half angle like some vampire on the loose, he felt like an endangered panther breathing fire into fire. He felt no need to apologize for being sexy ---
"Adios amiga -"

At Harvard Horace had stayed away from racial politics. In high school he often was accused for being a white man pretending to be black.

And all Horace ever wanted was merely to get along. He recalled the girl he dated back in first year, a white girl named Jennifer. The relationship was somehow tentative because according to Jennifer, "He just was not black enough." It had come as a surprise one early morning before class, "Horace, I like you but I can't go on, what I am trying to say is that if I wanted a white man I would have got one. I wanted a black man but you act whiter than Snow White. Listen to me --- I want nothing to do with you." And that was the end, Jennifer gone – The next time he saw her she was with some African exchange student from Nigeria and dressed in Yoruba traditional attire; she was also pregnant and leaving law school.

Her father was livid. He wrote her out of his will and banned her from his presence stating that she is limited to coming within only fifty feet of his presence. In the event he is in the house, she has to wait outside until he gives the go ahead for her to come in, a kind of low level cease fire…

"Anything else someone would be paying the price," said Jennifer's father -his face looking like a bright lantern in a lighthouse. By which he meant that he might punch her black husband in the face if she keeps pushing it.

Two years passed and Horace had again ran into Jennifer. She could not have looked happier.

"Ha, Jennifer, good to see you," Horace exclaimed.

"Good to see you too," Jennifer said.

"Where is the hubby?"

"Ohm George is at the UN, he is an international prosecutor now."

That was definitely not the answer Horace was fishing for. Horace had expected to hear that they had broken up because of cultural differences and that she had gone back home heart broken by the black man. Instead he had just been told in many ways, 'That the African was taking care of me,' and this hurt his ego.

He quickly changed subjects.

"I never knew why it did not work, you and me," said Horace now more direct.

"Ray don't, you are a good man but you always seemed to presume that being white was better, I never understood why you were not yourself, just an intelligent black man. Why do you have to act more white than white people? What I love about George is that he loves his African heritage and is successful in what he does, that's organically who he is. You don't need to be white to succeed, look at the Japanese, the Chinese, the Africans, the Indians, but Mr. Bates, the big black man on campus wants to be white."

At that the atmosphere became cold. Horace then said, "I am my self, perhaps you wanted a different kind of man, that's all. Why is being Horace so much of a black and white issue for so many people, I'm just me; your assumptions are totally unfounded. No one is really white or black until they are told so; I am Horace Arthur Bates." Interesting enough, that was his vintage way of saying – bullshit. As Jennifer walked away Horace remembered the jazz musician Coltrane's song: *Tanganyika Shuffle*; he heard it playing in the background; the drumming and menacing beauty; he could not account for both, maybe Jennifer could?

CHAPTER THIRTEEN

At the Hilton Hotel an eager crowd awaited the democratic front runner. The mildew and mist on the tarmac covered the poster - Reuben Howard for President - it read rather declaratory. The poster, a colorful mixture of half blue and half red, was similar to the one the Bolsheviks used to indoctrinate Red Russia into formation. The crowd that had gathered stepped over the poster blindly reminding the ubiquitous face on it of the symbiotic relationship between politician and the voter. The voters can destroy you!

Further away from the crowd there was a stage. Already dressed in celebratory star and stripes; the blue and the stripes were counted that day to almost fifty. Every corner had a flag flying high in the air creating the feeling that something historic is in the air. Horace observed the commotion from a distance; he imagined and concluded that the stars and stripes together with the star spangled banner could ultimately make a man do anything. There is a beauty in it.

Horace sat back stage, the setting behind the flood lights was as immaculate as the setting in the crowd. The crowd resembled ice cream, every second melting away, changing shape with every exerted pull from the gate crashers. Horace sat back stage, a man on the watch; his face visibly uncertain of his role. A close group of Reuben's handlers were also in the back; these were the big shots and Horace did not want to step on their feet. The money movers, all of them with grey-white hair like a uniformed battalion.

"Is he ready...how soon...ten minutes...is the speech ready" was uttered by various handlers like a picking at the auction. Horace could not put a face to the words but they had come from way ahead, very close to Reuben. As for Reuben Howard, the candidate sat in the back, very astute; he did not move but was like an actor rehearsing the final touches to a momentous piece: the biting lines of the cadence; the redundant free speech, the memorialized Anglophile all rehearsed by Reuben. For Reuben it was but an art form, for thirty years he had rehearsed his campaign speech. "Every politician begins by imagining being president," Horace said to himself.

Ten minutes later the crowd was electric once the tall figure known politically as Reuben Howard stood up. He put the cards summarizing the speech in his suit jacket. Reuben jogged on stage with his bodyguards like a rock star. But then he came back and started talking to Horace, as if to acknowledge him. Horace did not know how to address him and said, "Good evening Mr. President."

"Not yet, call me Reuben. You are at Harvard. Is that right?" said Reuben Howard.

"Yes sir, one more semester left," Horace replied. From close up Horace noted that the man was skinnier than in his pictures. His face looked like a younger Ronald Reagan with a deep Greek tan. The back stage was filled with smoke and this added to the ambience giving the moment the sort of intense backdrop between two actors.

Reuben sized Horace up and said, "I hear good things about you."
"Thank you Mr. President."
"Ever consider working for the government."

Horace wondered what good things Reuben was hearing; this was his second day in California. This surprised him and he said, "I hope that it's the truth..." "Oh yeah, very reliable," Reuben said. When he spoke he tended to make abrupt pauses designed to give the correct dramatic effect, very polished, thought Horace.

The question affected Horace at a deep level for he did not know where it came from. "Yes I would but doing what?" This came out excitable. Reuben leaned forward so that the security detail could not hear the conversation but only the whizzing sound of the tame less crowd. "A good president is always in need of political advisors."

Before Horace answered the question, a member of Reuben's security detail, whispered something in Reuben's ears. Reuben's ears turned towards the agent and were glued on the agent like an antenna. Reuben's eyes were still on Horace as he walked back on stage. This time he did not jog but walked slowly.

Bruce Springsteen's classic, Blood Brothers, played over a folksy harmonica. Horace observed, thinking how much of this is choreographed and how much is actually spontaneous. From a distance he saw Reuben's silhouette shadow gesticulating, Reuben lifted the microphone and out came the mellow voice of the next U.S. President. Reuben said, "Ladies and gentlemen, good evening California, it's been a long time coming I tell you."

In the crowd there were some who felt that Reuben was an opportunist and that Dr. King's words, 'I might not get there with you, but I want you to know I have seen the Promised Land,' were not targeted as political insistence for high office. The critics concerns were that Dr. King was saying there is a place of justice he sees, a place where the color of one's skin is immaterial and a person's skin color is not important and people are judged by content of character. Whether judging someone by his character meant election to higher office was all subjective. For one thing Reuben's detractors were quick to pinpoint that the words of Dr. King refer to a group and not individuals and that the oval office can only be occupied by one person at a time.

To his opponents Reuben remained unmoved; he suggested as rebuttal that he was as much a politician as any other white politician and those accusations of stealing Dr. King's dream were unfounded but born of the political drudgery south of the Potomac. An article that later appeared in the paper summed it up.

December 28, 2008 *LA Chronicle*:

    Today in Los Angeles, democratic front runner Reuben Howard, when asked whether he sees himself as fulfilling the legacy of Dr. King, that iconic civil rights leader of the '60s. He responded by saying, "The words of Dr. King do not refer to any single human endeavor but to the total result for African Americans." These words by Democratic front runner show that Reuben is leaning away and dissociating himself from the more radical notion that Dr. King was referring to presidential politics in his 'I Have a dream Speech.'

    When Horace read the piece he agreed with Reuben, now that he had met the candidate in person he could see where that sentiment came from. The group in the Hilton was getting rowdy and Reuben was shouting, "What do we want?" to which the crowd yelled back, "Howard."

    The speech lasted for forty minutes but it sounded like the most Hegelian thing – historic – he had ever heard. The man was the messenger, and he made for an impressive walking telegraph. Reuben went on to contrast himself with good old Philip Butler, his opponent, a man he termed a Washington insider. Ruben put it bluntly, 'My opponent is the kind of guy who buys a beer and asks you to pay for the tip.'

    Throughout the speech the crowd roared like a tidal upsurge in the Atlantic, moving forward with homegrown placards of… 'Go Rube Go'…it approximated a medieval bread riot shined upon with electric flood gates.

Fifty minutes later Reuben returned backstage, calm as before, as if he had just taken a stroll down Park Avenue New York; as if all this was preordained. His face lit, arms relaxed and eyes whitened to the limits of the jaguar in early winter.

CHAPTER FOURTEEN

"There is something about power that makes it attractive to people like Reuben Howard, a man who never had anything in his life. Power by itself is an abstraction...," said Jamie, the campaign coordinator. He adjusted his seatbelt in the fifteen-seated van used as campaign transport. "Reuben sees this as the height of his existence, without the presidency this man is nothing."

Horace looked intently at the verbiage coming out from the lips of Jamie.

Three days in and counting; Ray started to feel that Jamie was always trying to impress people with how much he read, and inadvertently showed how little he actually understood of the little he read. Today as the van pulled away from the Hilton hotel, Jamie was reminiscing about the philosopher – Aristotle the Great; Aristotle who begot Socrates.

It became clearer by the moment that Jamie did not share Aristotle's views on power. For while Aristotle never intended power to be merely limited to individuals, for Jamie the individual was the center of any discussion concerning power.

"You see, Aristotle has it wrong. Unless a powerful individual embodies power...power is just an idea, one has to wield power."

"What of the different branches of government?" challenged one volunteer who was wearing a purple sweater.

"Total rubbish; look at a man like Mussolini, now that was something there."

"Mussolini!" the volunteers exclaimed.

"El Duce, that's the one, that's what we need here, Reuben to take charge no more congress what-about------what-about."

The campaign members were astonished, one said, "Are you serious?" To which Jamie answered, "You better believe it."

The van picked up speed and the group was swept backwards by the sudden acceleration.

"Jamie, who are these powerful individuals?" the driver asked looking backwards.

"People like Reuben ...who know what to do with power."

The whole thing started to irritate Horace and he shut it out, letting his mind drift to the sweet smell of Maria, somewhere out there in Boston.

At the compound Horace started thinking about what Reuben had said, the man had actually offered me a job, he agreed with himself. "But what exactly is making people so gun-ho, first it was the law firm, now Reuben."

If he worked for the president just before graduation at the age 29, it would be historic in terms of age. Unfortunately, if the president turned out to be disastrous he would he forever linked to that failed black presidency. Horace rested, putting the decision for another day and time.

After two weeks of campaigning which involved going to supermarkets, standing late at night to meet the work crew and going to college campuses, Horace was ready to resume his final semester at Harvard. Jamie handed him a note on the day before his departure, straight from Reuben, he knew his calligraphic hand writing by now, the note read:

"Ray, see me before you go."
- Reuben H.

"How does he know I am called Ray?" Horace thought holding the note perfectly. "This is a collectable, very brief – such is the communication of the political ascendant," he agreed with himself.

Five minutes later Reuben's security detail entered the compound, four of them with wires sticking out of their ears.

One of them said, "1020, target, Roger that." He walked right to Horace, and said: "Are you Horace Bates?"
"Yes."

"Come with me." The security service agents and Horace disappeared into the secretive world of presidential epiphanies. The ride to the undisclosed location was pleasant, it felt like someone had been called for: code language for five star chauffeur driven treatment. "Yeah, I've been called for; wait till I tell those cats at Harvard next week." Horace said to himself.

Horace and the security agents got to the undisclosed location and entered through the main entrance. It turned out to be the Sheraton and Horace was disappointed, he expected some cottage on the outskirts of a hidden lodge. When he entered the hotel entrance a group of tourists, because he was black, waved at him thinking he was the presidential candidate and Horace did not miss a beat, he waved back… the secret service agents rolled their eyes and one agent said, "Really dude."

The Sheraton with its majestic allure gave the feeling of hitting the big time. Horace entering the hallway wearing a Harvard T-shirt and sweat pants made him look the part of the presidential candidate enjoying a lighter moment. Horace began thinking that perhaps he should have dressed more formally. "But this is not a job interview," he said to himself and he adjusted his T-shirt so that it was loose on his shoulders. This was a social meeting, the kind of thing between two men testing the waters of friendship and equality.

Horace was further escorted through what ended up being a meandering path of hallways, obviously chosen to confuse the low-IQ would-be-assassin; that virulent path, a common part of American presidential politics. Horace thought for a second, about the many assassins throughout history and this made him conclude, "You never know, it has happened before, don't take it personal."

The pathway continued; two turns left, one right, turn another left; the labyrinth pattern continued for close to two minutes, then Horace realized that the agents were really serious about getting him confused. If taking someone for a ride was meant literally, this was one of the times, thought Horace, sensing his head getting heavier as the dizziness from the elevator motion started kicking in.

Finally, the door opened in the presidential suite and there Horace saw the future president, again relaxing with his immediate family. His wife Barbara, acknowledged Horace with a caustic nod; also present was their daughter Christina. The whole Howard clan ready for its ascendency. While the room looked un-presidential from where Horace was standing, this was quickly corrected by presidential ornaments; the American eagle; the star spangled banner played out in the background like the opening to a musical on Broadway. Everyone seemed so relaxed that you could attempt to count their toes and there would be no objection. The room smelled like a new car, a new house; something not yet soiled by people's occupation. Horace took it all in, his brown eyes shifting left and right, he readied himself for a conversation with the future president.

Inside the lounging area, Horace stood, stationed by the security agents who had remarked, "Please wait here," the air thickened as the gashing lore of the evening's tempo melted into the ghostlike walls. The future president did not want to mix his words. His dressing perfectly communicated his mood; a smoking jacket — that rare garment used by the affluent while relaxing.

"Well come in Ray," Reuben said. He did not move an inch from his sofa, only turning down the TV volume and making sure that no confidential papers were lying around. Some of Reuben's actions were intended as relaxation but most of his actions seemed robotic, thought Horace...routine. A water glass rested in the middle of the table and this suggested some leaning towards healthy habits. They say a president ages five years for every one thought Horace, looking up at the ceiling...wouldn't like that idea to come out, he said to himself.

Reuben continued standing in one position and said to Horace, "Thank you for coming so late to see me. I understand that you did well, extremely well, they tell me. How do you like the political life?" Reuben asked, motioning for Horace to take a seat and relax.

"It's fun Mr. President, I should say, a bit demanding," Horace replied.

"You will get used to it some day," said Reuben, his eyes more communicative than his words. These words were spoken like a slow automobile driving with its hazard lights on. Reuben took a deep breath as the security agents dispersed to their tactical positions.

"I want to offer you a job when you graduate, I have won the primary election for the Democratic Party as you know and I want to offer you a job after the spring semester." Horace's heart shot up and pounded, he could not believe it. Being offered a job by the future president felt like being asked out by the most beautiful girl in the room, the one you least imagine; the girl next

K
E
N

S
I
B
A
N
D
A

door. But this is not the girl next door, it was the next president of the United States, he exclaimed to himself.

After an uncomfortable pause, Horace said, "What is the job sir?" His voice partly anxious and the other part frightened.

"Advisor Ray, I need a young advisor in my office, someone with a link to the younger generation. One needs to know how everyone sees things…your position would be Special Advisor to the President for Domestic Affairs."

The offer sounded too good to be true and Horace said, "Sir with all due respect, I am a novice in politics, I have not even graduated, remember?" "Are you worried about the job at Zimmermann?" asked Reuben.

"How does he know all this…" thought Horace as he answered, "Yes, very much so."

"I know Timmy. He is a Harvard boy remember…he won't hold it against you and guess what - you will have your job back should you ever resign from the White House."

To Horace the job offer tasted sweeter than Greek poison, he was hesitant and something deep in him told him to say no.

"Okay Mr. President, I will think it over during the spring semester…" As Horace walked out of the room, Reuben said slowly, "And something else Ray, let go of Maria…that's not you."

How does he know these things about me, what's going on here, Horace said to himself.

"With all due respect sir, is there something else going on about me that I need to know?"

Reuben thought for a moment, and his eyes began to shift in their sockets, "One day Ray, all in time."

The answer made Horace feel like he was bait being used to catch something lurking in deep waters.

"No for now, Mr. President, but I will think it over sir." The two men parted and Horace prepared to take the first flight back to Carthage. Horace remembered that he was due to meet his incarcerated cousin, Dixon Bates, in Plymouth County upon his arrival back home. The words of presidential hopeful Reuben Howard were playing in his mind. 'Either this guy is high on sometime or something else is going on,' Horace thought. The words continued to haunt him; 'One day Ray, all in time.' Was this a riddle, was Reuben Howard trying to tell him something?

CHAPTER FIFTEEN

There is something about leaving California that cannot be put into words, thought Horace, as he boarded the flight that would take him to Charlotte, North Carolina. The absence of Venice Beach; an end to Hollywood; a weathering of the abyss of liberal America ---- Horace could not put a finger to it…this is an enigma, he said to himself, letting the thought rest peacefully like a deer panting for water on a ranch's foliage.

Horace waited for his plane while reading USA Today. He wanted to catch up with the rest of the world, and the rest of America's political pulse. Reuben had made history, big history…the first black presidential nominee of a major political party. The news was bigger than the bombing of Pearl Harbor.

Fifteen minutes before Horace boarded the plane he received a phone call on his cell phone.

"Ma…." Horace answered.

"Yes dear, and so you forgot about us little people? No calls from you. How many times do I need to tell you…how did everything go…is he charming as they say?

"I can only answer one question at a time. Ma, yes to all your questions and I did think about you. I met him several times; he is a good man!" Horace answered, firing back as many perfect answers as he could, "And what was the other question Ma?"

"Charming…" Pauline Bates reiterated. This appeared to be her most important question.

"Ohh…yeah, very much so, only the best… ma."

"I called R because we miss you," she said, tying to appear like her other questions were merely peripheral.

"I am fine Ma, actually you called at the right time, I am boarding the plane back to North Carolina."

"I was checking on you, you know as a mother. They always say that with kids these days you miss a day you have missed so much. The next thing you would tell me is that you cut a rap CD and are quitting Harvard."

"Funny ma…"

"No that's true; you kids think you are invincible and that you are the first ones to be that age." The words could not have come at a more correct time and Horace found them prophetic.

"I am still going back to Harvard, I did not accept any job offers Ma," he said with the determination of a cornered bull.

"Good, you have one more semester left. Remember that and then you can play president. Finish one thing first and then do other things. There is something else I wanted to tell you, I can't remember what it is."

"I am sure you will Ma, you..." and then Mrs. Bates interrupted spurting through...

"I remember, this Dixon, your cousin, wants to see you when you get back...something happened in the penitentiary."

"But is he okay Ma?" Horace asked. A part of him did not want to hear the answer.

"Just go and see your cousin — it's sad what happened to him. Now why did he have to rob a bank? When you see him don't let him talk you into any trouble!"

Horace found the idea of a convict talking him into trouble rather absurd but then he remembered that there were cases where lawyers have gone to jail right with their clients, he smiled - the big shot criminal defense lawyer types.

"Will do Ma, see you soon."

When Horace hung up the cell phone, the boarding call sounded throughout the airport.

"Final call for flight XII23, final call, gate two, now boarding."

Horace boarded the plane and sat on his designated seat. It was a good seat from an online discount sale and again being a Harvard boy had paid in dividends. Horace acknowledged the pleasant thoughts of the last two weeks. He had hobnobbed with the top echelons of society, the year had changed to 2009 and he had spent the year hankered in a corner of a night club drinking German wheat beer, some hefeweiszen (yeast/wheat). It surprised him that his mother had not wished him happy New Year and that she seemed more preoccupied with sounding an alarm bell.

Horace held his head in his right hand thinking about his life.

Midway into the clouds, just as the plane found itself in the middle of the thickest seam of clouds; Horace started thinking about his cousin. Dixon like many in America, incarcerated for the quintessential American crime: bank robbery. Robbing a bank seems to be as American as apple pie, thought Horace; something in America suggests that if you want it hard enough then take it, he thought. The name Jessie James shot out of his mind; Bonnie and Clyde; the bandit in Chicago...perhaps the founding spirit is very much alive he concluded.

But in reality Horace did not have an answer to why so many black men were in and out of prison like it was some coveted gentlemen's club. Dixon's case was impossible to fully understand. Growing up Dixon did not show any signs for a future career in robbery. Actually, Horace said to himself, at one time they were both star students in the ninth grad. What had gone wrong?

Horace recalled his mother telling him about the bank robbery. In her peppered voice, like petals falling off a tree, Mrs. Bates had said, "Dixon, your cousin has just been caught trying to rob a bank... Ray, you hear me? He strolled into the First National downtown, and put a 0.47 to the teller while his friend jumped over the front and made the withdrawal." Horace knew that his mother knew a lot about guns so if she could name the gun used, this was for real. Mrs. Bates continued, her voice pained and strained, "Your cousin says, give me the money and the teller opens the safe, I think the other robber is called Mookie…Mookie then said, 'Hit the ground like a fast ball is coming.' …where do you kids get this stuff from Ray--- from TV?"

"But ma it was not me," said Horace in his defense as he closed the door. He owed a lot to his mother for her ability to make him learn from the mistakes of others.

Dixon had then proceeded to take ten thousand from the safety box. In the South anything of importance is kept in a safety box. On this particular bank robbery, the minds that had planned it, Dixon in particular, had not considered an exit plan. In fact the pair planned to spend the money locally…duh.

The bank robbery immortalized itself on Horace as the plane continued flying through the clouds. What did Dixon want, he thought to himself. I am not a lawyer yet and already I have to bail out bank robbing cousins.

*

At the airport Horace took the Jiffy Taxi home. He met his parents at the door and this started a conversation that seemed primarily to be about Reuben Howard. The election was around the corner and every poll had Reuben leading.

"This is historic." Mrs. Bates said.

"Never imagined in my lifetime Ray; this is a good example for you knuckleheads to follow," said Horace Senior.

After he took a shower and changed into khaki fatigues, with boots, he hurried back out heading for the penitentiary which ironically was nick-named CONGO, like the central African country.

"When you get to Congo don't stay too long, I don't want any of his tricks rubbing onto you" his mom called out the door after him.

Bates Senior laughed, "That's your mother Ray… see what I have to deal with."

"Ma…criminal behavior does not rub off. People learn these things."

"Then explain how it is that when you place a good kid around criminals the next thing he is trying to be a criminal himself."

"That's called peer pressure ma," said Horace trying to cut lose.

The bus pulled up in front of the prison quarters. Like most Southern prisons, the smell of urine mixed in with the local skunk permeated the area acting like a poor man's alarm system. The smell would probably have made the all time trial defense attorney Clarence Darrow cut down the number of jail visits he made, thought Horace, as he looked up into the sky trying to inhale some descent clean air.

When Horace walked into the prison he was surprised at its cleanliness. All the visitors lined up in front of the visitors' entrance. The family members with half a tear in their eyes; the wives thirsty for conjugal grace – their faces flashed out in anticipation. Horace stood in line with some goodies his mom made for Dixon. At heart Horace really thought his mother means well even though she might state things rather bluntly, but most women do, he agreed with himself. The women he knew in his life if you insisted on getting 'Bitch' from them then they did not mind obliging the request. The goodies Horace's mom had prepared included; smoked ham; some organic coffee for late night reading; some candy and cookies. Comfort foods designed to diffuse the monotony of prison food. Which would all be thrown out as excessive 'inmate gifts.'

After something of a long wait in the waiting room, Dixon was marshalled in with his feet chained. There is something about seeing a loved one chained that makes it intelligible – unable to put it in words; whether it is the measure of punishment or the wish for forgiveness or the emphatic nature of humans, Horace seeing Dixon in that state made him wish for Dixon's freedom.

"Dixon needs all the help I can give him," Horace agreed with himself. "But I can't promise him heaven on earth…"

Dixon approached Horace and Horace got up as respectful as he could.

"What's up son…how you feel?" Horace said, breaking the ice. He managed to remember that Harvard speech would be offensive and in bad taste.

"Good Ray, man good, look at you boy, some big time lawyer now son," said Dixon. As he spoke he tried to hide the shame in his face. A black man looking into the mirror at what he could have been… Dixon could not blame white people for his predicament. After all, none told him to rob the bank, he said to himself. Maybe it was this hip-hop and gang culture…

Somewhere along the line in hearing all these gyrating drums and lyrics made me feel like this is right, thought Dixon. Those videos with big time gangbangers and 'Phat' bosomed lead singers…

…All I did was play along with the music, Dixon said to himself.

Dixon's mind went to the fact that the gangsters who lived in Carthage, North Carolina were admired. Mickey, who sold cocaine, drove a 745 BMW; Keith whose specialty was crack cocaine of a cheaper taste drove a 545 BMW… and these cats did not flip burgers at McDonalds; all the ladies wanted these cats, who is this cat Reuben Howard any way…said Dixon to himself.

Dixon had wrongly concluded on that fateful day that his American dreams have to begin by, 'Getting some money son.' When he was caught eating fried chicken, the police officers said he was the most frightened bank robber they had ever seen. The police officers then took Dixon and Mookie for questioning; again the two were eager to confess their sins at the police station. Days later Dixon would retract his confession through his public defender. Dixon's public defender argued in a motion to suppress that the confession 'constructively was not voluntary,' and freely given but by then it was too late. Dixon pleads out and received ten years with three years suspended; Dixon had seven years without parole perhaps more.

"How are these knuckleheads treating you here?" asked Horace.

"You know Ray, prison is not the Sheraton. What can I say man?"

"Did you just say Sheraton?" Horace asked, remembering that two days ago he had been chauffeured to a Sheraton.

"Yeah man, prison is not the Sheraton man."

"Interesting, it's not Sheraton indeed Dee."

"There you go Ray, what does 'indeed'…supposed to mean?"

Horace laughing says, "nothing Dee, prison is not the Sheraton, I hear that."

Horace had grown apart from Dixon, so apart that their conversation was struggling to go beyond the mere introductory stage. The two seemed to have nothing in common: one lived in Sheraton and the other in prison. The thought of running into someone like Dixon at Harvard made Horace conclude that he would probably hide behind those fine hedges dividing the lawns. He felt embarrassed for Dixon but it seemed like Dixon was not embarrassed for himself.

While Horace now saw himself as the white collar man, he was having problems with seeing Dixon as anything but a thug.

He said, "Man don't take this the wrong way but, prison has become a place where black men receive education or reeducation on how to properly commit crimes, how are you really doing Dee, no fronting." He turned his head around and continued, "Right here in these walls, some black men graduate with PhDs of the wrong sort and some vow never to be taken in when they are caught. I don't know what to tell you Dee. Speak, what's on your mind son."

Unbeknownst to Horace, Dixon had taken the same oath – 'Never get caught again.'

*

Horace continued to look at Dixon; he noticed that prison attire did not fit him well and that the bulging muscles were those of a man bench pressing upwards of two hundred pounds. The bicep in particular was over worked like an old rotor. The chest was tight, full like an over packed grocery bag. In all, Dixon appeared to have achieved physical perfection…

"I see that someone has been working out," said Horace.

"That's how we do in here, you have to protect yourself; one of these dudes might want to play you for Miss Anne; you have to fight back. It's a zoo in here Ray. We are being trained to be animals." Dixon then looked around, making sure he is aware of his surroundings. "They threat us worse than dogs man…that dammed bank man…" said Dixon, his eyes rolling backwards, his lips pinched together and his hands shaking because they were cuffed. "I have so much anger in me now, the moment I come out I am getting mines son." Horace listened with an attentive ear not wanting to come across as paternalistic.

"Come on Dee…let it go," said Horace.

Dixon pushed a letter towards Horace from the local county prosecutor. It had official mail stamped on it in red and had the smell of recycled government paper.

"Look at this son," said Dixon.

Horace opened the flaps of the envelope and saw an indictment underlined... Dixon was being indicted for murder, felony murder...

"Can they do this son, I know we fired a round by mistake and it hit one of the tellers, but that was Mookie. The teller has been in a coma for two years, and now they say he is dead man. Is this not double something for the same crime?"

"Hold on Dee...hold on." Horace then quickly read the indictment. "They are saying it's felony murder Dee. Felony murder happens when some-one dies during a felony. Yes they can do that, it's the law...and the life is the law Dee...and this is not double jeopardy; it's a separate crime." The news was not well received by Dixon and his eyes started to tear up.

"So what are you telling me man, don't let them kill me Ray..."

"Come on Dee get a hold of yourself, they are far from doing that...we have to defend this...you could get the death penalty; that's true. Look, I work for a big law firm in Boston, I will convince them to take your case...hold on Dee..."

Then Horace looked up with resolute in his eyes like a razor cutting through hard board, "I will do the representation myself Dee!"

"Time's up lads," the guard said pointing to the clock in the room. Horace stood up slowly as if to acknowledge Dixon's humanity. He watched Dixon walk away thinking many possibilities that were now floating...only if you had left that bank alone Dee. Horace's face froze up, his pupils constricted and the exhaustion from the flight together with the heaviness on his shoulders came flooding in. His body now weighed heavy and the pain of what he had just witnessed seemed to go to his inner self...the real Horace Arthur Bates... he walked out of the dusty visitor's room, leaving behind his cousin and friend, soon to be on death row --- Dixon Bates.

CHAPTER SIXTEEN

The rustling noises of the provincial squirrel were neither muse nor ruse. For Horace they provided some measure of coming back to familiar surroundings. "That's Harvard for yah," he said to himself, heading for his apartment on Wendell Street.

This would be Horace's final semester in law school. The final year to hit the ball out of the park... It did not matter that the world was bending inwards and sandwiching him with opportunities left, right and center. Horace felt much like a man arriving at the summit of a very high mountain. His law firm; the offer by Reuben and then there was Maria; at last a Harvard boy. All just so, a mixture of elemental destiny...

For the final semester Horace chose classes more difficult than the previous semester. He learned that ironically the cute girls gravitate to the most difficult courses and so he chose *Conflicts of Law, Commercial Law; International Criminal Law and Legal Theory.* The hardest subject in his curriculum was Legal Theory – known affectionately as the science of law. The reading list in that subject read like a who's who in legal philosophy: H.L. Hart, Joseph Rawls; Dowkins; Stuart Mill and the Philadelphia lawyer David Kairyns.

There is some debate, thought Horace, on whether legal theory is really a law subject or philosophy. Horace took the view that law was not merely procedural courses; criminal procedure, evidence and civil procedure. It was also legal theory which according to the syllabus, seemed to open the back door of one's head like a telescope adjusting to infinite telephoto; seeing the many stars and their relationship to planet earth "One needs to analyze all this information," Horace agreed with himself, as he signed up for class. "What's the use of a lawyer who can't answer a simple question like ---- what is law?"

Spring also brought back Maria. On his way to see her at the restaurant Horace ran into Maria.

"Hey Maria," Horace said, giving her a kiss on the cheek. The relationship was still very under the cover and he kissed her in such a way that a passer by would conclude the two were study partners. Any suggestion that the two were involved would be disastrous, even Reuben said so, Horace said to himself, letting his vintage smile go from one end of his face to the other.

The kiss was the kind that never raises eye brows and is intended as social lubricant aimed at cushioning the tinctures of day-to-day living. The maître d' observing from a distance thought the gesture by Horace rather gentlemanly, she was impressed by the man with manners and wanted to know more.

"Good Ray…its good to see yah." Maria said, increasing her step so that she walked in step with Horace.

"I had one of the most amazing breaks ever…" said Horace, not wanting to blow his own trumpet.

"I am sure you will tell me about it…"

"Tonight, my place…6:30."

Some students had started looking and The Greek came from no where, "Mr. Bates - glad you could join us at Harvard."

Maria and Horace burst out laughing. The Greek continued like a field marshall.

"Man, every time I see you, you're trying to talk to Maria."

Maria started walking towards the college restaurant and pretended that she never heard a single word The Greek had said. There was that type of silence that only leads to the conclusion that the truth has been uttered.

As an actress Maria learned that the most effective acting was saying nothing at all and merely pretending you never heard anything --- and that pantomime speaks volumes. In this case Maria aimed at saying, 'mind your own business.' And it worked perfectly.

The Greek was so-called because he hailed from a rich Greek family in Athens. No one really knew what the family did, some suggested his family had a stock in Africa's blood diamonds, and yet others suggested his family favored black liquid, the oil business. But the closest Horace ever got to this truth was that The Greek was actually from the Papayas family and was descendent from that lineage. His real name was Andrioso Papayas and because most students found this difficult to pronounce they called him The Greek. Andrioso did not mind the name, it was better than hearing his name mispronounced every two minutes.

When Horace thought about this, he found it ironic that the most educated in America at supposedly the best institution could not properly pronounce two Greek words correctly: Andrioso Papayas.

"So how was your break Mr. Bates," said The Greek, with his usual fan-fare of warmth and sarcasm.

"Good Andrioso, and I still can call you that sir," said Horace, in a catch-22 sort of way.

"Mr. Bates, the only man who can properly pronounce my name at Harvard and should I say in the Good Ole U S of A."

The Greek had an oval face that best could be described as similar to a vase stationed in a very large room. The kind of face women find endearing; but he was also unexpectedly tall, he used cologne like he invented the stuff. Horace had already told him on several occasions to, 'Lose the cologne Papayas.' But somehow the Greek always went back to half a bottle per squirt. The man just would not bundle under any sort of scientific proof. "Maybe it's because he can afford it - sonnofagun," said Horace to himself.

Later that evening Maria walked through the half open door at about the right time, Horace impatiently waited, like a starved bull dog that has not eaten since its master left home.

Then came the unexpected utterance;
"I am a woman Ray, I need romance."
"I know." Horace said, turning away from her. "Maybe this is not a good thing."
"Is that what you were thinking about throughout the break?"
"Kind of...I have to get Harvard out of the way and get that paper sweets."
"Please stop calling me sweets."
"Okay Maria, what do you..." said Horace almost getting up.
"I want romance Ray."

Horace could name a dozen brothers who had fallen short of success because of a women and he did not want that to be him. He could name professional footballers who signed an NFL contract with the left hand and then gave back all the money to the woman with the right hand, much to their family's despair. It was simple, moving forward something had to give...
Maria said, "And don't give me that maybe we should take it slow crap," interrupting Horace's thinking. Her face communicated the mental exhaustion of the conversation.

"Maria can we just be friends for tonight. Then...then we can catch a movie this Friday, how's that?"

The words sounded off, a fluttering of lies pithily bouncing off the apartment wall. Maria took one look at Horace and said, "Cool Ray, have it your way." Behind her words, was the cold emotion of someone now detaching from their lover.

*

A confluence of meetings and perfect timing gave Horace a chance in life. And so he imagined, seeing himself, as the pioneer from Carthage. He wanted to make something of himself. At Zimmermann, the law firm, he continued to understand the inner workings of the criminal justice system. Why do ex-convicts go back to crime upon leaving prison when they vowed not to? Case after case Horace found the same pattern --- disjointed families, poverty and an opportunity for crime.

The first week was uneventful and Horace prepared for the great romantic dinner with Maria on Friday. "I have to dump her, let her go, she is becoming too needy," he said to himself; reinforcing the shallowness of his planned departure from romantic life.

On Friday, Maria and Horace sat watching a movie entitled, The Great American Train Ride. The movie's premise - a group of female bank robbers stealing from passenger trains. Horace found the title rather appropriate for what he was intending to do and that is take a one way ride out of the relationship. He sat silently in the movie theater anxiously waiting for his rebirth back to bachelorhood. He went over his game plan, over and over like a high school football coach.

'Two receivers from QB---strong in the center ---rush on the left --- circle defense---over shoulder, tight end--- wide receiver moving on left--- throw right.' The moves played in his mind, but Horace was not rehearsing a football match he was rehearsing a break up.

Once Maria had settled down, Horace indicated he needed to use the rest room for good measure, he said "Just in case." His face brightly animated. He darted out and left her hanging. "That's it," Horace said to himself, "Hopefully she gets the message."

When the movie was over Maria called Horace on his cell phone only to get the answering machine. She left a message spoken delicately with no hint of anger, this impressed Horace. The message said, "Hey babe, what happened; just checking."

The next day as if the fix was in, he ran into Maria having changed his usual route. "And on the day I decide to change my route look who I run in to?" Horace said inwardly, "Hey what happened at the movies?" Maria asked.

"The job Maria, got a call from the job."

"I thought so. But you never called me back." She said standing firmly and pulling her legs back the way women stand when their blood pressure is about to boil.

Horace could not do it, he just could not cut her off. There was something in her spirit that was too beautiful. He decided he would not follow presidential advice.

*

The next day Maria was waiting for Horace at his apartment. Horace's apartment had the flowery scents he had first observed when he entered the Sheraton Hotel. When Maria walked into the apartment she was happy that the room had 'That oriental cologne,' better that, than the smell of another woman, she said to herself.

"So, Mr. Harvard what's going on here?" She asked standing up and straight faced.

Maria looked intently into Horace's eyes giving him that 'Look me in the eyes baby look' popularized by Raquel Welch in the movie '100 Rifles.' It became clear to Horace at that moment that Maria was onto him. After all Maria's previous boyfriend had been a guy by the name of Ronaldo Hernandez, he was a sometime drug dealer in the Red District. A drug dealer who wore flashy bling-bling clothes. Currently, Ronaldo was serving time in the state penitentiary pending bail. Ronaldo could not afford to post bail for the indictment - conspiracy to distribute crack cocaine within a school district. Horace had concluded from a legal perspective that, the only benefit Ronaldo had was that under the new Fair Sentencing Act which changed the mandatory minimum for crack cocaine from five grams gets you five years to 28 grams gets you five years, he wasn't looking at more than five years in prison.

The police found Ronaldo, Maria's former boyfriend, smoking a cigar in his "Den;" street lingo for an apartment stuffed with the latest electronic gadgetry. Inside the den he had a prostitute and was spending some of his excess income. The police officers busted Ronaldo on an outstanding warrant and for soliciting. The search that had followed revealed white cocaine power stashed under an envelope and underneath the envelope was an illegal 0.44 caliber. Maria heard about the arrest from her cousin who also dealt in drugs;

Christopher Espinoza, who everyone called the Duke because he resembled El Duke, the Cuban Yankee.

Maria had continued telling the story of how she no longer dated thugs to Horace.

"The Duke's voice came through the cell phone late into the night," she said, "What do you mean he was arrested?"

"I mean he was arrested, what else can I say about someone being arrested?" The Duke said.

"For what?" Maria asked.

"I can't say over the phone, but you know the usual."

"Where is he being held?" Maria asked, her voice becoming angrier like a broken overheating drier.

"Downtown courthouse, the one next to Picknet Street."

The Picknet's reputation was the most notorious in high flying arrests. The who's who of Boston's criminal underworld had all been processed at Picknet. One time the police had arrested a drug dealer with one hundred kilos of heroin, the largest in the state. The police who worked that precinct were said to be able to smell drugs a mile away. When you were stopped by the Picknet crew, you better not even smell of Bourbon," Maria said to Horace. "The crew were not racist; not sexist; not anti-capitalist either, they did their job and this they did well," she emphasized.

Maria visited Ronaldo in his jail cell. The jail visits had cemented her decision never to become a lawyer. The hordes of Black and Latino men standing idle like produce at the market...

As soon as she saw Ronaldo, she asked him about the rumors about the prostitute.

Ronaldo was silent, the same arrogance he had shown as a drug king pin had not faded. "He still has the charisma," Maria said to herself. "Most criminals do "

"Ronaldo I am moving on, this is not for me," Maria said.

"Now that a brother is in jail see how you do me," said Ronaldo, indicating that he knew it was coming.

"But what did I do Ronaldo? You did this to yourself."

"No, you the one who's leaving," said Ronaldo.

Maria found the lack of personal responsibility rather surprising and said, "You gonna tell me you here in prison and it's because of me..."

At that moment Ronaldo yelled, "Guard, get this bitch outtahere...fuck this."

"No Ronaldo, fuck you --- asshole," said Maria in a very calm voice, not the least bit angered by being called bitch. "You want bitch – okay, I got something for you when you get out, my cousins are gonna fuck you up."

"What's this bitch talking about, guard – didn't you hear me, I gotta move man, this is wasting my time. I got better things to do."

"Like what Ronaldo, even in prison you 'Got better things to do'. Get real," Maria said looking away from Ronaldo.

As Ronaldo got up she said, "My family did not come here from Venezuela for nothing, I want more for myself. America is not about being a gangster and rap music artist. You're from Mexico home-boy and you don't even like black people so why act like them!"

After the visit, she ended it all. The relationship had made her gain close to thirty pounds.

Ronaldo then uttered something about Maria being a lose lady and entered the confines of the jail cell, a turtle returning to its shell.

Since then Maria had vowed she would never date another well-heeled drug lord, 'too much drama.' She was done with drug trafficking. While the fun is good, she agreed with herself, most of them were perennial losers hiding behind an expensive facade – the visceral lie of having made it. Their fortunes, the drug lords, were merely as good as the next good detective; one paper away from being busted through a government issued search warrant. Once arrested Maria noted that the drug lords often turned childlike and started to suggest that the police officer either planted the twenty pounds of marijuana or that the police officers were vindictive and racist.

After Ronaldo, Horace seemed to be a perfect fit for the new picture Maria was painting for her life. After all he was Mr. Black Harvard – At this time though, as the two sat in the apartment, Maria wanted to confront Horace about being dumped at the movies. Horace had already made up his mind to continue with the romance and said, "I apologize, a lot on my mind." The two hugged and a primal bond seemed to take shape. Apparently pushing some things away brings them closer, Horace said to himself, stroking Maria's hair.

Horace recalled his mom:

"Horace my dear, the greatest gift God has given you is the ability to forgive and see the redeeming qualities in others." Tonight the two, Maria and Horace seemed like metal melting together, as their emotions started to cool down. He felt like Beethoven, deaf but playing his life's passion, unscripted but intuitive, the music of love.

*

The unchanging circumstances called for a new plan on the part of Horace's assuming romance. He would not rock the boat but allow life to dictate the terms. Maria left that morning and everything seemed to have corrected itself, the two love birds were back to square one; the alpha of their romance. Those memories of how the two had met began to take over and now the rational attorney to be could not explain why the attraction had just deepened.

Horace turned his full attention to finishing his Harvard law degree. The spring semester of the final year is never easy, he had heard. The professors make sure that they hit you with the right amount of punches to knock out the last bit of irrational civilian left, 'you have to be a Harvard lawyer' they say. The duty of the Harvard law professor is to make sure that you understand the social thinking in the country and not just practice law, Horace said to himself. Now looking at a picture of Maria his heart felt light and at ease, gone was the impatience and the frigidity of dating someone new.

Unlike the previous semester, Horace did not see much of Abdullah Salem and the man kept his distance. But towards the end of the final semester, two weeks to be exact an interesting thing happened that would forever change the life of Horace Arthur Bates.

As Horace exited the lecture, the normal routine having unfolded, he walked towards the library and was deeply engaged in understanding the theory of justice from his legal theory class. He was engaged in fully understanding the theory of jurisprudence as espoused by the theorist Joseph Rawls, when he ran into Abdullah.

"Mr. Horace." Abdullah said.

Horace realized that for most of third year he had not seen Abdullah's investigatory face. And he had forgiven him for something, but he could not remember.

"Mr. Abdullah Salem, how can I forget the man and the name; I gotta go. Congratulations on Harvard sir." This was Horace's way of saying, 'It's you again, better not come close or else.'

"Don't run Horace, I want to apologize, maybe I was too pushy, I am from another country you know."

"No need to apologize Abdullah," said Horace in a way that made it clear to Abdullah that he was not into the apology game.

What does he want from me now, thought Horace and he clinched his face into a tight adverse expression.

"No problem, it's over," said Horace, maintaining the statute-like face. Abdullah seemed surprised at being forgiven and had nothing to say. The atmosphere was both sullen and awkward at the same time. Horace returned to what had been occupying his mind and concluded that, perhaps, the meaning of law the professors want us to arrive at is that the world is filled with man like Abdullah: men who are interest driven to the extent of breaching the rights of others. Horace continued walking, graduation day beckoned like a light at the end of a tunnel.

CHAPTER SEVENTEEN

The year ended on a lighter note and Horace graduated cum laude from Harvard school of law. He managed to scrape through the rigorous academic demands by scoring all A's in the final semester, this naturally raised his grade point average to 3.3, enough to receive an honors aggregate.

The call from Carolina was lukewarm. "You did it." Mrs. Bates said. She sounded delicately balanced like a fine-tuned violin.

And with those words Horace began thinking about taking the bar exam. The bar exam is the qualifying exam every lawyer must take before they can call themselves an attorney. He registered for the July exam and continued to retain his apartment on Wendell Street.

Preparation for the bar proved demanding and Horace took four weeks off as a junior associate at *Zimmermann* to prepare. This involved practice questions all laid out over a bar course of eight weeks.

The bar exam produces the type of obsessive-compulsive routine that often leads to isolation of the exam taker. For Horace this was no different, the cards written out and suggesting the brief answers at the core of the American legal system all made for quick memorization.

Horace studied for eight hours a day, returning to his apartment for dinner and the occasional Maria rendezvous. In July he took the bar exam and in October to his amazement he passed, surprisingly scoring high on both the multiple choice and the essay portion. It was now official, "Hello, Mr. Horace Arthur Bates, Esquire," said Maria when the results came in.

Now Horace was a full-fledged lawyer, no longer a law student having to answer to the Socratic Method, he was fully entitled to stand in any Massachusetts office and declare – 'mistrial.' He had standing; an all too familiar legal word denoting that one now could argue in a court room and that argument taken seriously.

In North Carolina things were different, under the iron curtain of capital punishment Dixon waited to hear from his freshly minted cousin attorney, Horace A. Bates. Dixon's case had become a felony murder and Horace was yet to enter an appearance thereby becoming the attorney-on-record. So far Dixon had managed to enter pro se motions, legal jargon for as your own lawyer. Most of the motions Dixon entered were inappropriate and would best be considered appellate in nature.

Later in the fall of 2009 Horace tried to convince his law firm to take the case of his cousin for free as pro bono. It was on a Wednesday and Timmy was seated alone in the conference room, drinking his patented water. Horace entered quietly and said, "Hey Timmy, have a moment?"

"Horace, how nice, how is everything."

"Good and you?" Horace said, as he took a sit directly opposite Timmy.

"Good." He carried on looking at the stack of papers in such a manner that he was suggesting this better be good.

"I wanted to talk to you about something," said Horace, pouring himself a glass of water, "I have a cousin in North Carolina and his name is Dixon." Horace proceeded to retell the story about the bank robbery. He made sure that the story sounded sympathetic.

"He never had a father...A student in eighth grade..."

"I get it Ray. You want the firm to take his case," said Timmy, at the end of the presentation. His check bones rose up. "Look, if we take this it's your baby, right. You are the principal; do you think you can handle this? It will be good exposure for the firm and the kind of stuff I talked to you about last year remember."

"I remember." Horace answered.

"Good, you can represent your cousin through our firm. Let me know if you need anything?" asked Timmy in flat-voiced speech.

Horace left the conference room and went back to his office. "True indeed, ask and you shall receive," he said to himself, agreeing with the biblical instruction.

At his desk he brought up the screen for computer filing; he electronically filed his notice for appearance under *North Carolina Rule 2:13*. At the other end, in Carthage, the superior court clerk received the notice and entered the name Horace Bates Esquire (very important person) as the attorney on record for the felony trial of Dixon Bates. "Probably his brother," said the clerk to another clerk in the same cubicle. The other clerk turned back to his work uttering, "Maybe, you never know. You have all sorts of apples in one family."

On that day Horace decided to start exercising again and to try and regain back the muscular frame of his early twenties. "I am almost thirty," he said to himself in amazement. He walked to Boston central park for a forty minute high pace walk. After thirty minutes he had had enough and went to the corner Star Bucks to get a coffee.

He left the counter and started sipping his coffee on his way back to the law office. He sat on a bench and did not even notice the many pigeons around him and even strangers who greeted him in his new Brooks Brothers 1818. The coffee tasted good. He raised his head only to be met by the sight of none other than Abdullah Salem.

"Hey Horace," said Abdullah in the usual gruff and rough voice.

"Abdullah, what a surprise," Horace said, staring him down like a bad cabbage in the fridge.

"Thank you..."

"For what?" Horace asked.

"For saying you are happy to see me."

Horace remembered that this was Abdullah after all and things usually have a different meaning and he said, "You're welcome I think." He got up and while preparing to leave he said to himself, "This cat is not the coldest beer I tell you." He looked at Abdullah and walked ten feet away.

Abdullah noticed the unexpected departure and said to Horace, "Please don't go Ray, we need to talk."

"Oh yes, I need to go, always good talking with you buddy boy, manyana."

"Your life is in danger," said Abdullah.

"Oh no, yours is in danger, especially since in Boston, extortion is putting someone in the apprehension of future violence."

Horace felt like tearing Abdullah into pieces, shredding him into cabbage for salad. "I don't know who this kid thinks he is," he said to himself, his face registering the unpleasant thought.

"You are out of your mind Mr. Salem. Get lost now."

These words never moved Abdullah who was acting more like a jilted lover than an attorney from Harvard; as resilient as the criminal in prohibition. Abdullah made sure his target understood the sort of obsession he had.

Horace ignored Abdullah and strolled away. He did not see it coming, nor hear Abdullah's light steps. He did not even see the handkerchief rise and cover his mouth but Horace fell to the ground and a van whizzed to the spot; the two men assisting Abdullah quickly put Horace in the back and the van disappeared into the lunch crowd.

The crowd which saw this thought it a prank. It never crossed their mind that anyone would really want to abduct a black man. The sun cut through the streets, closely connected to the van's powerful get away it simmered through the van's gas emission creating an illusionary moment. Horace never felt a thing, only blackness and a falling feeling. His eyes quickly shut to the animal type chloroform and he fell like a bag of potatoes. Abdullah's decision to abduct Horace had not come easy, but that was the only way.

CHAPTER EIGHTEEN

A rancid smell swirled up and filled the room. Blind folded, Horace became visionless. He could not see anything, only the blackness and when he tried to open his eyes the cloth covering his eyes was tightened like a hangman's noose on Thanksgiving. A figure entered the room; the echoing steps from the expensive shoes were amplified as the sound bounced around the room. Horace knew something about the sound of expensive shoes; his daddy had made sure of it...

As the figure approached, Horace readied himself for pain; a slap on the face; pinching of the ears; anything that would confirm he was still alive.

A second figure also entered the room, this one with cheaper shoes. But this was punctuated by the smell of expensive Italian cologne. Horace remembered that a week ago he had smelt the same expensive smell at Saks Fifth Avenue. Now that there were two figures in the room he wondered what the next move would be. There was silence and a third figure entered---he could not place this figure and concluded that it must be a woman.

The three figures stood for a moment. Then one figure said, "...Is that him?"
"...Yes."

"Definitely Harvard, look at that suit and neck tie." The others laughed.

At this point Horace's full memory kicked in and he recalled that the last thing he saw just before the darkness was that kid, Abdullah. Horace said, "Abdullah, what's going on here?" This was said in a calm and gentle voice.
"...So he saw you bonehead."

"He turned his head and saw me," said Abdullah, trying to explain that necessity had taken over. "He is a very smart guy."
"We might have a problem."
"But I thought he is our only option," said Abdullah.

The other figure got angry and said, "Abdullah, why don't you just shut up! Do you want to explain to him everything that we are doing here!" said the mysterious figure who appeared to be the boss. He thought for a moment and said, "Alright then, remove the blinders."

A figure approached Horace from behind and struggled to loosen the blinders. After a few seconds, the figure said, "Okay Horace."
"Abdullah," Horace said, his eyes showing the anger he was feeling; deep rooted and menacing. "Abdullah, you are going to prison for this, as soon as I am done with you, you will be building pyramids in Egypt my friend."

Abdullah and the other two figures starred at Horace, letting him vent out his emotion. It seemed like they were taking it as collateral damage to their job.

Then the figure that seemed to be in authority, wearing a white doctor's coat said, "Mr. Bates, good afternoon…"

"What's going on here?" said Horace. He tried to move but his hands and legs were tied to the chair tighter than a wedding knot. Even his neck pulsated from the tension of the tight rope around him. The position was so uncomfortable that Horace almost threw up; this forced him to say:
"Water, soda please…"

"Give him some water," said the figure in a white medical coat.
To the surprise of Horace the figure then said, "My name is Dr. Zinner." His voice seemed to fit the room's rough look.

"Sir, you and Abdullah here will have to untie me immediately please. This is false imprisonment; a crime in addition to the kidnapping charge."
"Horace …Horace…we already know that you are a lawyer, so shut up and listen for a moment." Dr. Zinner wanted to make sure that Horace understood who held the keys to freedom in this situation. "Mr. Horace, understand that you are not in a position to state your usual legal editorials."

*

"How much do you know about physics?"
"Not much, Dr. Zimmer…"

"It's Zinner, how about time travel, ever read science fiction growing up in Carthage, North Carolina with your cousin-brother Dixon."
"You guys are lost," Horace said.

"No, Mr. Horace on the contrary it's you who needs help in this situation. Again Mr. Horace, what do you know about time travel?"
"Look man I am a lawyer. I don't know what Abdullah told you but you have the wrong man. Abdullah tried to introduce me to some physics professor one time ask him --- Abdullah?"

"Again leave Abdullah out of this Horace. What do you know about time travel?" It then dawned on Horace that this Zinner was actually serious. "You serious man?" Horace asked.

"No, I am playing - Horace," Dr. Zinner sarcastically snapped.
"Then…sir…with all due respect, I know nothing about time travel, nothing at all. I saw some movies but that's not the answer you looking for I believe."
"Again, lose the lawyer stuff, we know you had one of the best results in the bar exam. We know that you have a good head on your shoulders," said Dr. Zinner.

"Who are you people?" asked Horace, but what he really wanted to say is ---- I need a lawyer.

Dr. Zinner approached Horace and looked him straight in the eye, intending to communicate some primal fear.
"Listen to me; we have been following you for quite some time. We sent Abdullah but for some reason you didn't like him; I should say I don't blame you."

Abdullah shook his head and Dr. Zinner continued saying, "We tried other subtle ways but Mr. Horace is a stubborn individual."

When Dr. Zinner realized that Horace was getting angry and the veins on his face were starting to make him look like a primed tomato he said, "Relax Horace, relax please."

Horace resumed shaking his head. The adrenaline could be smelled coming out of his nostrils. His blood seemed to get hotter and he started to believe he had the power to break loose from the rope…the adrenaline speaking to him. He looked out at the window.

Zinner saw Horace looking through the window and said, "Don't think about that. The flight down from nine floors will kill you…relax."
"No, you relax Zinner," said Horace not wanting to relax. As soon as he relaxed he would lose the adrenaline, and he needed it. He wanted to remain awake and venomous like a cobra in some African desert.
"You are a very interesting individual," said Zinner.

"…And what exactly is that supposed to mean; look I have never met you before."
"That's just an observation Horace."

"Since you have me here, tell me about this time travel business so that I can go home."

"Mr. Horace, once I tell you, there is no going back home; home becomes everywhere." Dr. Zinner smiled and looked at the others.
"I don't have all day. Please tell me so that I can go home. There are people looking for me right now."
"We already have that under control Horace. No one is looking for you."
"Okay what do you want man?" Horace asked
"We have an offer to make you. We have developed a heavy lift machine that flies back into the past."
"For real…"
"Yes, for real Horace, the science behind this is complex to say the least…but certain individuals can time travel because they do not disintegrate when travelling through one lunar system to another and faster than the speed of light.

And you are one of those individuals Horace."
"That must be a mistake; I am just a brother from Carthage, North Carolina."
"No you're not. You have the correct sequence in your DNA that allows for time travel."

"And how do you know this?" Horace asked.
"Mr. Bates, we researched and sampled you for many years sir, in fact now is as good a time as any to say this; we are not the only ones looking for you."
"Who else is looking for me?" Horace asked now with the inquisitive stare of a high school teacher.

"Let's just say, you don't what to ever run into them and introduce your self as Horace Arthur Bates; that could be the end of you."

*

For many years the group had been watching Horace; from when he was a little boy in Carthage, North Carolina; where it turned out that the superstition about the water had a scientific explanation after all and Carthage's water had something special in it. The group had found an interesting human frequency emanating from Carthage. When Horace was in California, the group had rented a room next to the compound and continued their surveillance. Their whole science and research had at its core the name; Horace Arthur Bates. But Horace never knew it, except for Abdullah; he really never saw anything unusual about the events that were unfolding; even when he had got to a prestigious law firm with a C- aggregate; and when the future U.S. president had offered him a job... now the pieces were forced together by his abduction. Horace could only see half the picture and he interrupted Zinner's speech with, "...what do you want from me sir, it's all fair and good but what do you really want from me? Don't get me wrong, I wish you much success but I am sure if you do your DNA numbers lottery another name will pop up. After all I am not a science junkie."

"My Horace, you are likeable - that I can see..." Zinner said. The process of torture is seldom planned, thought Zinner, and never goes according to preconceived notions of how the tortured will react... here the plan had been to instill in Horace the fear of God but the young man had remained in control putting them at the receiving end. Everyone expected Horace to be flattered and to accept this as a once in a life time opportunity.

"I am not interested in your games," said Horace, spitting his words out.

"Mr. Horace let me rephrase something here, this is not a take it or leave it situation, it's a take it or else!"

This had the effect of making Horace more taunt like a ballet dancer. He decided to engage them a little in case he should have to reveal the men to the authorities.

"Tell me more about your program."

"I like that, your words Mr. Bates, 'The Program.' We are part of a group of scientist known as the Houston Group. Are you familiar with the black explorer who climbed mount Everest, Charles Houston?"

"Yes."

"We were formed in his spirit Mr. Bates, and are dedicated to his pioneering spirit."

"Again I am not a pioneer but a lawyer?"

"Mr. Bates, will it be of some help to know that if you do not join us then that's the end of you. Either sign up or we will destroy you."

"Not the least bit interested."

Zinner slapped Horace across the face several times. "Zinner, that's enough, we need him," said one of the other two men who had said nothing up to now. "If he insists let's give him a taste of things and he will come back running for our help. The other group will get him soon enough."

"Okay Ray, I am sorry man, no hard feelings... When the time comes you will find us. Remember that The Russian will come for you and unless you are with us we cannot protect you. We only protect members of, in your words,

'The Program.' Good luck Mr. Bates. Try telling the police and see whether they will believe you..."

When Horace woke up he was back sitting on the same bench. He felt a terrible pain on the back of his head. Looking at his watch, he saw that two hours had gone by. He wondered what to do next; whether to report the incident to police or to let it go as if nothing happened? He got up from the bench and across the bushes he saw Abdullah dashing across the hedge and into the van. Horace confidently walked towards the local police precinct.

CHAPTER NINETEEN

The alarms sounded off on the sidewalk, blindly creating the immediacy of a traffic jam and because the noise went up and down, this gave Horace a dizzy feeling. He felt like someone high on heroin in the sixties. He staggered towards the precinct and thought about the torture he had just received...this Zinner fellow and Abdullah, he said to himself.

Horace entered the precinct and began to offer his story as succinctly as he could to the police officers. Within seconds it became clear that the police officer was not buying the story. The officer said, "Are you currently under any drugs or medication?"
"No..."

"How about drugs mixed with alcohol; drugs and roots..?" the officer asked.

"No...hell ..no. Are you serious?" said Horace. He realized that the police officer wanted to tease him out of his police station.
"Look here young man, relax, go home, you have a girlfriend don't you; don't be like one of those lawyers who cracks up just after passing the bar, go home. I don't want to have to arrest you for being a public disorder. Your story does not make sense, it's like picking cotton from a cotton bud."

Horace left the precinct and walked back to the law office. He still would have to account for the absence of about three hours and the raggedy look.

It felt as if he had left the office two days ago, and the minutes were adding up like a stack of pancakes.

Horace thought for one moment ...the mind of a man tends to flicker towards self-defense, like in this situation. But when there is no one to blame then it starts to make things up...rationalization. Horace decided to let it go. Maybe this was Abdullah's way of getting even. They do say that jilted high school friends have been known to do strange things...

The days that followed were an anvil heated against his skin. Horace could see Abdullah everywhere, everytime he turned he saw that silly smirk and heard that characteristic accent, 'Hey Ray.' Sometimes he saw Zinner...

In the next week Horace went to the alumni office to get the contact information on Abdullah from the register. He wore his Harvard alumni cap, so that he would be unrecognizable, to any one making a follow up.
"I am sorry but we don't give out personal information," said the register's secretary.

Horace left the register's office and waited until the secretary went out for lunch. He then went back to her desk. He pretended to be a work-study student working in the office.

Horace typed Abdullah Salem and the curious contact address of the law firm of *Zimmermann* came on the screen.

"What's going on here?" he said to himself.

Horace left the building with more questions than answers. He felt isolated and still considered all this as one elaborate joke. He resolved however to buy a gun and applied for a gun permit at the sheriff's office. "Next time that cat comes near me, I have something for him," he said to himself folding the permit and placing it in his pocket.

Still more days went by, until Horace decided to lose the investigation and see what happens next. He did not like being a passive agent in his life after all he was…

Ray jammin' never bammin'…

He never told anyone about the event of the past days; not his mom; not Maria; and definitely not The Greek. He kept it all in, hoping that somehow it was all an elaborate joke. "But if it's a joke, why is Dr. Zinner the only one laughing?" he asked himself.

CHAPTER TWENTY

D r. Zinner was not his real name. He had changed it from the Russian of Zyvesisky. No one seemed to know what his first name was and never bothered to ask him. He was an astronomer who had deflected in the eighties charmed by Ronald Reagan's smile. His colleagues had not believed his stories about being anti-communist. They always suspected that Zinner came to America for other reasons, perhaps to finish off a PhD with a lower pass mark. "Couldn't cut it in Moscow," was often said behind his back.

He did some consulting work for NASA, motor design and jet propulsion; and anyone willing to pay him in hard cash under the table. "Where Uncle Sam will not find it."

In addition to wearing the same plaid jeans for what seemed like eternity, Dr. Zinner stuck to himself like a cirrus cloud against the backdrop of a clear white sky; always there, but not really consequential. The most prominent feature about Zinner was his nose, it appeared to go on-and-on with no end in sight; surprisingly, women found it magnetic.

His income was mainly from grants, the kind of grants given in six figure increments. Zinner's research had gone from astrophysics to quantum and to relativity. He saw himself taking over from, 'Where Sir Einstein leaves us.'

In his research papers, the ones he hid from everyone at NASA and did in the early mornings at around 3 A.M., Zinner had jotted down a series of theories and equations and was shopping his junk science for funding.
The sepia folder, hand written on top, *For Dr. Nicolai Zinner Only*, was where Zinner kept his greatest conclusion. He wrote: it is agreed science that light bends; and because time is determined by the movement of light. If light bends, then time travel backwards is possible. Relative motion should include the principle of relative position or geo-coordinates.
From this rather didactic reasoning Zinner had concluded that depending on where you are in the world, time changes. And that means light from one place has not reached another place on earth. This was a major breakthrough for Zinner and he continued developing the theory...

Page 76 of his papers read, "...The general reasoning at this time is that moving from Greenwich meridian creates different time zones; but my conclusion is that at certain positions the same pocket of light is yet to arrive there. So as light travels so does time..."

Zinner remembered that his role model Sir Albert Einstein had said, "...Imagination is greater than knowledge," he went all the way and declared,

K
E
N

S
I
B
A
N
D
A

time travel using light as the medium is possible for all humans. Now he was faced with the problem of actually proving all this imaginary science.

For proof Zinner embarked on a secret research station in the Dominican Republic where he was aided by the locals who believed his statement that: 'he is retiring to the sugar cane business.' They helped Zinner build a research station… Zinner now wrote in his log that here in the Dominican Republic is where I have made the leap of faith from scientist to pioneer. He underlined the next section Dominican Experiments and wrote, 'See Zinner for explanation.'

In the Dominican Republic Zinner had managed to get two balls to travel faster than light. This was achieved by a high propulsion system which Zinner noted would revolutionize the manufacturing of sugar. In reality, it was a gun type device in which the object released traveled slightly faster than the speed of light.

The results of the Dominican experiment were legendary in underground science circles. One ball fired at a speed less than the speed of light from position A, a marker, went straight as expected. The second ball fired faster than the speed of light got to the A marker and turned backwards in a circle in the same direction from where it came. Zinner thus concluded that the ball turning backwards can actually see its previous path and that essentially is time travel. Zinner started sending out grant proposals in which he outlined that he needed more money to send a human being back into time. And that because of the success in the Dominican Republic he was confident and knew what he was doing. To many he was dismissed as, '…That loony Russian scientist.' Zinner's theory of going faster than the speed of light would take us back in time was not taken seriously, until one day he received a letter from a man who referred to himself as, Head of the Houston Group – a Boston lawyer by the name of Timmy.

CHAPTER TWENTY ONE

Dixon Bates remained incarcerated and was starting to grow impatient. He had not heard from his cousin in Boston. Horace had yet to argue the case and he started preparing late at night at *Zimmermann*.

Horace's defense was that Dixon had withdrawn from the felony and could not be charged with felony murder.

Voir dire; the process of selecting jurors, would begin next week and Horace planned on being there. He gave himself two weeks for the whole trial. This would be his first trial.

Horace looked at the facts, meticulously peering through them. "Bad fact, good fact," he agreed with himself. His relationship with Maria continued to deepen and he could sense an impending engagement down the line.

In the law firm, the partners were impressed by Horace's work and wanted him one day as a partner; but there was only one thing standing in the way – he was staring to feel burnt out; like rubber on a Mustang.

At the Plymouth County prison Dixon awaited the decision that would determine if he continued to live or not. Horace contemplated the process at hand: the criminal trial for murder normally raises the stacks to a heightened theatre. The state party seeks to rid society of an unwanted element while the defense is usually centered on giving a fair and humanized defense for the defendant. All gamesmanship without justice for the victim…

On that Monday of his arrival at the downtown courthouse, the accentuated feeling of being tested consumed Horace. His sinews adjusted to the thickening smell of the jailhouse when he visited the cell.

"How are you doing?" asked Horace, sitting on the bench. Dixon approached the bench wearing the usual striped chain gang attire.
He dragged himself, somewhat pulling himself, stalling, the way an old broke-down machine does. His face timidly flashed a sigh of being cornered in a rat hole.
"Good." Dixon answered, after what appeared to be eternity. "How you feel about the case?" he said in street lingo.

"I feel confident", Horace answered, looking away; he had learned that the more confident one sounds, then the more confident people felt around him.

Horace had come a long way. He had second chaired a case with his mentor. He recalled the case, when the detective, was asked, "Was the stop based on reasonable suspicion?"
"Yes," the officer had replied.

K
E
N

S
I
B
A
N
D
A

"How then do you explain that the informant information only said, I quote, 'White male.' About how many white males fit the description?"

"Many."

Horace knew he had to ask the right question in order to get the right answer.

Now in court, Horace steadied himself, making sure that he seemed as calm as he felt.

"I think we can win, my withdrawal defense is air tight."

"How about the other defendants? Mookie said I was there."

"I will deal with your friend Mookie, let's concentrate on you," said Horace like John Wayne at Rio Grande.

Now the conversation started shifting to more personal stuff and Horace adjusted his collar to indicate that he was relaxing.

"Dee, you would have made one hell of a lawyer, you were smarter than me. Every lawyer in this country knows someone who would have made a better lawyer than them."

Dixon had scored all A's in the ninth grade and this always haunted Horace. Something had gone wrong, he said to himself. Dixon started hanging out with the wrong crowd; taking rap music literally; he was initiated into petty crime. Horace remembered that in the sixties and seventies black America had seemed to have found itself. Then hip hop seemed to come out of no where ---- no more soul music, no more black empowerment, just quick money and phat ass…and a lot of jail bound kids in between.

Horace continued thinking; looking at Dixon…Nothing seemed to matter in this gangster mentality, just the result of more money. The hipsters are attractive to some women. Maybe that's the problem; these women who find the whole idea of gang bangers exciting…that is until they are gang banged. And then they have to file a police report for sexual assault…In Dixon's case he was now a star in the hood. He had some of the most beautiful women sending him naked pictures taken while in the bath tub.

Horace absorbed the atmosphere and concluded that humanizing Dixon is the only chance of staying execution.

"The electric chair is the ultimate for criminal education known to mankind. It does not purport to correct anything but merely to exterminate it…one hundred kilowatts of electricity enough to light up a medium sized city and enough to brew a cup of coffee for every coffee aficionado in the states," said Horace to Dixon. He then got up and walked off the thoughts about Dixon receiving the electric chair. He turned towards Dixon, looking over his shoulder and said, "That's what we face cuz'."

The prospective thirty six jurors from which twelve would be selected were seated in the audience section. Taking jury dynamics at Harvard helped Horace a great deal. He learned that a jury with women is a thinking jury. Horace's intension was to select all jurors who want to give Dixon a second chance and to be weary of the types who like punishment and 'Fixing people.' Those who believe the only person capable of an honest mistake and redemption is them… It was giving the jurors enough rope and seeing which one hangs.

Friday came soon enough – the court resembled the Titanic on that fateful day when it sank, packed to the corner with people waiting in anticipation of the proceedings. The judge, a local boy, John Ambrose, entered the court room, as usual, with the right mix of reality and substance. He proceeded to speak in what appeared to be a monotone, "The matter of *State v. Dixon Bates* will begin."

He lifted some papers and read fast like an atomic processor, he maintained eye contact as he went along.

"Please enter appearances."

"Todd Michaels, judge, for the state," said the neatly dressed assistant prosecutor.

"And Horace Bates for the defense your honor." Thus began the age old duel known to man said Horace to himself...throwing down the gauntlet.

"Well then, seems here like we have a local Harvard boy come to make good. Mr. Bates, you are aware of criminal procedure down here?"

"Yes, your honor," Horace said. He did not know whether the judge was piggy backing him or whether the judge was making a valid point.

"Yes...I know your honor. The rules are different down here."

The judge looked around in acknowledgement of the answer and said, "Then let's proceed..."

The process of selectively choosing the jurors went on until close to noon when all members had been selected. At its conclusion the judge piped, "Tomorrow, gentlemen, we move for opening arguments."

An opening argument is like a road map in a court case; it gives the jurors the 'game plan' of the advocacy intended and lets the court know what the evidence will be. "It's like telling a story, the beginning is the most important – getting the correct analogy; a song; a quotation...anything," Horace said to himself when penning the opening argument.

The next day arrived like a running water buffalo. Horace was unexpectedly upbeat. He began his opening in a slow and concerned tone, and wore the trademark grey with stripes. Not tailored but J C Penny.

Horace waited for his turn after the prosecutor; he made sure to ignore the prosecutor's themes and conclusions. "Ladies and gentlemen of the jury, this case is about someone who got out...got out of the car just before the car ran a stop sign; just before the car hit the pedestrian. Through out this case, I want you to think about someone who gets out. My client Mr. Dixon Bates, a straight 'A' student in eighth nineth, got out of that car before it hit a pedestrian." Horace looked at the jurors, one after the other, sure not to offend by looking at one juror too long. "Mr. Bates got out of the conspiracy to rob just before the gun went off. Yes, he said the words in the beginning to start the bank robbery, but he had a change of heart and left the bank. Human redemption is for everyone..."

The assistant prosecutor looked at Horace with his deep sepia eyes like a meandering ocean in its depth. He said nothing, silent, after all he was nicknamed, the Mongoose. The nickname seemed fair enough, Horace agreed with himself. Horace raised his voice, "So this case will tell the story of how

THE RETURN TO GIBRALTAR   117

Mr. Bates is not accountable for the actions of others."

Now it was the prosecutor's turn for a rebuttal. The assistant prosecutor had put in fifteen years at the office. Mongoose walked slowly to the juror's bench and smiled, "This case is not about blaming the wrong person, it's about what the defendant did; Bates the defendant and not his cousin Bates the Harvard educated lawyer!"

"You honor, I object to that," said Horace.

"Grounds..." The judge asked.

"Relevancy and argumentative..."

"Sustained!" The judge was impressed, 'This kid actually knows the law,' he agreed with himself.

The assistant prosecutor now started walking towards Horace. "This case is not about blaming the wrong person. It's about starting a car and the car has no brakes," he said.

Testimonial evidence was presented in only two days: it did not consist of a lot of evidence; three witnesses, which Horace cross-examined to the fullest of his abilities. He made sure that the arresting officer told the jury what he wrote in his report that it 'Appears the Dixon fellow was taken for a ride.' He made sure that the teller talked about how remorseful he looked after saying the words and that it was the co-defendant who jumped in and started putting pressure on her. He made sure that the bank's security guard on cross-examination admitted there was an argument between Mookie and Dixon.

After the closing arguments, time came for the jury to render its verdict. Horace felt good about the whole case. He gave his closing after the State rested and it took the jury only two hours to arrive at a verdict.

"What is the verdict?" the judge asked, taking the verdict form, from the jury foreman. The jury turned to face the audience who by now included Horace's mother and father. Tears swirled in Dixon's eyes and the jury foreman said, "Not guilty."

For a moment the universe seemed to end, to completely stop and the room became as silent as a baby taking a nap.

Horace turned and looked at his cousin; he could not give anything in the world to see what he saw --- a broad smile plastered on Dixon like a baby receiving an early morning thirst quencher of milk...they say that after you win a trial it feels like an elixir, Horace said to himself. His face glowed with the joyous realization of having thrown the Mongoose under the bus.

The Mongoose approached Horace and took out his hand, "Congratulations Mr. Bates; you did well." He did not show the slightest sign of resentment. "When you come down to North Carolina, consider joining us, some day." He gave Horace his business card.

An interesting moment occurred as a juror looked at Horace, it was if they were saying, "We did this for you," Horace thought to himself, while packing his lawyer brief case. The mood continued in its upward swirl; spreading like a wild camp fire. By the time Horace reached the door, the whole of Harvard class of 2009 had heard the news. The fire continued spreading and by the time he was at the door leaving the building, the law firm of *Zimmer-*

mann had heard the news. Horace had earned the nickname… "Sharpshooter." He was a man on the up…

Even Maria heard the news and decided that her man was, "The man." Now Maria had validated the whole relationship and she agreed that she had chosen the right man.

Horace was on the expense paid business class plane heading for Boston and as he looked out of the window a sense of calm became present. Undeterred, motionless, and unearthed by the sun's percolation, he was the black eagle taking a moment before his final ascendancy.

CHAPTER TWENTY TWO

The victory came as no surprise, it tasted sweet, like nectarines picked in their prime and eaten with a smothering of vinegar. The respect that seemed to come with the win pointed to a future as a litigator; a high stakes litigator defending the man as the cause. At the law office in Boston, Horace was surprised to hear even days later that a man, with an accent was here to see him, a Mr. Abdullah Salem.

Abdullah entered the office – a rat, trying to make sure he has all the corners of the room in sight. There was something that bothered the secretary about the gentleman she was walking towards the office of Bates Esquire; whether it was the eyes of Ali Baba and the Forty Thieves or it was his slow walk, as if climbing uphill at the end of a long journey. The secretary felt bad, because she did not want to judge the man...but it was not judging, it seemed like an animal thing to do; to protect one's self, she said to herself.

At the door she was brief. "Ray you have a visitor. A Mr. Abdullah..." "I don't want to see him," said Horace with the calmness of a man ready for anything. He kept his 0.45 caliber semi-automatic close, so he did not fear that Abdullah might try another one of his tricks. "This time I have something for you," he said to himself.

Horace kept a photo of Maria on his desk and he turned away to look at the photo. It showed Maria in some theatrical costume and grinning from ear to ear.

The practice of law had already hardened Horace to the point where he was beginning to see the world through logic points and explanations. The miniature moments for creativity seemed like wasted human energy, perhaps it's true what they say about lawyers... That they are calculating ...Horace said to himself, maybe I am not giving Abdullah the benefit of the doubt. Horace raised his head wanting to break the cycle of thoughts and said, "Tell him I do not want to see him."

Jennifer weaved her hair backwards and said, "He said to give you this." She handed him a khaki envelope. The envelope looked as if it had seen too many winters; it was bent at the corner and coffee stained and had the smell of cheap new paper.

Horace hesitantly took the envelope. What was inside would forever change his world, he imagined. He pushed the fear aside and opened the envelope and in it was a photo. In the photo was Horace pausing at a courthouse...some old castle really....Horace said, "I never posed for this." Jennifer answered, "What did you say..."

K
E
N

S
I
B
A
N
D
A

"No, I was just saying...never mind."

Horace looked for a date on the photo; it had none. Then he looked on the back of the photo and whoa! He had signed it. Horace's heart started racing and Jennifer noticed the changes.

"Are you okay Ray?" she asked.

"Yes, just a thought or two... If he is still here tell him to come in."

Abdullah walked into the office softly and passed Jennifer, without looking at her.

"Mr. Abdullah sir, this is really starting to annoy me. This photo here, is it doctored?"

"No." Abdullah took a seat in the chair opposite Horace.

"Don't get too comfortable. This won't take long – how did you do this photo."

"I see Horace, we have realized that you are a man of seeing-is-believing; that photo is not doctored, it's you ...I will leave the details to Zinner."

"Dr. Zinner!"

"Yep, that's the one, Ray."

"Why me Abdullah? This is getting ridiculous, you know?" asked Horace his voice strained.

'It's about your frequency...'

"Frequency?" Horace asked.

"Yes...frequency."

Perhaps it was the word – frequency used so charlatan. Horace agreed to meet Zinner again and for once and for all give them a big NO. This would put an end to all the nonsense that was in the air, Horace concluded. Horace's eyes relaxed for the first time in the last ten minutes and his face became like that of a chess master anticipating the English Opening on rematch.

CHAPTER TWENTY THREE

Abdullah Salem was born in the dry and textured plains of Eastern Egypt; close to the pyramids but not close enough to have any direct contact with the world's wonder. Abdullah's family was well off and he wanted for nothing. As a practicing Muslim, the kind Nasser adored, the family's wealth reflected divine blessings filtering from the very top --- Allahu Akbar. So it did not seem impossible that the oldest son to Sarah and Yusuf should attend an American private school, a prep school.

The old man could not understand what drove his son to love America so much, a non-Muslim country. All of Abdullah's toys were surreptitiously replaced by American ones: the cow replaced by Apollo 13 astronauts; the pyramid replaced with the speed racers; and the wooden musket replaced with the toy water gun.

Things came to a head when his father asked, "You know that Egypt is greater than America?" Yusuf Salem was considering his son's petitions for western freedom.

The son, Abdullah, kept quiet and was unable to answer his father's authoritative questions.

"Answer please, Abdullah...why do you like America, so much, ha?"

The Salem's were unlike most Muslims in Cairo. For starters, they could afford a TV set and broadened their children's understanding of the world with American books like, Look magazine. For Abdullah, he felt that Egypt was invisible and that the pyramids had been replaced with America's triumphant history. He hoped for a day when Egypt would return to its triumphant days.

"It's that Abu," said Abdullah, using the honorary Islamic prefix for father, "We have disappeared from the world."

"Where did you hear such a thing from, that's not true, where?"

"Hawaii Five-O..."

"You see Sarah, what did I tell you about American TV? No more TV for this one."

"But daddy, they have gone to the moon and back; and granddaddy says..."

"What does granddad say, he is another one brainwashed by American television."

"Granddad says that, a man's actions speak louder than his words; this is more important than what people say about him."

"The young man has a point," said Yusuf to himself. 'America made good and is a successful country. Maybe Abdullah needs to see America up close and then all this TV will be washed out; the inequality concerning the Negro; the division of labor; the disparity of wealth. Maybe Abdullah needs to go there and come to the sad realization that America is not great,' Yusuf said inwardly.

Yusuf knew that from his own expatriate experience that America on paper and America in writing were two separate things. Yusuf had attended university in America in the heady '60s. That period in American development that seemed to awaken a new "frequency"....thought Yusuf. He arrived right in the era of civil rights; the assassination of Dr. King; the assassination of the Kennedy brothers; this preempted the '70s and gave rise to Mr. Richard Millhouse Nixon. Yusuf pealed together various historic moments in the sixties. Does he even understand the science that went into the building of these pyramids? What does it help to build on the moon and not here on earth?

It would be evening soon in Cairo and the setting sun teased the numerous tourists. The tops of the pyramids looked like a fork pointing towards heaven suggesting that they are a work in progress. "To be continued at a later date," Yusuf said to himself.

No, he would be the father his father had not been. He would allow his last born to leave and go to America and stay with his cousins and like a prodigal son one day Abdullah would come back. This is what Yusuf concluded: there was no need to try and convince the young man through words alone, after all you heard him - 'Actions speak louder than words.'

Abdullah left for America in the summer of 1994, boarding the luxurious Egypt Air. He arrived in Brooklyn, a skinny and ambitious fellow: Cassius in the play *Julius Caesar*. And immediately he fell in love with America. Instead of developing the noted fanatical hatred of America which characterizes the Jihadist, he had fallen in love: love at first sight - الحب وال لوأل وقلة in Arabic. Yusuf was shattered. A father's prayer that his son hates certain people or develops a disposition to others seldom occurs, thought Yusuf. Once alone the human heart bends towards love. Yusuf had learned this lesson the hard way, it was not Abdullah who learned the final lesson; he agreed with himself, it was him, the father.

The laws of nature appeared to have worked from a position of removing darkness from the cissoids of light, Yusuf thought. The age old realization that hatred seldom ...becomes one's heritage.

Now, Abdullah waited for Horace dreaming of the past, the future and the pyramids with lights. A light in his eyes had a hint of hesitation and expressed his concerns with an understanding that Egypt would never be America, and America ---Egypt. "When you are growing up it's like everyone can be the same," said Abdullah to himself, as he waited for the man in the middle of it all - Horace Bates.

In Egypt, Yusuf had made a grave miscalculation. From the outside world, America appears to be self-centered but from the inside that view is somewhat distorted for the average American. No country offers so much personal freedom, said Abdullah to himself. In Egypt he was held answerable to someone; he had to give someone power over him and this meant that decisions on his life were taken by others. Even as a young boy he recalled how his father seemed to be terrified of the government, as if it were a dinosaur in the middle of a play ground. In America, this is not so. Even the poorest man-of-straw can criticize the president; you don't have to be rich to be a critic. It's not a must to celebrate the president's birthday.

The thoughts continued banging in his head like drumming in the middle of the night. Abdullah said inwardly, when wild animals interact they determine who is king. In America it's the competition that produces the goodness. Look at me now about to embark on time travel...the new frontier. He continued to wonder what the pyramids would look like from outer space...

CHAPTER TWENTY FOUR

Two years ago in the winter of the primary election before Reuben's sudden unannounced ascendency, Timmy, as head of the Houston Group, wrote to the man he had been receiving letters from, a Mr. Nicolai Zinner.

February 7, 2006
Mr. Zinner:

> *I represent a group of business men called the Houston Group. We are looking to invest. Please elucidate your theories from the, "Dominican Experiments." Our group, as you may know, is named after the black explorer Charlton Houston who climbed Mount Everest and so, we find an interest in all forms of human endeavors, especially those geared at advancing the limits of human civilization.*
>
> *Yours truly,*
>
> *Mr. Timmy Teague*

Zinner did not take a day to digest the letter. He wrote back the next day sending the reply express mail, signed delivery.

February 8, 2006

Mr. Teague,

I am in receipt of the letter you wrote. Thank you in advance for your kind words. My theory, which is attached to this letter, is really a continuation of the work of Sir Isaac Newton and Dr Einstein --- a Unification of Physics.

The idea in a nutshell is that we are now in a position to project waves of a speed faster than light onto an object and transport that object to the past. As long as the initial frequency of that object is keyed in to what I have invented as alpha waves then the object travelling beginning at ten miles an hour will be locked in for time travel.

Please find attached my paper: Frequency and its Relationship with Time..

Yours,

Dr. Nicolai Zinner, scientist and scholar;
NASA advisor.

Zinner's handwriting resembled that of a president in a hurry, highly ineligible and scribbled on the page. Timmy struggled to make sense of it. But once he noticed that the circled zeros with crosses were actually Os, he was able to conclude rightly that the letter came from quite an intelligent individual. The paper used by Zinner was indeed expensive and designed to give the impression of comfort. On the whole, the letter was well researched, textured and with enough footnotes to sink the Titanic for the second time.

Zinner's letter had some coffee stains on it. Later it would become common knowledge that Zinner liked morning coffee at Star Bucks. Here, he would observe the early crowd and start to plan his events for the day. Because he had sent random frequency checks, he had narrowed one individual in Boston with the exact frequency pattern needed, right at Harvard. 'What you know,' said Zinner to himself. Next thing, he rented an apartment very close to where this frequency was being generated, very close to Wendell Street. It did not take him long to realize that the patterns of the frequency moving corresponded with what appeared to be a class schedule. "Bravo," said Zinner. It was the jackpot when he realized that the subject also was a law student.

He had informed Timmy immediately, "The subject for our experiments is attending Harvard law school; this is perfect for us. And he is the only one in America."

Zinner continued with some minor tests set up at a test site in California's Palm Spring desert. He would pretend to be a '60s hippie enjoying the desert's unrefined torture. On these expeditions to the far west, Zinner carried with him unwilling volunteers; these included rats and hamsters. But for the most part he preferred the hamsters with their brightly colored and expression filled eyes. He had created a track and positioned these hamsters to receive "Alpha" rays ---courtesy of the Houston Group, and then just like that the hamster would disappear into the past. To get the giddy hamster back, he would do the same thing; fire the gun, lock in the frequency, coordinate, date, and the hamster returns back. This back and forth pattern made him feel like he was engaged in the most pertinent of human activities since the fall of mankind.

"It's all simple," Zinner inwardly agreed, "The problem with people is that they make life complex. Life is about as simple as you make it." One time, Zinner had sent the hamster back into 1820 South Africa. When one of the hamsters returned, it had with it a spear edge. Zinner concluded that it must be from, 'Those Zulu warriors.' Zinner later authenticated it as a Zulu fighting spear. He wondered what the local tribesman must have thought. 'White magic,' he said, and laughed like a college frat-boy high on cheap beer.

Zinner continued thinking, now the only thing missing was a human guinea pig. Someone actually dumb enough to volunteer. Someone who is naïve would be a good catch; perhaps this Harvard chap will suffice... Zinner wrote in his treasured note pad; the one he carried with him and held tightly for dear life...must show a sense of innocence.

...must show a sense of innocence.

A month later after Zinner sent the initial letter to Timmy, he received a reply.

Dr. Zinner,
Good day,

We received your letter and are happy to award you a grant of unlimited spending. Now that you have used the two million dollars I gave you as gratis for your research, I am letting you know that you can bill the group for anything related to, "Time Sequence." Because of the nature of our arrangement please refer to Time Travel as Time Sequence in further dealings. We don't want information to fall in the wrong hands.

Congratulations,

Timmy Teague,

P.S. The Nutcracker by Tchaikovsky is at the Boston Metropolitan and I hear it's pretty solid.

*

Now three years later, at a local Star Bucks, across from the law firm of *Zimmermann* - Timmy, Abdullah and Zinner waited impatiently for their human guinea pig. So far the three men had maneuvered perfectly, giving Horace a job, identity, and threatening him. It would be a matter of time to finally have someone human to add to their ongoing experiments --- the thought floated from Zinner and Timmy as the two looked at each other.

"About time Zinner, we got this thing up and running."
"Yes, this is all we need and then we can be guaranteed of possessing the only system of time sequence known to mankind. Imagine the power to that." And at that moment the impressionable Horace entered - it took him a minute or two to notice the three men, including his boss Timmy Teague.

K
E
N

S
I
B
A
N
D
A

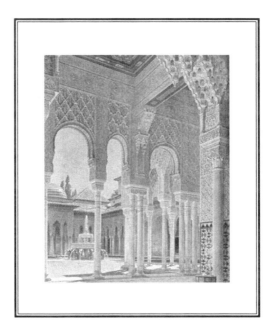

Innenhof der Alhambra. duesseldorfer-auktionshaus. 1892

BOOK II

CHAPTER TWENTY FIVE

Trust is something that needs to be extended to everyone, said Horace agreeing with himself after seeing Abdullah, Timmy and that incongruous Zinner. He was timid but bent on showing some courage, a deep sense of courage derived from meeting those whose veracity you doubt.

Some hours earlier the night had ended at the law firm of *Zimmermann et al*; Horace wanted this to be the end of it...No more strange men looking at him through the hedges at Harvard, and no more secret surveillance at work.

It was evening and the crickets and the squirrels performed in an orchestra that only a listener accustomed to Boston might recognize. Their full honors and musical talents on display, they seemed to sing complimentary to the night's mood. Horace arrived at Starbucks and entered the heavy set doors. He scanned the room, looking for those delicate spots where lukewarm characters have been known to hide. The dark spots behind the art work, the table in the corner next to the sugar pot: all the places that the casual eye ignores. Off center towards the sugar refills, Horace noticed Zinner, Abdullah and Timmy waiting for him with the patience of a toad. His eyes rested on Timmy for a second longer than the others.

"And what are you doing here Timmy?" Horace asked.

"Relax, Ray, all this will make sense as we go along."

"Are you a part of this?" asked Horace.

"Again...wait," Timmy said. He looked at the others raising his eye brows in a 'See-I-told-you-so' way. Timmy removed the medium sized coffee, known in Starbucks cycles as grande, and looked at the edge of the coffee table; his eyes had the lambent look of a sailor in rough terrain. Timmy did not want any coffee spills on him, especially since his wife, Nancy, suspected him of not dealing with a full deck. Timmy was playing cards like a bandit on LSD.

There was a silence and anger shown on Horace's face.

"These people are my friends Abdullah and Zinner," said Timmy. "These are my colleagues; we work together."

"You got to be kidding me!" Horace said.

"No, I'm serious, my friendships boarder on the eclectic; we have been watching you for many years Ray."

"But gentlemen I really have nothing for you; with all due respect, this is beneath you Timmy."

The other coffee drinkers at Starbucks looked at Timmy talking; they were becoming more curious by the second. Timmy became aware of the stares, noting the dirty looks behind the grande coffee mugs.

"Maybe this is not the best place for us to hold court gentlemen," Timmy interjected. This was said as if he were a steam engine forced into the industrial revolution.

"I think we chose it because this is public and safe," said Abdullah like a student passing an overrated standardized test. "Horace needs safety." Horace looked at Abdullah his eyes thinking ------ 'boy, here we go again...' "I think Abdullah hit the head on the nail! Ha, Abdullah!" Horace said, sarcastically raising his eyebrows.

"Let's go back to the office. I am beginning to think this won't do," Timmy said.

Horace agreed with Timmy. 'Who has confidential meetings at Starbucks any way?' he said to himself.

The four left for the law office of *Zimmermann et al* and the air thickened like overcooked grits on a malfunctioning stove. They took a taxi and arrived at the law firm in only twenty minutes. In the taxi cab the men had maintained a controlled silence. 'Over speech is a killer,' thought Zinner to himself, adjusting and loosening the tension on his waistband iphone.

Horace did not want to hear anymore talk about this time travel nonsense. He was done and was about to call the FBI anonymous tip line. 'Who is this Zinner fucker anyways?' he asked himself. Probably some dissident from the former Soviet Union on some blacklist, who slipped through the tight claws of the Kremlin, and Timmy, now that's a surprise... that explained the low grades and the job. I get that part. Horace knew what he wanted to say to this group of losers, but what he was getting ready to hear was a different story. Was all this talk on time travel really Timmy teasing out whether he was partner material and trying to see how he reacted under fire?

Horace continued thinking, '...Every endeavor needs its own unique individuals. Am I being primed in a pressure cooker for some experiment or was this all just a big elaborate joke?'

Horace continued playing it cool. Steady to the end, he held tight, his emotions evened out.

The four got to the law firm and entered from the rear door, taking the elevator to the third floor and into the conference room. The room was named "Washington," after the first American president and did not appear to be the conference room to which Horace was accustomed. Horace soon realized that in fact it was a different conference room. How had he missed it? It had just appeared out of nowhere.

'They say that enemies are born from requests,' Horace thought to himself. 'Once I refuse their request we have become enemies.' The thought made him reconsider his game plan. '...maybe I should go along with the project.' He looked at Dr. Zinner's face. Dr. Zinner was skinny and loose like an old shoe lace; that was the most dangerous-looking of the three. Horace remembered the proverbial warning from Shakespeare:

Let me have men about me that are fat;
Sleek-headed men, and such as sleep o' nights;
Yond' Cassius has a lean and hungry look;
He thinks too much. Such men are dangerous[1].

i JULIUS CEASAR (I.ii.192) 1623, 1st Folio

K
E
N

S
I
B
A
N
D
A

CHAPTER TWENTY SIX

Timmy's burly voice cracked through the conference room's forbidding silence, a buffalo's bell ringing into all four corners. "This meeting is the start of something," he said, eyes looking at George Washington's portrait. "Everything has a beginning; the women's rights movement..."
Zinner listened with the alertness of a choir boy during morning assemble, - upright, stiff, gluey, while Abdullah looked ahead of him as if to contemplate filling the empty space with something more meaningful.

"Look..." interrupted Zinner, "What Timmy is trying to say is that you are our test pilot and we have carefully selected you to fly a test jet. The reason..." At this point the laconic looking Timmy made sure he was the one calling the shots.

"That's enough Zinner. I will take it from here." He looked at Zinner and frowned like an old lady reluctant to argue.

"America-101, Horace --- take a look at Boston for example. How many firms actually hire minorities for junior associate places? And Horace you're a smart kid. You know it was not the grades that got you in; we moved mountains to hire Mr. Bates and you know that."
"What about my references..."

"Those were doctored," Timmy said, sharp and perfunctory.
"You know you could get disbarred for something like that?"
"Now Mr. Bates you know that will never happen. Let's just say, some people are the law! Look, here is the bigger picture that you need to understand." Timmy got up and buttoned his suit. "This time travel thing is real. It's not fiction. Abdullah and Zinner already told you but it seems like you have told yourself that this is a joke. Well it's not Horace...there is a lot of science the average person does not know about in today's world."
'I read that once...' Horace thought inwardly.

"...there are many things taking place in America, Horace; like alternative fuel, the average person does not know about that; stem cell research; people only know what they read in the papers."
This seemed to take Horace by surprise and he said:
"Get to the point."

"We have invented a high lift jet, one that goes hypersonic and also faster than light."

"Again Timmy, you missed something. I do not have a license to fly and have no interest in learning. Look, even if you helped a 'brother out,' the only thing I can say at this point is thank you and resign." Horace started getting up.

"Sit down Ray. We are prepared to use other means to get you into our program. Let me explain something to you."

"Other means like what?" Horace asked becoming serious.

"You wouldn't want to know." Horace for the first time was seeing a different kind of Timmy Teague, a man with a past dark enough to give the effect of doom in a poorly produced B-type movie.

He said, "Timmy...all this time man..." Horace clinched his fists like a featherweight about to launch into combinations.

Timmy moved his seat further away from Horace and also clinched his fists under the table.

"The machine we have computed is a baby. It literally flies itself; artificial intelligence at its best," Timmy said.

"And the fun thing is that..." Zinner said, only to be interrupted by Timmy. Timmy shot in not wanting Zinner to finish his statement. "The whole thing is nothing Ray." Timmy then looked at Zinner with a stiff stare, almost to the point of making the others feel uncomfortable. He did not want Zinner finishing off his thoughts.

"You are wondering why we chose you. What Zinner is trying to say is that your DNA and the resulting frequency of light is unique; there are only two of you in the world who have this unique mutation, almost a grounding that enables you to time travel and remain in tact. The rest of us would disintegrate if we ever attempted anything that approximates time travel," said Timmy in a rhetorical sounding voice. "The other good thing is that you are also a lawyer --- you see, we hit two birds with one stone."

Horace's eyes blinked as he absorbed the information; a sponge soaking in the watered down information from a once hearty rotunda. He could tell by the fluctuations in Timmy's voice that he was telling the truth, at least about the scientific part.

"I beg your pardon ....what are you talking about, repeat that?" Horace asked.

There was a moment of silence, half operatic and half staged. It felt like a rehearsed opera performed by amateurs in-between waiting jobs in some Manhattan restaurant.

But for Zinner he would not disappoint. He sat back and said, "How much do you know about physics sir?"

"Not much," answered Horace.

"What...eight grade, five ...what?" asked Zinner.

"More like 12th grade."

"We have some work to do, let me start by saying - do you know that matter expands when it reaches high velocity?"

Horace thought for a second. Nothing was more humiliating than for a lawyer to say: 'I don't know that'...especially a Harvard educated one. "Yes I know that, it's $E = mc^2$."

Zinner looked at Horace for a moment and decided that he would heighten *the Schadenfreude* – joy from the misfortune of others - "No kiddo

$$m_{rel} = \frac{m_0}{\sqrt{1 - \frac{v^2}{c^2}}}$$

the right equation is:

This is for objects in movement…the relative mass is defined by that equation. This means the greater the velocity the greater the mass! Mass expands - All praise to Professor Einstein – when matter approaches the speed of light it expands. This is the exact equation used to calculate how much uranium the atomic bomb needed during World War II."

At this point Horace interjected, "Please stop calling me kiddo for the record."

"Okay Mr. Bates; the mass equation is the main reason why you alone can do this thing. The majority of us, me included, cannot time travel, and obviously would expand and blow up when we reach the speed of light; but you my friend are an entirely different ball game; when you get to the speed of light you adapt and the frequency of your blood reconstitutes itself, it's called a mutated gene of the 22 Chromosome."

"How do you cats know all this about me – you stole my medical records? I remember getting a call from my family doctor and he just hung up one time?" Horace asked.

Timmy interjected, "We did our research. Look Horace, we don't need to beat around the bush; money can buy anything. We have been searching a long time for a person just like you. We ran a world wide search and only two people were identified."

"Who is the other person?" Horace asked, now appearing to become his intellectual self again.

"It seems that the other person lives in Africa and we really don't have the time to bring them in."

Zinner jumped in and said, "You don't really need to know this Horace."

"You see Ray; too much is invested in this project… 'All in good time,' is what they say. 'Waste makes haste.' You get the picture,"
said Timmy.

"It's haste makes waste," Horace reminded them.

From the corner of his eye Horace could see Abdullah, the Egyptian watching like a contender from the ropes. Something in his eyes seemed queer but not in a sexual sense.

Outside the night continued to deepen in its darkness. Horace looked outside. 'It's darkest most when it's closest to dawn,' he said to himself. Something is about to break through. The truth…

CHAPTER TWENTY SEVEN

In a village on the eastern part of Sudan, a girl, dark as coffee beans fetched at their prime, walks the path that will take her to a river. Nola Gumelo walked towards the river from her family's hut, her steps barely touching the tuft of African savannah grass; the type of grass that litters the woodlands of eastern Sudan; the grassy patches that show the possibility of a desert someday. Nola kept to as much of the green patches of grass as she possibly could. It was a matter of being kind to her herself and not scraping her feet.

At the river, a bird flies past and Nola stops, perhaps she should have waited for the other girls to accompany her. But she had to do this on her own terms and given that the cut on her right hand had to be rinsed she could not wait. The night before she had fallen hard over the corn miller: a wooden drummer designed to take a baobab piston stick. Then she looked for her mother who sat at the evening's fire-gathering listening to stories of how the country was torn between two groups: Muslim and African.

"Don't worry," Nola's mother said to her daughter. "The cut will heal itself; you are special. Go to the river tomorrow and wash it off. Every time you cut yourself you can heal faster than most people."

"But ma..." Nola protested.

"Because you have different blood..."

And that was the third time Nola's mother told her about this specialness that was a gift from God. When water touched her wounds, the flesh was renewed.

At the river Nola waited and waited for a sign that she should put her hand in the river; perhaps, a flash in the eyes of a baboon to scare her, a lion's roar, or fish swimming inland. After some seconds she put her hand into the river and raised it and it was healed, fresh like new. 'With age the power to heal seems to get stronger,' she said to herself. But what were all those colors and flashes she saw when her hands were being healed?

The flashes were like flint striking steal. When the other girls got to the river it was already too late for them to have seen anything and to be witnesses to the miraculous event.

One of the girls said, "Nola, you quite fast today."

Nola turned her head and said, "Have to - because momma said so. Sorry."

"Next time let us know please."

"Yes, but if mama says go I can't promise," Nola insisted, her voice delicate and soft.

The river dancers as they imagined themselves, were a close knit bond in the local village and Nola played intermittent leader for the group. In the mornings, especially on Saturdays the river dancers would fetch water from the village river, the Basa. Since the civil war, there were only a few places that were safe from the fighting and the Basa was one of them, as well as their village known as the Minadora.

Here at Minadora, a Sudanese word for enlightenment, it was safe. The government protected it from the rebels to a radius of fifty miles and the rebels then took over and protected it from the government for another fifty miles – a cat and mouse game, Nola would often imagine. 'We protect what you protected yesterday!'

Nola then said to one girl, "Let's go. We have enough water." At that the girls began to walk away from the Basa. Nola then decided to drink some of the water. As soon as she tasted the water there were more bright flashes. These proceeded with the intensity of a hammer thumping a finger nail.
'I will become a doctor to help people with this problem,' she said to herself holding on tightly to the water pail.

Little did Nola know that it was not a medical condition, but the same condition peculiar to Horace Bates, the American.
In America, often the revelation that Nola existed gave Zinner a second option in dealing with the difficult Horace. The thoughts on Nola as an easy subject, made Zinner see an opportunity. He had told Timmy, "The fact that she is in some remote village in Africa works to our advantage."
"And the fact that you have far reaching schemes is to our disadvantage Zinner." Timmy replied, shaking his head in mild disapproval.
The two often tossed wisecracks and each hoped to outsmart the other but today it was Timmy who had won the innocuous fight.

In Africa, Nola continued imagining her fate as determined by medical cures. Nola's counterpart Horace entered Harvard law school without once thinking of his 'Special sickness.' But that pendulum had now been forced to the center and Horace seemed to see himself at the mercy of greater miracles to come.

The group of African girls walked away and for a moment they sang out in Akola, the local language:
"Some suns are bright while some are not," sang the girls. Nola considered herself now too old for the songs, she preferred to read. In two years she hoped to enter the local university ---- The University of Sudan for pre-med, then med school, the thoughts encapsulating her as she walked back home; others had done well from her village, like the minister of finance --- she was from the same village, Gertrude Makundo; known as GM, she too had once been a skinny African girl like herself and she too had walked to the river on Saturdays. Now GM worked with the president of Sudan, making sure the water was safe from tapeworm and all sorts of water born diseases, Nola thought inwardly. She is in partnership with the president...

"Let's see your hand," Nola's mother said to her when she arrived back at the village. Nola's mother, Catherine, gently touched the hand and said, "See, I told you."

She did not want her daughter to imagine herself as awkward and peculiar but to think of herself as special.

"This is good Nola," Catherine said, rubbing Nola's hand with Shea butter.

Nola rushed into her mud hut. It resembled a small mud dome similar to the one used by the Eskimos of the Baffin lands. She bent her head and entered. When night came she picked a book GM had donated to the village when GM visited on a presidential mission. Since it was Saturday, it was also her chosen day for reading. The book was entitled: *Anatomy of the Human Species.*

CHAPTER TWENTY EIGHT

In the conference room, the four gentlemen continued tousling in torrid verbal jabs. "Gentlemen please leave the room," Timmy said to Abdullah and Dr. Zinner. He then turned his head momentarily to the subject of his monotone, "You and I have known each other for some time now. I feel like you are my son Ray."

Abdullah and Zinner closed the door behind them and emptiness perched where the two men had previously sat. Horace took the message as an invitation to tender...

"You lied to me, and I thought your act was for real man, the references, all doctored huh?"

"Come on buddy boy, nobody hires you based on references anymore. This is America. You don't get hired on merit alone for the big jobs. Who knows you Ray? We knew you before you knew yourself."

Timmy's face glistered as he spoke, like some slimy cheese dripping off a window pan, Horace found it hard to ingest anything said.

"What are you gonna do Horace? This means your family will be taken care of and you will be a great man like Houston, the first man to walk on Mount Everest."

"But is it not debatable since the mission was organized by Steven Peters?" Horace asked.

"By chance or call it what you may, Steven could no longer walk and so he sent Houston as an advance scout. Houston planted the American flag on the highest peak," said Timmy.

"I guess factually he was the first man, but it was Steven's resources that got them there, what a shame." Horace thought about the story for a few more seconds and said, "In all fairness the glory should have gone to both."

"But you see - Steven's position was that since Houston had only been a servant and ultimately was not entitled to any glory. It could be him or Houston but not both. But Houston was vindicated as you now know; in 1956 Congress awarded him a silver medal."

"Interesting," Horace said.

"Some people chose Steven while others chose Houston. It's a free country Ray."

"Still, I think both man needed each other for such an achievement!"

"Free country..." Timmy said raising his hands in the air.

"But that's not what I want for my life Tim!" Horace retorted.

"I see that you need to think this over. Take some time off. Go to the

K
E
N

S
I
B
A
N
D
A

Bahamas…we will cover the trip; go to France."

"You can't buy me Timmy…"

"That sounds more like the cry of an infantile bug." Timmy imitated Horace, "You can't buy me…' Grow up Ray! Everyone needs something! We're not yet in heaven!"

The two gentlemen outside, Abdullah and Zinner, tried to listen through the thin wooden door but could not hear anything. Zinner's eyes were becoming tired and signs of wear and tear started to become evident. It was like watching a baby about to doze off for a mid-afternoon nap. Zinner was taking medication for a condition, known succinctly as chronic venereal disease. Since no women would have him voluntarily, Zinner resorted to escort services and because of the slow moving medicine, nights came earlier for him.

Inside the Washington Conference Room, it was a different story: the peaked voice of a bludgeoning inquisitor resounded. Timmy said, "Talk to me kiddo," his hands thumping the conference table.

"I am afraid, it's thanks, but no thanks, and I will put my resignation on your table first thing in the morning."

"Don't do this Ray, not like this, you will regret this…"

"Your warning is nothing to me," said Horace, getting up. "Anything funny and I will make sure that you are at the receiving end of the FBI. I am sure you have violated a lot of laws pertaining to outer space travel without government permission." Then Horace continued sarcastically, "If not out of your mind!"

The chair roared as Horace got up; intrusively ending the conversation. Horace walked out slowly and on his way out he saw the two stooges playing listen-in-at-the-tea-party.

"Gentlemen, good luck… I hope to never see you again. And I no longer work for this law firm."

At his apartment, the door was already open. For a moment Horace had forgotten about Maria and he thought this the work of Zinner and Timmy and Abdullah…this Houston Group…

"Honey is that you," said Maria. "I entered just a few minutes ago. Where have you been?"

"I worked late at the office dear."

"Work never hurt anyone. I tried calling the office."

"We used a new conference room."

"Something is wrong. You always return my calls and I am sure you have ways of hearing the phone go off in your office while you are in the conference room."

"Actually that would be a great idea, but it's a new conference room. I never heard the calls and my cell phone was turned off."

It was part women's intuition and part of it was that Horace was not a good liar. Maria did not believe the story. When Horace lied his heart beat faster and faster, until his heart started pulsating like a Sumo wrester panting for dear life. His hands would sweat profusely. After being in his apartment for thirty minutes Horace received a phone call.

"Horace here. Hello."

"It's Reuben Howard!"

"Sir …honey it's the presidential candidate Reuben…what a surprise…and what good timing."

"Good to hear your voice," said the president in waiting.

But Horace did not believe it was him, probably Timmy trying yet again another plot to coerce him.

He said, "Sir please give me the number of your hotel and I will call."

"Here is the number 202-133-0877. Call directly."

"No problemo amigo." Horace put the phone down and said to Maria, "Where is the president-elect staying?"

"At Blair Hotel…"

"I need the number?"

A few seconds later Maria said, "The number is 202-133-0877."

It was him: the President elect in person hopefully. Horace dialed the number and the receptionist picked up.

"Blair Hotel, good evening," said the receptionist.

"May I speak to president-elect Reuben Howard?"

"And who might you be?" asked the receptionist in a not-so-fast tone. She laughed, "So does everyone else." Her voice was sarcastic, like someone who is suggesting they neither have the patience for such a question nor the time for it.

"Seriously, I need to speak to him, tell him it's Horace Arthur Bates, Jr."

"Sorry sir, it does not work like that, N-I-G-H-T."

Horace looked at the phone as the voice on the other side went silent like lightening at its end. A few minutes afterwards the same number came up from the caller ID. It was him, Reuben Howard.

"I tried calling him they did not want to take my call," said Horace.

"Horace, still naïve, do you really think you can pick the phone up and talk to the president of the United States, come-on now brother! I represent the aspirations, ideals and hopes of the free world."

"I know sir, what may I do for you sir? You obviously have fifty million things to do."

"I will keep it brief," said Reuben.

"Brief is good sir."

"Do what Timmy is asking or we will have a problem one day. That's just how it's gonna be."

This caught Horace napping and he said:

"It's nonsense sir, their science, absolute nonsense."

"Horace, it's not nonsense. They are aiming at ruining you and I still would like to talk some sense into you. I already owe you for California and have offered you a job…your country needs you."

Horace was flabbergasted, 'Was everyone in on this?' he said to himself.

Horace then said, "Call me tomorrow sir, and we will talk…."

"I won't call you Horace. I am a busy man. Have a good night, but remember the options are limited. You will start calling people and only bring harm to your family. You no longer have the option of saying no."

And just like that the future president of the United States hung up. There was an eerie feeling that something serious had been aborted and that he had no choice: it was death or the Program. He looked at Maria and she did not want to ask – 'who is that?' She overheard some of the words the president had spoken. She did not want to know and get dragged into muddy terrain. With that the conversation was over. The day's end produced the convulsion and the untimely obtuse words. As he lay there in bed, his mind held a full conversation on its own. Horace in bed, eyes shut was like seeing the calm ocean tide; Maria noted that Horace's body gave in and totally collapsed due to exhaustion. He was no longer running.

CHAPTER TWENTY NINE

The future president of the United States wanted him to do it and so it was only a matter of time before Horace reached a similar conclusion. He agreed to participate in this new social experiment known as time travel. The skeptic resistance was now replaced by presidential overtures.

Horace continued with his job at the law firm of *Zimmermann et al*. The meetings with Timmy now seemed intense and less friendly. No longer was there the friendly fellow Harvard alumni; instead their interaction was substituted with the cold knowledge the two belonged to a secretive group aimed at scientific research. True to the fact, Horace said to himself, secrets do not create friendships but deepen the distance between the truth and honesty among those who know the secret and those who don't. Horace arrived early next Monday morning to resume his job, much to the surprise of Timmy who arrived at 10:15 a.m. Timmy's fresh faced countenance did not show any loss of sleep.

"Good morning sir," Timmy said to Horace in a jocular manner – half question and half cross-examination.

"Good morning..."

"How are you sir and how are things?"

"Things are very well. Thank you," replied Horace.

Horace did not know how to break the news and said, "I will do it..."

This communiqué irked Timmy and he replied, "That's the ticket; you will never regret a single moment; this is the best decision in your life." This came off ironic especially given that Horace's heart was not in it. It was all smoke screens.

Horace said, "Thank you. Thank you."

In Horace's mind he wanted to belt this sucker all the way to the beltway...

Soon enough Timmy was heading out of the office. Horace wondered to himself, as he watched Timmy's gaiety quickly change into almost a jogging step, like Mussolini inspecting a presidential guard. Who was Timmy in the first place?

*

Timmy was born in Galveston, Texas to a single mom working as a waitress in the local deli, *Peters*, which was located just a block away from the coal mine owned by American Fuel Company, Incorporated. She had 'hooked up' with a trucker by the name of Leroy Richardson, known locally as 'Big Bones Leroy.' The result of that brief liaison was Timothy. The 'hook-up' put

Timmy in a fix – he had that unfortunate sociological station in life where he knew his father but also never really knew him. At school, when he was asked about his father he would often say, '...Daddy is an industrial developer...' A lie because being a truck driver and driving trucks does not qualify one as a developer, his mom would often remind him. This became awkward, especially since in Galveston, Texas, folks take pride in what a man does for a living - that's if he does anything at all.

Timmy had only met his dad Leroy for a couple of minutes when he was two. Soon after Leroy disappeared and was never seen again. Folks in town joked about the whole affair...suggesting that the trucker might merely have changed his route.

Sometimes in the evenings, Timmy would even take the 45 bus to Dallas, and ask the truckers if they had ever heard of a Leroy Richardson. Because Timmy's mother was a single mom she was treated as such; like a cast-out with leprosy: Jonah in the belly of the whale. Timmy's mom, Tracey Collins, never again saw 'Big Bones.' She became an outcast in a puritanical Babylonian era: a gypsy made to pay for parental hubris. Everyone talked about 'Poor Timmy.' They talked so much about him that his ears started to hear his name when more than two grown ups were present in the absence of his mom.

In order to give her son a better life, she took him to her sister, Jane, in Dallas who was married to a physician named Paul Teague. This was despite the fact that one time Paul had asked Tracey, 'What size panties do you wear?' She had replied, 'None of your business.'

At Teague's house Timmy seemed to strive like a light bulb in a cold night; shining through the mist. In time Timmy became part of the family and eventually like a son to Paul; who granted Timmy permission to call him daddy. Timmy started acting the part of a physician's kid: a trust fund baby. The icing on the cake was when Timmy entered Harvard on a full scholarship. Now the Teagues' completely rewrote family history and referred to Timmy as their biological son. Months later when Horace heard the biography re-told by the ever present Zinner he could not help but say, "If personal history can be re-written so much, how about the history of peoples and nations." To which Zinner said, "Horace, why are you constantly seeing the unwritten lines in everything."

"Because, because..."Horace said.

"Because what...?" Zinner asked.

"Because all good things are unwritten, it's sensory."

"You have the right name Horace, deep thoughts...," said Zinner dusting his usual apparition of pen and recycled paper. The thinking man's tools, Horace concluded...

After Harvard, Timmy realized the American dream: a house, a dog, a wife and two daughters. Now he could offer the world something more... science.

'They say time heals all wounds,' thought Horace as he listened to Zinner. Soon enough Timmy forgave 'Big Bones.' Timmy often thought about his mother and would reach the conclusion that women, unlike men, bare the effects of men's bad decisions and the mistakes they make.

But Timmy's heart had healed fully and he had rid himself of the bitterness and the anxiety that comes with wanting revenge. He played a lot of squash and golf and this helped reduce the stress. Thirty minutes of a good sweat for a life time of merciless plots and traps for his father. Timmy often felt the shadow of his mother and wife; both strong women preening from the past. It was his conclusion that because of these women he was standing on solid ground...after all he concluded, "When the lion feeds it's because of the lioness."

In the afternoon Horace met Timmy to discuss how things were supposed to progress moving forward. 'It was the coming together of many histories and personalities this moment,' thought Horace - like the founding fathers each playing the piano to the correct intonation, anticipating the coming tumultuous storms ahead. Love with no physical contact... Horace felt like a man about to walk the moon.

*

K
E
N

S
I
B
A
N
D
A

CHAPTER THIRTY

Two weeks passed since Horace agreed to enter "The Program." And each day he would contact Timmy at the office only to be told that he should wait; until one day Timmy initiated a conversation. "We will have to go out to California, that's where we have built our station," Timmy said to Horace; his head still inclined to a picturesque Rembrandt tilt. The California trip seemed good, thought Horace - to further see what they are up to.

"We will arrange for your tickets. Make sure you're at Boston International on time now," said Timmy. The relationship between Timmy and Horace had quickly gone from employer and employed to co-conspirators. Horace started to feel like an unindicted co-conspirator. He wondered whether this whole affair was even legal and how many laws had been broken. "Almost seems impossible to do anything new without offending the old ways," Horace said to himself, agreeing with the realization that two sides will never merge seamlessly into one.

Horace leaned forward like a horse at the race track, ready for top speed.

"Are we breaking any laws here, international laws especially, how about the Geneva Codes on Science for the whole of humanity? You know what I am talking about. I know you do."

Timmy took a glance at Horace, a glance that easily reflected his inner thinking on the experiments.

Timmy said, "Nope."

"Someone can get hurt with this kind of thing don't you think?"

"Nope."

"Changing things - Timmy come on. It affects a lot of things."

"Nope, look kid you have more questions than Santa trying to decide what to get for a kid that is asking for a Rolex. Relax."

But the law is the life Tim…"

"You always seem to amaze me speaking in riddles…the law is…It's nothing to me, complete shit actually."

"You're serious!"

"Oh yes, in order for humanity to progress, there are always laws to be broken kiddo."

"Man's laws or God's laws."

"Man's laws---- I think God's laws should never be broken," said Timmy finally considering that Horace needs a victory that would shut him up. "Yes, Horace, never break God's laws." Timmy's voice was sarcastic and Horace turned away, unable to think of a counter-question. The truth was that Horace was talking about both, one - man's laws; gets you in all sort of trouble with state and federal government; and the other ---God's law, can condemn a person to purgatory. Horace's mom had said, "Never break God's law R, never!"

The mood seemed to change. Timmy looked at Horace, "Initially, if it helps you. Zinner had hoped for a total decomposition and re-composition mechanism for time travel. You become dust and we reconstitute you in the past, but we thought this as too dangerous," Timmy's camp-side-eyes had a naughty glare. "No one would know for sure if you were coming back. We could not guarantee your return, you dig." Timmy had that ingredient in man that makes them use military terms gratuitously.

"Confirm Horace," Timmy said.

"Confirmed," Horace replied and bit into a health snack bar. This was a good way of maintaining his energy levels.

"We need your vitals to be one hundred percent, nothing less of that, and lay off the sugar. That sugar is your blind spot, it can slow us down."

Horace imagined the heavy lift engine shattering, crashing and he saw vexing images of him crashing. He looked at the snack bar, at 48 grams of sugar it packed a powerful punch. He threw the bar into the trash can.

"Good, I put the fear of God in you didn't I?"

"Not really," Horace refused.

"Not really is good enough."

Horace hated the way he was out of control. He liked determining his future. This was not his call; he had about auctioned his life to three desperate men who had ideas, maybe grandiose – maybe idealist, but ideas that seemed otherworldly. What ever these ideas were Horace was at the center like a spider, each side of the spider web pulling in a separate direction, the result was that he felt his limbs starting to acquire an independence of their own.

Horace was in a fix and he did not want this to be the case. After all, he had Harvard behind his name. Somehow the name Harvard did not fit well with someone whose fate is determined by others. The biting irony of it all - like snow in a desert.

Time seemed to pass and Horace said, "I have one thing to say Timmy before we make this great trip to California. By the end of tonight, I want four million in my mother's bank account or else…"

"Or else what, are you still trying to muscle me kid?" Timmy said in a prosecutorial voice.

"Or else, it's no go Jose…" said Horace, "no way Jose!"

Timmy thought for a moment and then picked up the phone, his face starting to look like an old pair of wrinkled panties hidden in the corner of a closet. Timmy's eyes straightened out like Augustus the warrior and his hands became firmer holding the phone.

He uttered into the phone, "Get me Bob." A second later he said, "Yeah Bob sorry to bother you, but I needed to call you."

Timmy opened a drawer as he spoke and pulled out Horace's banking information – he pointed a piece of paper at Horace, who nodded yes – "Transfer four big ones to a Ms…"

"Mrs.!" Horace protested!

Still speaking into the phone, to Bob, Timmy said, "Mrs. Pauline Bates, PNC bank number 088892475; and call me back once it's done."

Timmy hung up and looked at Horace, who sat staring at Timmy throughout the telephone conversation.

"You still have not accepted it, have you, this thing is not a joke, and it's real. I know that for the educated, seeing is believing. Even Jesus said this …but look kid, faith is more powerful than seeing. If you insist on seeing everything you will ultimately rub most people the wrong way. You will see it but lose the relationship – I'm gonna let this one slide because you are young blood. But get it through that Harvard educated head on your shoulders that believing is more powerful than first having to see… that's the weapon of the believer. Remember this, that you are not going to the past based on superstition but based on science…science Ray."

At that moment Timmy almost burst out into an improvised song… 'science, science, science'…it sounded like Andrew Lloyd Webber's third act in some Victorian opera centered on scientific invention.

*

The San Bernardino International Airport was crowded with the usual affluent crooners. From a blind spot Horace emerged looking for his luggage. The flight had been shorter than he expected. From there he aimed at getting to Palm Springs Desert, 37 miles east; right in Riverside County --- the Coachella Valley. He took a taxi, telling the driver promptly, "Get me to Palm Springs Desert."

The cab driver replied, "But that's 37 miles east from here. Are you sure you want to take the cab?" He had a heavy Arabic voice.

"If I was not sure then I would not have asked you. Now please, get me to this place," said Horace, handing the man what resembled a dog bitten exam paper: an address in Palm Springs.

He then said to the cab driver as he handed him the piece of paper, "Greatly appreciated."

Horace looked carefully at the cab driver. The driver had Asian features. Horace could not place him; his best bet was Sri Lanka, maybe Mongolia. Horace recalled being told that a quarter of Mongolian men can trace their ancestry directly to Ginghas Khan. The thought brought a smile to him and he sat back for the long taxi ride.

The cab driver still provided Horace with a sense of interest; he was gracious, like Abdullah. 'Perhaps he is a lawyer or doctor,' thought Horace. The man's real name is Ibrahim Mossoud. Horace read the name thinking he was reading it to himself only to realize he had just read it aloud.

"Can I help you with something?" Ibrahim Mossoud asked.

"I was just reading your name; you're not Egyptian are you?"

"Actually I am from Egypt."

The proverbial, never ask a question you don't know the answer to was in play.

"Do you know Abdullah Salem?" Horace impulsively asked.

The driver looked at Horace from the rearview mirror and there was a fire in his eyes, as if he was saying, - don't test me. "That depends; this is a very popular name." Ibrahim started laughing, "Which one? There are millions of them."

Horace decided to tighten the pressure because he was detecting some deception.

"The one who works with Timmy and Dr. Zinner!"

Suddenly out of the blue, Ibrahim became serious, his body tightened like the wolf sensing the initial kegs of gunpowder; he went from night to day in two seconds and said, "I don't know that scientist…"

"I never said scientist," Horace quickly shot back.

"I meant that I don't know the two men."

There was a lie in the man's voice yet again, similar to when the words --- I love you so much, are uttered immediately after the placement of a six carat diamond ring, thought Horace.

…honey I have a surprise for you, imagined Horace; the ring comes out and she answers:

I love you…

'These bastards are watching me all the time,' thought Horace, as he momentarily looked out of the taxi window. The two men, Horace and the taxi driver, would barely utter a word to each other for the remainder of the trip. It had been established that one was lying and so the ground rule in this situation is to remain silent, least you say the wrong words…I know who you are; either ante up or shut up, imagined Horace.

Horace looked at his copy of the San Bernardino Herald, with the big Palatino typeset. The heading was unassuming, something on immigration; Horace turned the page and kept the driver in his peripheral vision. The driver appeared to become deeply engaged in driving his car. "Mr. Ibrahim Mossoud!" Horace said to himself as he turned the news paper.

Thirty seven miles from the airport the taxi cab seemed to slow down as the gears clammered. The taxi pulled to a halt in front of the address; that resembled an outback cottage. Horace handed the man one thousand dollars without even looking at the meter reading which read, five hundred dollars. He was now by all accounts a millionaire and so the high tip seemed appropriate in keeping with the Joneses.

"Mossoud, see you again soon. I have a feeling your face will show up one of these sorry days."

Horace hated the way he was beginning to sound. Like the rich trust fund kid who believes that he does not need to be polite because his daddy owns the town. He made a mental note to himself - 'Stop the airs.'

Horace knocked at the cottage and Timmy answered; the gate keeper as usual. Timmy wore khaki safaris resembling some tourist from Africa.

'What's going on here?' thought Horace. He then said, "I thought this was supposed to be serious and you are dressed like a tourist in deep Africa."

"I am glad you could make it Horace and I have no idea where that statement came from."

"I just had an encounter with one of your men Timmy, an Ibrahim Mossoud?"

"I have never heard of the name," Timmy said in shock.

"You mean he is not with us!"

"Yep, that's exactly what I mean."

Horace looked at Abdullah and Zinner in the cottage who shrugged their shoulders simultaneously, like two cheer leaders simultaneously saying that they both did not sleep with the football quarterback.

"Look Horace, we are already through with rudimentary innuendo; this man Ibrahim belongs to a very bad group seeking to do the same thing that we are seeking to do – time travel." Timmy stopped and looked around; every time he said 'Time Travel' he had developed a subconscious desire to look around. "I am surprised you even made it here alive," said Timmy.

"What's going on here?" asked Horace. "You mean you have never heard of this man? Well, he certainly knows you..."

Timmy looked around the room, he said to Zinner who was looking at a Playboy magazine, "Get me Bob."

Zinner handed Timmy a cell phone he had just dialed.

Seconds later Timmy was holding court with the mysterious Bob on the other line, he said:

"We might have a problem." Timmy then in characteristic fashion disappeared into his study quarters.

The air became dry and Abdullah got up to greet Horace. He looked genuinely happy to see Horace.

"How was the trip otherwise?" asked Abdullah.

"Good...California ...what can I say?"

"I see that you brought yourself a Brietling, Horace...very nice," said Abdullah, his face gregarious.

Horace remembered Harvard and how he first met Abdullah – the memories seemed distant.

"Yes, you know the Brietling, have to keep time; a man is as good as his watch right?"

Zinner interrupted the conversation. He regrettably put down the Playboy and said, "The watch, why did we not think about that? That's your constant when you time travel, good. That way you know what time it is and you never lose track of the 24 hours in each time zone, very nice."

Timmy came back out of his study looking happier than before, almost like a pre-pubescent kid who has seen the first signs of mustache on his upper lip. "We don't need to worry about this Ibrahim guy; no offense Abdullah but Bob says he will take care of this..."

Finally, Horace entered the cottage and looked around. He poured himself some water at the liquor station. "Who is this Bob guy anyways?" asked Horace, "I have been hearing a lot of Bob this, Bob that!"

Timmy did not wait for a second to pass and said, "He is a fixer, that's all you need to know...our fixer."

Horace found the answer to be evasive and asked, "Is he in with us or what?"

"Of course, this whole thing was Bob's idea, his money," said Timmy, his eyes flashing. "Take a shower and we will all have dinner in a second. What kind of food do you like; Chinese, Italian, or Japanese..."

"American...I actually like American food...burgers, French fries; all the unhealthy stuff you can dish out in one serving." Horace answered with a hint of sarcasm in his voice. "I love our goodole American food gentlemen. I am the last American standing!"

To which Timmy said:

"Horace Bates - ladies and gentlemen."

The others especially Zinner were taken back by the cool headed answer. 'Maybe there is more to this kid, light at the end of a tunnel,' said Zinner to himself, 'after all they say that – a man is not what he appears to be on paper...he is a combination mostly of how he acts and what he says! Resumes are written and re-written all the time.'

*

Horace went into his designated bedroom upstairs and closed the solid looking door behind him. It made a clinking nose and locked shut. The sound of the rusted door hinge closing created in the adjacent room a grim like ambience, almost approaching the prelude to a ghost town. For Horace as usual, thoughts and ideas continued floating in his mind like the forbidden money exchanged in a synagogue.

"This is a mistake...I want out...what have I gotten myself into; I am only a guinea pig, so it seems..."

A short while later Horace's cell phone rang and it was his mother.

"R, honey, I just received a phone call from the bank; are you in some sort of trouble." The voice sounded fragile; a glass breaking.

"Mom; I forgot to tell you –I forgot to call you."

"You wired four million into my account and forgot to call me; I am still your mother you know; what's going on here?"

Horace's mother could be heard saying, "I will tell him dear..." she then spoke directly into the phone saying, "your father wants to know where you got all that money from?"

Horace never liked lying; it was not him and he struggled with himself, he finally said, "Mom, can I call you back?"

"Don't lie to me junior you hear me, don't lie. I know it when someone is about to tell me a fib...liars usually need time to think. Are you selling drugs like some Harlem hoodlum up there in Boston?"

"Ma...I will call you back and why does a black man need to sell drugs to be a millionaire, maybe I am selling textbooks?"

"Don't hang up on me junior!"

Timmy walked in and rescued Horace from the impending embarrassment. He said in his usual top voice - think former state secretary McNamara under pressure - "Everything okay here, I hear shouting."

"Yes, it's my mom..."

Then Horace got back to the phone and his mother asked him, "Who is that you are talking to?"

"Ma, I really can't talk. I will get back to you later," said Horace and he hung up the phone. Now he had two problems on his hands. One: the four million in his mother's bank account that had to be explained; two: having dropped the phone, he had to explain himself to his mom. Horace did not know which one of the two problems was a bigger obstacle. Outside the cottage, the night seemed to impeach the cottage and corner it tightly. The smell of high-grade Angus beef frizzled on the stove, and in the living room where the three men were seated for a before-dinner- liquor, the tapping noise of the CNN late Cable News was overheard. Timmy left feeling snubbed and ignored.

*

The memory of Bates Senior came back to Horace as he looked at his travelling bag, readying himself to unpack. At such moments it seemed Senior had all the answers and anecdotes. He recalled one disturbing conversation he had with the old man...

"That the days had gone when American blacks were treated any sort of way by white Americans," said Horace Bates Senior seated on his patio bench in Carthage. The well lit evening night - and outside the smoking chimneys of black ruined chimneys, formerly plantation homes, lined the outskirts. Old man Bates had a vivid image of life in the sixties and fifties, even the forties. The stain of humiliation and rejection littered his voice. But today he spoke candidly and even lovingly about those times, his narrative drawing from the deep blues roots of black culture – the forgiving fig tree transplanted to the western world.

"That blacks are their own worst enemies; you know junior in the sixties we had soul music, good music, now we have a different sort of music that's all about booty. It encourages blacks to act like fools and be irresponsible. Tell me, what can possibly be the end result of any one becoming a gangster?" Senior asked Junior, unintended as rhetorical, the question demanding a quick answer. "Huh? Tell me junior"

Horace knew when his father wanted a yes. He said, "Jail."

"A pimp?"

"Jail!" Horace replied.

"A gangbanger?" Senior quizzed.

"Jail sir!"

Horace trying to fill in the missing gaps to his father's communiqué; today, the old man was serious like firewood in a steel oven.

Senior said, "We as blacks have gone back forty or even fifty years in terms of self help: we receive freedom in one hand and give it away with the other. Our very music is jive and booty calls..." he was now getting angry and under the froth of his voice Horace found the words starting to create an imprimatur for lucid images drawn form contemporary black culture; the recherché of beats, hips gyrating, thick lips, curse words and guns reloading.

Horace conceded that senior probably was right, "He usually is on these sort of things..."

Coming back to his present predicament, in the cottage, the conversation reminded Horace of his responsibilities as one of the few who made it through the tight cracks of both black cultural suicide and white institutional racism.

He unpacked half his bag and then put his toiletries back on the bed. He took a quick shower, the one-minute shower the military encourages. The three men in the living room, Timmy, Abdullah, and the evasive Zinner, were eagerly waiting for him.

Horace looked again at the three-tenors. Timmy: authoritatively macabre, always on the verge of selling a strategic doctrine, a fix it yourself attitude. Abdullah: his sycophantic and irritating smile and then there was Zinner: his eyes swirling in his sockets like a bowling ball.

The mood in the lounge, fairly requiem had what the English, and Union Jack, thought Horace, might term pleasantly as 'splendid airs surrounded.' On this pleasantly splendid dinner table were foods from a gourmet chief, something that was expected from a high end restaurant, Horace agreed with himself. But where did it all come from? The roast beef lumped together; the greens: southern and textured; the potatoes: fluffy. Horace concluded that there must be a professional cook who had pieced the meal together.

"Who cooked this?" Horace asked, his eyes searching for a hidden clue.

"I cooked the meat and the others all chipped in," Timmy volunteered the answer, lifting the bowl of potatoes into mid air. The words were uttered quick enough that they suggested an elaborate cover-up. "This here is Zinner's handiwork."

Horace impressed by the cooking said, "Nice, not only can we think but we can also cook, what a combination!"

Zinner found the observation by Horace rather accurate and said, "Are you saying it's either one or the other?"

"I am saying that great thinkers usually say they don't have the time to cook, that's all," Horace replied, maintaining enough eye contact with Zinner to suggest that he actually meant; 'Don't even try...'

Timmy put his fork down, almost in slow motion and said, "We are glad you are with us Horace, really glad sir."

Moments later Timmy repeated himself, almost in a robotic manner, "Very glad."

Outside the cottage, the darkening and moody night seemed to eventually unveil itself like a lucky lotto number. The four gentlemen ate their dinner slowly, like men enjoying each bite. The jocose Timmy could not help but comment, "Tomorrow --- we go--- we start training ---- more roast beef please ----ha, this beef is really good ---- Zinner, tomorrow is good right ---- what time do we go?"

"Eight o'clock in the morning is good. Let's start as early as possible," said Zinner. He then turned his head towards the subject of his conversation. "Mr. Bates, how are you feeling? What do you know about test pilots?"

"Not now Zinner, let the kid enjoy his dinner. Tomorrow we go over everything," said Timmy. "I have never liked using the dinner table for planning sessions. Dinner is dinner gentlemen. It's not a place to make decisions." Abdullah nodded, smiling in agreement.

'Timmy, just like Union Jack likes those big words,' said Horace to himself, looking at Timmy through the corner of his eye. Horace recalled how Union Jack had the appropriate word to describe every minute detail in life. Once he had referred to a murder case in class as: 'electricity.' Union Jack then qualified the statement by saying that, 'not electric as in Jimmy Hendrix, but as in Con Edison...."

Timmy noticed Horace staring and asked, "Is there anything else you want to say Horace?" He remembered that Horace had to make up something to tell his mother, "Tell your mom it's a bonus and that she should call me directly to clarify why it's so large."

"No disrespect intended, but my mom will never believe that...never."

"Then tell her you won the lottery and that you were holding out on them."

'That's even worse, she can verify that."

"Relax then Horace. Just take care of it your own way."

Dinner came to an end and the jaunty house was ready for relaxation. This resembled the sprawling of a giraffe in the African Serengeti: slow and contrived. 'Mick Jagger would be impressed,' thought Horace, admiring the group's lack of inhibition. Timmy went over to the stereo and put a cold tempo of jazz, a bohemian tune by Coltrane. The music floated softly around the house. While the music circulated the house, the cottage's walls appeared to absorb each note and to transcend it --- time travel is beginning, Horace said inwardly.

K
E
N

S
I
B
A
N
D
A

CHAPTER THIRTY ONE

Rochester, New York; with its swan lakes and affluent theatres, there one finds a giddy college, the University of Rochester, known primarily for its school of medicine. In 2001, an African exchange student from Sudan became the talk of the small campus. When she arrived at Rochester seven years ago she did not know why fate had favored her, or who her benefactor was. Only the initials D.I. seemed to be declarative of the caustic relationship.

She lay in her bed with no familiar people and a few black men willing to date an African exchange student; thinking about whom the D.I. initials belonged to. Who ever the D.I. referred to was immaterial. All that mattered was that D.I. had a heart of gold and it showed through the anonymity.

She had enrolled as an undergraduate at Rochester College and majored in Pre-Med. That was the only thing she ever dreamed about - being a medical doctor, especially given her 'special secret.' Her decision had been the talk of her village. 'She wants to be doctor. Who ever heard of a girl wanting something like that?' It also became the talk in some political circles. She appeared on the front page of the 'Sudan Times,' after receiving a scholarship from an American organization.

She enrolled at the school of medicine four years later, the natural progression of her intellectual rigor. Now, the bells of graduation rung out into the world announcing her fiat accompli. 'What to do next...' she said to herself. Then she received a letter from D.I., she had almost forgotten about D.I. and the fact that someone out there was to thank 'for all this.' The letter all typed, read:

Dear Nola Gumelo,

We are pleased with your progress and hope that this letter finds you well. You have progressed to becoming a doctor and we are eager to offer you a job. If interested you may write back at the address attached.

SIGNED,

D.I.

She tore up the letter and put it in the garbage bin. "I am going back to Sudan," she said to herself. America was just too much for her. She missed

KEN SIBANDA

the smell of familiarity; the Sudanese flora, the dry heat as it evaporates, and small things that are overlooked in the States.

*

But Nola's friend, Elizabeth Hammer, saw the letter in a different light. Elizabeth, a biochemical student at Rochester University, encouraged Nola to see the letter as the best news she had received yet.
Elizabeth secured a job as a biochemical engineer, designing fertility drugs for the Asian market. She inquired from Nola in her room, "So, are you going to take the job offer?" she said.
"Don't know."
"We value jobs here in the States."
"I don't know really, everything seems to have come so soon," Nola said while trying to maintain a serious face.
"Why don't you apply for work at the local hospital? I hear there are always looking for doctors like you," said Elizabeth.
Nola leaned her lean body forward until it was about to fall over, "I need to do research. I am not certain what kind, but research."
"Suit yourself!" Elizabeth shouted. "You are not in a position to pick and choose Nola."
Sudan had its share of problems. One coup after the other made Sudan an irrelevant place in the world's hemisphere. It was a world of its own, faraway from the developed world. A world where superstition seemed to occupy a prominent place in the hearts of its people and Nola wanted to change that. Science is second fiddle, thought Nola. Sudan is frozen in the early Iron Age; iron cut tools. Developed countries, conceded Nola, had progressed from Iron Age to Plastic Age to Space Age. Africa on the other hand was still frozen in the multifaceted world of small shape instruments known as – *tools of the Iron Age*. Space age never arrived for the African. The African's world was not based on technology ----taming the environment----- but the environment, taming the man. This was Nola's realization, having already spent several years in the United States and so she found the invitation for a job as tempting as a second serving of an unhealthy slice of almond pie with ice cream added ale mode.
Nola felt her thoughts starting to wear her down. Her friend left her to be alone but she felt Elizabeth's presence.
"The need to prove a point perhaps and make a difference; ideals have to be embodied in flesh, not books – the problem with Africa is too much influence of intellectuals – and not enough scientists. Science was almost non-existent," Nola said inwardly, closing the door behind Elizabeth.
A few minutes later there was a knock on the door. It was Elizabeth still wanting to convince her dear friend to take the job.
"Do you like what we do here in America, Nola?" asked Elizabeth. "After we accomplish something we explore all avenues, every thing and then we make a decision ---- you need to do the same."

Nola considered the thought for a moment and her haggard face brightened at her friend's words. She decided to take the job and now looked at her velveteen dress, its colors could almost betray that she had taken the job not because of what Elizabeth said, but because of the 'deep secret she had;' a secret only known by people in Africa and people like D.I., her benefactor. A secret that produced visions of a brighter tomorrow.

K
E
N
S
I
B
A
N
D
A

CHAPTER THIRTY TWO

The river of sweat dripped down his head slowly. For days Zinner wondered whether Horace is a good pick. Maybe we should have gone with the African girl, he thought, she would be easier to control. But something about the African girl made him buckle up; those Africans have pride in their poverty…

He locked himself inside the warehouse. The warehouse had written in black on all outside walls including the roof: 'Churchwell, Inc.' A parameter was maintained with the advance warnings 'Keep Out — Private Property.'

Now at Palm Spring Desert in California, the experiment test sight, Zinner waited for the arrival of the other three; Abdullah, Timmy and Horace. Since he was an early riser he had taken an early drive to the site while the others rode shot gun in a sports van.

The sun seemed to rise on that fateful day with a tortuous burning, insisting on penetrating everything in the desert. The result is a convergence, thought Zinner, of warmth and the pioneering spirit.

"This has to work. I have invested my whole life – I will be the first – like Einstein," Zinner spoke inwardly as he readied the timer and metallic gauges in front of him. He was an old type of physicist; unless he saw it in his eyes then it was merely ideas.

Then the sports van arrived and the three men exited. They were all dressed in safari khakis and resembled an African safari expedition.

"Zinner, the early riser, what you know!" Timmy said getting out of the driver's seat. "The time gauge is prepped?"

"Yes, the machine is ready; ready like Sunday."

"Did you go through all the calculations? We don't want the engine shaft to have insufficient power."

"It's done, I redid the internal wiring so that it has a backup circuitry solely on electromagnetism."

"Good, we don't want a Tyrannosaurus Rex running around from some bygone age."

"Very funny," said Zinner. "We have our share of dinosaurs in current time," looking at Abdullah slyly.

The look was disingenuous and Abdullah said, "Zinner, Zinner…what are you talking about man, We have our own share of dinosaurs?"

"Yep, I'm curious to know also, what that means?" asked Horace, walking away from the sports van.

Zinner's eyes started racing left and right, he finally said, "All that I am saying

K
E
N

S
I
B
A
N
D
A

is that, some people tend to behave like dinosaurs." His opinion fell flat and the question still remained unanswered. Everyone shook their heads.

"Let's just talk plainly folks," said Timmy, "no more deep philosophical bullshit Zinner. Back to business now, remember what we are here for." Timmy then turned his head at Horace. "We will do the science part for one week and then the legal part for the next week."

"What legal part?" Horace interjected.

"You never told him?" Timmy asked as he looked at Abdullah, who was supposed to be in charge of the legal preparation.

"I never had the chance. Remember that Horace here has been doubting Thomas from day one."

Timmy looked at the Dunkin Donuts coffee next to Zinner in the inner room of the entrance to the warehouse. He lifted a pitcher and poured himself a cup. "Okay everyone just relax. Let's drink some coffee."

Zinner watched closely as he continued polishing a prototype in his hand. A die cast prototype of a stealth heavy lift jet. Moments later Timmy said to Zinner, "Let's see it."

Zinner marshaled everyone to the center of the warehouse and said, "Gentlemen. I introduce you to Troy, the fastest heavy lift carrier capable of time sequence: he can go supersonic; hypersonic and supernova!"

The grey metallic jet glowed with the finish of perfect aeronautics engineering. Every corner seamless, every rivet flushed flat like a frying pan. On its nose it had a protruding bar of five feet and around the middle was a metallic blue strip.

Horace approached the middle of the jet and saw the word---Troy written, this had been achieved by making imprints through the blue middle fold to expose the grey metallic undercoat. The whole thing looked as if it had the power of a bear breathing and panting in the forest. Horace raised his head.

"Troy ha.."

"Bob's idea!" Zinner said.

Troy, is the mythical city; site of the Trojan war – 1250 BC according to Herodotus; located northwest of Anatolia, now Turkey, thought Horace to himself. He smiled...

"So this is a war machine?"

Zinner shrugged his shoulders and Timmy answered, "No. It's entering a war zone, I can't speak for Bob but that's probably where he is getting this from."

"Interesting, the Trojan wars are just beginning..." said Horace.

"You think too much," Timmy retorted.

"No I don't. You don't think enough."

Horace couldn't wait to see more of Troy. Further towards the back he saw the American flag emboldened and the motto: *In God We Trust*.

Horace said, "Don't we all," and carried on inspecting the heavy lifter. Its wings looked close enough to be mistaken for an F35, but there was a definitive characteristic in which the wings split at the tip like the claws of a crab. Zinner saw Horace looking at the wings and said, "That's a defense mechanism; once activated the wings appear to be flushed!"

"Nice...who designed this?"

Timmy looked at Zinner and said, "In time Horace; trust is earned here, not declared. All I can say is that this is tested science...tested in Dominican Republic and we have used the best materials known to man; Rhodium, Titanium, and Aluminum."

*

Towards mid-morning, the four men stood at the opened doorway to the warehouse like yeomen eager to see how their invested energies would play out. Horace entered the heavy lift jet by means of a portable pair of stairs and fastened his seat belt. Inside the cockpit he marveled at the glistering and fine fitting buttons. He could only compare this to a Mustang; a very high end Mustang. This machine was seamless, thought Horace, every detail computerized.

Horace cocked open the cockpit and said to Zinner, "Impressive, very good."

"Thanks Ray, for the first time I feel..."

"Feel what..."

"Like it's been worth it, you know."

"I can only imagine," Horace said, shutting the cockpit door.

Then Horace opened the door again, "You have the American flag on it, so the government knows about this?"

Zinner remained silent and Horace continued, "I get it, top secret." He shut the funnel door and shook his head. 'Crazy sonnofagun,' he said inwardly.

Earlier on Zinner had briefed Horace on the auto-pilot method to be used:

"It's a simple enough endeavor, because once the machine is locked in you have to do nothing; it uses your oral voice print; only yours now." Then Zinner had Horace speak into a speaker that translated Horace's voice into a mathematical formula and pattern.

"Nice..." Zinner said. He read the printout.

In the cockpit Horace heard the booming voice of a scientist in his ebb. Zinner said:

"To test run the machine we have selected a flight to 1948 India...."

"Right now?" Horace asked. His voice carried the surprised loudness Zinner did not anticipate.

"Of course not, just get a feel for things today and two days from now we will do the test flight," said Zinner. The retraction loosened the friction between the two men.

*

Two days later the group was ready to run a test run on the heavy lift jet. Troy hangered in the warehouse and was soon rolled out into a landing field that resembled a football pitch. Zinner stood in the control room looking at the computer screens. All the buzzing was like an old fax machine; lit with super luminova the buttons glowed in the dark. Zinner said, "Shuttle trotter engaged…here comes the throttle." And the jet lifted vertically into the air.

He jotted down some notes on a pad and continued, "…fuel injector engaged, set India June 6, 1948."

"Set," the computer responded and Horace sat in awe of the totality of the project.

"Set coordinates, Calcutta."

"Calcutta," the computer on the jet replied.

"Here comes the lift kid, ten-nine-eight-seven-six-five-four-three-two-one."

Then like a comet leaving the earth's lunar system the jet whiffed into the sky: it went from supersonic to supernova in less than five seconds and it had disappeared from the sky.

From the inside Horace only saw colors intermittently changing and no physical boundaries. Then the colors changed for the final time and he started a slow descent into a dusty, murky place. A recherché of sounds accompanied the landing. He landed on top of a mountain far from the populace city. *India, 1948 –*

Troy, confirmed the destination:

"India 1948."

Horace looked outside and all he could see were the tips of mountains stretching outward like a colony. He turned his eyes to the cockpit release switch and disembarked from the jet.

"It works, my God, it really works," Horace whispered to himself. Fear starting to form in him made him feel like a man working solely on adrenaline. An Olympiad…

CHAPTER THIRTY THREE

C alcutta - 1948: the dredges of an Indian summer entered the heavy jet lifter and created a feeling of having encountered the exotic, thought Horace as he inhaled the smell of curried rice. The jet lifter had landed at the correct spot as Zinner had predicted; a tad bit too much would have meant that the machine is visible from the northern trenches in the high affluent suburbs where the British live. *Wouldn't want that now…*

Horace put some olive branches over Troy, making sure that it was covered and disguised from any on looker. An unwelcome visitor would think it trash from a pagan ceremony. Horace was dressed in traditional Indian garb of some Hindu persuasion. He looked the part; the Indian merchant going about his day and undeterred by the sight of poverty everywhere. The clothes fit like a tailored outfit. Horace tried not to seem surprised at the inequity.

Horace started downhill towards what looked like a town. He had been walking for just a few minutes when the smell of spice started to intensify. This naturally meant a change from residential to a kind of common market thought Horace, dusting his nose off. From a hundred feet Horace could now see the dusty contours of the market and hear the strange language being spoken, mostly Hindi and Urdu.

Before arriving at the market, a stranger approached Horace. The stranger had the lambent look that's routinely associated with the homeless. The stranger put his uninvited hand on Horace and said, "Do you have five rubes?" He took out both hands and held them in a cup.

From the way the words were pronounced, Horace knew it was Urdu. But then it dawned on him that he did not know a single word of Urdu. He said what most people say when they don't know a language, "yes."

The beggar continued talking for a good five minutes and then he stopped in an irritable pause and said in a hotchpotch of broken English and Urdu, "why no answer me - you spy."

Horace thought for a moment, now his mind catching up with the magnitude of the whole conversation. "Am I now being accused of being a spy?" he said inwardly. His greatest fear was that if he tried to speak the beginner words of Urdu it would become obvious that he did not speak the language naturally and that it was learned; a cello playing off beat to the thumping insistence of a piano. The beggar shrugged his shoulders and walked away in the opposite direction. Horace then saw the beggar talking to two police officers dressed in the sort of British hardtops you would expect to find in London. The two officers started to approach Horace and he walked away almost in a jog. Two seconds later Horace broke out into a complete sprint and the police officers blew the whistle.

One of the officers yelled, "Runner! We have a runner!"

Horace hit the streets, convulsing into a full sprint. The streets of Calcutta have a width that is almost a third of American streets, Horace said to himself as he tried to make as quick a turn as his feet would allow. He did not have an escape route; a plan B. He ran in a pointless sprint, as far away from the police officers as his feet could carry him.

Before leaving for India, Zinner had briefed Horace accordingly. "1948 is an eventful year in India," said Zinner, "when you get to India, write a report about this Gandhi fellow as your assignment." And so Horace continued to run, while the thoughts and images of Calcutta filled his mind to the brim. He saw an abandoned church and entered from the backdoor. Just as he was about to close the door, he heard the voice of a lady say, "What are you doing here? Are you the one the police are chasing? You must be guilty of something. The police would not be chasing you unless you have done something wrong. Get out." It seemed that news had legs in India...

Horace did not utter a single word and left through the same door he had previously entered from. He went past a group of Indian school kids and then right into a mansion type of house, an old castle.

Horace entered the house and tightly shut the door.

From the creak of the door he could see the police officers, now numbering a baker's dozen, snooping around. Inside the house, the dark skinned ladies in high knit underwear looked at him and in a collective utterance seemed to be saying, "welcome." From the dresses; the make-up and the low lit chandeliers Horace concluded that this must be a brothel. The many English officers leaving further confirmed the conclusion.

Then one of the ladies, who resembled a burlesque from the old west, said to the other girl seated next to her, "Should I tell the police?"

"No, let him stay," said the lady who appeared to be in charge. "Let him stay!"

Ten minutes went by and eventually the police officers decided to backtrack. From the cracked window in the Madame's room upstairs, Horace could see the police officers reluctantly retreat. They appeared to have a strong aversion to the brothel, Horace noted, maybe it's owned by the chief of police? Once the police were gone, Horace had a chance glance around the brothel. He had entered the Madame's living quarters.

The head of the house approached Horace. She was slightly overweight and had the sumptuous look associated with those in the business of sensualities; a giddy confidence like an advertisement for expensive jewelry. "What do you want in my home sir? We do not hide prisoners here..." said the owner, in perfect pitched English.

"Good, so you speak English."

"Are you here to monitor the elections; are you a journalist; you were told to all leave the country remember?" she said, informing Horace of the current state of India.

"I am actually a journalist from America," said Horace.

"Are they trying to arrest you because you don't have a license to write, is that the reason; you need a clearance to be a writer here, you know that don't you?"

"Yes, I guess that's the reason."

"You don't sound too confident."

"I meant yes, but I am leaving soon; that's why I don't have a license, but I mean well."

"Well, you can stay here one night, that's all; I have a business to run you hear. I need to make money here."

The Madame then sized Horace up from head to toe and said, "The girls charge forty-five rupees for thirty minutes and that's if you can make it to thirty minutes."

"Thank you for the vote of confidence," said Horace pulling out some money.

"No, I am out of the league; choose the other girls from downstairs."

"No, oh no…this is for letting me stay here for the night."

As Horace rolled the money the other girls started to gather at the Madame's room. It seemed that the money was becoming a source of interest and there was now competition as to who would be chosen for her services. The thought made Horace appreciate the finer intrigue of time travel. He smiled…

As Horace rolled the money the manager said, "Wait for him to be ready please, wait." The women in the room all turned their heads and she repeated herself, "Wait for him to be comfortable please."

Horace was then offered tea and biscuits by one of the ladies; the lady resembled a super model on a photo shoot. Within the last two hours of his life Horace had gone from being a test pilot, to a fugitive on the run and now, a man at the center of the action. Horace then looked at the super model and motioned his head. Soon he was shown to his bedroom and he walked with the supermodel wondering how best to handle the situation. He still had Maria on his mind. In fact Maria had left several messages for him on his cell phone prior to dispatch.

Horace and the girl entered the room and he poured himself some water. He looked at the feline shaped girl and said, "Here take this," giving her one hundred rupees. The lady started to undress and Horace said, "No, come back in the morning, I am tired."

"But…."

"No buts, tomorrow another one hundred Rupees."

She left the door and there was a silence in the room. Outside the dazzling image of Troy seemed a distant dream.

The next morning in the early hours Horace sneaked out through the back door. It was becoming obvious to him that the back door is always the first choice if you need an air tight escape route. He peered into the dusty road heading in the direction of Troy. His watch served as a campus navigator and tracking device for Troy. Horace arrived at the jet and a sigh of relief plastered on his face; the haggard expectant look was replaced with the look of satisfac-

K
E
N

S
I
B
A
N
D
A

tion. He unlocked Troy and engaged the shuttle throttle; he disengaged the time key; and committed the count down. Ten seconds later, the colors started…and then a desert….and Troy landed safely back to 2009; just a couple of minutes from when he had left.

"All this happened in just three minutes," Horace said to himself, unlocking the cockpit. "It's a mystery; time sequence."

Horace opened the cockpit and in the background a happy Zinner started shouting, "He did it!" Horace looked at Zinner in the control room jumping up and down like a kid who has witnessed his favorite cartoon in Disneyworld.

Horace turned back and looked at Troy; a bond was beginning to take shape. "This is the beginning," thought Horace. He jumped the wingspan and walked slowly towards the other three who had been patiently waiting. It felt like crossing the Red Sea barefoot…

Chapter Thirty Four

Acelebratory mood punctuated the room –"How was it kiddo," said Timmy wanting to sound laid back. "Your vitals are in order and everything went according to plan," added Zinner, removing a magnetic index fork from Horace.

"Except for one thing; you did not prepare me enough – somebody forgot to mention that they actually speak Hindu in India and that it would be a good idea to know the language. Also – 1948 is a political year in India, some fool forgot to tell me that. This is their 1776." Horace piped, his forehead all wrinkled up.

The words uttered killed the mood, the realization that everyone pitching was not ready for the majors.
"Next time I promise you!" Timmy said.

"Next time I am doing my own research; I need to know where I am going and for what; it seems gentlemen we have already proved that …that Troy is solid; now, we need to make sure I come out alive; did someone forget that part?" Horace insisted.
"That sounds fair enough," said Timmy, unmoved by Horace's expectant words.

"I need to rest, all this time zoning business has got me unbalanced."
"That's one of the side effects," Zinner said. "You lose track of where you are and need to be reminded that you are not still in India. Just look at your watch for now," Zinner's voice sounding bland.

"Is there anything else I need to know gentlemen? This is a need to know affair right."

"When you go to sleep, we will wire you to a machine I have made for that particular purpose, it will demagnetize you."
"Always something," said Horace, shaking his head. "Is there anything else I need to prepare my body for?" Horace asked.

"Congratulations Horace, the first man to time travel," said Timmy.

Horace walked to his bedroom and closed the door behind him. He hit the sack and fell into a deep sleep; soon after Zinner wired his body to a special machine capable of demagnetization; the localizer. A machine Zinner invented to make sure that time travelers maintain a piece of sanity from one year to another. It outputs the subject's subconsciously retained fears and anxieties from the past and substitutes it with what they had before leaving, explained Zinner, entering the room.

The next morning Timmy walked into Horace's room.

"Morning Horace, we want to make sure we are on the same page here... okay," he said.

Horace looked at Timmy wearing his usual tight fitted and tailored khakis.

"Morning to you Tim. In high school did anyone ever punch you in the face?"

"I want to talk to you about something sir; your next mission -- we need to start preparing for that. We need you to help the Moors in 1491, ever heard of the name Rashid Muhammad."

"Yes, I studied that case in my international law class."

"You know the case. Then you know that Muhammad gets hung and that this ends the reign of the Moors leading to their surrender on January second 1492. We want you to defend him in his case and reverse that decision; and for the Moors to win in 1492. In other words through your intercession the Moors will win in 1492; re-writing history kiddo!"

Horace had wondered why he was so interested in *Spain v. Muhammad* during his Harvard days. He said to himself, 'Nothing amazes me anymore.' Then he looked at Timmy, eager for a new frontier and said, "You know I got stuck on that case at Harvard, it's like my mind got obsessed."

"Sometimes the world knows where you will later travel."

"Are you a religious man Timmy?" Horace asked.

"Sometimes and you?"

"I believe in God and his love; God is everything; his laws through Moses; who can ignore that."

"You not only a law man but someone who believes in God's law - interesting." Timmy noted.

"*The law is the life*...without it we are lost; those laws; what was said on the tablets on mount Sinai is for the benefit of humanity and not for God's benefit."

"God's law?"

"Yep, there is no life if his laws are breached sir."

"Okay Horace, what we are doing is merely changing man's laws..."

"I hope so..." said Horace. He doubted the answer; he doubted most of what Timmy said anyway. "God's laws help us, they don't hinder what ever it is we think we are supposed to be doing; take "Thy shall not kill' for example."

Timmy was starting to feel like he was in a religious sermon and he noted almost a sort of halo around the young man as he spoke.

"We need you to learn Spanish amigo, enough about the laws of Moses."

Horace looked at Timmy intently and said, "Why the Moors Tim?"

"Because we believe that the world would be different if the Moors had won in 1492 against the Recon Questa Spanish Monarchy."

"And why..." "Because the Moors were set on a certain line; so this is actually God's work Ray; you can see yourself as a missionary here!"

"Very funny Tim."

"No seriously, your efforts will make the world more civilized. Is civilization not the ultimate goal these days? One civilization..."

"One center of civilization is what you want?"

"Not entirely in those words but culture divides us, let me put it that way."
Horace thought for a moment, he said to himself, "Sounds like bullshit shoveled in snow to fertilize the frost beaten roses; this man is a bad liar."
"Okay, one civilization through the Moors, Tim."

"That's a boy, I knew that someone like you would pick this up right away; you are amazing I tell you."

"And so I imagine," said Horace, looking down. The sarcasm generated a freeze in the room. He continued and reluctantly nodded to Timmy and sat back into his bed. Nothing about his recent trip seemed to be available for him to contemplate. Those memories were now distant.

After Timmy left, Horace strung his Nike shoes and headed off for a jog. A two mile route that would take him into the desert's countryside. Now it dawned on him: it was Spain they wanted him for – not India.

K
E
N

S
I
B
A
N
D
A

CHAPTER THIRTY FIVE

For Horace, it soon became evident that in increments the journey had begun. This was acknowledged by the four gentlemen who were masterminds behind the Spanish operation. It would take Horace one month to master Spanish; in between dodging questions from his mom and Maria. He fed the two with the usual, "Out of state case investigation," and stayed evasively away from Boston.

Horace had mastered the dialect, a natural student of Spanish; the language started rolling off his tongue like dynamite leaving the hand of Billy the Kid. Horace found the Spanish language to be romantic, balanced; maybe that's why Maria is so affectionate he thought.

Soon into his Spanish lessons, Horace remembered how his Spanish instructor, courtesy of the mysterious Bob, an elder gentlemen going by the name of Pablo, had said, "Remember that all words that start with Al are actually derived from the Arabic...*Alframbra...carpet; Alhambra...The Palace; Aljibe...water reservoir; Alfange...a sword; and Alberge...a home.*"

"Nice..." Horace replied.

Horace re-read the case of *Spain v. Muhammad.* Now it would be different. He was not merely studying the case but Muhammad would be his client in 1491-92, he thought. The moment almost had a dream sequence to it and Horace found himself looking up just to catch the color of the sky and for a reminder all this was really happening. "The human being is probably one book away from a complete change of how they see the world," he said to himself. *"One's reality is nothing but the dream one has decided to consider as the truth..."*

Then Timmy visited him in his room on the fifth week, with some cocoa in hand.

"And so how is it going? Almost ready kid?"

"Almost; but I feel I need something else..."

"You can never be too prepared now," said Timmy.

"I know but remember India; I can't have that happen again Tim."

"India was a mistake. We should have been more prepared..."

"Now I am travelling five hundred years back to represent a brother, talk about fate and getting what you ask for."

"Horace ....Horace...that head of yours always spinning; you are definitely the why guy!"

"It's my life you know..."

"I know Ray; you are the only one who can do this and we are four million dollars grateful."

Timmy did not want to rock the boat, by now, he had already sized Horace up and Timmy's conclusion was that Horace was a man of some principal; some integrity...

"Tomorrow we fly..."

Timmy exited the room and there was a lightness that punctuated his departure. The cottage lightened and there was a Bloomsbury flora smell percolating the cottage. The wooden turpentine was not completely dry. The compound resembled, from a distance, some remote NASA outpost instead of an independent research station. It is too much into the desert to be bothered by the local residents, imagined Horace.

Horace recalled the taxi driver who had brought him in on that eventful day he arrived at the cottage; that brooding implant, unable to maintain his cover.

The next day at the barracks...

By this time Horace had accepted this as a fait accompli – something done and beyond alteration. He jumped into the cockpit. He then adjusted the seat belts and noted the new super luminova touch on the controls.

Horace remembered the conversation with Timmy just a few seconds ago.

"Go to Al Hambra's library and get some information about law practice...in Spain in the 15th century."

Horace turned up the volume on his ear phones and in came the blistering voice of Zinner.

"Can you hear me kid?" said Zinner.

"Positive Zee..."

At that time it seemed appropriate for Horace to say, "If anything happens to me tell my family I love them." But he did not say this, he kept it to himself.

"Okay you know the drill," Zinner said, his voice operatic, "let me know when you ready for the shuffle." The silence thickened. Zinner remembered that Horace had never called him Zee before and in fact no one had ever called him that and so he said, "Don't worry kid, you are a pro in this."

Thus, a brotherhood seemed to be developing at the eleventh hour...

"Here we go Ray." Zinner confidently leaned forward, "Looks good from here, all systems are check – EAP switch on, Roger."

"Roger that," Horace said.

"Arms switch on – shuttle breaker in. How does it look?"

"Looks good chief."

"Here comes the stutter kid... and we have lift. Counting down for supersonic...ten, nine, eight, seven, six, five, four, three, two, one...we have supersonic. Roger that..."

"Roger, supersonic confirmed," Horace said.

"Going hypersonic in ten." Zinner counted downwards to zero, "Roger hypersonic..."

"Roger that chief," Horace said.

"Okay kid, going supernova in ten," said Zinner and after counting from ten to one he asked, "confirm supernova?" By then Horace had transgressed time and the computer print came through the fax machine.

...confirmed supernova, we have Spain 1491...

In the jet lifter, Horace slowly watched the colors changing every one hundred years; this was the most beautiful thing he had ever seen in his entire life. "It was not so much that one saw the color but one felt it as well..." Troy's computer screen flashed, "*Spain 1491*" and the jet started a slow descent onto a mountain valley. The valley overlooking a province by the name Grenada.

"Zinner is accurate yet again..." said Horace inwardly like a child confirming their parent's prediction about the demerits for not doing homework. Horace disembarked from the jet wearing his Muslim garb and carrying the holy Quran in his right hand. He looked at the cockpit where the screen saver read: Horace Bates. This would be the last time anyone would be calling him by that name, for now he would answer only to the name...*Mustafa Al Mutaseed: the lawyer from Malaga*.

He walked a few yards and the parting words from Timmy came through louder than before, "go to Al Hambra library..." Horace began walking in the direction of Al Hambra using his gps locator system courtesy of Zinner. It was still mid-afternoon and there was enough time to adjust to the city's menacing but romancing seduction.

At the entrance of the great castle, Al Hambra, Horace was greeted by the guardsman. He replied, "waliakum salaam," and entered the castle, slow and confident. If India had taught him anything it was that if you run, people will chase you...

A thought crossed Horace's mind as he entered the castle: now he was Mustafa; a name he found rather prodigiously elusive. "It is always the first place in any civilization to find out how capital punishment is minted out, this determines a society's level of sophistication. How one group is excluded from the majority..." Horace said to himself. "What would lead the Christians to want to defeat the Muslims and for the Muslims to want to defeat the Christians?"

Horace buried himself in the ancient texts of the forbidding Kingdom. He noted the obscene, the profane, the religious, and the sentimental. Horace looked up from the book entitled, *Early Moors in Spain* by Mayad. He agreed with the author's thoughts, "The sentimental in Spain are the religious clergy, but then what are the institutional places for logic?"

"The Monarchy," Horace answered himself. He lowered the book and thought now in real terms:

Perhaps, capital punishment provides some insight as to how developed a nation is technologically.

"...traditional peoples use spears to met out capital punishment; some use machetes and the developed countries do it using lethal injection and remote control devices. In Spain 1491 Muhammad was looking at death by hanging from a rope...hands on..." Horace's conclusion was that justice in Spain is real and deadly.

Horace closed the book and took his written notes with him. He thanked the guardsman who had looked at Horace with a measure of interest that made both men feel uncomfortable. "It's like being looked at by an attractive lady. You're not sure whether she is looking at you or just stretching her head backwards…"

Horace left the Al Hambra and headed for the dungeon that housed all prisoners who commit crimes against the monarchy. The dark dungeon implied that this was hell for anyone who dared transgress Spanish law.

Horace went to visit Rashid Muhammed and found the former general staled in a corner of his cell like a Count that has not paid her majesty's taxes; plying away, pouting and sullen, removed from the center of politics in Spain. Muhammad was once a formidable general in the Moorish army, in reality the commander of the forces; and now he was just a prisoner, with an anonymous number and a date with justice.

He entered the dungeon and smelled the rotting litter of garbage; the wounds of those who soldiered and the remnants of overcooked food. Horace recalled the prison that housed his cousin Dixon and concluded that prisons never seem to change. In any era they are the same - dilapidated and insanitary places to live. "No wonder no one ever gets rehabilitated here…" he looked around again and said to himself, "even when it comes to punishment, since it is not immediate, the delayed response does not benefit the victim…"

As for the inquisition that was rumored to be happening while Spaniards were targeting the Moors, Horace thought the whole affair a very delicate political game of cat and mouse. He vowed to leave Spanish politics alone for now…concentrate on the case. Now Horace's eyes were dry like gun metal. His skin suggested the earlier stages of dysentery either caused by malnutrition or caused by poor eating habits. Horace approached Muhammad's cell for a closer look and found the man rather calm for someone under intense scrutiny. The petals of his destiny rested flat in the hands of his enemies. Horace thought it through and continued towards the cell door still adjusting to what appeared to be a bad case of jet lag.

He got to the cell bars and leaned forward, "So tell me, why do they want to kill you ahir?" asked Horace, unhesitant and delicately balanced like a flute playing in the wilderness. *Ahir meant brother in Arabic*

CHAPTER THIRTY SIX

The belligerents were all imprisoned in the dungeon and this made Horace contemplate the high possibilities for a defense career in antiquity Spain. In the dungeon; the humid grey rains plastered on the wall; Rashid Muhammad wondered whether this new man in his presence is the final answer for his freedom.

"Allahu Akbar..Allahu Akbar…Allahu Akbar…Allahu Akbar, Ashadu Allah ilaaha ill-Lah," said Rashid in slow tones and beginning the Muslim prayer – the Salaat.

This was familiar to Horace and he found the softening call to prayer beautiful as the birds moving from one hemisphere to another. Horace compared the salaat to *The Lord's Prayer*, the Christian cornerstone. He found both prayers evenly balanced. He said to himself, "Such words do move us all at some point in our lives."

Rashid turned his formidable head and faced Horace. The stunted gaze of a man searching for a clue in the new acquaintance.
"Pray with me brother – ahir – pray with me….let's make Salaat," Rashid said.

A few hours ago Horace was the perfect all American and now he found himself in the funnels of the greatest Islamic events; he was in a different world and with different rules. He felt the thunderous melting of two worlds joint at the hips by convenience. Now he was in Spain and the role he was playing demanded prayers of beauty be made. He answered, "Inshallah…if Allah wills it." He knelt down and felt the crusted cemented floor, its coldness and grit, a floor that almost seemed to encapsulate the word dungeon.
"Maybe this is where the word comes from," Horace agreed with himself.

"I will pray with you. It's an honor ahir," said Horace.

The two men were now kneeling side by side divided by the cold metallic bars. Horace looked at those dreadful bars. "Even across time zones and centuries of human grit the cell bars were making him nervous at the purported loss of freedom. One feels not only the loss of freedom but also the loss of humanity," Horace said inwardly, biting his upper lip like a virgin at the prom. His mind on occasion drifted back to Plymouth Correctional Facility and to his cousin Dixon.

The prayer continued and the two men started upright, bending at the correct juncture. This was done until the final verses vibrated against the dungeon walls, *"As Salaam 'Allakum wa rahmatulaah ---- peace and God's blessings be with you."* Even though Horace was not Muslim and was merely pretending, he felt an inner peacefulness; a serenity; a jocose mellowing; like a river flowing into an endless ocean. He rose from the cement floor and felt rejuvenated.

"That is something ahir," said Horace to Rashid, shaking his head in astonishment.

Rashid did not understand the question and said, "Always ahir, always." He folded his prayer mat and said, "Excuse me brother but I never caught your name. Who are you by the way."

"I am Mustafa Al Mutaseed," said Horace trying to hold a perfect Spanish accent---Grenadian in origin.

"Have we met before?"

"No," Horace replied.

"For some reason your face looks familiar."

The remark caught Horace off guard and he said, "You too ahir; you too."

Rashid appeared puzzled saying, "Let me get your background again; who did you study law with ahir?"

"I studied in Grenada under Al Said."

"That's good, Al Said, is a good legal scholar," said Rashid turning away in a respectful reflex.

"I volunteered for your case; and want to help you," Horace said. He moved closer to the cell bars holding tightly the rails that seemed to be ice-cold. Then he lifted a nearby stool and wobbled over towards the cell's bars.

"Do you know much about this Spanish code they use; the cannon law; I know they are not using Shari a law."

"I am familiar with it," said Horace. "They use a unique system and we have to prove that you are innocent, right now you are guilty."

"Do you have experience with this sort of law - canon law?" Rashid asked, his voice having a hint of dehydration.

"Canon law," said Horace. This got the attention of the prison guard; a stocky looking potentate who appeared to belong to a vaudeville show. *The kind of medieval show that goes around with tents offering home remedies along an English countryside…*

The guard stooped over saying, "Everything okay."

"Good, everything is good," said Horace in Arabic.

"Don't speak to me in that language; use Spanish." The guard raised the butt of his musket and changed his mind. "Spanish please…"

Horace felt the tingling pressure from the guard's rebuke and held his ground, "Okay."

Horace now waited for the guard to disappear into the shadowy anonymity created by the lack of light in the dungeon.

"I see that we are being forced into a tight corner," said Horace.

"They want us to use Spanish as the official language; it's a problem."

Horace remembered that a question remained unanswered and said, "Why again, do they want to kill you ahir?"

Rashid seemed to want to ignore the question for a second time.

"I said….ahir…."

"I heard you," interjected Rashid, "this is hard, you never imagine as a great general that we will lose; once they hang me, the Moors are finished, this is the end. And as for Islam here in Spain, it is doomed."

Rashid's eyes were those of a man who has seen the years becoming a decade and a decade slowly slipping through his fingers like sand in a sandbox.

"The world of one's childhood ending," thought Horace, looking at the former general. He could see that Rashid was once held in high regard by military types; the forbidding presence, the sunken eyes - like deadly landmines.

Rashid saw the look and said, "I am being framed for buying a gun; I never bought the gun, that's not me."

"How did they get the seller to say this is you? Who wanted to buy the gun?" Horace asked. By now he had already settled on accepting the thin line a defense attorney must throttle. One of advocate and the other of being objective; "Never doubt your client's facts," Horace agreed with himself. He smiled as he normally did when thoughts became too condensed for him to hide.

"They say ahir, that they found a man who looks like me to do their bidding," said Rashid. Anger set on Rashid's face turning it crimson; this communicated that words were not enough and that what he was suffering a burden to his heart.

"I see," Horace said. He toggled on his wooden stool making a scratching noise and repeated himself, "I see, so this is how it's done here, they frame the generals!"

"Oh yes, remember what happened to the Toledo three; you were young."

Horace remembered…he had read the story in his debriefing papers months earlier. The Toledo three were three Muslims who were accused of heresies in Toledo, Spain and were summarily executed while waiting trial because the prison guards felt that the evidence was 'enough to hang them.' Horace felt an overwhelming indulgency in the matter, from the way Rashid spoke he already concluded that he was telling the truth. "People who tell the truth seldom emphasize looking others in the eyes and it is often their body language that reveals the inner conflict taking place," Horace noted, he kept the thought in mind as he asked Rashid, "These things still bother you general?"

"How can this not bother me? I am supposed to be the starting point now I am the end."

"You're not the end. You are not done yet."

"How can you say this, they will exclude all evidence of my alibi as specula…"

"…speculative."

"Thank you, as speculative evidence…"

For a moment Horace was equally surprised. This is Spain 1491, and it appears the legal system just left the dark ages; superstition, intrigue, and a good dose of cultural bias. It did not appear to be an *imprimatur* of legal notions but a system of crimes and their rewards.

There was some silence and some moving of air in the prison quarters. Horace said, "I believe you. Do you have any enemies?"

"Is that a serious question," replied Rashid; for the first time his bearing rose to a threatening tempo.

"It is, I have to make sure our defense is believable and we have to make sure that we present as much of your innocence as possible."

Rashid looked at Horace with the stare of a cornered man. "If you get me off, then I will reward you with a position that will change the position of your family; you will become someone important in the Moorish empire, Mustafa Mutaseed."

Horace almost asked who is that but held himself. "I have to go, we will continue tomorrow."

"Assallum Allakum," said Rashid, his face sullen like a great leader who realizes that his hands are tied. "I don't know. I have many friends and many enemies."

"How about people who look like you?"

"Not that I have heard of; try Toledo. I understand some people there have been known to favor us Moors." Rashid breathed in some fresh air. In the background he heard the slow beat of the flamingo dance….cha, cha, cha….the music played in:

…Oh Spain, the night is young, the evening so bright.
The life is young…

This reminded Rashid of the beauty of Spanish culture. "Why did it have to be like this?" he thought.

Horace got up and shook Rashid's hand. Spain reminded him of '60s America – the 'Us and them' mentality. Exiting the prison, he gently walked in the direction of the tumbling drums.

CHAPTER THIRTY SEVEN

Back in real time America, the mood seemed to resemble the barracks of an army soon to be attacked. The events unfolding in California were like an old tale about a Scottish man exploring the African interior, in Eastern Africa. Timmy found the tale appropriate given the news he had just received about Zinner. He remembered the tale from his high school history.

The tale about the wandering Scotsman gave new light to the unfolding events. The story is that the intermittent wanderer, David Livingstone, spent a sizeable amount of time trying to get back to his original trek. The local authority then sent a gentleman to find Mr. Livingstone; a sir Henry Morton Stanley from the *New York Herald*. Stanley later found Mr. Livingstone in the town of Ujiji on the shores of Zanzibar. It is reported that Stanley upon seeing Dr. Livingstone said: 'Dr. Livingstone I presume,' to which the Scottish Missionary uttered in response, "yes and I feel thankful that I am here to welcome you."

This tale is juxtaposed with what Zinner experienced at his mansion in the suburbs of Orange County, California. Unknowing of what happened to the Scotsman Livingston, Zinner retired for the evening. His thinking was to relax and enjoy the fruits of his hard work, having given it all…Horace was in Spain!

Zinner's Californian mansion overlooked a dozen gold mines, from its top floor one could see the old squalor locations left by the immigrant Chinese workers. Littered on one side of the residential area they resembled a Polish ghetto about to explode inside out. Zinner relaxed unaware of the weather outside, his mansion had windows so large they could be mistaken for doors. A day after Horace traveled southwards, as it was coded; Zinner bought the architectural masterpiece, writing a cashier's check drawn from Chase Bank.

From the mansion Zinner had started working on a book based on time sequence. He entitled the work-in-progress ----*Time and Space*. This work is revolutionary he said inwardly. On early mornings when he was typing hard with his Royal typewriter from the sixties, he would reminisce about how the whole project had come together. A mathematical formula; some hyperbola and the rest, an ability to think it through and dream.

In between writing his book Zinner continued to use the escort service business as a stress remover. Whether it was the massages or something else he was looking for, could only be answered by the obliging *masseuse* who enjoyed the close attentiveness of the intellectual scientist. On days when his greatness was but a shadow, he would call his favorite escort service, *"The*

KEN SIBANDA

Room," requesting someone who is conversant in Swedish deep tissue massages.

Zinner's schedule was rudimentary and involved very little exercise. The time spent writing was treasured as if it were a commune with Zeus and Apollo. Zinner was always a loner but this was taking it to another level. he was becoming agoraphobic. He began to fear that people might come into his 'space.' Even the mysterious Bob soon heard about the crippling phobias to his number one scientist, and he saw an opening; Bob being the planner he was, started plotting and soon the phobias were an advantage. Thus when Zinner needed to buy a house he funneled the money.

As for the phobias they became so great for Zinner that his mansion had twenty bedrooms; which Zinner enjoyed changing on a day to day basis. He never slept in the same bed more than once in twenty days. And in each bedroom he kept a clean pair of under garments, *Esquire magazine* and the morning *Wall Street Journal*. Each room had a flat screen TV and a wine cellar. Since the ladies Zinner invited were naturally in awe of the man and his achievements, namely wealth and the cleanliness and decorum accompanying a five star hotel, the escorts imagined Zinner as an engineer who had made well on a patent.

And still the other girls saw him in his cushioned Lakers slippers; his smoking jacket and Calvin Klein t-shirts as a yuppie who made good in the stock market. The ladies all competed to out do each other and become the first Mrs. Zinner, or so they imagined. Zinner saw the competition and with a gingerly grin on his boyish face manipulated the situation to his advantage promising most of the escorts marriage 'Come next week.'

On the fateful Tuesday after Horace's departure and during an evening where he felt particularly lonesome as lonesome goes, Zinner rang, "*The Room*," requesting an East Asian or Vietnamese masseuse, 'Proficient in this deep tissue business.'

"A broken shoulder done me, still recovering..." said Zinner to the front desk consul.

"Sounds like trouble," she said.

"Big trouble." Zinner then awaited his request in jolly mood, almost like a musician in receipt of a new electric guitar.

The great Zinner, as he imagined himself, poured himself a gin and tonic and waited for his escort's arrival; Jackie Yaakozuki. Whether his pains were imaginary or were rooted in medical proof was up for speculation. As soon as Zinner placed the call to the escort service his shoulder muscles tightened and his back felt like a quarterback who did not warm up for the initial throws.

Zinner did not notice on his video surveillance the two men in black military fatigues jump over the gate as the masseuse reached the front door. The two men had been prying around the place for sometime and had arrived at the conclusion that this was indeed the Zinner himself. Zinner did not see the two men take out the masseuse by knocking her out with the back of a 0.45 caliber.

Now the masseuse lay sprawled in front of Zinner's door and breathing heavily, suggesting a recent injection of a sedative high in nitric-oxide, any one of many stimulants prevalent in Japan. The two strange looking men, stranger if viewed from the side because of their asymmetrical chins, waited patiently for Zinner to answer the door. Both men looked as if they had been force fed an unhealthy dose of push ups since the age of twelve.

Zinner heard the knocking on the door and said to himself, "about time, these escorts take their time I tell you." He walked gentlemanly to the French designed door whistling and half listening to his favorite musician, Miles Davis. Zinner did not even look through the peep hole nor ask, 'Who is it;' he merely pushed the forbidding door open like a colonel demanding respect at a basic training rendezvous for the impetus.

When the door opened the two gentlemen looked Zinner straight in the eyes and the taller of the two said, "Dr. Zinner I presume!"

To which Zinner thinking of Livingstone in Africa replied, "yes, and I am pleased to make your acquaintance."

These words punctuated the conversation and the short one of the two men fired a bullet into Zinner's left side. Down fell Zinner hitting the interior Persian carpet; his body sounding like a bag of potatoes falling from a market shelf.

To the surprise of the two men, Zinner fell heavier than they had expected and the short one who had pulled the trigger said, "He is heavy." The accent was French, almost Burgundy but closer to Southern France.

The two strangers, half robotic and half animated, then went into the lounge room. They knew exactly what they were looking for; the secret book Zinner was supposed to be writing.

The taller of the two entered last and said, "Look for a study room." To which the short one, whose face resembled a wrestler on generic steroids, pudgy faced and plum replied, "Oui."

A few minutes later and after overturning the mail in the living room and all the writing material scattered across Zinner's work station, the shorter of the two lifted a manuscript of an almost complete treatise entitled: *Time and Space*. He yelled to the taller one, "Trouve il...found it." The two assassins exited the mansion and got into their 2000 BMW. They left in the sort of hurry that usually accompanies bad blind dates, but also the sort of rush suggesting criminality. The BMW sped off and turned a corner, leaving behind it, the scientist, the escort and a perfect alibi --- money.

Timmy concluded that Livingstone must have been better prepared when he met Sir Henry Morton Stanley in Ujiji, Zanzibar.

CHAPTER THIRTY EIGHT

The Moors arrived in what is termed *Al Andalusia* in early 711; Rashid Hussein Muhammad's forefathers crossed over the badlands of Morocco's Atlas Mountains. This history told to Rashid had never really registered; the oral history seemed elusive and imagined. Now Rashid sat hunkered like a ferry in some desolate port thinking about his roots.

Of the stories Rashid Muhammad heard, the most seminal were those that informed him of Moorish history. His grandfather would relate the stories in a methodic manner, drawing lines and animating the major highs:

"Moor is the term of art that means any person practicing Islam and dark-hued, it refers not to one tribe or group but to a set of ideological and political beliefs. There are Moors and there are Christians, we are Moors."

Still yet, Rashid's grandfather would continue, "The Moors are descendents from African Berbers and look more or less like cocoa with some milk." Throughout his youth Rashid played in the dusty paths of Grenada and heard the stories told over and over again of how the Al Hambra was built and how mathematical accurate it was; "square root of two, square root of three and square root of four, are the incremental increases of the squares." He was told of how the word Moor was derived from *Maurie*, a word used in the ancient city of *Numinbria*. It all made sense like adding up the minute figures on a match stick ship. "The Moors are Muslims and the others are Christians; like water and oil Rashid," the old man insisted.

Now in the dungeon, Rashid could not really pin-point the reason behind this ordeal, "perhaps, it's because they are one thing and we are another." He sought refuge in religious differences, but he had known a Christian family once growing up. They had been kind and good people. "The whole thing is a travesty..." he concluded.

They say in prison every second appears to be like an hour and Rashid sat reading his Quran. He felt a lightness beginning to avail itself. There was something about the young man Mustafa. He could not put a finger on it; perhaps it was that in manner he did not come across as a Muslim or maybe it was the realization that he did not seem to have urgency.

"Oh Moor..." thought Rashid, his mind trying to explain the predicament. He continued, "Allah, you are great. Please release me from this bondage. When Rashid finished saying the words, the name Mustafa came to him again like a bolt from below sea level. Maybe Mustafa is Allah's answer he thought. He wished he had been more cooperative with the young man.

Rashid got up and walked towards the prison bars.

"Guard…"

"What is it now Rashid?" the guard asked, dragging himself to the cell, "remember you are no longer some big time general. We don't answer to you here."

The guard's sole interest in this affair was to make sure that Rashid, the great Moorish general, knew his place and that his spirit breaks; slowly but surely. "The best way to destroy someone is from within…within," thought the guard.

"I know, I want you to call that young lawyer who was here…abogado," said Rashid, endearing himself to the guard by using the Spanish word for lawyer. "You know how we old time generals behave once caught." This was exactly what the guard wanted to hear – nothing like a good loser who knows his place.

The guard said, "Don't be too hard on yourself Muhammad; don't be too hard, strangulation goes fast." The voice was laconic but bitter sweet. Rashid froze in thought and said, "Please hurry before he leaves the prison… please hurry…"

The guard dashed out, in high pursuit. He could be heard saying, "This arrogant Moor, he is a prisoner but is making demands."

Outside the prison, the guard did a 360 degree rotational look of the outside quarters. The dungeon, located in Southern Spain, the coldest part of Andalusia; here, King Ferdinand and Queen Isabella constructed the dungeon as a palace for dealing with 'social misfits.' It was said the overriding sentiment was that the Moors had to be put in their place; once and for all…put them in the coldest part of the country. It was rumored the King was planning an inquisition as to who the heretics were in Spain, thought Rashid.

The guard looked for a good three minutes and then saw the shadowy silhouette of Mustafa in the far distance.

"Stop!" he yelled, "stop…"

Horace considered the day's events as pleasant. He planned to spend the night at the motel and then start looking for Javier Mendez, the gun seller in Toledo; and for Rashid's look alike, if ever he existed.

Behind him, Horace heard the screaming and wondered --- is he calling me? When Horace eventually turned his head the guard was within walking distance and he could not run.

"Got you," said the guard to Horace. "Your general is asking for you; he wants to make a confession I suppose."

Horace sighed with relief, around the guard the ladies passing by curtsy; then the guard says, "Why are you so nervous Mustafa?"

"Oh, that's nothing, it's cold out here!"

"Are you afraid of the night? It's as dark as you!"

"No."

"What was your name again?" the guard asked Horace.

"My name is Mustafa Al Mutaseed, and I am from Malaga."

"Mutaseed," the guard quibbled, and his beefy hand pulled out a piece of

paper, he wrote the name down. "Mustafa Al Mutaseed," he uttered again...
"now then, let's see what the general wants."

The two men disappeared into the thickening hue of darkness; in the evenings the smell of Spain's magnetic flora floats, thought Horace, enticing and joining all commoners in a flamingo dance.

K
E
N

S
I
B
A
N
D
A

CHAPTER THIRTY NINE

The moment was brief and Horace had not been animated nor reacted to the bulging hands of the furtive guard. In the dungeon his head almost hit the hanging lights and he said, "I have to be more careful!"

The guard did not respond. He was not interested in being friends with any Moor. His study on the Moors gave him a polemic voice. "They are belligerent and intransigent," thought the guard, who had acquired some elementary political jargon.

He neither wanted a Moor in his presence nor in Spain; he represented the overriding feelings of the Christian majority – 'The Moors must go, back to whence they came; there can only be one religion dominant in Spain.'

"Wait here," said the guard to Horace, his eyes twinkling from the shadows of the evening lights in the dungeon. He then moved dotingly towards the prison cell.

The guard looked at Rashid seated on his cement bed and said, "You see, I found him."

"Thank you," said Rashid, looking timid and despondent. He got up and walked towards Horace, whose face glowed from the assured nature of what he was observing.

The guard did not like being seen as un-Christian and yet he did not want his country to be shared with Muslims; and so being nice was out of the question. He heard the stories of how the Moors had crossed over from Morocco gallantly; across the Mediterranean Sea and into the southern tips of Spain. The guard was insistent. He wanted a Christian country; and not a country shared with Muslims. Sharing a county with a people you despise is not easy, he thought. He looked at his crystal rosary and seeing its reflection became light-hearted almost to the level of being elevated.

The guard did not know that by stopping Horace he had helped Horace avoid a wasted trip all the way to Toledo. He moved back to his chair and sat down, looking at the two men beginning a heavy and intense conversation. There was a brotherhood between the two men already, thought the guard. A meeting of two halves, this he seldom saw in his Christianity. Muslims were not co-congruent but seemed to become one indistinguishable family, a brotherhood. A band of warriors… moving like masses who believe in the purity of their leader. The guard shrugged, this is the greatest strength of Islam, this insurmountable and inscrutable brotherhood that cuts through national identities and creates armies.

The guard, now seated, on a chair a size too small, saw the lips of the two men moving. His pride could no longer bring him to be a spectator; what you hate you destroy and so he shouted, "Two minutes and then you have to go Mutaseed." Horace looked at the guard and felt the coldness of his iris penetrate the very nature of his being.

Horace and Rashid turned away from the guard after acknowledging the sacrosanct voice. From a distance the guard resembled the Hardy part of the famed Laurel and Hardy troupe; from closer the guard seemed to favor an unfed bulldog with itchy toes; the kind of dog one avoids when jogging in the mornings, said Horace to himself. The guard silently turned away – ferociously diplomatic.

"I called you back because I wanted to tell you something," said Rashid, a magician taking in every second.

"I am open to hearing everything you have to say ahir. The more you tell me, then the more I have to prepare for this case; law is about the facts, not rules..."
"You abogado..." responded Rashid, touching the yellow tuft of his beard.

Horace looked closer at the man in front of him. Rashid Hussein Muhammed was fairly tall. Slim built, he carried himself almost like a gymnast. Because Rashid did not smoke, he had the eternal glow of youthfulness. At forty two he looked thirty two, but since he had the countenance of seriousness, this gave him a look of middle life in his eyes. Rashid was healthy looking, but so were the other Muslims Horace had seen. His textured hair was kinky and his lips were like an African from Sudan. When he moved his whole being seemed to be moving, not merely physically but spiritually and he imbibed his space.

Rashid raised his head like a hippopotamus in the Niagara Falls, "I want you to talk to someone who will guide you to Toledo," he said.
"Better still ahir!" Mustafa said.
"He is one of my advisers but he is in hiding," said Rashid, "I can't talk too much because the guard has ears like an elephant's." Across the tunnel the guard was dozing off.
"Who is this man?" Horace asked.

"He is one of my closest advisers...Zaniweri. Please make sure you keep this to yourself, he will guide you to Toledo. When you get outside, look for the inn closest to the road, on your right— *Medina*."

"Be well, and stay with Allah," Horace then looked at the guard and said, "Guard...I am ready."

"You Moors always making demands," said the guard getting a hold of his keys. For a moment he realized he had been sleeping and became embarrassed.
The two men made the realization that if they had wanted to escape they could have taken the keys from the guard.
The guard walked towards Horace and said slowly, "Let's go."
"Thank you," replied Mustafa.

Horace now walked out of the dungeon for the second time and into the evening's fresh air. There was something about being imprisoned underground, he thought; something that made you feel buried alive. Horace recalled the Soviet premier Khrushchev during the cold war, *'we will bury you.'* This sent cold chills down his neck.

K
E
N

S
I
B
A
N
D
A

CHAPTER FORTY

To get to Toledo from Andalusia, you take the travelling carts to Joen; from there you take them further inland to Linares, and from Linares you turn eastward to Cordoba. From Cordoba you continue northward to Toledo. But first he had to find the general Zaniweri, thought Horace acknowledging the map's directions.

At least that was what the little piece of paper in Horace's pocket read. He carried the piece of paper in his brown leathery satchel. In the satchel were pieces of paper to help him make the transition from roving American to Moorish adviser. The trip to Toledo was necessitated by Horace's investigative legal ethic. He had to find the gun shop owned by Javier Mendez. He had to dig deeper than the surface and uncover the hidden facts. He learned from the Dixon case that law is like a tidal ocean, the deeper you dive the dimmer it gets until alas there is no light only the oceanic sea weed, invisible from the very top of the ocean. He was gutty and hungry for answers.

The directions from Rashid were not the best and had been dictated in high monotone, as if Rashid was trying to leave the episode behind him, but this has become him, thought Horace reading over the notes. Horace walked for a few blocks through the dusty streets leaving the dungeon. The roads away from the prison were narrow as if leading away from a romantic farm in Australia. Horace observed there were no skyscrapers, the tallest building would be the Al Hambra for a good forty minutes. All the other buildings surrounded the Al Hambra giving it a droid sort of big brother stature.

Soon Horace was lost and he stopped to ask a Muslim lady for some clarity to the directions. The lady, dressed in Islamic garb from head to toe, did not utter a single word, she only motioned with her head that she is not allowed to speak. A burly looking man approached Horace. He had the look of disdain and his eyes seemed somewhat out of place.

"You know Shari a ahir, why get her in trouble; you can't speak to the sister. Are you from around here?" the stranger said in a coarse and bitter voice. The words were juxtaposed by the realization that the stranger also had the face of a detective, that genteel face at which many have been known to offer involuntary confessions.

"Yes, I am from Malaga, but just visiting. If you can brother, where is the inn in this city," said Horace, walking towards the stranger. "I need a meal; something to hold the stomach together."

Horace was learning or unlearning to speak in a sort of metaphorical way when speaking to people in Spain. The lessons did not come easy since

Harvard had offered him the best education in formalities. Every sentence Horace spoke was punctuated by a testament to faith. He said, "Inshallah, please advise me where I can find these things?" The stranger replied unexpectedly, "Come to my house and have something to eat.'

"I am in a rush ahir — brother, I need to be moving."

"Please come with me," said the stranger, "what is your name?"

Again Horace almost said Horace Arthur Bates but he didn't, he said, "Mustafa Al Mutaseed."

"Son of Mutaseed please let's go, my wife is cooking something."

"No ahir, I really have to be going."

In between talking with the stranger Horace kept reminding himself that he was an amateur to this world of espionage and that he potentially could forget everything and end up speaking like the old Bates. He did not want any slip ups. A slip up would be deadly, especially given the realization that everyone carried a government issued sword.

The stranger was insistent, "Come to my house and break bread, you know what the prophet Muhammad, peace be on his name said; *'a stranger is worth a million prayers,'* and helping a stranger is merely helping the many faces of God." The stranger smiled boldly and his teeth glowed brightly.

Horace contemplated everything within the past hours; there was something beautiful about Islam to the human spirit…perhaps this is what makes Islam so powerful…I am my brother's keeper.

"I am working ahir, I need to be on the road," Horace protested. He did this in grand fashion raising his hands: *bopping and weaving like a boxer.*

"But it's still quite early," the stranger said, his stance changing to that of someone who is no longer in a rush. The woman had disappeared into the many faceless people on the road. She had shyly bowed her head and left without saying a word.

"Next time ahir," Mustafa said. His face had the fractured emotional weight of having to convince the emotive stranger.

"Okay Inshallah. Have it your own way ahir, but next time, we are breaking bread," said the stranger.

"Next time ahir," said Horace. He felt the growing need to escape the conversation.

"You asked for directions," said the stranger. "Continue with this path until you get to a brown villa, turn and walk in that path and cross the wall and walk towards the market. You will see an inn." The stranger thought for a moment and asked, "What brings you to this part of town ahir, in the first place?"

"I am exploring Hispania ahir," replied Horace delicately.

"Exploring…is that right, you have time for that?" The stranger's mind appeared to be racing like an electric train sliding through the meadows of some farmland. He said, "be careful, you know that the world is out to suppress Islam; you know that, please don't explore the wrong corners! Maybe I should accompany you; I am sure you heard what happened to Rashid Muhammad. You need a witness here. By the way I am Isaiah Ali."

"And I am Mustafa Mutaseed," said Horace for the second time.

"Ahir, you appear to be headstrong, then go with Allah."

And so Horace left the stranger, disappearing into the wilderness and the dusty trail like a gunner in the old west. In the distance the perfect horizon was infected by the smell of flowers. This could be the perfect national flower for Hispania, thought Horace admiring the reflection of the sun's rays on the petals. The smell of the flower floats from one village to another, connecting and uniting, forging an identity, concluded Horace.

Horace arrived at the inn and could see from a distance what looked like a police quarry; different law men walking in and out with thuggish individuals. He smiled…and waited. Moments later the coast was clear and like a chameleon trained to blend in with the surrounding, he approached the inn. Although Horace did not have any military training, the whole affair was starting to resemble some crack-pot commando mission. The thought almost made Horace burst out in an explosive gut. He remained calm and slowly approached the inn. India had taught him that situations soon escalate because of rushing.

He entered the hotel like someone who has found a precious ornament and said in Arabic. "Assallum Allakum."

"Allakum sallum," the woman replied.

"Who is the manager of this place?" asked Horace. Old habits are hard to overcome and Horace had just transgressed Islamic tradition. *Hadith, says that there are no managers in a home, only Allah.*

"Excuse me, ahir have you lost your mind."

"Crazy," he heard one of the guests say as the guest walked out of the inn.

"May I speak to the person in charge," said Horace, trying to correct himself.

"Are you Muslim ahir?" asked the man in the reception area. He seemed to be the one with authority over the others.

"Yes, very much."

"You sound like an unbeliever; we don't have managers in inns ahir, I will get you the keeper of the house."

The man walked slowly and confidently to the other room. He soon came back with another stumpy looking fellow, who uttered, "And how may I help?" He did not even bother to give Horace the respect of being greeted in Islam, it was straight to the point; an arrow fired by a determined archer, set to pierce any hardened soldier. The new gentleman had the posture of a soldier and Horace remembered that Rashid's closest general Zaniweri, lived around these parts and so he carelessly asked, "Are you Zaniweri?"

There was a cold silence and everyone turned to look at Horace.

"No and who might you be?" he asked in a strained voice.

"I am Mustafa Mutaseed, I am abogado; and I am working to help brother Rashid." Horace uttered the monologue with great enthusiasm; so much that some of the guests looked away feeling a sense of naivety for the young man.

"Wait here," the brooding man said and he motioned to the other gentleman. The two men both left for the ante-room of the inn.

Horace did not seem to notice the men coming from behind. But he felt the cold metallic poking of a musket; a Spanish flintlock.

"Move ahir, Allah hu Akbar, move."

It was the gun doing the talking and so Horace had to obey. He was taken to the back and into a room that resembled something from a sixties horror flick; purple, unclean and unsanitary.

"Who are you exactly," asked the soldier, his eyes zeroed into Horace. "I am Mustafa Mutaseed, I was sent here by Al Said, to help brother Rashid." There was a hint of coldness in Horace's voice.

Then came the flattening with the musket and Horace's face jerked sideways. It's one thing being tortured and it is another to be hammered by a musket from antiquity, thought Horace, looking at the floor. As a teenager, Horace and Dixon had been pistol whipped once; this had taken place at the normal time for such confrontations and that is after school. It had been a territorial violation; the big bully asserting his territory. But this was different - *to what did he owe this ass whipping?*

"I am talking truth," Horace said in Arabic.

Now the torturer moved closer to Horace, his eyes menacingly unpleasant like red plates on a coal stove. "Okay, you are tough." He swung the musket straight into Horace's nose splitting the skin on the tip of his nose. The cold dripping blood created a river moving downwards towards his lips. Horace's body became consumed with wanting revenge and he felt the hands holding him back tighten with emotion.

"Let me take you back to see Rashid tomorrow and then you can hear him speak for himself, please ahir," said Horace in protest.

Again, the flintlock musket came, this time Horace blacked out. The blow came from no where and like thunder in summer. Horace fell forward and to the side crunching into his stomach like a soft pillow.

He woke up to the pained feeling of a man walking on the moon with no earth in sight; a druggy and spongy daze. His head hurt and seemed to become a mountain. He touched it just to make sure there was no battery acid on his head. The rest of his body felt lethargic.

Horace scanned the room and thought, 'there are a limited number of ways to deal with your torturers and most of them end up in compliance.' He asked the man wielding the musket, "What happened?"

The torturer did not hesitate since he had already put in the heavy lifting by pounding his target. He said, "We want the truth Mustafa. There is a war taking place here my friend, a complete war."

Horace thought again, 'either answer or ignore them.' He looked at the friendly gentlemen, who reminded him of Abdullah; the one staring. He seemed to be saying through his eyes, he is going to finish you, tell the truth please. Horace turned away and looked his torturer straight in the face.

"Look," the torturer said, "you need more meat to your story, cook up a better one. Your story has more holes than the Al Hambra's irrigation scheme." The men in the room laughed, all five of the cronies seemed to appreciate the horsing of their leader. Their laughter had looseness and suggested that it was practiced as apposed to a knee jerk reaction.

"Don't cry now, you were doing so well," said the torturer in mockery.

Even within a different history; a different county, Horace could feel the human element in its entirety. He thought, '*Union Jack would be impressed with the amount of sarcasm in antiquity Spain.*' The thought plastered on Horace's mind and his eyes became laconic like someone in need of medication.

"Don't you dare look at me like that!" The torturer screamed. "You are the one who is asking for it! Gentlemen, is that not so, asking for it!" The cronies acknowledged the torturer's lukewarm outcry by nods and a certain slimy smile that appeared to come all too easy.

Then there was a silence in the room. The earth seemed to shift. Horace felt the moving silence blow into the room and he saw the torturer becoming calmer.

The taller of the cronies approached Horace. "Maybe he has a point," he said to the main torturer. "Maybe we have over reacted." This was said with the tone of someone testing the waters, someone unsure of the outcome of his words, just the emotions behind his words.

"Maybe you shut up Zahiri..." said the main torturer, and then he noticed that he had made a mistake by saying the tall torturer's name in front of Horace.

"...Okay Senore Mustafa, later today you take Zahiri to see Rashid, and if there is a problem with your story, you are salt in water my friend." *Salt in water*, thought Horace, he had never heard the metaphor so bastardized and because of this he replied, "Sea salt, thank you al hamdillah."

The two torturers left the room; Horace had time to re-think. The day was eventful so far; the room's reticence continued to climb and now he had been put on the spot and had to figure out an escape route. A zero-sum game, he thought.

CHAPTER FORTY ONE

"Maria, Maria…" the call emerged from the balcony window and sailed onto the truncated streets. Outside, the morning's foggy sunrise beat the pace and created a hallow effect on Boston's impatient roads.

Maria, still busy fixing herself for her daily morning jog when she heard her name belted out in discord. Horace was on Maria's mind. She had last seen him a couple of weeks ago. *'His absence and the reasons he is giving don't add up,'* she thought, as she laced her sneakers and tied her shoe strings.

The voice yelling was that of Maria's ever present mother. "Don't forget you have an audition today!"

"Okay mom, I know, I am going out for a jog and will be back in a second," Maria said. She waved good bye to her mother delicately like a Parisian in the streets of Paris.

Inside the apartment, the smell of Spanish bananas and the coffee brewing punctuated the house giving the apartment the edginess of a frequently visited home.

Moments later Maria turned the corner and was heading towards Boston's central park. From a distance she did not notice the two French looking gentlemen watching her and writing down notes. One wore a thick woolen pea coat and the other wore a green military bomber jacket, the kind worn by US pilots in World War II, courtesy of Eddie Bauer's ingenuity. Both men were wearing Boston Red Sox caps, but none could tell you what an *inning* was, or who *Big Papa was*! The things that betrayed their foreignness were their noses and chins; the elongated chins that stretched out like an exclave to a commandeered territory. Maria merely glanced at the two men as she jogged by, her sneakers tapping on the tarmac.

Maria noticed their chins, and that did not bother her. But, from their chins one could have foretold the world. The one going by François Degualle seemed a professional, an ex-military type. The other going intermittently by the nickname Jerome or Jerry also seemed to be military with an inclination to leadership. Their orders were to watch the girl and not to repeat what happened to Zinner.

The day before, the two Frenchmen had left California with the stolen manuscript and headed eastwards towards Boston. As to their previous target, they had sufficient circumstantial evidence to conclude that Zinner was now safely a no go. They related this to the higher-ups; only to be told this was not the case.

In California, Timmy started to get worried; the number of calls going unanswered from Zinner were increasing. Now at four calls, and counting, Timmy knew that if Zinner removed himself from the program then they were in a fix. 'It is imperative that Zinner is at all times accounted for,' Bob had told him.

Timmy called for the fifth time and rung the plastic cord around his finger in anticipation of an answer on the other end. When the answering machine keyed in, Timmy spoke, and for a moment his heavy Texan accent got the better of him.

"Look son, you have to call me at some point, we need to run a signal check on Troy and see whether Horace is in distress; it's not just science you know. Horace needs us down there."

Timmy hangs up and thinks for a moment. "Something is off..." he calls for a taxi.

A few minutes later the taxi arrived, quick enough by Californian standards. The traffic on Minister drive was beginning to mushroom and Timmy wanted to go before it all became haywire.

"Take me to Palm Spring Acres; you know the suburbs east of the Palm Spring Desert?" Timmy asked the taxi driver who did not like the questioning; this made him feel like a lackey. Now insulted, the driver sped off and a few minutes later Timmy pulled up at Zinner's mansion.

"Right and if I may ask, can you wait for me?" he asked the taxi driver who only obliged because he needed the extra money from the slow day's pick ups.

"Okay, but hurry you know," he said, biting his finger nails.

Timmy went past the half-opened gate.

He felt the edges of his hair line lifting up and goose pumps crawl across his arms. He looked around the sprawling villa which resembled that of an expatriate in hiding from those he left behind in his homeland. Timmy approached the door. He saw a body lying at the entrance of the door. It looked like a log. Timmy started running towards the log, his high school track days kicking in. He got to the figure and confirmed its identity.

"Zinner," he breathed in disbelief to himself.

Timmy peeled open Zinner's jacket and saw the Hawaiian shirt soaked in blood. The bullet had gone in sideways and instead of severing the aorta it merely bruised Zinner's side. "Lucky... Zinner must be unconscious," thought Timmy, dragging the body inside.

Timmy went into the kitchen and came back with a glass of water. He splashed the water onto Zinner's face and thankfully his eyes started blinking like an old Oldsmobile receiving power after months of neglect. Zinner's eyes peered open and the quintessential Zinner was back. His lifeless body now seemed alive and animated.

"Good," said Timmy, "just you hold on Zinner."

He lifted Zinner with the skill of an amateur weight lifter. He stumbled for a moment, perspiration dripping cross his forehead. Since Zinner was far skinnier than first imagined, Timmy had no problems dragging the scientist to the taxi.

The taxi driver did not notice that Timmy was dragging a human body. He merely assumed it was a sack of potatoes or some tools. 'There are so many film producers here.' He imagined.

The taxi driver had until now been busy listening to a brand of music best categorized as 'Indian rap music,' and enjoying the suburban breeze. Timmy interrupted the driver's relaxation and barked, "Take me back to my house in Palm Springs West." Then Timmy reconsidered his next move and changed his mind, "...No, take me to see Robert Churchwell, do you know him?"

The taxi driver replied in a heavy Indian accent, "I would be a fool if I lived in California and did not know where to find Bob's house!"

The taxi raced off, the exhaust fumes combusting into the air like a chimney smoking in the country side. In the taxi, Timmy looked at Zinner lying on the taxi floor and for the first time he had empathy for the brilliant scientist ----- Timmy understood that from here on it was war and Bob had to do something. *Ivanovich has gone too far*!

CHAPTER FORTY TWO

Horace's head throbbed with an aching pain in the area where he had sustained the most slaps from the torturer. Dawn soon broke and the sun's first rays started kissing the Spanish badlands. Then the torturer had entered the room for a second time and approached Horace. This man walks with the perfection of the elite, thought Horace, observing the torturer's grand entrance. The torturer continued walking like an English man in Montenegro.

The torturer said to Horace, "I hope you are telling the truth and that Rashid will be your witness inshallah." He walked behind Horace softly and cut the rope that held his hands together.

Horace's hands had been held tight by threadbare ropes and were starting to blister. The crude makings of the rope resembled something from a beginner's knitting class.

"Rashid is my witness," said Horace, trying hard to hold the Arabic accent. He thought about the defiant Arabian knight in turmoil and this helped him produce authentic sounding speech.

"Okay, go with him, since you already know his name, go with Zahiri." The torturer said.

¥

The walk back to the prison did not seem as punishing as the previous day's journey. It seemed shorter, thought Horace, or maybe it was because Zahiri was a fast walker. With his long legs like a giraffe, Zahiri matched forward, fearless and stoic. Horace remembered the term 'Jihad,' and that seemed to mean a sense of confidence and grace under fire.

"Soon," Zahiri said, "Mustafa Al Mutaseed, we will see which way the sun sets my friend." He welded his sword and then held his musket, as if to imply – if it's not one, it's the other.

Horace did not want any argument and kept quite, he merely looked at Zahiri in a toughened statute like coldness.

At the prison the smell of early morning food permeated the air. They got to the gate and Zahiri told the guard in a goaded sort of polite demand, "We are here to see the general, commander of the Moorish forces, Rashid Ali Muhammad, the Moor." Zahiri had intended to sound defiant if not rebellious.

The guard looked at the two men and said, "That one is fast asleep.

Come back later." He turned around to look at the other guard seated next to him, "Rashid is sleeping right?"

"Right!" The other guard yelled.

The guard-in-charge took this as a democratic consensus and smiled, "You see Senore Mustafa and your friend - I not lie."

"We really need to see him," said Horace.

"What is really going on here, every two minutes, 'can I see the general...' No more of this nonsense. He is going to be treated like others, one visit a day."

He lifted his hands like Giacomo Puccini the Italian composer in high conduct.

The guard who had been seated all along got up and said, "No more Rashid, no more, 'the great general' go home." He waived his musket into the air and appeared to derive some liquid satisfaction from being the bearer of bad news. He adjusted the flintlock to its firing position and the ambience became deadly, like a dragon getting ready to breathe fire.

"Don't do that please, I am abogado and I have to confirm something. It is the law. Lawyers are allowed in," said Horace. His head still hurt and the throbbing played in and out of his head like an '80s disco.

"And who are you?" the guard asked, pointing the musket in Horace's direction.

"I said I am Mustafa Al Mutaseed from Malaga!"

"Were you here yesterday Mutaseed?" said the guard, remembering that there was a sophistication and pause about the young man he liked.

"Yes senore!"

"What was that?" said the guard, making sure Horace was paying the price for access.

"I said, yes commandante!"

The guard liked the word *commandante*. It made him feel important. At his wages he needed anything that would make him feel important and valued.

The two guards looked at each other and then the one who had made the initial greeting disappeared into the underground tunnel. "Bang!" the door banged shut behind him and Horace as well as Zahiri could hear the guard's footsteps entering the tunnel.

There was a moment of awkward silence and Zahiri was beginning to sense that Horace might be telling the truth. He looked at Horace squarely in the face, like a butcher considering the price of a piece of lamb at Thanksgiving.

"How come you don't behave like a Muslim ahir?" Zahiri asked.

"Because, because my family never practiced, I converted."

The word converted seemed to elevate Horace to a higher pedestal and Zahiri said, "Inshallah you converted, what a blessing for he who finds the teachings of Muhammad rashulllulah."

"I don't know about you Muslims from Malaga, but here in Al Andalusia we are practicing and believers. It would be against hadith not to practice Islam," said Zahiri, his face animated.

"My Abu wanted to concentrate on my becoming a lawyer and on education," Horace replied, making up the story as he went along.

Zahiri looked away into the afternoon's warmth and said, "Maybe you are telling the truth, maybe!" he reached his hand out, "I am Zahiri Muhammad." "Good to meet you Zahiri," said Horace, imitating the humility of Islamic teachings. He bowed; his movements and eyes were stealth.

The guard could not have come soon enough because at that very moment Zahiri and Horace formed an initial brotherhood. An initial agreement to agree... the stumpy prison guard came back storming through the tunnel, his hair flying and his puffy face reddened by the brief exercise.

"Come this way you Moors! You people need special treatment all the time, this is the last time," the guard uttered. His words were sore because Zahiri and Horace had made him work. He did not like working.

Zahiri and Horace followed the reluctant guard back through the tunnel.

Soon the three arrived at Rashid's cell. They arrived at the right time as Rashid finished his mid morning prayers. An empty plate and cup from breakfast sat on the floor.

Rashid studied the two men. He was a good student of the emotions of men when close to warfare. He said, "I would offer you bread but I have eaten every single crumb these bastards give me." He reached out his hand to shake the two visitors.

To this the guard yelled, "No, no please!"

Rashid retracted his hand and said to Horace, "That's all they think about these hooligans. They think I am about to escape, like I am waiting for the right moment." Rashid's face turned serious, the seriousness of a leader writing an unofficial edit, he laughed, "maybe they can see through us."

Zahiri and Horace laughed and the air's tension diffused.

Horace looked at Zahiri, waiting for him to make the inquisition; he decided to take charge of the exchange. "How are you ahir, otherwise?" "Otherwise, good," Rashid said.

"Assallum Allakum," began Zahiri, to which Rashid responded, "Wallakum salaam ahir."

The ever vigilant guard hearing all these pleasantries yelled out from a hidden corner across Rashid's cell, "Don't waste time with greetings, you have two minutes left...Assallum Allakum this and that!"

"This is like traveling with a child," mumbled Horace in disgust. "...or traveling with a nuisance," agreed Rashid.

The three locked smiles and there was a silent agreement as to the mental health of the general – he was still sharp, in fact sharp enough to lead the Moors back to victory, thought Horace.

There was warmth in Rashid's laughter and the three felt relieved that his spirit had not been broken. Prison is that rare institution that can either make or break a man, thought Horace. Rashid certainly was regaining much needed composure and this was a perfect time for re-tooling.

Then Zahiri spoke, "Rashid, do you know this man? Yesterday he came to the motel looking for Zaniweri."

Rashid looked down like a disappointed Catholic priest contemplating the correct amount of contrition for mortal sins.

"Of course I know Mustafa. He is helping me, and I sent him to find Zaniweri."

"Zaniweri did not believe that," Zahiri replied shamefully.

"I don't care what he thinks. Mustafa is with us now. He is my abogado, the first counselor. Now go back and tell him what I said. We don't have time for games."

"We are sorry to have wasted your time," offered Zahiri in apology. "Don't apologize. The guard here will see you out."

Even in prison, Rashid was using the guards as secretaries. He said to the guard, "Thank you that will be all for this morning!"

The guard looked at Rashid in astonishment and shook his head, "We are going to hang you Moor."

"Thank you gentlemen," Rashid countered, unmoved by the insult. "Guard, show these men out please."

Zahiri and Horace got up and waved good bye to Rashid. For a moment the dimly lit tunnel gave the appearance of four men instead of just two. Soon enough, at the motel, it was discovered that the torturer, the one who had belted the shit out of Horace was Zaniweri, the second in command of the Moorish armed forces. Fate had crossed paths with Horace and Horace was just getting a sense of its many layered pathways; of how long and narrow each path was - he could only imagine. Zaniweri never apologized; he only informed Horace that tomorrow the two would head off at last to Toledo, up north, 'to find the imposter.' In the distance Horace thought about his heavy lift jet and the consequences of being discovered. He turned his face away from Zaniweri hiding the thought, like a spinster on a Caribbean vacation.

CHAPTER FORTY THREE

The path to Toledo would take Horace and Zaniweri close to three days. The two men were well acquainted and the initial lobotomy like introduction had worked in Horace's favor. Now he was in the inner circle, the sanctum sanctorum. The air had the imagined stiffness of diesel in mid summer; in turn, the two men looked at each other with avarice and jugular fixation, something you expect on a blind date or from an ex-spouse.

The next day the donkeys were rounded up. It was still early morning when Horace and Zaniweri started to advance northwards, first to Cordoba, then continuing north to Toledo.

As the journey progressed Horace began to feel nostalgia set on him. He missed Maria, his parents, the bustling noise of Boston and its provincial squirrels. He had become a transplanted man finally emptied of all hubris. He had no past, just a present and a future.

The two men rode on donkey back; and as they headed out from a distance they looked like a ragtag outfit of some bandit organization from pre-independent Latin America. The dust rising did not help with the characterization, nor did the fact that occasionally the wind blew upward onto their faces sounding like a countryside carnival. The two men did not talk to each other and Horace maintained his distance, as if to suggest that cat and dog were the assumed mascots for the day. "After all, this man has not yet apologized," thought Horace. Zaniweri was proud, the pride of someone who has lost a father in early infancy, imagined Horace. He was a descendent of the great Tariq Ibn Ziyad, who hailed from the Umayyad caliphate.

Tariq Ibn Ziyad, Zaniweri's ancestor, was an En Maziyn or Berber from the dust lands of Morocco, he had in 711 ACE led a successful overthrow of the Visig-oth ruler, Rhoderic and thus established a Moorish Kingdom. From Morocco, Tariq ascended into then Hispania (former territory including Spain) from the curtain drums of North Africa. He was victorious because his ambush caught Rhoderic off-guard and partly because Rhoderic was what you would consider a leader only by name. These memories were held preciously together by an emotional battery from which Zaniweri was sourced; it was clear to all who encountered him that he venerated his legacy.

Horace on the other hand was starting to have the kind of itch uncommon to Marylyn Monroe: a desire to be left alone and an eternal thirst for freedom. He wanted to explore Spain, its tall immaculate buildings. He wanted to let go of Rashid and all this talk on antebellum belligerence. Inside, Horace knew that besides the video games he had toyed with growing up he

KEN SIBANDA

THE RETURN TO GIBRALTAR 213

was not ready to be plunged in a war zone.

"How are you feeling?" asked Zaniweri, as they arrived in Cordoba. "I feel good, how much more do we have to go?" Horace inquired, holding the donkey's mash of collar-bone hair.

"We rest for the night and tomorrow we touch Toledo just before sun set," said Zaniweri, his oval face while unremarkable remained stern and unchanged. Horace noted how impressive Zaniweri's face was – "He has the face of leadership," said Horace to himself, "The face of sitting bull ---- Tatanka IyoTanka." Still looking at Zaniweri's face, Horace concluded that this was the kind of man that when you crossed him you knew that you had walked through fire and that there was a price to pay. He glanced at his satchel and remembered he was carrying a 0.45 automatic and this reassured him of his ability to walk the walk with Zaniweri.

"This man is not to be messed with," thought Horace as the two jumped off their respective donkeys. Horace tied his donkey next to what he imagined to be a jacaranda tree and Zaniweri tied his donkey to an oak tree.

"Do you like the motel?" Zaniweri asked and looked at Horace with the impassioned gaze of premeditation. "Do you have many motels in Malaga? I have never been there." This was uttered playfully and Zaniweri's lips bit into the word Malaga, in a playful monotone.
"Yes, many."

"Are you still angry with me?" said Zaniweri. He had noted the sarcasm in Horace's answer.

"Usually when we punch someone with a musket in the face, we apologize," chided Horace, deciding to run with it.
"How nice, Mr. Mustafa is also a big baby, is he not?"
"No, we have a man here," replied Horace, getting nerved by the gutsy utterance from Zaniweri.
"So if you are going to be a man, then complain, at least, like a real man."
Horace's cheek bones perked up as his teeth exposed a grin half reserved and half sincere.
"And how does a real man cry?" Horace asked.
"A man cries by not crying, that's how!"

Zaniweri and Horace then entered yet another motel, this one more dome shape than the others, the walls had bricks sticking out and the mortar showed bad craftsmanship. "This one was built in a rush," thought Horace.

"Assallum Allakum, where is Musa?" Zaniweri asked the attendant maître di.
"Wait here," replied the maître di.

Seconds later Musa arrived in jolly fashion; Zaniweri and Musa seemed to be reunited like two high school friends who once shared a common girlfriend. They clapped hands, hugged and even kissed.

"Musa, this is Mustafa Al Mutaseed, an abogado from Malaga. He is here to assist the general. Mustafa trained with the great Al Said."

Horace shook hands with Musa and noted that the man's hands were sweaty as if he had been chopping wood. Horace withdrew his hand and dis-

214

creetly wiped off the sticky grim of sweat.

"Mustafa," directed Zaniweri, seeing that the handshake had become awkward. "Sit here while the men talk."

Horace became surprised at Zaniweri's guile.

"The men... ha!"

An animosity between Zaniweri and Horace was continuing to take shape and every piece colluded together in anticipation of the final duel. This is the kind of cold war give and take that kept Ronald Regan trim and fit Horace concluded to himself. This reminded him of his responsibilities and the great burden he carried on his shoulders as an ambassador from another day and time.

Horace took a seat at a center kitchen table in the motel. He was served onion soup, bread, and a dish he could not fully comprehend but which had as its base - *cumin and barley*.

In the background he could hear the two men chatting off...the sound of a musket loading. The conversation piped through the room divider giving Horace a sense of being hunted.

After a good while, Zaniweri came out of the other room and said to Horace, "Here is your key ahir, for the night."

Horace grabbed the key and said, "Thanks."

"Don't thank me," said Zaniweri, "thank Musa, our host, he is also a descendant of Tariq like me." Zaniweri turned away slowly and walked off. He held a glass of water in his hand and in the other hand a Quran, he did not even invite Horace to make salat, *Muslim prayer*.

*

The next day the cock crowed, and with that coldness seemed to hover over the town of Cordoba. "The mornings here in Spain, have a sense of the mellowing transcendence," thought Horace, looking outside from his window. The night before, Zaniweri and Musa had spent the whole night talking and he had heard their brawny voices ricocheting off the wall, the echoes of two grown men enjoying middle age the best way they can – through oral history. The mornings in Spain, appeared to come in spasms, playing through like a trombone. And with it hesitantly the life of a Spaniard so commences.

Horace was always thinking about Troy, his heavy lift jet, which served as a time machine vessel. He was getting deeper and deeper into 'This country.'

'What if Troy is lost and I end up trapped in antiquity Spain?' thought Horace. Over and over the resilient thought kept coming, an ominous hurricane chasing the banks of Louisiana.

Close to mid day, Zaniweri and Horace left for Toledo.

Zaniweri was busy with Musa for most of the morning, talking, comparing muskets, comparing stories about their wives and future wives.

During the trip Horace would on occasion catch Zaniweri starring at him. He thought to himself, 'they say Islam is the religion of brotherhood,

KEN SIBANDA

but they also say Muslims make the best enemies because they fight you to the end – jihad.' It was becoming clearer every second that Horace was now an enemy of Zaniweri – the looks, the sourdough eyes and the gorged gaze like Rasputin in court defending his reputation.

"Maybe Zaniweri is onto me," Horace imagined and turned away from looking at Zaniweri in a quick reflex.

Now Zaniweri disembarked from his donkey and said, "We rest and then we go to the shop where Rashid bought this musket – or where the imposter bought the musket, and we ask many question. You are abogado after all, wait - I will ask all the questions."

The last statement was said in a declaratory manner and it struck Horace that Zaniweri had some education under his belt. "This cat is something I tell you…"

Horace looked Zaniweri squarely in the face and said, "Thank you very much Mr. Zaniweri but I am competent enough to ask questions."

The reply made Zaniweri fume in anger and he looked hard at Horace. Zaniweri took a step back, like a ballet dancer leveling his balance; he swung his left fist at Horace who ducked just in time. Horace in turn, now panting like a deer, threw a right hand lead that caught Zaniweri napping. It threw Zaniweri on the ground.

For Zaniweri, it came as a surprise that he had been floored by Horace. Like most bullies, he had never expected Horace to fight back. Zaniweri was expecting the tousle to go like a whipping of a naughty child reprimanded by his parents, but now he was floored and dazed; dry eyed, crimson and approximating an amateur boxer who neglected roadwork leading up to the fight…

Zaniweri was on the ground with dust in his face and his pride half deflated like a party balloon on the ceiling. He looked up at Horace and whimpered to Horace, "You did not have to do that…

"Ohh yes, I did…Mr. TARIQ-is-my-ancestor!"

Zaniweri got up slowly and said, "You will pay for this ahir, I will fix you one day."

"You already fixed me," said Horace, "you just don't realize how."

Horace rushed into the motel and checked himself in. This one was better looking than the previous one. And since he was new in Toledo, Horace reasoned that he did not need the company of a breathing bison ready to attack at any moment; the whole suspense was getting out off control. The corral was just too small for two bulls.

"This cat will never outsmart me; I am Horace Arthur Bates from Carthage, North Carolina. He will never outsmart me." Horace agreed with himself; entering the motel, a new resolve seemed to follow him and he wanted to succeed like never before.

CHAPTER FORTY FOUR

The next morning, Horace went 'Sight seeing' –put more plainly, in search of the missing evidence. He had slept well, nothing sinister about last night, he conceded, except for that crackling noise that seemed to originate from the top. Horace was curious about the noise, so the next morning when he met the motel keeper he inquired in a glucosidal matter of speaking.

"Ahir — brother – that noise last night, what was that?" he inquired, looking upwards at the ceiling.

The keeper did not want to be bothered and said, "That's the irrigation system, and you don't know this?"

Bit by bit Horace was giving himself away and it was becoming clearer to anyone who can see through smoke screens that all was not well with the man calling himself Mustafa Mutaseed. Horace remembered that in Spain, the irrigation ran through the roofs. "I should not have asked that question," he admonished himself.

The keeper shook his head and hurried off. "Allahu Akbar," he said as he disappeared into the anteroom of the motel. There was an uneasy silence that remained with Horace.

"Now, how do I catch an imposter?" Horace said to himself, his eyes communicating the inner turbulence he faced. He was like a rhinoceros trapped between a fence and a hunter.

He continued walking and eventually found himself outside where he was met with the usual morning smells.

Still in a bit of a daze, Horace remembered that Rashid's imposter had bought a musket from a gun store so that logically was the place to begin. After a good ten minutes he arrived at what appeared to be a gun store. It had the redundant feeling of having gone through history untarnished. The gun store was neighbored by a food store. Outside the store there were bags of coffee beans, salt and spices. He walked right into the gun store unhesitant.

"Assallum Allakum," Horace said in greeting, his voice rising to the occasion in crescendo.

"Wallakum sallum," replied the woman. She wore a hajib and looked away from Horace. This was done in keeping with Hadith and Sharia law.

Conversation between the opposite sexes is kept at a minimum. "My husband will come back and make you some coffee," she said in Arabic.

"Coffee would be nice, no sugar and no milk," Horace said, in his brand of hotchpotch Arabic. The lady grouched at the bad Arabic and said: "Allahu Akbar!"

Soon enough the lady came back into the room with a big cup of coffee and said, "You look for musket ahir, to buy a musket?"

"I look for gun yes," replied Horace, his voice quivering. Meanwhile his hand reached for the coffee on the counter. For a moment he almost burned himself with the coffee. He thought, "seems like Spanish coffee is served one hundred degrees fahrenheit."

*

A man entered the gun shop and the wind from outside came in with him. He carried a wooden box, covered with a reddish silk cloth and had the congeal look, as if he were an owner. Horace realized that this must be the gun shop owner. From the way the lady and the man looked at each other Horace concluded that the two must be husband and wife. It seemed that the strange man entering was being looked at with endearment and a strange sense of the de ja vu. The man and woman exchanged greetings and then the man turned his full attention to Horace.

"I hope you are not a Moor," he said coarsely.
Horace was caught off guard and answered, "No."

By now Horace got the feeling that not everyone shared the feeling that the Moors were noble Islamic soldiers, and so it appeared that some regarded them as a public nuisance for the monarchy.

"Good," the man said unpacking the box, "these Moors will get us Muslims all in trouble, we are guests here in Spain," he said. Spoken uneasily the utterance came across like a conflicted doppelganger.

The wife sensed her man drifting into dangerous waters and quipped, "Don't start with that dear, please."
"What brings you to my store my dear friend?"
"I need a musket, a flint, the one that Rashid Muhammad uses..."

"Hold on, Rashid Muhammad... so you are really a Moor, aren't you?"

Horace was fishing and baiting the man to get enough leverage as possible.
"No, I just admire the man! He is a good general."
This took the owner by surprise and he seemed to enter a dreamlike mood.
"Go, leave my store. You are not welcome here senore, not welcome."
"But why, ahir?" Horace asked, knowing full well what the reason was.
"Don't you know that man is trouble? He is in prison as we speak! That name, don't utter it in my store, please."
"But why?" Horace persisted.
"That is enough."
"Some say, he was framed and that the assassin's gun purchase is the work of an imposter. They say that in Toledo there is a man who looks exactly like Rashid."

The man's wife shook her head in astonishment, the guile and eloquence of the young man.

The pot just about boiled over and the store owner's face started to resemble someone annoyed at having to answer the same question fifty million times. He piped, "What's wrong with you, out boy!" His face tightened like a nut on an old bolt needing repairs. Horace had seen that look before; he had seen it when Zaniweri took a shot at him.

*

Horace hurriedly left the store and headed towards a tent type bar. There are no salons here, he thought, just a tent and people. It struck Horace as a surprise that there would be a bar in the middle of holy land. Horace entered the majestic looking tent and took a sit. He felt the dryness of heavy unventilated covers; he inhaled the hard liquor and adjusted to the awkwardness. There was a dancer on stage doing the flamingo. He watched the dancer momentarily without any sense of time and place; just a hollow gaze starring into thin air.

Something was amiss and Horace ran back to the store. Breathing heavy like a marathon sprinter, he entered the door. Immediately he sensed an eerie, unwelcoming feeling. "One gets this feeling when one enters a shooting range," he thought. He recalled India and the chase. "Damn, why did I ever agree…?" thought Horace.

The store owner and his wife were surprised and without words.
"I want to ask you a question ahir?"
"Ahir, get out please," said the store owner, pulling out his musket.
"Who framed Rashid. Who is the imposter?"
To that the store owner replied, "You are lost my friend. Ask his own people. They know everything. Get out please."

And from that Horace's mind raced like a stallion at the Derby, "his own people…" what does that mean?'

Horace looked intently into the man's eyes and he could see that there was innocence about him. Something seemed to come together and Horace concluded that this must be a classic case of betrayal for Rashid? 'Ask his people,' repeated itself, like rejection from a beauty-queen.

Horace had read some classics and he knew that betrayal in power is what sugar is to tea – an essential part of the brew. Betrayal is the greatest liability of the powerful, thought Horace. *'Caesar's memorable muttering: etu Brutus – you too Brutus!'*

Horace seemed to finally get the picture and understand why Zaniweri hated him with so much passion. It was not the monarchy who wanted Rashid out but it was the proud and boastful Zaniweri and his junta. This also meant Rashid's enemies had automatically become his enemies. That thought was enough for him to remember that Zinner had packed a 0.45 caliber in his leather satchel for him.

Meanwhile at the motel in Toledo, Zaniweri and his cronies arrived a moment too late. Apparently he was looking for Horace with his cronies and said something about, 'settling old scores like real men' to a foot soldier. Zaniweri left the motel thundering off towards the gun store.

"If you see him, don't admit him again; very bad man, very bad," said Zaniweri writing the editorial on Horace.

Zaniweri then disappeared into the musty lands asking anyone if they had seen a man going pejoratively by the name, Mustafa Al Mutaseed.

Across town, Horace had to return back to Rashid and inform him about the sabotage and the internal problem he faced.

Horace began his sordid journey back to Al Hambra in the south. He remembered the Rock of Gibraltar, its permanence and its symbolic history. From here the Moors had ascended, but now, like the tail end of a comet, the Moorish star dimmed. Horace jumped onto his donkey and struck it gently; soon the donkey was set in the direction of Al Hambra. Behind him Zaniweri had yet to patch up the pieces and realize that Horace had escaped and that Horace now knew of his plot to unseat Rashid. But at half a day's end that would all change; Zaniweri gathered his men and headed after Horace.

The sky seemed to darken, the two men becoming enemies was now itched in stone, perhaps the Rosetta Stone.

CHAPTER FORTY FIVE

Back in real time, the man known as Robert Churchwell was about to retire for the evening. His lush mansion seemed to cap a life well lived. Robert Churchwell looked at the television set; his eyes had the glare of continued enjoyment with the finer things in life. Robert carried himself like Lincoln at Gettysburg; ready and presidential, friendly but unabridged like a dictionary. Known for often indulging in fanciful clutter, he seemed to live in the refined epicure spot that money affords the wealthy. The tailored suits he wore were all an assortment of the pinstripe, grey with white stripes; blue with charcoal black...a wardrobe better suited for the Antarctic penguin.

In the evenings he would wind down by pouring himself a glass of expensive brandy on the rocks, which was imbibed slowly, as if to say life is best, lived at zero miles an hour. He was physically fit, a Tory (conservative) perhaps, running for higher office and when he smiled his face remained stern. By simply looking at Robert Churchwell, one could tell he was well-oiled. He had more money than the whole continent of Africa put together and including the hidden stash put aside by the despots. Twice divorced, he was neither misogynistic nor a debauch. He only liked women of a certain delicate nature. To get Bob's attention, one would have to combine expensive 'Parfum' with persuasion.

Few of his friends imagined Bob, as they called him, as a future presidential type. He was Yale class of '70, graduating with the Bachelor of laws, L.L.B, as it was then known and not the J.D. He was not book smart but was well read and knew that Zimbabwe used to be Rhodesia and that *Mandela* was not the misspelling of *Mandel*.

He liked to read pulp fiction: Grisham, Paterson and DaSilva, but he also had a keen interest in heavy reading like, *The History of Law, The Law of Relativity* – all titles that found themselves in the western ante room in the gated suburbs of Orange, California.

He was Californian elite, the way Nixon was after his return from a failed presidency in '78. His enemy list was minimal; the usual competitors and high-strung former-friends. He had keyed in to the cause of enemies and would say, ...*it's a result of people wanting the same things; and most people do not have anything that I want in life*.

He was a banker, but never carried a business card with him or identified the bank he worked for. As a banker, he often would take three month long vacations into the most exotic places. The Caribbean sun always seemed to surprise him in its magnanimity and it's energizing spirit. He was known as a brilliant man. Once he had said the prophetic words that proved true; "you see that South African Mandela, one day he will come out of prison a martyr."

Bob was then asked why he was saying these things and he replied. "You can't keep a good man down without holding yourself down buddy boy," he said, clapping his palms together like a kindergarten teacher emphasizing the K in 'Kick.'

On that fateful evening a commotion got Bob's attention while he was in the living room. "Who ever it is must be familiar enough with the guards," thought Bob. The security guidelines had been breached - *'No visitors after seven P. M.'*

Bob left the sofa with the comfort of a man who does not have to report to any one. He walked down stairs, offbeat and yet relaxed, almost whistling Dixie. He stopped at his gun cabinet and removed a 0.357. The gun had seen some action during World War II and retained the pristine look of oxidized lead.

Bob neared the door and shouted, "Who is it?"

The words appeared to bounce off the door and Bob felt like he was talking to himself.

"It's me, Tim, open please."

"Timmy, what the hell is going on here? Didn't I tell you that seven is a no show for me? You know that by now."

"Open up," came the insistent monotone from Timmy, "it's an emergency, it's Zinner."

The word Zinner was like mentioning the price of gold, after all it was Zinner's science. Without Zinner there was nothing.

Bob continued thinking as he opened the door. 'Mr. Timmy again,' he thought, 'for some people, the whole idea of life is urgency.'

*

Timmy plunged into the room, he walked right in pulling the scientist with him. There was coolness in the room which Timmy was expecting. He looked straight at Bob and said:

"It's Ivanovich, they got to Zinner. I knew this would happen and you said so yourself."

"What's going on Tim, Ivanovich? I thought they were out of the picture by now. Don't they get it! We beat them to the punch and we have the science they don't," said Bob. He looked at Zinner.

"Zinner was never careful as you know by now. I found him on his door step breathing for dear life."

"Is he alive?" asked Bob, helping Timmy carry Zinner into his house. Zinner's legs scraped and hugged the carpet as Bob pretended to be helping, but in fact he wasn't. Like most wealthy people, he found it extremely hard to do any manual labor – even tying his own shoe laces.

"I am feeling a pulse," said Timmy.

"Pulse is good, let me call my physician," offered Bob, making his way to his study. Bob kept a personal physician on salary.

He entered the study and speed dialed his physician.

"Jackie, get down here ASAP. It's an emergency."

He nodded his head and then said, "Thanks Jackie."

Bob walked into the other room where Timmy and Zinner were waiting for him and said, "Let's take him to the fourth floor."

Timmy motioned towards the stairs and Bob interrupted him saying, "I have an elevator, this way. Now did you really think an old horse like me has the stamina to walk those steps? You gotta' be kidding me."

But what Bob did not tell Timmy was that the elevator was actually a situation room designed to survive a nuclear attack. It went upwards to five floors and also went downwards 1200 feet to the water line, where there was a direct input into the oceanic cervix.

When they got to the fourth floor, the silence of the whole mansion seemed to make its invasion known and again Timmy was struck by the loneliness of high money.

Bob interrupted and said, "I know what you thinking. I get that feeling all the time - the house is too big."

"How do you manage this, all alone like that," asked Timmy. He struggled with placing Zinner's arm back to the rest of his body as the scientist was dragged across the floor.

"I don't know. I don't think about it and I enjoy my personal space. There are too many people in California. It's good to have your space, once in a while. What can I tell you. I need my space," said Bob raising his hands and unlocking a guest room. "Space, space, space…"

Zinner was taken into the guest room, his mouth frothy and his eye lids occasionally fluttering in spasms. "Set the bugger here," said Bob. Timmy was surprised at the laid back behavior of Bob and said:

"Bugger!"

"That's just slang for good man."

Timmy looked away. Something about Bob seemed to change every other night. "Maybe money makes you immune to emotions," he thought. "A complete vaccine to human bonding…"

Soon Zinner was placed on the guest bed and Timmy checked to see whether he had the pulse rate from earlier. "Anytime now the doctor should be joining us," said Bob, trying to make up for his previous cold words.

And before the words had left Bob's mouth there was a knock at the door and Bob said, "That's Jackie."

The doctor approached Zinner and placed her hand on his wrist. She nodded to herself and Timmy watched through the corner of his eye like a wolf in hiding. He said to the doctor, "Be careful. He is all we got."

The doctor turned her face towards Timmy and locked eyes. Her brunette hair and slim frame made her look younger than she was and there was something in her eyes; the same thing that he had noticed in Bob's eyes. *Something hidden…*

CHAPTER FORTY SIX

The sunscald parchment of grass and vegetation littered the pathway back to the dudgeon adjacent to Al Hambra. Horace rode on his donkey and kept an ever vigilant eye for Zaniweri and his men. Ever so often into the journey, he would stop and look back, absorb the sun pressing on his back savoring its cooling effect and continue unabashedly into the wilderness of the country. It was like picking gnats from pepper and hoping that the taste was not too repugnant.

Horace's diet by now resembled the basic keys to the food pyramid; bread supplied the grains; goats' milk supplied the calcium; raw veggies gave the added boast and finally a lot of falafel evened out the palate.

In the distance, Horace could hear the cry of Al Adhan, the Islamic prayer. He would stop and look around to make sure that he was not ambushed. As soon as the call was silent, he would continue his journey.

The call to prayer, thundering through the Spanish sky like a bold eagle lost in flight:

Allahu Akbar,
Allahu Akbar,
Ash-hadu an la ilāha an la illa llāh
Ash-hadu anna Muhammadan-rasūlu llāh
- *Allah is greatest*
I testify that there is no God but Allah,
I testify that Muhammad is the messenger of God.

Surprisingly the journey back to the Al Hambra was shorter and seemed to be short circuited; Horace had not even stopped at one of the inns lining the road. Instead he had continued for fourteen hours on donkey back like an outlaw chased to the outer fringes of a sheriff's locale. Throughout the journey Horace was consumed by thoughts of futility. He said to himself, "Perhaps this mission can't be done; perhaps Rashid is already dead like the Toledo - three."

Horace arrived at the prison towards the late hours of the evening. He headed straight towards the dungeon without a moment's delay. Horace imagined the Italian poet Dante Alighieri and his writing on exile and this seemed fitting, given the fact that he was in hiding in a distant land away from his family. In Dante's case, thought Horace, exile happens when one is unable to understand the Florentine sentiment of the city they reside in. Horace's thoughts were getting crazier as the donkey started to show its tiredness. For the first time, there were signs of exhaustion. The donkey breathed heavier and its eyes were red.

KENSIBANDA

At the entrance to the prison, the guard on duty motioned for Horace to go in. But now he seemed not to even think of Horace as a threat. "The power of the law behind one's name," thought Horace, as he returned the sullen grin from the guard.

The guard was even generous with his time during this visit as he shouted in a bellicose fashion, "You have exactly six minutes, hurry in," the guard said. His face reddened by the sweetness of the cherry wine he was drinking. "Make sure you hurry, don't play."

Inside the dungeon Horace found the general asleep. As Rashid breathed, his stomach went up and down like a baby's. There was no snoring and Rashid was completely deadened in sleep. Horace thought to himself, "He sleeps extremely silent for someone with so much to say." The realization struck him as rather odd and Horace jettisoned, "Rashid, ahir, it's me, please wake up." Horace looked behind to make sure that Zaniweri was not behind him. The term, 'watch your back,' had become a living reality.

Horace tried again, his mind more determined, "Rashid, please wake up!"

Finally Rashid seemed to awaken to the calling of his name.

"Ahir, I am back! We need to talk!"

Rashid took a deep breath and said, "You made it back."

"We really need to talk, we have a bit of a problem," said Horace.

"What is it?" Rashid asked, getting up from the bed and throwing the blankets to the floor. His face had the seriousness of a man awoken from the enjoyment of an impassioned dream. "What is it?" he asked again confidently.

"Rashid, I am sorry to tell you this, but there is no imposter, your own people…your generals have betrayed you."

The words did not seem to shock Rashid, who by now was seated in an upright constellation. He said, "Betrayal, ha! The sweet revenge of the man who wants to be in charge."

Horace was taken back. The man was unshaken by the insult, and continued "How did you know that this would happen?" he asked.

"It's Zaniweri…I know, the look on his face; those parry eyes and threatening look, like quartz shining in the court yard. One never forgets that look, he has the look of a man who believes that his time has been quashed by lesser man."

Horace almost opined the findings of others in this matter – betrayal, but he declined the invitation. Instead he said with much enthusiasm, "We have to find another plan. We can deal with Zaniweri later."

"There will not be another time. After this, our time here as Moors, there will not be another great Islamic nation; they only have me as the final front, then it's over," said Rashid unable to comprehend the thought.

"Killed," said Horace and then he realized that he shouldn't have said that. "Maybe there is something we can do. I will do my best tomorrow to defend you in court."

Tomorrow was the date for the trial; the day when the magistrate would be hearing all evidence against the Moor, Rashid. The law used in Spanish court is a combination of ancient *Hammurabi Code, the Justinian Code*, thought Horace, the sort of law whose base is caustic in outcomes: if a man tries to assassinate the president he should be killed, so forth and so on.

Horace knew the law and how it applied. No defense could save Rashid. He turned away in a somber state unable to comprehend that two religions had collided so bloodily: Christianity and Islam.

Renewed by inner strength, Horace thought about the trial tomorrow, and said to Rashid, "We might have a chance. Sometimes the law overlooks things."

Rashid was adamant, "The only thing that can save me is a miracle my friend."

"Miracles have been known to happen," said Horace. "We are not too far from Lebanon, the land of miracles."

Rashid shrugged his shoulders, "Lebanon...you are well read."

"As a lawyer you read."

"You are a believer my friend. I like that - a true believer."

Horace got up and looked at Rashid for perhaps the final time. Next time he saw the man it would be in court and the man would be sequestered. Even as a lawyer, he would be unable to talk directly to his client. Horace found this to be insufficient for the minimum standards of justice. He remembered Dixon in North Carolina – he was in and out of the jail house and had met with Dixon numerous times. Horace was now becoming obsessed with finding justice for Rashid. For now, his hand reached through the cell bars to shake Rashid's hand.

"Tomorrow we win ahir...tomorrow we win." Horace did not notice that he had repeated himself.

Horace left the prison troubled. His thoughts weighed on him like a weight thrown at sea in hopes that it anchors the Titanic. "Friends now enemies...and enemies now as friends," Horace thought. "Painfully poetic..."

K
E
N

S
I
B
A
N
D
A

CHAPTER FORTY SEVEN

"May the defendant stand," said the magistrate, Thomas Sanchez, his wooden voice caressed the court walls delicately suggesting tenure in his judgeship. The black cloak he wore made him look regal.

"Monsieur Rashid Abu Muhammad, you are charged with treason and have already pleaded not guilty in this matter, is that correct?"

Rashid hesitated and then replied, "That's correct."

"You had enough time to consult with your lawyers – sorry, lawyer, and to have the known evidence adduced against you."

"Yes, your honor I have." Even at his lowest point Rashid sounded presidential.

"Do you still want to maintain your innocence in this matter?" asked the magistrate, his face sternly articulated.

"Your honor with all due respect…"

The magistrate interrupted, knocking his hammer onto the wooden plank in front of him. "Please just answer the questions, no commentary. Save the history lessons for the gallows, Rashid. I am sure you can talk fairness all day."

The judge then turned his learned face to the defense table where his eyes locked with Horace's.

"Mutaseed, you are counsel on record?"

"Yes."

"And your defense is still the same," asked the judge, his voice rising as if to be more respectful to another officer of the court.

The courthouse was aptly adjutant to the prison ward and connected from the rear to the great Islamic castle, the Al Hambra. It was shaped like a horse shoe and allowed for quick access by the defendants, the attorneys and the magistrate himself. In hind sight thought Horace, "This resembles an Elizabethan stage." For now, the dry air filled the corridors and gave it the humidity of Boston in summer. This was in tandem with the silence and Horace imagined that you could hear a needle drop.

The magistrate continued, biting his lips together and said, "Very well, prosecutor. Are you ready for business?" The prosecutor's name was Rodriguez Salinas. He carried himself accordingly, the perfect gentleman.

"Your honor, we are ready," announced Rodriguez, adjusting the assortment of papers on his table.

"Your honor we are ready," said Horace. From close by it was evident that Horace was anxious to get the trial moving, his face rectangular like laundry pegs.

Horace continued, "We would ask that circumstantial evidence be limited your honor, only direct evidence."

The magistrate looked surprised at the request and said, "May both attorneys please approach."

Soon Horace and Rodriguez approached the bench. The judge leaned forward like a mother admonishing a spoiled child and said, "We will have no mistrial here, you hear me. All objections will be at bench, no standing objections, you hear me senore Mustafa."

Horace reluctantly answered, "Yes."

"I don't know what Al Said taught you but in my court we will have no fancy lawyering," said the judge and then he turned his head to Rodriguez whose face by now glared to the extent of a flood light with excitement. The judge said to Rodriguez, "It's good to see you Rodriguez."

"Same here judge, always a pleasure to see you? How is the family?"

"Good, the young one is starting school…"

Maybe you should exchange recipes, thought Horace looking at the two lawmen. The exchange was so unprofessional that Horace began to conclude that Rashid did not have a chance. "This is mere formality," he agreed with himself and turned to Rashid.

Horace returned to his bench and the prosecutor stood facing the gallery, gallantly dressed in what resembled a three piece tailored suite. He said confidently, "Your honor, the Monarchy calls Javier Martinez."

The gun-shop-owner walked in as serious as the monsoon rains. Javier took the witness stand and looked at the prosecutor. It was clear he was avoiding eye contact with Horace.

"You solemnly swear to tell the truth, nothing but the truth," the prosecutor asked Javier.

"I do."

The prosecutor went straight into his direct examination trying to funnel out all the pertinent aspects of his case. It was Harvard vis-à-vis Spanish customs, thought Horace, looking intently at the prosecutor.

Horace listened carefully and soon it was his turn to take a shot at Javier. Horace did not hesitate. Somehow the idea of Rashid's face sitting with nobility gave him a confident bearing and reminded him that behind the title 'Defendant' was a real person. He remembered his cousin Dixon and drew strength like a bull facing an unlikely outcome in a bull-ring.

"Isn't it true, that you have an unpleasant disposition towards the Moors? In fact, you don't like them, and you find them contentious."

"Please no big words," said the magistrate.

Horace wondered what big words he was using and said to the magistrate, "Your honor please instruct the witness to answer the question."

"I am instructing you to rephrase the question."

"…would you agree with me that you don't like Moors."

"Yes, I don't like them."

"Please strike that answer out," the judge instructed the stenographer. "Mr. Mustafa please, that is irrelevant."

"Your honor, I would like to re-answer that question," said Javier.

"Re-answer, you gotta be kidding me," thought Horace in frustration. Javier, the witness then said, "I don't agree with you, no, I like the Moors."

It was clear now that Martinez had been coached, perhaps by Zaniweri, perhaps by Salinas the prosecutor, or was it the magistrate: someone had got to him.

Every question thrown at Martinez was met with a clear and intelligent but belligerent answer. By the second, it was clear who the witness actually thought had bought the musket and what he heard.

Martinez leaned forward for added dramatics, "This man here said he was done with the monarchy and that he needed a flintlock quick and his exact words were "…to shoot them both."

The magistrate interrupted in assistance, "…by two people, you actually mean King Ferdinand and Queen Isabella."

Maybe he means King Henry the VII of England, thought Horace, of course the Spanish Monarchy. Horace was getting irritated at the extra-judicial help Javier was receiving.

Midway through the cross examination, Horace tried again to ruffle Javier's feathers. Horace's legal education had taught him that the most difficult thing to recall when lying on stand is time and dates.

Horace asked, "When did you first see Mr. Rashid Muhammad?"
"…in the early morning hours around 8:30 A.M. on the first Saturday of June."
"And does your store open on Saturdays?"
"Actually, I meant the first Friday of June," restated the gun-shop-owner.
"Really, Senore Martinez…"
"Yes, I am sure."
"Are you not a practicing Muslim?"
"I am," said Javier.
"Then how is it that your shop is open on Friday, the holy day?"
To this Javier interjected, "I meant Thursday, your honor."
"Are you really sure senore? How about Sunday at 7 P.M.; Tuesday at 12 P.M. --- do these times sound familiar?"

Horace was content with the contradiction and proceeded to another area of contention.
"No…" said Javier, a moment too late.
"Okay senore, memory is not one of your strongest pursuits is it?"
"Strike that question!" said the judge, "Mustafa, I am warning you!"
"Sometimes I have…" said Javier
"No need to explain," said Horace, "but I will bring your attention to this gun here, this musket. Your honor, I would like it to be marked exhibit A for identification purposes only."

The watchers in the courtroom were impressed with Horace and seemed to be hanging on each and every word. For the first time, Horace eyed Rashid smiling with a sense of contentment; he imagined what was going through the general's head. The prosecutor looked away like a child looking for a toy that's gone missing.

"Marked as such," said the judge.

"You own a gun shop?"

"Yes."

"The record will reflect that foundation has been established. Is this gun one of those you sell?"

"Yes."

Horace approached the gun shop owner with exhibit A. He said, "Does this gun look familiar – is it in the same substantial condition as it was when you first saw it?"

The judge interjected like a public service announcement, "One question at a time Mustafa. Let the man answer, final warning, senore."

After the gun was admitted into evidence by proper physical authentication, Horace asked Javier yet another one of his cat-in-a-box questions.

"Can you please explain to me when this gun was made ---- you are familiar with guns and how they are manufactured and when?" asked Horace.

"Yes, very much such so," said Javier, in a boastful tone.

Javier's face was ecstatic, now he had the chance to show off.

"Sure, this is a flint Musket, made in the summer of 1490."

"Will you kindly tell the court please senore, how it is that you are off by twelve months? This gun was only released this summer, in 1491!"

A silence filled the court room. The prosecution was furious.

"I object to that line of questioning," said the prosecutor.

"He objects to all my line of questioning but at a minimum he must have a basis your honor."

The crowd burst out in laughter.

The prosecutor then said in anger, "May we approach your honor?"

"...approach Salinas and Mustafa please."

Moments later the two attorneys were half bent facing the magistrate.

"This is circumstantial," said Salinas.

"I have no clue what that word is supposed to mean but your honor, this is all relevant. You yourself spoke about relevance, didn't you?"

"I did," said the magistrate, hating that his words were being used against him, "and I am ruling the question be stricken off the record. I find your antics very displeasing senore."

"I strongly object to that decision," said Horace raising his voice.

"And I don't care that you strongly object."

The two attorneys returned to their respective tables and the judge said, "After hearing evidence from both sides and their arguments, I find the defendant Rashid Muhammad guilty and sentence him to death by hanging. Good day gentlemen!"

"Your honor I have not finished with the cross," said Horace.

"I really don't care. I am satisfied with the evidence. Good day senore. Mr. Salinas, please see me in my chambers to sign the death certificate and the required paperwork for this."

There was a booming voice yelling, "All rise."

Rashid was walked out off the court room. He turned around and looked at Horace with a sullen look of a man who has accepted his fate as just so.

Horace lifted the Spanish books on criminal procedure from his desk, as well as the Justinian code and walked out in the opposite direction from the judge's exit. The two men, Rashid and Horace, were now like two halves of a moon's eclipse, moving slowly out of place, one side the moon and the other, the earth. It was dated that two weeks from now, Rashid would hang.

Horace remembered that historically the Moors surrendered on January 2nd, 1492 – so this was the culminating event, he thought. Horace still imagined that there could be a plan B put into place ---- something equitable and fair...

K
E
N

S
I
B
A
N
D
A

CHAPTER FORTY EIGHT

Horace felt the sustained re-enactment of yesterday's deliberations beginning to settle. Outside, from what looked like a motel window, Horace could see the edged skyline of Spain in the distance; the tallest buildings were the places of worship; the church and Mosque. He shuddered at the sight, "so much love for God but in the absence of love for one's neighbor."

Another sentiment chopping at him was that he missed being Horace Bates. Just a week ago he had been in 2010 United States and he remembered Zinner, that giddy scientist. Zinner had said to Horace before take off, "Horace, my dear friend, since you are changing time zones your sense of space will be greatly affected."

In the back of Horace's mind were those strained words and in the foreground the spicy dinner from last night. 'Seems like every thing is spice this and spice that,' thought Horace. 'Zaniweri is gaining on me and my work is done. I have to leave. What about plan B? Get Rashid out of prison...'

Plan B was something Timmy had hatched up in commotion and lacking of detail. Timmy had stitched plan B together in less than fifteen minutes – explaining the finer points like a piano instructor. Horace found the whole idea rather fanciful in substance. It seemed to lack the detail for an operation Mongoose or Desert Storm, but it had the ambition for something military. "Something half baked," thought Horace, "like morning apple tart." Plan B would have worked excellent if it were a plan running parallel to diplomatic overtures. And since diplomacy had failed, thought Horace, plan B had to be activated.

"I need to get Rashid out," said Horace to himself almost audibly.

He looked around to make sure the words had not travelled into the distance.

Zinner had stuffed C4 into the bottom bunker of Troy and all Horace had to do was to surreptitiously remove it and make sure Rashid received it.

Horace had to go back to the jet, remove the C4, then use a remote control to blow an opening in Rashid's prison cell. It all seemed so simple, except that actually doing it now seemed like climbing Mount Everest. Impossible – he still lacked the resolve of military training and he knew it. He lacked motivation and this made him realize how his family contributed to his being motivated. He needed a muse.

There was loud thumping on the door that reminded Horace of Zaniweri. Horace walked to the door and looked through the peep hole. It was him: Zaniweri after all. He had a posse of angry looking flunkies and they all carried a hodgepodge of sword and machete. This was definitely not the welcome party his doctor ordered, thought Horace.

Horace thought for a moment and said, "Ahir...hold on." He said it like a Californian busy at work, very relaxed. He climbed out through the bathroom window. And in vintage Horace manner, instead of running away, he turned back towards the men. From his satchel Horace removed a 0.45 caliber.

One of Zaniweri's men, a stumpy looking fellow, said in a heavy accent, "He is crazy! What is he doing?"

Horace fired the musket in the air like an English man directing his hounds in the right direction.

"He has a musket," said one of Zaniweri's men. They were all dressed in an assortment of hand made white linen. The men soon fled into different directions scattering at various speeds like the segments of an angry volcano. It surprised Horace how effective gun fire must be. Horace's plan had worked and he proceeded in Troy's direction.

Horace walked for a good distance before he saw the particular pattern of hills and rifts. He looked at his watch which by now had its tracking device turned on. The watch read - one mile to Troy. After another twenty minutes Horace could now see the lumpy leaves covering Troy. He got to the jet and disengaged the alarm.

The routine of disarming the jet made Horace realize how much he was actually Horace Arthur Bates and not the time travelling man-in-Spain Mustafa Al Mutaseed. A few moments of being Horace was sufficient to give him the comfort level he was used to. He missed speaking English and the usual give and take American English affords. *What's up son...*

Horace lifted the C4 which had the whiteness of snow packed ice and was accompanied by the smell of sewage that needs urgent drainage. He lifted it out slowly. He had heard tales of how nitroglycerine seems to enjoy surprise explosions. He wrapped the C4 in a piece of cloth, making sure there was no exposure to sunlight.

*

Horace proceeded to the prison with the determination of someone who does not know what he is doing.

At the prison gate, he spoke rapidly, "I am abogado, Mustafa, and I want to see Rashid."

The guard said, "Okay, go in senore, once we kill him, we will have no more of this nonsense."

When he got to Rashid's cell, the general was engaged in prayer. Horace waited respectfully for the prayer to end and said, "Ahir, I brought you some bread."

"Mustafa my brother, you finally arrived. You were good yesterday, and where did you learn that from. I tell you what - I would give the world to

see you again in trial. The way you spoke… 'your honor with all due respect.'"
Rashid moved his eyes in mock imitation. "I am very proud of the things I saw yesterday. I just prayed for you ahir. I asked Allah that one day you too may experience the graces of his love."

"Thank you."

"Don't thank me, thank Allah."

"Allahu Akbar," Horace said.

"Now because of you the whole world will know that I died an innocent man. May Allah bless your name my friend. I am guilty only by name, not by deed."

"Thank you, ahir," said Horace and he started to feel that plan B should be cancelled, after all the man accepts his fate.

"So what do you have for me?"

Horace took out the C4 and said, "Stick this to the wall and at eleven tonight please step away from it. I will be waiting on the other side…"

At that moment, as if fate was tempting Rashid, the guard came closer to the two men and looked at the white loaf.

He asked, "What is that?"

Horace inhaled deeply and then said, "Oh, that's just bread, nothing really, you know us Moors, eating bread that is a few days old."

The guard felt ashamed and said, "Sorry senore, just making sure."

Horace left the prison and waited a distance of four hundred yards. From a distance he saw Zaniweri talking to the guards who were responding by telling him to leave. Horace laughed, "Good…at least someone shares my sense of insight," he said to himself.

*

At 11 p.m., the explosion occurred, it floored Rashid completely. It took a few minutes of the dust settling down when Rashid overheard Horace yelling.

"Here …please hurry."

The guards all ran away from the noise, piping something about Allah's revenge.

There was a lot of smoke in the dungeon and this served as the perfect diversion.

Horace and Rashid took off for the mountain veldt leaving behind them the dusty, smoky insistence of bondage. Rashid could not believe it, this man had saved him. In the distance the two figures began to slow down, it seemed like they had been running for eternity. Horace's face was lived with emotion; his brows were animated and his lips jocular.

"Rashid, you have to cross Gibraltar and into Morocco, go back to the land of your forefathers and return from there. I cannot accompany you. My work is done here."

It took Rashid a second before he shot back, "I know ahir. I will never forget you saved me, and the Moors. Tomorrow is January first, a new year… I also know Mustafa you are not with Al Said…he died years ago…but I know your heart, that's all that matters."

Horace was taken back by his cover being blown and said, "Go now," he looked at the ground, "please, ahir, go with Allah."

Horace watched Rashid disappear into the wilderness, into Juma Al Tariq ---- Gibraltar. Its is from here that legend has it, Rashid's ancestor, Tariq invaded antiquity Spain and established the Moors as a permanent power in Spain.

As for Horace he turned and headed back towards Troy. In the opposite direction he could see Zaniweri caging in. He turned and made a detour. Now his adrenaline was so pumped that his heart felt like it was directly pressing onto his shirt.

Horace felt content, knowing that he was going back to the land of milk and honey – the good ole U. S. of A. He ran, ran until the heels of his feet seemed to hover on the ground like a hovercraft. Then to his surprise he arrived at Troy. He got in the cockpit and closed it shut, the way a thief closes a cookie jar – recklessly fast. Horace then turned on the EPS switch; disengaged the stutter breaker ----Arms switch on; then he moved the stutter upward and Troy elevated upwards magically. He was in awe, "modern technology never lets you down, now back home."

He turned for the final time towards Gibraltar and remembered Rashid the General. In all it had been worth it ---- the price of justice. Troy roared like an old lion trapped in some hunter's menacing trap. It continued rising upward, like a determined hiker. Horace locked in the coordinates – Palm Spring Desert, 2010, United States of America. Nothing ever felt so good!

The bully machine continued even higher. It accelerated towards Gibraltar; going supersonic in three seconds and then hypersonic in another three seconds. In less than ten seconds it went supernova and like a star seemed to disintegrate. Horace was going back home. He could not wait to see the fruits of his hard work. He was leaving Gibraltar - never to return.

Alhambra Gatehouse, Tower of Justice, Andrew Dunn, 12 May 2006

KEN SIBANDA

BOOK III

CHAPTER FORTY NINE

Horace landed on the air strip in California at 6:30 in the morning, like a hawk finding even ground. He had no problems landing; there was the usual tingling sensation of a new pilot's final moment but Horace by now understood fully that Troy, not only made concurrent calculations to any instruction, but that Troy searched for alternatives. He secured Troy, the heavy jet lifter, and headed towards Timmy for further instructions.

He decided to take the LA Metro to Timmy's house in Orange County.

Something had been different on the return back to 2010 America, thought Horace, looking around. He walked away from the warehouse that now housed Troy. He was familiar with Palm Springs. Much of it was desert land. You had to catch a ride hitch hike all the way to San Bernardino. From Bernardino, Orange County is another one hundred miles. He was heading to Villa Park in the northern part of Orange City and prepared himself for a spacious welcome; something that includes Jacuzzis and looking over into the mountainous cliffs of southern California. But for now he was in Coachella County and he could hear the coyotes in the distance and smell the dried rot flown by vultures.

The difference was in the dissimilar colors. The arrangement of colors, something had changed…The arrangement of numbers had been reversed and things looked backwards. For the long ride to Orange City Horace bought the San Anna Times Newspaper and started playing catch-up on local news. Two weeks was enough time for him to lose track of events in current time but the two weeks was actually two days in real time.

"I already miss the general," thought Horace, thinking about Rashid. In the train it occurred to him that the train had only blacks in it and Horace reluctantly asked the gentleman sitting next to him.

"Where are all the white people?"

The passenger, a burly gentleman in his mid-fifties, looked at Horace and shook his head.

"Don't you read the paper…hey, you know who you remind me off….Mustafa, Rashid's lawyer in 1491, that jaw line. He became the first advisor to the Moorish Kingdom…"

Still Horace was frozen, "What's in the paper?"

"Do I also have to wipe the crumbs off your mouth?"

Horace looked away making sure that the words rubbed off.

"Okay let me spell it out. Their leader, Marthy Kenny, was making trouble; … the leader of the whites. So we banned white people from riding trains."

"You banned white people from riding trains?"

"It's about time I tell you! We should ship them back to Europe if you ask me. They are just wasting our time here," said one passenger.

Horace did not know how to take this gratuitous jab at white people; he did not appreciate any form of racism and so he said, "Come on man, its one person at a time you know."

The man seemed to be irritated by the suggestion that people should be taken one at a time.

"Look, one at a time my ass man."

Horace sank deeper into his seat and it finally dawned on him; a reversal had just occurred, black people were now oppressing white people. He decided to double check his discernment.

"Excuse me, I don't mean to bother you but is the leader of the whites doctor Martin Luther King?" Horace asked.

"Either you high on drugs or you just a dumb ass; what's your problem man?"

"Nothing" Horace said.

The man got up and started walking to another seat, he said, "I am changing my seat. Good luck." Then just as abrupt and as cunning as a fox, the stranger left the train.

As the stranger was leaving he uttered the words, "Their leader is Marty Kenny, you were almost correct. This Marty Kenny fellow is a very dangerous man." And with that all the black people seemed to share this viewpoint and nodded in agreement.

"Yeh, and the next thing you know these people will be asking us for equality and wanting to sleep with black women," said another passenger. All the black women in the train shuddered and curtsied in surprise.

"That's just not acceptable now," shouted yet another train rider and it all made for a symphonic discord.

"You know what they say about white men," said another.

Horace smiled to himself, even stereotypes had been reversed, "This is ridiculous," he thought, "I hope not all black people are this dim witted." The black women did not seem to mind and burst out in a collective gut.

Horace could not believe what he was hearing. Black people were indeed running things, as they say, if not running things into the ground. But these were some mean spirited people, he conceded. Reversing the polarities in Spain had put black people in a prominent social position; fate does have a sense of humor, he thought. Now he closed his eyes feeling the weight of time travel; his forehead wrinkled and he tried unsuccessfully to relax. The sleepy eyes could not hide the disgust and deep sadness of what he had just witnessed. He drifted into a kind of half-sleep – half awake moment. Something crossed his mind – he was the reason for all this. "I have to go back," said Horace to himself, "And fix this."

This thought tormented Horace and then he looked to his side to see an older white woman of close to seventy in age. The fact that the lady was seventy did not change the tone of the conversation as it continued to escalate to another level.

Before the lady could take a seat in the train the conductor approached her and said, "Excuse me mama, so where do you think you are going?" he asked.

"Young man, please, I have a condition," said the lady, "just for today may I ride with you black people?" She repeated herself over and over again, "I have a condition, I have a condition...I know I am white but I am also Christian like you, we are all God's children."

"No way, hosea," said the conductor without missing a beat, "I could get into trouble for this," he insisted.

"One more stop and I will be there. One...stop please."

The crowd in the train by now is silent in anticipation of the worst to come. Outside the train, the noise of the train's tracks grinding into the rail vested the moment with a theatrical impasse just before the sorrowful opening of a third act. Neither the conductor nor the white lady wanted to move away from the confrontation. Horace took the position of an impartial observer, his stomach started to turn because of the spicy soup from earlier on in Spain.

The spectacle between the white lady and the conductor progressed. Two spirits; the young conductor in his prime – fit as a fiddle, and on the other hand the women, frail and showing the first symptoms of dementia.

The conductor took those words as a declaration for war even though the lady was old enough to be his grandmother.

"I will give you one more chance before I call the police," advised the conductor. Then from out of the blue the conductor's supervisor arrived. The supervisor goose stepped, instead of walking and looked – over confident.

The older lady did not move a hair's breath; she remained fixated at the conductor's request, standing her ground. The supervisor's walk was reminiscent of that dreaded Nazi march at the party conference in 1938 – left, right, chins pointing at 90 degrees to feet.

"What's going on here?" proclaimed the supervisor, his voice carried through the train car. All the passengers seemed to listen to every word spoken.

The supervisor's name badge read, "Frank Stigler." He prepared his well rehearsed speech; and began in earnest, speaking like someone who is speaking down to an infant child.

The conductor leaned forward and said to the supervisor, "This lady does not want to follow transit law."

"And is that true?" Stigler asked the lady.

"Yes sir. Please, I have a condition."

"Mam, we have heard a lot of people telling us they have condition after another – if I let you in, I will have to let everyone in. It's just not fair to the others who are not allowed to ride the train. I am sorry but you have to leave, condition or no condition you have to go." This spoken in a kind of working accent designed to humiliate the old lady. The supervisor thought it through for another second and said, "Next time you try to pull something funny, it's jail for you."

Horace was astonished by the level of callous disregard for the rights of others. It almost felt like because there had been a reversal in the polarities the results were heightened vulgarity.

"Okay sir," said the lady, holding her mid-section. Her stomach growled and her face started turning pale.

Horace watched all this through the corner of his eye. A sadness engulfed him, raffling his inside. The sadness sank deeper – to a place where heartbreaks occur.

The train reversed back into the train station and out went the lady. As the train started moving forward, the lady fell into a diabetic coma. Of close to fifty passengers in the car, only two were even looking at the lady – and that was Horace and a younger black woman in her twenties. All the rest pouted in silence and seemed content that she got what she deserved. Then Horace had the misfortune of locking eyes with the conductor and he sensed in the man a bitter coldness with a hint of laughter, "Is he laughing at her," said Horace to himself. "What has she done to you brother!"

CHAPTER FIFTY

The atomic nature of Horace's scientific transgressions possessed him to the fullest and he felt a tickly sensation in his mind; a consciousness, beginning to weigh heavy on his heart. The reversal, mildly enough if not bluntly, had caused an exaggeration of racial polemics or positions and because of this he now found that, as a black person, he was in the fortunate or unfortunate position of belonging to an oppressive national group.

The first thing when Horace saw Timmy would be to question, "This after all was not what he signed up for." Answers from Timmy would lay the matter to rest. Horace intended to know why this reversal had even occurred and just why he had been sent to Spain in the first place!

The mission was still a secret. And like most secrets, the truth remained buried beneath a rubble of deceit.

Horace walked up to Timmy's house in Orange County with the zealousness of a hungry tiger about to lock its claws in some canine in the animal kingdom. He wanted answers 'from this cat.' The house, located in an affluent neighborhood, seemed to contrast directly with what he had just witnessed in Spain; giving him an almost comparative advantage from the previous untraveled Mr. Bates from Carthage, North Carolina.

The events from the previous day seemed to heighten the cacophony of confusion. For starters, Zinner had survived an assassination attempt; his book was stolen by the Ivanovich group; Zinner being stupid enough to contemplate a book on time travel. At least this is what Timmy would tell him later on.

Now the giddy Horace approached Timmy's house with the jaunty illusion that an answer would solve everything.

Horace wondered whether the change had affected anyone in the core group. Then he remembered that earlier that week in American time, he had categorically questioned Zinner or more accurately, cross–examined him.

"Zinner, what if the world changes?"

"There is no chance of that my dear friend."

"Usually, my dear friend, that means you don't really know what you are talking about sir." Horace said.

"…there is no chance that the changes will directly affect us. After all, we are the constant in this change." Zinner replied, unmoved by the fact that Horace was treating him as a hostile witness.

Zinner continued further, "$e = hv$; anytime energy moves depending on its speed, the constant is the same. Energy increases merely by multiplying this constant by the speed of travel, the Plank Constant, named after Plank, you get it?"

"Yep. I get it, it's all mathematics on paper!"

Horace was beginning to suspect that the emphasis on science without the humanity in it was getting out of control and his little cross-examination of Zinner had just confirmed this.

In the house, Timmy waited for Horace expectantly. Timmy checked his Swavkopia watch and drank some water. The overly clear glass suggested a proclivity for obsessive-compulsive behavior. Timmy profusively wiped the sides of the glass and poured some more water. Upstairs, Dr. Zinner had stabilized to normality. He was under constant monitoring from what appeared to be a private nurse. Bob had suggested security detail be stepped up in his usual fanfare baritone, like a steam engine hissing through the Mississippi Delta. The fifty paramilitary men clustered throughout the villa seemed to blend in so seamlessly that Horace did not notice them.

One of the guards met Horace at the gate, "May I help you please, sir." He raised the AK-47 upwards and for the first time Horace noticed the gun. It seemed that he began noticing all the other men who had turned the villa into a medium sized bunker.

"I am here to see Timmy," said Horace.

"Is he expecting you?"

"Yes, very much so!"

"And who should I say is calling?" asked the guard.

"Tell him Horace Arthur Bates."

"Okay sir, hold your horses."

"The horses were never released," said Horace looking at the guard with the acoustic stare of someone who finds the conversation awkward.

Until recently, Horace did not like repeating his name. But in moments when he felt threatened, he would restate the name in its fullest.

The guard hurried in the house and then came out and spoke to Horace in a more relaxed tone, "Come this way." The gate was opened and Horace made his way to the mansion's front door. He still had to knock on the door and Timmy took his time, calculating the suspense. The door was now open and Timmy said, "You made it Mr. Bates. How was Spain?"

"Don't patronize me. We have reversed everything man!"

"Seriously; first things first, how are you doing?"

"I am doing fine. Spain is good, but what's going on here Tim. This is suicide, complete madness."

"Don't be too hasty Ray. We made a miscalculation of sorts really. The ripple effect you are seeing is because the change was never calculated to localize. For one, a group we only know of as working for a Demetri Ivanovich, is trying to steal this science from us and they shot Zinner."

"Is he alive?"

"Oh yes, almost got to the guy."

Horace looked around and closed the door behind him. It now felt like he was in the trenches of a world war frontline.

Still speaking in a diatribe rendition, Timmy continued:
"The earth has shifted its grids and demagnetized itself. South is now north and north is now south."

Horace kept a firm silence and this made Timmy uncomfortable.

"Let me show you this map, as it stands today," said Timmy, rotating a globe of the earth. "look here - see where you have South Africa. Look here - and see where you have Iceland."

"This is not good Tim!"

"We know that Ray. Bob wanted to help Rashid and for justice."

"Our aims were noble but look at the outcome man. A lot of things will take longer and there is an extreme angle to all this; a nasty one. I just heard the most racist talk on the train earlier today."

Timmy smiled, "God does indeed have a sense of humor. As of yesterday Reuben was just a school teacher in some ghetto part of LA."

"No kidding…"

"Yep, good ole Reuben Howard went from president to school teacher."

"Interesting…"

"He was completely erased from history books; must be annoying really."

Horace thought to himself, "maybe that's why Reuben wanted him in the program so much. Maybe a part of Reuben knows!"

"The funny thing is that Reuben does not know about the program and us. I just spoke to him yesterday on the phone," said Timmy.

"Sounds like you are having fun with the whole thing," said Horace, his voice light.

"Sounds to me like you are out of line."

"I mean listen to me Tim. The man is in a fix and you are offering wise sayings."

"The whole thing was Bob's idea. He is the big man in town remember."

"Then he should reverse this. We can't push people backwards just for the fun of science."

"Don't push it boy," warned Timmy.

"Push it is just what I will do – boy!" Horace approached Timmy with his fist cocked.

"Maybe we should talk it over with Bob. No need to reach a solution today."

"Maybe I am going back to change things; Rashid gets the gallows. That's how God intended it."

Zinner had been hearing the conversation escalating and he walked downstairs to make sure no one was at the receiving end of a fist.

"Gentlemen, what's going on here?"

"Zinner, what happened to bed rest?"

Horace jumped at the opportunity, "Too many lies man. I need to know everything. No more blackmail." Horace did not like the words but he was calling it the way he saw it. He had been blackmailed into 'Helping' humanity and this was a continuing emotion playing like a concerto in the background.

Zinner's eyes opened and he said, "Tell him Tim, and tell him everything!"

"Zinner- what happened to the concept of bed rest?" Timmy countered.

"It died in bed."

Horace smiled and said, "Still the man with many jokes Zinner?"

"Still the one Ray…"

Timmy felt left out and said, "Okay, I will do it. Are you joining us for this impromptu debriefing Zinner?"

"Oh yes. This time I will add my input to your version of events." His voice had a 'gotcha' feel to it.

"Did you have a difficult time in Spain?" asked Timmy.

"You will have to go beyond that please! Tell him how it all started."

This annoyed Timmy who now regarded Zinner as the ringleader of what looked like a low level mutiny.

"Zinner, please, can we all get it together…" Timmy said.

"I got it is not enough. Would you please tell him about Demetri …or I will." Timmy took another drink of water to which Horace opined,

"That's about the fifteenth time you have taken a sip – are you thirsty or just nervous?"

Timmy looked at Horace with a growing anger. "You…don't."

"Gentlemen should I remind you of the price as they say – time," interjected Zinner.

Timmy took a deep breath like a professional swimmer threading through deep waters.

He then said, "The whole idea of time travel started when Zinner came to the United States from Russia, aged twenty two. He hired a research assistant by the name of Demetri Ivanovich; an ambitious fellow. Demetri was a Ph.D. student at U.S.C. He worked together with Zinner on the first formula – that did not succeed. You are familiar with the idea of trying to use light waves for time travel – well that failed. I will not talk about the second formula because I never understood it myself. After this there was a time of struggle for Zinner and…"

"Just the facts Tim, not the Hollywood version…"

"…The third formula came along and then as usual the fight happens after success, right Zinner?"

"Actually it was Demetri's fault- the whole thing…"

"Zinner here had a fight with Demetri and Demetri broke off and founded his own underground research team searching for the same formulas for time travel. Zinner never says what the cause of the conflict was, but I suspect that a woman was involved, right Zinner?"

"Asshole!"

Zinner flinched and it almost felt like the gnawing of his teeth could be heard a mile away.

"Now come on Zinner," said Timmy, "where is the love brother?"

Timmy rubbed it in like tiger balm sequestering a wound, "women, women, women…"

Horace empathized with Zinner for a second and then said, "Can we agree to skip the short and long term causes section of the infomercial?"

Timmy continued, a high school teacher, touching every detail, "Demetri, is not altruistic – or loving, like Zinner here. He has big plans for us all."

"So Demetri is trying to time travel. Bullshit! I thought I was the only one?"

"You and an African girl, Horace, remember!" said Zinner.

"This brings me to what happened to Zinner. Two days ago, Demetri and his crew broke into Zinner's house and tried to assassinate him. They stole his formula."

Horace calculated all the angles to the lies and said, "What is her name?"

"Who?" asked Timmy.

"The African girl!"

Timmy looked at Horace, "Her name is Nola Gumelo; she is now a doctor actually…"

"That's bullshit," Horace said.

"Nope. As you see, Demetri now has the formulas and the test pilot. "However,he does not have the jet, that's unless he steals Troy; but it will take three months for him to compute all this information in."

"What a mess…" said Horace, raising his hands in the air.

CHAPTER FIFTY ONE

At Demetri's bunker the melancholic preparation for war seemed effortless. He hunkered in the basement studying the stolen manuscript from Zinner his old pal. It read like the man himself, very thorough and concise. "Page 400 - *Time is nothing but perception*, Page 420...*time can never be compressed or found*," Demetri read silently to himself, like a jackal hiding from a predator. The man Demetri was still a mystery in the mind of Ibrahim, who had previously doubled as a spy on Horace's initial California arrival.

Ibrahim had gone downstairs and given Demetri a sandwich; the usual egg and sausage with black coffee. Now it was Nola's turn. While Ibrahim was downstairs, Nola heard the jabbing, stabbing and tensely liquid exchange between the two men in the basement.

Ibrahim said to Nola, "Congratulations."

"Congratulations on what?" said Nola.

"Beating the man at his game. Demetri is like that you know; he will ride you until you fight him off. He is insistent."

"Really," cried Nola.

"He assumes that because he is a scientist that others should wash his face for him and tie his shoe laces. If no one does that for him, he leaves it undone."

"Funny," Nola said, remembering the laziness she had seen at her village growing up - men and women who refused to participate in any communal activity. "Laziness sure is universal..." she thought.

The room upstairs was the main meeting room for Demetri and his group, unlike the bunker downstairs. Everyone was invited upstairs. In the bunker this remained the domain of Demetri. Here Demetri - in between plotting against Zinner - would meet with Ibrahim, Nola and the two French men – the mysterious two whom Demetri only spoke to in low whispers; like a man asking for a telephone number in a crowded rendezvous. Here in the bunker Demetri was busy calculating and meditating on certain death. The other notorious bunkerphile, Adolf Hitler, haunted Demetri's thinking on what to do should his plans fail. *Hitler had used his bunker to meditate on suicide and last minute emergency plots; for Demetri, it was the opposite; the bunker was a place to sow seed and to see whether this seed sprouted. Demetri saw himself as a living legend, an auto-icon from which humanity would later use to parry forward.*

Nola reflected on Demetri's misconceived world, and how he had funded her education through a closely guided maze of lies and grants. Nola learned the hard way that it was not her grades that won her a scholarship but the fact that Demetri wanted something from her. The thought often made her question everything, 'the whole idea of meritocracy is flawed,'...she thought.

A few moments ago Nola had told Demetri that she was not here to act as his servant and that she would not make anymore breakfast specials. Now Nola leaned forward and said "He wants to see you by the way." This caught Ibrahim by surprise and he said, "I hope this is not about the breakfast independence speech you just declared."

"Breakfast independence!"

"Just hold your horses," said Ibrahim and he got up from the fluffy sofa, more Soho than Los Angeles.

Upstairs, Nola would not hear the most disturbing part of the conversation between Demetri and Ibrahim.

"The target has to shift to Reuben," said Demetri.

"Reuben Howard?"

"Is there another Reuben that comes to mind?"

Ibrahim thought for a moment and said, "Why are you so driven to get these people?"

"...because, that's why..."

"You don't even have a reason?"

"I have it. You are dismissed Ibrahim."

Demetri lacked any measure of secrecy in his dealings; everything seemed to roll off his tongue like a ticker tape communicating some obscure telegraph.

As Ibrahim left the bunker, he wondered what the world would be like if men like Demetri ruled it. "Humanity is doomed," he thought - "no diversity, just judgment under his laws." The whole conversation made him irreverent; that was the case with Demetri – he drains the spirit.

CHAPTER FIFTY TWO

Next morning at Timmy's house, contrasted with Demetri's bunker, everyone seemed to be in a state of semi-acceptance. Horace had already made up his mind- he would take the most effective route in ending this madness. Outside, the forbidding noise of the crickets is outplayed by the squirrels testing their agility. For Horace, it felt good to be back home from Spain; but then he had walked right into a big decision. He thought about his mother and about poor Reuben – he had received the butt of the whole affair --- from president to inner city school teacher.

Breakfast is quickly served with the tenderness of a five star restaurant. Horace scanned the room trying to place everyone in their correct place. Zinner's complexion had cleared from the antibodies he was taking.

"I see you are doing much better," said Horace.

"I feel it too."

"Good." Timmy interjected. "Anytime from now, Abdullah is going to join us. He has been busy...you know...making sure Demetri is not a step ahead of us."

The murky room had the gritty feeling that accompanies the prelude to a poker match: that dry humidity of Kentucky. Abdullah had remained busy for all purposes since Horace's departure to Spain. Abdullah's duties involved monitoring bank balances, email exchanges, incoming phone calls and going to the Demetri compound. This kept him mildly busy and at the end of the day he would report back to Timmy; who in turn reported directly to Bob - *the chief architect*. It was a change of command, bitterly informal and effective. The bureaucratic paper shuffling replaced by the warmth of orally transmitted missives and coded messages.

"We are all here," said Horace.

"The team," said Zinner.

Zinner seemed to be imagining that the group was like a family returning for a holiday gathering.

The food always tasted good and Horace said, "Timmy, who is cooking all this food again?"

"I second that question," Zinner volunteered. He naughtily smirked and lifted the Canadian bacon from the plate. "Americans never fry their bacon, Timmy – we kind of warm it off," he said. This was ironic because it was spoken in a heavy Russian accent.

"Maybe it's the influence of our Russian immigrant population." Timmy continued with the ascorbic tone of reprehension. "Gentlemen we have to be serious. Please, no more clowning around."

Timmy's proclamation sounded like the words from an apprehensive mother, telling her most spoiled child to buckle down or else.

"I am going back," said Horace plainly. "Back to Gibraltar, I mean Spain!"

This was met with an excitement that bordered on the melancholy; an excitement that accompanies a beautiful woman wherever she goes; an aura, an emotional space; the continuing restlessness of imagination...

"That's good, really good," said Timmy, his checks rosy and plastered on a full mouth smile.

"Good decision kiddo, I had anticipated that," said Zinner. He patted Horace on the back. "Well done!"

"Alright now, lets not get carried away. I am not doing this for any of you but the seven billion humans that ask for truth at a minimum from those entrusted with leadership."

Horace sounded off in a dictate. "Seven billion Timmy, seven billion God given people; does the number even ring a bell up stairs!"

Horace was beyond angry, beyond the point of détente; he was ready for a fight with Timmy.

Horace continued, feeling like the heaviest star in the universe suddenly out of place. Midway through breakfast Timmy's cell phone ran, the quintessential loud bell. Timmy flipped open his cell phone and said, "Hey Bob...good, having breakfast...." then there was silence and Timmy said, "Always something...I know that school..."

Timmy put his cell phone down and looked at Horace, "We need to talk."

"What is it now Tim?" Horace rotor-mouthed.

"Reuben is in great danger. You have to get to his school as soon as possible and bring him here. If he is kidnapped, the changes become irreversible. Bob's thinking that probably Demetri wants to clone Reuben, so that when we change things back, there is a clone in the oval office."

"Demetri Ivanovich!"

"Who else?" Timmy asked.

"Do we have proof? Seems like we are just jumping to conclusions here."

"Ray, are you Demetri's lawyer now?'

"All I am saying is that do we have all our ducks lined up?"

Timmy ignored the previous interjection and said, "Reuben is in danger. He is a very big part of this puzzle. Certain people are important for the lives of other humans...you just said that yourself."

The words bit in like some rancid turpentine undercoat. Now it was clear that the situation was impossible.

Horace said, "After this, no more for me, no more."

"Ray, all we have been doing all along, is stopping Demetri by making certain changes ..."

"...changes..." Horace voiced.

"…the world is full of them."

"And all these changes are your changes Timmy; you and Bob's?" Horace replied, his temper rising.

For Horace it felt like the world was rejecting a bad kidney; like after harvesting the saphenous vein for a triple-by-pass, the attending physician realizes that the aorta is beyond repair.

"This is all my fault," said Horace.

Guilt weighted heavy on Horace's heart. He now resembled the convict awaiting sentencing.

CHAPTER FIFTY THREE

The bellicose building hid the reluctance of its students inside, giving the building a loose and dilapidated topology. The building, a low ended school in the most beat down parts of southern Los Angeles, was where Reuben Howard was teaching. Inside one of the classrooms he stood robotic:

"For a perfect algebraic expression to occur you need variables; in variables then you would need *pi, the golden mean*," he said.

The voice continued and echoed out of the classroom and into the green patched parking area. There the voice was only faint to the Audi A8. The Audi had three men enjoying their tête-à-tête - the two French men with the brooding shoulders and Ibrahim, Demetri's right hand henchman.

For the past couple of days the three men had been casing the school, *Public School 345*. The two Frenchmen both had the neck of iron Mike Tyson in his prime: the turgid stiffness, like nickel dried from the bowls of a black-smith. In the back, the team leader Ibrahim, sat waiting and watching the doors of the school. Their orders had been made perfectly clear, "Abduct and eliminate Mr. Howard."

For Horace his assignment from Timmy had been to go to the same school and to, 'see if you can talk to Reuben and get him on our side.'

"But Reuben, does not know about the program," said Horace.

"You Ray, are a man of much persuasion. Talk to him," Timmy said, his voice filled with authority.

Now Horace walked to PS 345 slowly. He entered the school from the backdoor. The days had been piling and Horace missed walking; he remembered walking as a law student in Boston; walking in Spain. Horace did not have the faintest idea how he would break the news to Reuben. After the change in polarity, Reuben's mind had become like mush and he did not know of another world in which he was a man of power. He only referred to himself as a 'Math school teacher.' The thought reinforced itself as Horace walked through the empty corridors. For a moment he felt like he was back in high school and Dixon was calling him, asking him to skip school so that they could go smoke a cigar he picked up over the weekend.

Early on, Zinner had told Horace, "the feeling of walking on space will disappear, after being demagnetized you will feel your true self." "Zinner, I have a feeling that a part of me is still in Spain."
"That will pass Ray."

Now having entered the school building, he again felt like he was in outer space, "perhaps a flashback from the past," thought Horace.

In the math class, Reuben busied himself explaining to the students the ground breaking significance of pi. Horace knocked on the class room door impatiently and then took a peek in.

"Howard, Reuben, is it?"

"Yes," said Reuben, "and who might you be sir?"

"I need to talk to you in private sir; I am sorry for interrupting the class. My name is Horace Bates. If you will come outside sir."

"Did you pass by the principal's office?"

"Yes, sir?"

"And what's the principals' name by the way?"

Horace was dumbfounded; the students in the room appeared to be changing their eye sockets like an audience at a tennis match.

"That's irrelevant."

"Relevancy!" Reuben repeated. A big word to be thrown around at a high school math class room he thought to himself – 'who is this kid?'

"If you'll come with me outside, you will see why I need to talk sir."

"Horace you say, your name is. Please go to the administrative building first," Reuben said, not wanting to lose face. Reuben did not want to appear weak in front of the students and so Reuben maintained a strict and stiffened demeanor. He saw that Horace was not moved by the empty threat and said, "Go and wait for me at the principal's office please. I will see you in about five minutes."

Reuben did not know why he was giving the black kid two minutes even though he was lying. There was something about the kid; maybe it was because he was black like him or maybe the young man carried himself with an irradiated aura of being educated; how he pronounced his words - the searing demeanor of an intellectual sage. Reuben was used to being surrounded by gang bangers and pimps. He did not expect a young visitor to the school to actually speak proper English.

*

In the Audi, the smell of Camel cigarettes clustered the windows like a smoke screen. "We move at 1 P.M., when he goes for his lunch," said Ibrahim, getting off his cell phone. He had just finished making the eleventh call to update Demetri.

"Make sure we put this on his nose --- that's chloroform by the way. It will knock him out."

"Nice," said Francois, the bigger of the Frenchmen.

"We will need to move pretty fast, as fast as we can go," said Ibrahim.

In a matter of correction, the other Frenchman, known pointedly by his first name, Jerome said, "Fast already means fast."

"Just move fast enough, gentlemen!" Ibrahim said.

"Oui," said Francois.

Jerome nodded his head like a doll at a circus.

"And the two of you better not burst out in French now, English please."

Jerome and Francois looked at each other slyly and in smirks appeared to accept Ibrahim's preemptive words.

CHAPTER FIFTY FOUR

Reuben's eyes were usually extremely tired by mid day. He left his math class and his eyes continued to retell the forbearing pressures of inner city teaching. His spirit was scorched by the teaching and so was his mind. At the principal's office he did not see the young man going by the name, Horace. He leaned into the office and asked the secretary, "You didn't happen to see a young man, a well educated college type, blue shirt and jeans, looks like a moving poster for Harvard College."

The secretary was so busy helping the students that she did not hear Reuben speaking; the additional voice was just another student trying to get smart.

Reuben got irritated and said, "Did you see a young man here?"

The secretary came back to her senses and finished typing the last sentence. She appeared to Reuben to be typing as fast as thunder blazing through the sky.

"I am looking for a young man. Did you happen to see a young man here?"

"What does he look like, there are many young men who pass by; maybe hair color – that sort of thing catches one's attention – eye color. Now Mr. Howard, you should know the key is in the detail. You are Mr. Math."

"Hmm, he is black, about 6' 2"," said Reuben, obliging the secretary. The whole exchange looked more Sesame Street than high school.

"That would be no, Mr. Howard. No I did not see the aforementioned gentlemen," said the secretary, trying to sound official.

Reuben left the principal's administrative offices and headed for his car. He was starting to get worried. "Who was that young man?" He called his wife on the cell phone and asked, "Barbara, do you know of anyone looking for me from your end."

"Not that I know off dear, why?"

"Some kid stopped by my office. He seemed familiar, as if I have seen him somewhere…"

"You know what they say about L.A., Rue; stay here long enough and you start looking familiar."

Outside in front of Reuben's car the sun's rays were bursting forth solidly covering the school area and creating a blanket of softness. The Audi was now silent and the three men sat impatiently enjoying the sun's rays. It felt like a good day to take a break for the three men, but that was short lived when Ibrahim spotted Reuben entering his car.

The three would be assassins exited the car and headed for Reuben.

The bigger French man, Francois, led the way. The atmosphere became creepy as if they were burglars trying to short circuit entry into the Democratic hotel –Watergate. Walking slow like turtles, prodding forward inhibited, Francois approached Reuben from behind and put the handkerchief with the chloroform over Reuben's mouth. The handkerchief was then force fed into his mouth to give the sedative a stronger effect. There was a slight scuffle between Reuben and François but nothing major.

Ibrahim said, "totally out of shape," he said to himself. The passing students seemed to suspect the whole thing to be a prank. Francois then threw Reuben over his shoulder while Ibrahim and Jerome played defensive surveillance.

A blonde cheerleader walking past noticed the incident as peculiar and for a moment wondered what had happened to Mr. Howard, her math teacher. She would later report the incident at the principal's office.

When Ibrahim saw that the cheer leader was watching he said, "Not feeling well, we are taking him home."

The cheerleader had stood there dumbfounded and then she ran into the school heading towards the principal's office. Reuben was then placed, with the help of Jerome, in the back seat and started to resemble a business man taking a cat nap and being chauffeur driven in a high end Audi luxury car. The Frenchmen even waived at a group of students, trying to pretend that it was all a game and not real. The car soon raced off, its powerful engine climaxing to fifty miles in less than three seconds. Inside the car, Reuben was unconscious, his breathing slightly irregular and his body limb, unmoved by the dangerous driving taking place.

CHAPTER FIFTY FIVE

Horace felt an airy sense of disappointment. He had walked away, unable to bear looking Reuben face to face. The mendacity of the action, its cowardice all played on his face giving him the look of impermanence. He was not a coward but courage had certainly left him. Horace concluded that it was the weight of everything; India, Spain and now the introduction of Demetri to the equation.

Horace entered the house trying to sneak in and saw Timmy and Zinner waiting for him. He had no choice but to talk to them.

"How in the world do you do something like that Ray?"

"I never signed up for this," said Horace angrily, "Gentlemen I have not had any covert operations training."

"This is not a game Horace – we need you to understand what this entails," said Timmy. Bob just called and says his men are tailing the car, but that does not excuse what you did!"

"I never signed up for paramilitary crackerjack operations," said Horace, turning his head to lock eyes with the two men. "Maybe you and Zinner need to do the heavy lifting for a change."

"Look, let's not get smart here buddy boy. That was a pretty dumb thing to do," said Zinner, touching his left side and the contorting muscles.

"I have to look out for me. I saw a suspicious Audi with three men in it, but look, three against one, that's not how I roll...."

"You are pushing it, Ray," said Timmy, in the usual magisterial voice.

"No, I'm not pushing it."

"This kid has balls like a bull I tell you," said Zinner raising his hands in mid air like a belligerent cheerleader.

The two buried themselves in the suggestion that Horace was a coward and that he had run away. Some how this did not move Horace and he remained intransigent. His calmness stemmed from knowing that he is the eye of the storm and that without him the program can never advance.

He spoke politely, "Gentlemen, let's see where they are taking him... but in the future I need some backup."

Horace had resolved that he would take responsibility and now had the impassioned zeal to see this project come to end.

"I am taking my gun and tell Bob I am on my way tracking his men. Tell Abdullah to get ready." He stopped and looked sternly at Zinner who by now had lost a couple of pounds, "...and you my fellow American, try slowing down, will ya?" said Horace.

The Audi carrying Reuben pulled into an abandoned warehouse, screeching to an abrupt halt. Reuben jerked forward and went back into his comatose state; the chloroform had completely knocked him out. The two Frenchmen, Francois and Jerome, hurried out and went to the passenger side. There, they removed Reuben and carried him to the loading dock. The warehouse was partly marked out and there were indescribable words followed by, "...well." Some one must have gone a long way to cover up something thought François, as he looked at the detached painting. In the warehouse, Reuben was thrown onto a pack of boxes and landed flat.

"Don't hurt the man," said Ibrahim.

"Oui, boss man," said Jerome.

Ibrahim looked at Jerome and said, "Close the car and ..."

The noisy stepping of a light footed man was heard making way to the four men.

"Who is that?" Ibrahim asked. There was fear in the air like baked soda from an old bakery, reminding everyone that chocolate croissants were once sold here.

"It's me..."

They recognized the voice as that of none other than the chief instigator himself, Demetri Ivanovich.

"Demetri!" Ibrahim exclaimed.

"Yes, Ibrahim, I am here, who do you expect? I have to make sure you follow through on my orders."

"We just arrived boss," said Ibrahim.

"I know, I saw you come in. I was watching from the other warehouse. I also have cameras installed here." He pointed at the cameras. "All the angles are covered."

"And let's hope that you really do have all the angles covered," said Ibrahim.

Ibrahim still had a Saudi accent that refused to mellow off, even after twenty years in the United States. He still had the deep brawn of a villager on the banks of Mecca.

"Very well...Ibrahim, sometimes, I just don't understand what you are trying to say," said Demetri irritably.

Demetri took out a hand sized pistol and said, "Finish him. He had it coming." He handed Ibrahim the gun. Ibrahim took the gun looked at it for a second and said, "no..."

Ibrahim motioned that the gun be handed to either Francois or Jerome. "The two French men know how to use guns."

Francois took the gun like a kid grabbing candy from the kitchen sink. He did not show any hesitancy.

"Where do you like it boss, in the head like this, in the ear, right here perhaps, in the mouth, out the back of the head?"

"I see that we share a similar hobby," said Demetri.

Demetri had a secret hobby for all purposes. He liked to see people cringe in the face of insurmountable torture.

He looked at Francois and said, "Let's wait until he wakes up and then we can gauge the look on his face when you pull the trigger."

Outside, the swat-like team assembled by Bob was busy surrounding the parameters. Bob had called in a favor from a former marine by the name of Frank Perkins. Frank had called more old friends, until there were fifty men strong. The fifty men were waiting for the go from Bob.

Frank the leader called Bob closer and then told him, "All is in place Bob."

"In three minutes we go," said Bob.

Inside the warehouse Reuben did not have three minutes, in about a minute the sedative would clear up and he would be awake. Demetri and Francois were eagerly waiting to see any semblance of him being awake.

Then Bob nodded to Frank Perkins, who motioned by use of an index finger, 'Go.'

The black dressed paramilitary team swamped the warehouse and readied to enter though the high flown windows.

'...Three, two, one...'

The crew could see Frank counting and when he got to one, they burst in, just in time. Francois had his finger tightened to the trigger and the pressure in the gun's combustion chamber had started to heat up like motor oil entering an old engine.

When Reuben woke up he could see Demetri and Francois; in the background he could see the swat team running and chasing. He heard, "stop..." and he ducked to his left side, just in time to dodge the bullet from Francois.

"I missed," said Francois.

"Stupid." Demetri said.

Francois got ready to fire a second shot and Demetri said to him, "You fool! What are you doing? You only get one bite to the apple! Let's go, stupid."

Still Francois's trigger tightened but the trigger seemed heavier than before or it was Reuben's innocence, but he just could not do it

"Abort stupid, let's go."

The arriving swat team seemed to swarm into the place in seconds from all but the back exit. The team's leader, Frank Perkins, found the whole thing rather peculiar...he thought to himself, 'our arrival has conveniently created an exit strategy.' He looked behind him at Bob, who turned away like a swan flying past a group of nudes at the beach...overweight nudes. "What's Bob up to..."

Frank and Bob went back a long way. He was Bob's handy man; but this one felt different. It felt contrived...smoke screens. Frank had direct orders to scare the men away but not to kill them.

A block away Horace and Abdullah heard the noises of the swat team; the Audi roaring in the distance as it accelerated to automatic transmission. Horace looked at the departing car. Again he remembered Timmy's orders from Bob were not to chase Demetri but he wanted to see this Demetri fellow up close. His eyes scanned the car. He saw two men of European descent,

KEN SIBANDA

rather athletic, a man of Middle Eastern origins and then he saw another man who he placed as eastern European and that man was staring at him and looking. This must be the Demetri fellow, thought Horace. There was stiffness in the air, a defeating resilience of the departing car as it swapped past. The four men looked like fugitives fleeing a bank robbery.

Horace looked away from Demetri; there was something about Demetri he just could not place: A quality of dictatorship, a closet despot, a reign of terror, fire in the abasement of an empire, something. Horace felt haunted and invaded…he never wanted to see that face again.

CHAPTER FIFTY SIX

Thumped and invaded, that was the gruesome feeling Reuben felt when he finally recovered at Timmy's house. Abdullah and Horace had removed Reuben from the warehouse and raced him off to the safe house. Now it was evening, with all the expensive flood lights glowing in the front yards. The area's quiet majesty percolated everything.

At the door to the house, Timmy was waiting for them in his quintessential – never-rock-the-boat patented demeanor.

"…Is he still awake, must have taken chloroform," said Timmy, holding a Padron cigar in one hand. Horace knew the smell. It was the odor he smelled when he was drugged by Abdullah when he was being courted for the program. Timmy's cigar had the fullness of tobacco without the embers of dry English tobacco; it was perfect for a day that had ended favorably.

"He is here, getting to it. What's that stuff I smell on him by the way?" Horace asked.

"Good old chloroform," said Timmy.

"Is that not difficult to find?"

"Yes, it is Mr. Ray. We are dealing with professionals. Now you see why you have to go back my friend and fix all this."

Reuben's head rested on the sofa's arm and Abdullah did the unpleasant task of removing Reuben's shoes. He noted that the school teacher was wearing cheap shoes, a far cry from the expensive campaign shoes he wore before the earth was depolarized. Abdullah looked closer at the shoes and said to himself, "Buy one, and get one free."

"Get the man's shoes off and stop day dreaming," said Timmy looking at Abdullah.

Soon the shoes revealed socks with holes in them.

Timmy said, "Poor guy, Mr. President, ha!"

"He got the blunt end of the stick," said Horace. "Hold on Reuben."

Horace, looking at Reuben, felt responsible. "I have to get back to Spain…right away," he said.

"I see, you have a conscience--- maybe that's why God gave you the gift after all," said Timmy.

Conscience is that rare thing that makes a man think twice. The glue that holds and binds human interaction together, thought Horace. Without it we are like ships sailing in an ocean without a keel or a sail, subject to the mercy of the winds. Horace then looked away at the coffee pot. The brew was done and the steam oozed out of the culinary coffee maker like a steam boat.

Horace thought about his parents and Maria, but then he could not get in touch with them. That would contaminate them at this point. Plus, it was meaningless. *There was probably a mirror image of another Horace running around in current time, a different Horace.*

The idea made Horace think, 'perhaps, they had all become invisible shadows, disguised within human existence and trying to help humanity.' The thought made him quiver. He did not want to be invisible but to be alive and real; to have an emotional connection with others and not to be hiding while solving the newest threat to civilization. He now carried the weight of memories like an old widow battling with memories of forlorn husbands past; husbands who were once romantic but have now become bitter enemies.

Horace poured himself a cup of coffee and staggered up stairs. He needed the rest before departing back to Spain.

"Wait Horace," said Timmy. "He has to see your face."

"Why?"

"Because," said Zinner. "Your face will have to be the first thing he identifies as soothing and comforting; then at least he will be on our side."

"But I have to prepare. This time I am taking a machine gun to Spain."

"Oh no! That would be a problem if it fell into the wrong hands."

"I need fire power, that's all I am saying.'

"Troy will have all the fire power you need Ray."

"You sound like a hired gun instead of a lawyer," laughed Timmy, "Funny how time changes everything."

Horace looked away. There was something pretentious about Timmy. He still could not put a finger on it. Maybe it was just the wise-ass remarks.

Timmy passed the cup of coffee under Reuben's nostrils; this made Reuben's nostrils tighten and his eyes appeared glassy like a reflection from a dejected river.

"Bulls eye, that's a baby," said Timmy.

Horace looked on with the unimaginative eye of an understudy whose role keeps changing.

"Come closer, Ray," Timmy said to Horace. He always called him Ray when he wanted something done.

Soon enough Reuben was fully awake and he turned his head in the direction of Horace.

"Now what's going on here?"

"Relax please…" Timmy said.

"Who are you people?"

"Relax, will you, you could go into cardiac arrest," said Zinner.

Reuben reluctantly stopped talking and then tried to force himself up and was met by the brutal force of three men pinning him down.

"We can either do this the hard way or the easy way, sir," said Timmy. In the other room Zinner had been finalizing some more calculations for the return trip. He was curious as to what caused such a grand shift in the earth's historic polarities.

Zinner said, "Give him time to aclimate, some breathing space."

Timmy reached his hand out to Reuben with a cup of black coffee. He said, "That's the mother of all remedies Reuben, coffee."

"How do you know my name?"

Timmy dodged the question like a police officer dodging bullets from a pellet gun. "Please take a moment to look at all the men in this room. That man over there," he said pointing at Horace, "he is the one who saved you." Timmy then nodded his head and Horace left the room. Horace did not want to be in the room anyway. He wanted nothing to do with the lies Timmy was getting ready to tell.

Downstairs, the debriefing would begin earnestly. The room made for the perfect place for freelance debriefing exercises, especially with its militaristic architecture, thought Horace, as he walked the steps up to his room. After all, he was intent on getting those machine guns…

Timmy, as usual, was doing all the talking; fast talking like a Texan negotiating an oil lease. The others would merely nod their heads at the appropriate place, to give the illusion that Timmy is a well read man; like a snow ball rolling and picking up vistas of knowledge with every tumble.

CHAPTER FIFTY SEVEN

At the bunker, it was another story. Demetri Ivanovich was fuming mad. The smell of rotting egg filled the bunker, and Demetri walked through the basement thinking.

"This was not supposed to happen. Now we have double trouble. You could not follow the instruction to merely pull a trigger, stupid..."

"Perhaps, we have underestimated them boss," said Francois, who now took being called stupid as part of his on the job American training.

"...that is to never happen again. You hear me. Never François."

Demetri eye balled the two French men to leave. "Go."

Now he looked through the manuscript for more answers in recreating his own heavy-lift jet, which he wanted to call, Troy II.

"Francois!" Demetri yelled; his voice an octave higher than usual. Francois dashed downstairs, adjusting the upholstery holding the Uzi machine gun.

"I made an executive decision. When Troy II is ready, you will accompany Nola. We do not want any problems, if we cannot destroy them here, we must do it in Spain."

"Boss, this has gone too far. Why not just bomb their Troy and stop this nonsense. We know where it's located. You cannot fly something broken."

"You Frenchmen have a peculiar love for dynamite; here in America when you bomb something, your neighbors call the police." Demetri shook his head in annoyance.

Demetri resembled a dictator in some tin pot African county holding on to power for dear-life. Francois noted the inflexibility and the animated mood of his boss; he wondered – what's really going on in that tin head of his.

"Francois," said Demetri, "the problem with men like you is that you do not know that to arrive at greatness you have to sacrifice something. Men like you can only conceive of things being given to you, you hear me?"

"Loud and clear boss," Francois replied obediently, shaking his head.

"That's settled then." Demetri said, almost in a conclusive tone. He was running out of time. All the cards were stacked against him and he felt it. The gunmetal bunker resonated and appeared to become one with him. Demetri also wrestled with different variants of the same plan; Plan B and Plan C. He retreated deeper into his mental cocoon but before Francois departed Demetri yelled, "Do Not Disturb!"

Upstairs, Francois, Jerome and Nola had become like family, bonded by some dark secret in the closet. The general thinking was that Demetri had degenerated to a directionless and repetitive dance, like a lone gypsy still playing to the tune of a pianist long gone.

"I think we need to slow down. This is for science. What we are doing."

"I for one think you need to shut up," said Jerome. "We are the guns in the operation. You are just the doctor."

"What!"

"The old man needs support and we have to give it to him," said Jerome with the pinch insistence known to Frenchmen.

"Watch your words Jerome. This is America. We don't tell women to shut up here!"

From those words, Nola began to conclude that the household was like a house falling apart; a dickered assortment of playing cards. It was a matter of time before the deck tumbled over. Once the powder keg was lit, there was no telling what would happen.

Nola looked at Jerome and her eyes narrowed. "Don't ever tell me to shut up again," she demanded in a calm cool voice.

Francois did not return the look: he had decided that he was not going to Spain.

*

At Timmy's house, the mood remained celebratory. Timmy, for one, was sincerely happy something had gone in their favor so he reverted to his usual 'High-class self' wearing expensive jewelry and imagining himself as the tycoon from Texas'.   Horace could not stand him for more than two seconds, maybe it was because of the way he had masterminded Horace's entry into the program, using the lure of a legal job as the bait. Now Timmy was in the kitchen fixing his usual brand of gourmet meals when Horace walked in.

"I have been thinking," said Horace.

"Here we go again Ray. Did any one ever tell you, you think too much. It must have been divine to be named Horace after Horatio the poet – you think too much my friend. You are just about the most thoughtful kid I have ever met….boy-o-boy I tell you with this one."

"I will ignore that, but I need to say something. After today, I realized I need some kind of military training man. It's a war out there. In Spain I am a hunted man dude."

Timmy thought for a second, adding some pungent spice onto the fillet mignon.

"…Basic training, the usual stuff, specifically Navy Seals!" said Horace.

"Why Seals?" Timmy asked.

"I did some homework. Their training focuses on projecting force from the sea."

"Horace, Horace, Horace….we just don't have time. Demetri is almost ready to fly in!"

"Then Timmy, Timmy, Timmy, my friend, as you say --- it's a no go for me."

"Come on man." Timmy said.

Horace left for upstairs, steady and confident that Timmy would think over his request for military training.

Chapter Fifty Eight

Horace tried relentlessly to listen to the rusty noises of the chairs accommodating the four men downstairs: Timmy, Abdullah, Zinner and Reuben. He heard according to him, the sounds of a question and answer session in progress.

It was too much to take so Horace resolved to stop eavesdropping. "Let Reuben reach his own decision," he thought. His agreement, though silent with Timmy, seemed to be that by next morning. It's either a go with the military training or it was all cards off the table. Horace liked the shift in the balance of power and retired for the night with the relaxed look of someone seeing his way out of a hunter's fox trap.

He postulated, "funny, freedom is the thing that when it's taken away seems to have the most value. Perhaps the founding fathers had a point; freedom's value is only to be found in fighting for one's freedom and making that demand and not in the mere presence of freedom." He then retired to his bed and noted that his room resembled an old abandoned dormitory.

Downstairs the wiry noises of interrogation had ceased. Reuben had come to terms with the predicament. He now understood that he was trapped in a hole because of a scientific experiment. He understood that the man with the power to help him was the young man upstairs, 'that hot headed Horace,' at least, that is how Zinner put it. Reuben looked at the house. He looked at all the men and for some reason it was Horace he seemed to believe and trust. He said to Timmy, "Call the young man back."
Timmy then looked at Abdullah, "you heard him."
Soon enough Horace had arrived in his pajamas, which smelt like tobacco from a fire camp.
"Yes, Timmy."
"He wants to say something to you."
Reuben looked around, and said, "In private, just him and I."
The others left the room and then Reuben blurted out, "Man, brother to brother, is this real man?"
Horace burst out laughing. He would not have framed the words better.
"It is, and I tell you what man, when I was in Spain, I asked myself that question, over and over again."
"So I am supposed to be president."
"Yep." Horace said reluctantly.
"You gotta help me." Reuben said.
Horace leaned forward exerting his flexible tall frame, "I will...I am going back."

K
E
N

S
I
B
A
N
D
A

*

In the morning Horace was awoken by a ferocious knock. It was Timmy chopping at the pit like an inflamed pancreas.

"Wake up kid." He knocked as hard as he could. "Wake up will you? All the sleep in the world won't save your ugly self."

Horace instantly recognized the voice as Timmy's and the sardonic humor as either Timmy or Zinner. He bet on Timmy.
"Timmy, what do you want man?"

"I have news for you. Your dream has been granted; remember, you asked for military training? Well, I have news for you. The leader of the assault squad from Tuesday, Frank Perkins, has a farm in Yorba Linda and you are going. Three weeks cowboy…three weeks of eating spit actually." Timmy burst out laughing like an maladjusted Thomas Edison phonograph from the '20s, screeching a ballad.

CHAPTER FIFTY NINE

Horace headed toward Yorba, Linda in Eastern Orange County, California; still in the thick of the affluent zone twelve miles north east of Santa Ana. Again he found himself in yet another part of the Orange County. The brick walls smelt of money and he could imagine how the furniture looked inside. He had seen on the outer parts of Yorba Linda, three farms with hordes of illegal aliens. In the past, thought Horace, looking at the illegal workers, picking cotton was the quintessential American activity; now it is picking potatoes.

Fifty yards from the main road as Horace branched onto a dusty path following an arrow pointing with the words: Perkins Farm, Horace immediately spotted an individual standing in the middle of the main door. His long silhouette seemed jaunty, like a kite flown concurrent to a windy day. The individual was built top heavy — sumo wrestler, and his head was rectangular like that of Abraham Lincoln. Horace approached and started to see that the individual had blonde hair. As he approached closer he now started to see that the individual was fairly tall.

Horace turned from the dust path onto what felt like gravel from a construction site. On the other side, the individual could be identified only as, Frank Perkins. Perkins saw that the young man wanted to approach quietly and he shouted from the top of his voice, "Don't mind the gravel; been there a thousand years! It's not egg shell you know!"

Moments later Horace was a handshake away from Perkins.
"I am Frank Perkins. They call me Frank."
"I am Horace Bates."

"They told me about you, Bob told me all about you," said Frank, sizing up Horace. "You do look like you could use something to eat. Come in will yah."

Horace looked pertly at the man. Before he could continue with his scan and adulation, Frank said, "You do have an interesting name, I tell you."

"Thank you and you sir do have a name for yourself. I heard people talking about you on my way here."

"I hope it was good talk," said Frank with the blurting synergy of a lawyer on trial.

"All good – something about *you can always find work at Mr. Perkins' place.*"

Frank burst out laughing like a drum rolling downhill. "I try, you know. A lot of illegals here in California. Some pennies here and there; some rice and beans here and there, and you get loyalty and hard work."

Frank's towering voice echoed into the field and from a distance the plantation field hands turned to look at who this new comer was. They were used to seeing a female knocking; one of Frank's many 'mulattos' retiring for the night. Frank kept a steady flow of women coming in and out of the house for what he termed - 'Sustenance.'

So it was quite a surprise to see from a distance; a figure that resembled the physical bearing of a black man; a brooding black man entering Frank's house.

"I must have forgotten my manners, come in Horace. So what do they call you when they are not using this grand name?"

"Ray, they call me Ray." He entered the house and then said, "Looks good." The house looked like something from the Victorian age; its curtains delicately matching the cushions and chandeliers. That in turn, balancing the light outside as if to suggest that heaven on earth is a possibility.

Frank saw that Horace was checking the place out and said, "I see that you are falling in love."

"In love?'

"Yes, with the place."

"Ohh, that kind of love," laughed Horace, his voice sounding younger than he looked.

"Yeah kid. We fall in love differently when we get older you know."

"I hear that. It's a nice house; very old school."

"My daddy gave it to me," said Frank in a joyful and mellow tone. This made Horace think of how many black men could actually say their daddy gave them anything.

"He must have been something."

"Who..."

"Your daddy!"

"Ohh, yes, he ...had the money as they say."

Horace was silent and searched for a comeback. Frank said, "Old man Pickens did know the value of a good dollar. The man owned but just a few clothes you know. All his money tied up in this investment and that. You ask me, he was the most frugal sonnofabitch I have ever known."

The two entered a room that served as the reception area and Frank looked at the stairs, his eyes glared, like flint from a village mine. "Go up here and to your right. You can call that your home for three weeks."

"Thanks." Horace said.

"By the way, you were named after Horace the poet weren't you?"

"Something like that..."

"I studied Latin you know; back in the days when everything was not made in China."

Horace almost burst out laughing.

"Laugh kid, but I am serious. We don't even make cars any more, and we started them ...the Ford. Anyway, where I was going with this is that ..." Frank stopped like a buffalo panting for glory, "*Dulce et decorum est patria mori*...it is a sweet and fitting thing to die for one's country."

"Who said those words?" Horace asked.

"Your namesake, the Roman lyrical poet Horace – *Odes* III.2.13. Today's kids - you're named after great men and women but you have no clue who they were."

"It's a beautiful saying," said Horace. "Do you believe in that?"

"Yes, one hundred percent, unequivocally."

*

That evening the two men sat down for dinner in a room that resembled a kitchen of an old farm estate. One of Frank's cooks had prepared a Spanish cuisine that seemed to take on a reality of its own. This had the effect of reminding Horace of his brief Spanish conquest.

From the way Frank looked at him, Horace had a hunch that Frank knew all about the "Program". Horace had reasoned that according to the formula $E = hv$; H, which is the plank constant, does not change, and Frank would have to have known of the formula since as a white person he still retained his position in time and space. That caused some uneasiness with Horace and he said, "So we begin tomorrow."

"That's correct and like clockwork. It's not easy taking a civilian from civilian to soldier."

"Especially the Navy Seals program."

Frank looked intently at Horace with a smile on his face and said, "I'm gonna' give you what's called hell week in Navy Seal training." Then Frank changed subject and said, "What is good old Bob up to?"

Horace did not answer. He carried on eating the curried rice and beans.

Frank's house maid entered and said, "Senore, some more tea?"

"Mochas gracious…Horace this is Candida. Her cooking is still the best I have ever tasted."

"Se, bonoas diaz esta mucho caliente escudia…" said Horace.

"Some Spanish on your side; not very good, but at least you try."

"Yes, you try Mr. Horace, but need more practice," said Candida.

Frank then turned his full attention to the young man sitting in front of him. He found him to be pretty relaxed for his age.

"Horace Bates, I'm gonna give you the whole Navy Seal deal and teach you every thing you need to know, copy?"

"Copy that!"

"You have a law degree from Harvard, so you naturally do not need three months. You will improvise as you go along. But I want to tell you a story…"

Horace felt like he did not have the patience for stories and quibbled, "Right now!"

Frank ignored him while saying, "The use of chemical warfare was pioneered by Fritz Haber, a Prussian Jew who went on to win the Noble Prize for Chemistry in 1919 for I believe, - 'the synthesis of ammonia from its elements.' Haber later invented Zyklon –B, the gas used by the Nazis to affect the Holocaust…"

There was a deafening silence in the room, a meeting of silent minds perhaps, thought Horace. Then Frank said, with the insistence of a general at Normandy, "Remember, there is good and bad on both sides of the aisle."

Horace looked at his food and Frank's words seemed to be suggesting that maybe there was even poison in the food, or maybe not! Horace put down the fork and knife and thought, 'what have I got myself into...'

Outside, the potato fieldhands continued working late into the evening. When Horace looked through the window, he could hear the cold winds shuffling past the workers and imagined how that must feel. He admitted he was being mentored by a giant of military history; outside seemed perfect and served as the enchanted chorus of a ruse, gently touching the fledgling timbres of a protégé. He looked up at Frank and the two men seemed to understand that an unwritten contract was now in place – *learn, I will teach*.

CHAPTER SIXTY

Horace was awakened the next morning by Frank's discomforting knocking; kindling noise, like a rusty door hinge.

"You have twenty minutes, suit up."

Horace got up and took a quick shower. Moments later he entered the vestibule of the patio for what he expected to be a delightful breakfast. He took hold of a muffin but just then Frank's voice came through from behind.

"Hold on now. After the training. Who ever heard of someone having a muffin for training. You Harvard guys - man." He looked at Horace like a grandfather looking at a grandson, "We want to replicate the actual thing, as much as possible, hear me. Memorize the Navy seal creed. Take this."

Horace looked it over and put the booklet in his pocket.

"That's life and blood, in your pocket, now."

"I can imagine." Horace said, removing his hand from his pocket.

"First thing is to get that Harvard degree out of your head. Out here I am the law. Ask all the questions when you get back to Bob's compound. I have to make sure you are alive after the program."

Frank had called it by its code name, 'Program', and now the two men exchanged uncomfortable glances.

"He knows," thought Horace. "Maybe he knows some information, not all of it, and how could he possibly know!"

"Most men," said Frank, "either make good soldiers or not." "You have to make up your own mind whether you are going to be a soldier or whether this is all for show, feel me!"

After dodging breakfast the two men made way for the training ground. The blue pick up truck cruised through the dusty pathways. Fifteen minutes later, Frank asked, "Can you fire a gun?"

"Yes." Horace said, in a manner that felt like he could not fire one.

"Which one?"

"Magnum…"

"Not bad, especially since that gun is hard to find." Frank looked at Horace with that 'got-you' look he was accustomed to giving his field workers. "Look at this for a moment; no in fact, hold onto this. I will test you on it at the end of two weeks."

The book was entitled, *Essential Weapons for Warfare*.

Frank then looked at the rearview mirror, old habit from Korea and said; "… making sure kid, look, read that like it were your Bible, you hear me?"

Another five minutes later the two men arrived at a field barn; at least

KEN SIBANDA

that was Horace's first impression. But behind the front, Horace observed that it was a hidden training barracks from some military relic. The barn in front seemed to serve as a diversion, once you got past the front part, you could see that it was a minute military barracks. Horace looked surprised and Frank said, "This is how it's done."

Frank then looked at Horace's feet, "You have the Nikes so give me three miles, pace yourself."

It took Horace almost an hour to do the three miles. Frank watched, shaking his head in disapproval. He was close to sixty but could run the distance faster and with better overall conditioning. Horace paddled in after one hour exhausted like a man who has been bench pressing excess weights.

"You need work. When was the last time you even exercised? You are a mess kid, a complete mess, and you have to go on a diet, you hear. No fried foods, no excess sugar, no desserts."

"No sweets!"

"Yep, sweets are the problem. They take away from your nutritional stock."

Horace tried giving Frank the requested push-ups and could not even do ten.

Frank shot up like frothy ice cream on top of soda, "More work here, that's enough. I have seen enough of this for one day."

"Can we stop!"

"Not yet," said Frank, changing his mind and threw Horace some Poland Spring water. He opened a closet. "This is my private war chest. I have the *Washington Flint replica*; the *Magnum* – thank you very much Mr. Eastwood; and the *Walter PPK*. Your first gun is like your first kiss, you always remember it."

Frank started dismantling the 0.45 caliber and the AK 47 until the two guns were nothing but a heap of parts.

"Tomorrow we assemble them. I think it's time for that breakfast you wanted this morning" It was close to noon and Horace felt like his arms weighed more than the rest of his body.

At the house Candida offered Horace a muffin and Frank intercepted saying, "Not for him, let's put him on the high protein, needs to lose weight."

"High protein, senore?"

"That's right, until he can hold his own weight!"

Frank walked out of the room and then came back with a stern look on his face as if he had forgotten something. The grey hairs on his head looked like they were standing up, he said, "Always remember, veni, vidi, vici ---- *I came, I saw, I conquered*; the words of Julius Caesar in Asia Manor."

He then departed the room, and Horace thought, "What a performance, Frank Perkins ladies and gentlemen."

CHAPTER SIXTY ONE

ater that evening, Horace is met by the music of the field hands busy at work. He could barely lift his feet courtesy of Frank's training regimen. He retired to bed and fell into a deep and restful sleep. He did not even take his clothes off.

The next thing he heard was shouting from Frank.

"Horace, wake up sleepy head!"

"Okay," said Horace now turning his head away from the door.

Frank still continued, "...you have the name of the great poet Quintus Horatius Flaccus, but you don't have the spirit...not yet."

"Okay Frank!"

Frank entered the door and said, "Bob is not paying me to watch you sleep!" He went into the bathroom and started pouring water in a bucket. Horace heard the faucet running; Frank wanted to douse him in cold water; and that was enough to get him giddy and ready. When Frank returned to the bedroom ready to throw the cold water onto Horace, Horace was awake and said, "Ready when you are."

"Come-on, stop playing, next time I want you waiting outside kid!"

"Okay Frank."

The two men rode to the manmade barracks without eating any breakfast and Horace's stomach, not used to self-induced starvation, rounded off like a bad tire running off heavy gravel. Horace could also see that Frank from close up had a couple of scars on his face. The kind of disfigurement that happens when napalm touches the skin, he thought.

Frank saw Horace starring at the scar and said.

"...that's Vietnam."

"Did not mean to stare."

"No need to apologize. Scars are good for men. Everyone wants to know where they came from."

"And what do you tell them?" asked Horace looking outside and into the distance. - *This place is good farm land, Horace concluded.-*

"I tell them that I was a prisoner of war..."

"And is that the truth!"

"Absolutely not."

"So you lie to them to get away from explaining the truth."

"Something like that!"

"Military psychology?"

"Yep - need to know basis kid."

Horace was left hanging; of the scars he could only conclude that they must have come unexpected as they seemed to have a particular pattern like glass cut with a sharp diamond.

At the barn, Frank repeated yesterday's routine. While running, Horace noted Frank talking on the cell phone.

When Horace passed Frank for the first time, Frank looked so content with himself that he said, "That was your good friend Bob, and so Mr. Horace is a valuable commodity."

Horace ignored the statement.

Frank watched Horace jogging and concluded that the kid was naïve. He reached for his tobacco pipe. As soon as the smoke touched his palate his eyes became teary. Tobacco was a good choice for Frank, at least it was better than heroin. Heroin had left him feeling exasperated, emaciated, lean and mean. "At least with tobacco, one always remembers his name and address…"

CHAPTER SIXTY TWO

The routine continued unabated for a good week. Horace started to feel his muscles re-programmed into those of a soldier. His body had adjusted through muscle shock to the demands of a desert warrior eagerly searching for yet another oasis.

A week later, Frank's tone of voice seemed to mellow as he became less combative. He said: "We have some improvement here."
"Glad to hear that!"
The complement flowed somewhat guttery after the usual morning jog.
"You have it."
"Maybe I will be a Navy Seal like you soon?" Horace was fishing for some answers; was Frank Navy Seal, Marine or Special Opps. He still did not have a clue.

"Not yet. You still have two more weeks here." In the barn, Frank commanded, "Give me a total disarm and armament in one minute."
Horace spoke as he completed the mission, "Hand, shaft, trigger, connector, safety…"

Frank said, "Funny how you Harvard boys start off slow but finish strong."

*

In a different part of California, close enough to Zinner's test cite in Palm Springs, Demetri was still irritated about having lost his greatest bargaining piece, Reuben Howard. He now instructed Ibrahim, the Saudi, to look for Horace. Ibrahim had reported a week ago that, "Seems like Horace might have already gone back to Spain."

To which Demetri said, "Nothing appeared on the kinetogram, so Troy is still here! He is hiding some where! Find out where and eliminate him; that's plan B."

Plan B had come sublimely as Demetri read the manuscript for the eleventh time. He concluded that since only Nola and Horace can time travel, then eliminating Horace gave him an upper hand. It was simple calculus; high school elementary stuff.

Ibrahim was starting to get word that a young black man meeting the description of Horace was seen around Yorba, Linda in California. Ibrahim had paid some change for the information but he trusted the informer.

It was the same dark figure who had fingered Reuben.

Ibrahim conveyed the message to Demetri, who sat in his bunker surrounded by chemistry funnels and metallic balls. Pictures of Horace, Timmy and Zinner cluttered his space and in the waste basket half eaten egg sandwiches.

"Boss, they say he might be in Yorba, Linda."

"About time; now please don't botch this one up. You have the go."

CHAPTER SIXTY THREE

The next day Frank seemed edgy. He kept on looking in the rearview mirror as the sports utility drove towards the barn. Military recognizance stuff, thought Horace. Frank noticed in the rearview mirror a glaring light covered by dust. He changed gears and route.

"We are being followed."

"That explains automatic to stick."

"...Something like that."

"I think it's time for you to go home Mr. Horace. I am starting to catch heat here. I am assuming Bob has the usual enemies in this one as well."

Horace was surprised at the abrupt refusal for continued training. "Look, I am a retired mercenary. I've already done this in Angola. I don't want any problems. I will talk to Bob about this!"

The car trailing Frank and Horace belonged to Ibrahim. He had no problem finding the 'Mystery military man who lived in Yorba.'

An illegal immigrant had told Ibrahim all bout the man named Frank, "...very good man, used to be army, good job at Frank house," said the man. "Look for a house that looks like a shoe that has seen better days."

Ibrahim waited outside the house for two days until he spotted Frank and Horace leaving. He tailed them on the second day. That is when the truck started to go slow and in a different direction. Ibrahim was certain the two men had seen him. He slowed down and unclipped the safety on his gun.

Frank looked at the car trailing him for a third time. "We're making a U-turn. Actually, we're taking a different route."

Frank looked at his gun in the back seat, a rifle.

"Maybe this is good for you. On the job training never hurt anyone."

It was day ten and Frank was starting to feel lethargic. The smell of gunpowder and Horace's morning sweats were taking him back to Vietnam – Saigon. He was starting to see helicopter flashes. Frank had been stationed with the 52nd Marine Brigade responsible for forward tactical advancement. Back then, Saigon was not known as Ho Chi Minh City. It was an ancient city on the precipice of modernity. The memories of Vietnam became fluid; the marches into Southern Vietnam, strategic assault, high end maneuvers under the cover of night; air assault coordination.

Frank came back to mother earth and said, "That guy might be a scout for a bigger operation, an advance team." Frank made a U-turn. The whole idea behind the U-turn was to chase the enemy; they did it all the time in Vietnam.

Frank now shifted the truck into four wheel drive. He again took the path heading towards his farm. Soon, Ibrahim realized that the car he was trailing was now coming right for him. He was surprised, "What is he doing this man!"

Ibrahim made an abrupt turn and headed back for the farm house. He was running; running like a field mouse from a big cat. The truck chased Ibrahim's smaller jeep through a series of meandering valleys and roads. It was now clear that familiarity with the environment was working in Frank's favor. Soon Ibrahim jumped out of the car and started running. Ibrahim running for dear life made Horace say, "What does he think he is doing?"

"They all run kid. Get used to it." Frank got out of the car and said to Horace "Wait here. I don't want to deplete Bob's investment." He started chasing Ibrahim, running and puffing. Horace noted that Frank could well have been in his late fifties. The old goose was in good shape. Not once did Frank stop to take a deep breath.

Ibrahim headed towards the abandoned rail road steamer station and Frank closed in, his gun cocked for action. It was Ibrahim whose trigger happy self started with the firing. Frank ducked and aimed. He fired close; hitting Ibrahim on the leg and Ibrahim fell like a heavy bag.

Horace heard the exchange of gun fire and got out of the truck heading towards the abandoned railroad steamer station.

Frank was soon standing over a wounded Ibrahim. The pain in Ibrahim's leg was too great for him to even consider pulling the trigger.

"Now, who the fuck are you?" asked Frank impolitely. Frank's Czech American facial features had by now become more profound as the anger increased.

"You shot me man."

"That is the idea."

Horace got within hearing distance and he could hear that Frank was interrogating Ibrahim.

"Now you see this little baby," said Frank showing Ibrahim his gun, "the next shot will take you out."

"Please stop, I will tell you…"

Horace was within twenty feet and heard the words, 'I will tell you…' He released his safety clip and aimed at Ibrahim. Already the world was unbalanced because of his actions and now Ibrahim was getting ready to drag this mystery man Frank into it. "No," thought Horace as he fired two shots at Ibrahim. Frank was surprised and turned to see where the shots were coming from.

"Horace, what do you think you are doing?"

"That's enough Frank. I am going back home. I have learned enough from you."

"You just killed the evidence man."

Horace looked at Frank and the two men seemed to sign an invisible treaty, - "get off my property."

Frank hated the way Bob had used him in the past and now he hated the fact that the young man, his student, had stopped his freelance investigation of what Bob was up to.

"Man, I want you to leave today. I don't deal in secrets. Get your stuff out of my house and go." Frank said.

K
E
N

S
I
B
A
N
D
A

CHAPTER SIXTY FOUR

The bad blood between Frank and Horace seemed to spill over. Horace began to feel that he too was caught up in the middle of a deep hole and that perhaps Frank was really trying to help him, 'in his own way.'

On the train back to Timmy's house, Horace saw an article in the newspaper that caught his attention; almost as if it was being pointed to him.

The article was still freshly minted on paper and read:

Today the philanthropist and banker, Robert Churchwell, donated over 1.5 million to a group of scientist involved in new technology. In making the award, Mr. Churchwell said, "This is the beginning of a new era and we must utilize our science for progress." Mr. Churchwell has been known for his generous philanthropic giving. In 1989 he hosted a group of former astronauts at his house in Orange County, California. The proceeds of that event went towards the cure of unknown blood disorders in Sudan, Africa.

Horace looked at the accompanying photo that read: *Robert Churchwell and scientist Demetri Ivanovich.*

Horace found the whole affair off putting. "We are in the midst of a war and he is taking photos for the press," thought Horace. He then decided that from now onwards he would play detective and stop assuming that everything Timmy said was the gospel truth. Horace made up his mind that he would not utter a single word to the group about the photo - not a single word, and that he would not tell them about the bad blood between him and Frank. He was starting to see things differently - through the eyes of a detached observer.

*

Horace had not talked to his family for close to three weeks now. His mother Pauline was starting to get worried, and so was Maria - the passionate and adoring Maria. The thought made him almost quit on the spot.

He did not like how things had ended with Frank because he thought the man in his own way the first sincere person he had encountered thus far having anything to do with 'The Program.' Maybe I can patch things up in the future…

At Timmy's house, Horace walked upstairs, repeating the routine of two weeks ago. The others noted that he looked leaner and deadlier. Horace had finally realized that all cards were not on the deck. He had been dealt a half deck of cards and the other half was still hidden. He looked through the window, imagining Spain and seeing the other half of the hidden cards unfolding. Now he felt confident that he could return to correct his mistakes.

CHAPTER SIXTY FIVE

Horace's mom, Pauline Bates, had started to worry about her beloved Horace Arthur Bates, the apple of her eye. She had already began to acknowledge the shifting dynamic, 'the Maria girl had taken over.'

She approached her husband and demanded that they file a missing persons report. In the past, Horace Senior had always been the one to say let's wait it off and see, but this time was different; the money in the bank account, the Maria girl who was rumored to have dated drug dealers, the whole thing felt suspicious...

At the police station the couple were handed a missing persons folder that resembled a securities registration package with the IRS.

"Can this be done electronically?" asked Horace Senior.

"Come this way," said the female detective and showed them a computer screen. "Here, just punch in his social."

The application had gone from fifty pages to one computer screen. Horace Senior looked at the police officer like Galileo realizing that the earth is round and said, "The wonders of computers."

It took the couple only two minutes to complete the missing person's report and the Bates' left the police precinct feeling relieved. Fifteen hundred miles away in California, as soon as the missing person button was hit, Bob received an electronic transmission to his home telex.

Missing for three weeks, Horace Arthur Bates.

Aged twenty nine, hair black, eyes brown.

Bob was too busy listening to his classic music to hear the Teleflex come in. He was too busy listening to the Bavarian Mozart's *Eine Kleine Nacht Musik* – a little night music - and preparing for the final chapter in the program; making sure that all details for the plan were in place. Bob went to his bedroom and still did not see the telex lying on the floor having spilled off the telex machine.

His guest for the night, a Ms. Tammy Sullivan, did notice the telex. This happened at close to nine in the evening; the telex having gone out at close to four p.m. Carolina time. Tammy, for her part, did not tell Bob. She wrapped the message and put it in her purse. She would tell her handler, the mystery man - who had sent her roses and asked her to seduce the billionaire Robert Churchwell - the heavy accented Demetri Ivanovich.

CHAPTER SIXTY SIX

Since Tammy Sullivan had been recruited at such a late part of the counter-assault program, Demetri felt, that like a child, she could not be entrusted with too much information. He made sure that her every move was closely monitored. After Tammy told him about the fax, he was ready to launch Troy II into Spain. He instructed Nola to keep an eye on Tammy, to which Nola responded rather catty; "Do I look like a spy to you?"

"Nola, why so difficult," said Demetri. "As a woman you are in a good position to pick up on body language that's all."

"And as a man, you can do just the same." Nola shook her head no and walked away, saying something in her Sudanese dialect.

Demetri chose chivalry instead of confrontation. He turned the other way saying to himself, "Do what you like but once I am done, you are out." The thought of final revenge made him feel like he had the upper hand. All this time the thing he needed the most was her DNA.

"Okay Nola, you win. You always have the right answers. I still need another blood test to make sure that your vitals are in order for the trip."

Nola wanted to ignore that, but said, "Why are you such a lonely man Demetri? How the hell did you get this way, huh?"

Demetri shrugged his shoulders and said, "Science is a lonely profession!"

"I might be from Africa but I am no fool. Loneliness comes from a deep sense of pain. You imagine slants and insults. Loneliness breads contempt for others."

"And how did you get this smart by the way?"

"We are all smart Demetri. That's what Africans believe. There is an African saying that -wisdom does not belong to a single person."

"And who does it belong to Nola?"

"All of us!"

Demetri was in awe of what Nola had just said to him.

"Okay darling...anything else."

"No."

"Night, Nola."

"Night, Demetri." Nola left the room and Demetri opened a drawer, un-keyed the lock and wrote in a note pad ...*advise Bob of failure with Nola, time is of the essence. Soon they will know about us...*

He closed the drawer and looked around the room, like a cat peering through darkness.

Demetri then walked towards a closet. He punched in a secret code and the doors opened. Inside the room, were trays of blood samples. One read Horace Bates and the other read Nola Gumelo.

"Very soon, the cultures will be good enough to harvest and the program does not have to deal with these two liabilities."

Bob had given instructions to both Demetri and Timmy that the Troys', one and two, should be wired for a one way trip. He was done with Horace and Nola.

Bob had advised rather loosely that once the two liabilities were gone then he would install his own president and thus move one step ahead in achieving Omni-competent power for himself.

The only problem with the calculus being made was that Nola could smell a rat and as for Horace, he had already seen it – in the local newspaper.

All along, Bob had financed the two scientists: Zinner and Demetri.

CHAPTER SIXTY SEVEN

In the cockpit the next day, Horace felt the metallic stiffening of the controls as Troy locked in the coordinates of December 26, 1491. He now anticipated every move Troy was making and did not have the anxiety of the two previous missions.

Soon Troy had launched into the lunar system, gliding through it like a boat sailing upstream. He cruised slowing down through a group of cirrus rain clouds, the ones that usually come before a monsoon thunderstorm. From a distance he could see the rock of Gibraltar ...almost there.

Flying over the rock he noticed the many macaque monkeys swinging on the rock. The moment faded away and then he saw Al Hambra in the distance; the castle of justice that was adjutant to the dungeon he had been responsible for exploding. The thought made him remember that now he must be a wanted man. The task of putting Rashid back in prison would not be easy. The spot he chose to land Troy was the same as the spot from before. As he neared the landing spot appropriately, surrounded by green bushes and trees, he took over from auto pilot locking in the manual flier. Troy descended at twenty miles an hour, almost like a hovercraft flying.

Horace recalled that from his conversations with Rashid Muhammad that Rashid had headed towards Morocco to reboot for an invasion. Horace went over the details of his new mission the same way he had done just a few minutes ago with Timmy. "Get Rashid rearrested and leave him at the hands of the Spaniards." Timmy had said.

There was however the biggest problem of all; the Spaniards were looking for Horace as well and Rashid had decided, 'Mustafa is a liability more than an asset.' So Horace was trapped between a rock and a hard place.

Across the Spanish border and across the Alboran Sea, nearer to the Strait of Gibraltar, on the Morocco side, in Rabbit, Nola landed Troy II. For her, she found the trip bumpy and the color changes rather intrusive. She had shut her eyes to stop seeing the symphony of colors.

CHAPTER SIXTY EIGHT

A n hour before Horace left for Spain, the group was huddled in like an afternoon snack.

In Orange County, Bob had summoned the two ring leaders, Timmy and Demetri to his office. Now all faces were on show. There was no need to hide...

"Gentlemen, we achieved our plan. Those two are gone forever. No need to pretend. We are now one family." The only thing that seemed real with the facade Bob had created of two feuding groups fighting for scientific advantage was the death of Ibrahim.

"Ibrahim." Timmy said.

"Causality of war!" Bob replied. "That's right, we have reached the end beautifully. They say that the end is always sweeter than the beginning," said Bob, raising a champagne bottle. He also had in his sanctum sanctorum Zinner who closed the door behind him.

Bob continued unabated, "Gentlemen, we are closer to achieving our goal; I should say that I am sorry for all the confusion that this web produced and as for Ibrahim, he too like our friends Nola and the great Horace A. Bates, was getting too suspicious.

If we are to succeed we cannot tolerate men like Ibrahim, right Timmy!"

"Right boss."

Timmy continued clapping; his sycophantic ass-kissing self, eager to kiss ass even when it's unnecessary. The two Frenchmen, Jerome and Francois, were standing guard outside, and they two had accepted the ending at least from what Demetri told them, "as about time we worked together!"

Abdullah on the other hand had listened carefully when Timmy told him that they were now joining forces with Demetri with a sense of unease. For Abdullah it just did not add up. He was like a transplanted man who leaves his home for the wrong reasons.

"After what happened to Zinner!" Abdullah questioned.

"Let it go. We are one group now." Timmy had said.

Then Abdullah remembered the Saudi national working for Demetri, "...and Ibrahim!"

"Let it go Abdullah!"

The answers were enough for Abdullah to realize there was a plan from the beginning and that he had been played. Demetri was never an evil man. The whole thing was a set up...

Abdullah recoiled with the new information. For all he knew he was next; and then Horace, and then the African girl. He vowed that he would help Horace. He hurriedly scribbled a note and shoved it in Horace's travel case.

*

In the deep trenches of Spain, Horace was awakening to the gravity of the problem he was entrenced in. Abdullah, of all people, had managed to slip the note into his satchel and all that Horace had to do is read the note and this would inform him of the whole affair and how Ibrahim had been sacrificed as part of the cover. "The note is the key..." thought Abdullah putting the note.

In California, in Bob's lounge, the smell of roasted coffee continued to be a part of the proceedings. Bob leaned forward. "Gentlemen, coffee and champagne is always a sign of a life well lived," he said. "From today, see this as the beginning of your high status."

He continued, "Ich freue mich wir freuen uns ----- I am happy and we are happy."

"Bob, I had forgot that you speak perfect German." Timmy said. Bob smiled and said, "Only when I am in high spirits." He continued: "Now, more pressing matters gentlemen; we have to come to a consensus." Bob walked to the door and opened it, making sure no one was listening. "What do we do about Abdullah and the two Frenchmen? Do they remain?"

There was an aura of charisma and demagoguery in the air, as if Bob was entertaining the others. The aura you expect from a stand up comedian.

"Those in favor of his continued stay here please raise your hands." Bob said.
There were no hands raised and Abdullah's fate was sealed...die.
"The Frenchmen!"

All hands were now raised and this meant the two French fighting dogs would live. This about cemented Bob's role of Roman emperor in the making. Now everyone knew that he had to be taken seriously. Timmy loved the whole affair, 'Like law school; a bullet for the wrong answer!' He thought.

"Demetri," said Bob, "what is the update on the blood sample?"
Demetri staggered to his feet; the early signs of arthritis had resulted in a toughening of the knee ligaments - resulting in the gaity of a much older man.

"Gentlemen, in two days we can harvest the first generation of time travelers. We did it." There was in Demetri's eye, the flick of narcissism. He had actually meant, 'I did it,' but circumstance had tempered that to, 'We.'

Demetri said, "We can have one hundred time traveling soldiers at our mercy by the end of the month. That is in three weeks, and that means, I think we all agree, this means, good bye Horace and Nola."

"Well done," said Bob, sounding like an English teacher keeping a score chart for correct spelling.
"That's nothing," quibbled Demetri in heavy English, "the strand we harvested can be kept for twenty years."

Bob's face shown with an impressionable acquiescence to what

Demetri had just said. While Zinner had been the brains behind Troy and had taken the rubber bullet as if it were the real thing, to Bob's surprise, it was Demetri who had created the illusion of competition while actually investigating a strand for new DNA. Demetri had not only given the program its first breath but a life insurance. Demetri's role as a demigod creating a species was far beyond Zinner's mathematical jargon, thought Bob. He nodded at Demetri and Zinner took that for a slant. Before Demetri had entered the scene, Zinner was always the number one go to man. Now there was Demetri and everyone wanted to know when the first crop of time travelers will be harvested. He was the new kid on the block, innocently attractive. And then there was the history Demetri and Zinner shared; former student and teacher.

For Timmy, the whole affair seemed too good to be true. His mom had insisted when he was growing up, "that if it's too good to be true, it usually is."

Timmy recalled the somber sermon from his mom. "When things happen too easy or with deceit, they usually lack the humility of things obtained through the presence of God."

Timmy started observing in Zinner, Demetri and Bob, vanity in all its early stages. Each man wondered, who is greater? Who deserves the most credit?... Timmy looked away like a child looking away from an out of control flame. "Maybe, I should be running the show and not this Bob guy!" thought Timmy.

CHAPTER SIXTY NINE

Horace tumbled off the escarpment of meadows leading from the hilltop. With Troy safely secure, it was only a matter of time before he found Rashid hiding in the Atlas Mountains of Morocco. Horace wore a turban on his head made from pure silk; this gave him the Islamic look he had hoped to achieve. Horace headed for the Atlas Mountains high in Morocco, Midlit as it is known, and here he expected to convince Rashid to embark on an impossible mission back into Spain.

Zaniweri, Horace's nemesis, had given up finding Rashid and had settled back in Grenada, spending a great amount of his time preparing to do battle with Rashid in the event that Rashid tried to invade from Morocco. Zaniweri knew the invasion was inevitable, especially given that Rashid had a reputation to live up to ---- the great general. Zaniweri heard from the blowing whispers that Rashid was in the Midlit part of Morocco's Atlas Mountains and that Rashid was regrouping, so as to reenter Spain for a final confrontation with Madrid's Visigoths.

So, Zaniweri camped in Grenada sixty miles away from the unsuspecting mountains that housed Rashid; awaiting the moment to cross into Morocco. The name Rashid still infuriated Zaniweri because he regarded Rashid as the biggest obstacle in what would ordinarily have been a great career as a general.

Horace traveled on mule as he headed towards the Atlas Mountains. Seven hours later, he started seeing the mountains of Atlas high up; a region inhabited by Berbers or the Emagazhin. He patiently continued towards the Strait of Gibraltar and then ferried himself using the ferry boats that took people from Spain to Morocco. For this, he had to pay by means of gold coins neatly tucked in his bag by Zinner, as a last minute gesture. From a distance Horace could see the camp fire ablaze and hear the whispering of shepherds surrounding the distant camp fires. The smell of goat milk seemed to get stronger as he approached Morocco. Soon enough, Horace had arrived at the banks of Morocco and was approached by a local goat herder who noticed the turban and said:

"Assallum Allakum, where are you going this late at night ahir."
Horace did not miss a beat as he dusted his sandals and pulled his long gown from the water, "I am going to see my father...haven't seen him since last December." It was December 1491 and the goat herder's calculation meant that Horace had not seen his father for a year.

The goat header then said, "For one year, one full year!"

"And who is your father?"

Horace thought for a second and wondered which answer would be the best. "Rashid Muhammad."

The sound of the name sent a thousand ripples in the air.

The goat herder sneered his face with fifty million questions, and said; "You don't look like a Moor, you look like the opposite, describe Rashid for me?"

"Tall, carries himself like he just finished lifting heavy bricks."

The three goat herders continued to eye Horace and the leader of the pack lifted a stick.

"Go this way," he pointed intelligently.

"Thank you ahir inshallah, thank you," said Horace. He walked a distance and looked behind him to see if he was being followed. The goat herders then headed in front of Horace.

Horace offered the herders condiments made from chocolate and dates. That was the information he was looking for...But just to check he walked in the pointed direction and in a few minutes eyed Rashid and his men eating what appeared to be dinner in tin plates. He made a u-turn and started back for Spain. Horace hoped to find Zaniweri and relay the message, and that would mean Rashid is ambushed - an end to Rashid. Horace tried to justify the whole continuance of events by weighing seven billion people against Rashid's life. It just did not add up. The balance shifted against Rashid.

Horace now headed towards the water taxi, looking for the ferry service that had placed him in Morocco just close to two hours ago. The ferries were rumored to be reliable and consistent. At the Strait of Gibraltar, Horace found the same ferry he had boarded close to the previous spot, as if it had never moved. The whole thing irked his sense of happenstance.

"We go back so soon ahir?"

"Yes, father not very happy," said Horace.

"May Allah bless you. You are a blessing. Today from you alone I make good gold."

In the boat Horace started to feel tired. The jet lag from Troy was beginning to take effect.

He asked a stranger. "Brother, do you know any motel I can use..."

"You asked the right person! When we get off, thirty minutes by mule and turn to face the moon for ten minutes...*al Mecca* is the name...we like remembering *Mecca* here."

"Thank you ahir..." said Horace in the usual dose of patented Harvard manner of form.

The boat traded in and the low tides encroached inward on the shoreline. As the boat slipped forward, Horace had to pinch himself to avoid falling asleep.

Soon Horace felt the edge of a letter prodding at him from his satchel. He looked into his satchel and found an envelope, sealed and written by his former nemesis, Abdullah.

Chapter Seventy

Nola's entry into the goaded night did not mirror that of Horace. She did not have a clue where she was and men kept commenting on how attractive it is to see a women wearing hajib. Demetri had given her a watch that could trace Troy. From the beeping she could tell that Troy was close by - so close that the signal was up from two nods to five. After a day of what appeared to be effortlessly looking for the character known as Horace, as Demetri had put it -----"Horace, remember Horace!" Nola was getting tired. She raised her eyes to the painted sign of *Al Mecca*. Her mission was either to eliminate Horace or to destroy Troy. She had decided to take the former route and eliminate Troy by means of an explosion.

According to Demetri, "If explosives are placed in the cockpit, the jet is compromised." Demetri had given Nola the codes to open Troy by means of remote, "This is like hot wiring a car parked at a K-Mart," he insisted. The first motel Nola laid her eyes on was the one she decided upon - *Al Mecca*. It was seven thirty and the night was just beginning.

*

Al Mecca seemed to send off a welcoming light into the distance. When Nola arrived it was still half crowded and the place had the faint smell of Spanish perfumes floating in the air. She checked into her room and soon after that as if fate was testing its limits, Horace arrived and was given a room adjacent to Nola's room. If Horace had arrived a minute early he would have run into Nola. The problem was that Nola knew about Horace and could identify him but Horace did not know what 'the African girl looks like.'

Horace walked to his room on the second floor. He saw the adjacent door to his room close hurriedly. "Whoever it is must be running from something," he thought.

This all made Horace think how difficult the life of an undercover agent must be: the shutting doors, the secrets and the unseen enemies lurking in every corner like a dormant volcano. Then he thought about Frank Perkins. He remembered the man's dry Bourbon voice, 'remember to always have an exit kid.' He considered Frank a friend and the events on the farm as unfortunate. "It's a pity," thought Horace, "the friendship never blossomed. What was that all about?"

Horace again felt a nudging shape in his satchel; the corner of the letter from Abdullah. The ominous letter from Abdullah. After Horace had marked his territory in a pristine manner, he washed his hands and his face in a bowl. He used a piece of cloth to wash his face and this felt like using the corner of the carpet. In bed Horace could hear the noise in the adjacent room – Nola's room – he wondered what the noise was all about. Then, he leaned back and opened the letter from Abdullah.

The letter read:

Horace:

I hope that Allah may bless you and that you may have the opportunity to read this letter one day. I am writing this letter out of fear and regret. The Program is not what it appears. All along Demetri, Timmy and Bob have been working together, as sad as it sounds you have to know this. It's all been a big cover and you were used to develop the correct DNA sequence for a high-bred time traveling clone.

Horace stopped reading. His eyes raced over the letter and his heart beat faster than two horses running the Derby. He was not surprised with the Demetri and Bob connection, but had not prepared himself for the whole revelation – Timmy, Demetri and Bob, as one group.

The letter continued in a melancholic tone:

Secondly, there is someone hunting you down, a lady by the name of Nola Gumelo. She is the other time traveler handled by Demetri. She was recruited, trained and fixed by Demetri. They blame you for the death of Ibrahim; remember the taxi driver who worked for Demetri.

Third and final, my involvement with the program has always been in order to advance scientific research, climate control in Africa and disease antibodies, but now I realize that I made a mistake.

Forgive me,

Abdullah

When Horace finished reading the letter the rattling noises of the town's merchants seemed to get louder. He was angry and his eyes squinted. The instructions to enable Troy's return flight seemed too complex to figure out single handed. He got up and started walking the room.

He could not sleep and decided to take a walk outside and to absorb the evening's majestic airs. The idea of being cloned was sickening. He imagined one hundred Horaces walking around. The thought made him angry again and his eyes tightened like a wire on a ranch fence.

Adjacent, Nola was also settling in. She unpacked her turban and looked at the C4 dynamite and at the gun, all wrapped neatly in khaki cover. She removed the picture of Horace, smiling, from her bag. Somehow the man's face did not correlate with the editorial comments given by Demetri. She looked closely at the picture. The man was somewhat handsome... he did not have the poise of power hunger Mussolini nor the ambivalent desire to conquer everything. Again she put the picture down and lifted it up, looking into Horace's eyes.

"Harvard," she thought, "looks more like GQ to me."

She put the photo away for a second time and then fell into a deep sleep, almost a comatose meditation, in which she dreamt of meeting and confronting Horace.

In the courtyard in front of the Al Hambra, Horace continued walking for another hour or so. Everything was now wrong, he thought. Not only was he responsible for time travelling depolarization of the earth's magnetic poles, but he was also responsible for supplying DNA for a new high breed race of time travelers. The thought created a certain indigestion and he stopped walking, looking into the distant sky – the stars shining and the moon half full. There were no answers to be found there. He felt guilty. He had courted the dragon, shaken hands with it and now become its meal. Horace looked into the Spanish evening and far into the sky his eyes searched for an answer from God.

"Give me strength God," he said to himself and then continued thinking, "maybe Nola is watching me right now?"

In the adjacent room little did Horace know that his would be assassin was dreaming and in that dream had found Horace asleep inside Troy. In her dreams Nola found Horace asleep in his Troy and simply placed the C4 inside Horace's jet. Nola woke up in the middle of the night around 2 A.M. with a smile on her face. At that time Horace's mind was starting to get lighter and he was finally getting into bed. Still, he had no answers; somewhere out there his enemies and this Nola woman seemed to hold an upper hand. He breathed deeply and fell asleep. From in between his eyes, at his temple, one could notice that even though he was fast asleep his mind remained restless and preoccupied.

THE RETURN TO GIBRALTAR   303

CHAPTER SEVENTY ONE

The red matter in the test tubes had a glow to it and glistened when Abdullah turned the switch on. He was now looking at the harvested blood from Horace and Nola. Demetri had harvested the blood strains and created one hundred vials of test tube cultures. Now, within a matter of hours, the first fully formed fetuses would start to resemble human embryos and from thereon they could be termed test tube babies, thought Abdullah.

He proceeded into the freezer looking from one test tube to another. "These are the future time travelers of Robert Churchwell, and no doubt they would be answerable to him alone."

Abdullah did not want to go down in history as one of those despotic men who had contributed to the demise of mankind. He recalled how it seems that humankind had an even sharper memory for remembering the power hungry individuals from the past. And so Abdullah carried a bucket with hydrochloric acid in it. He started pouring the vials slowly onto the bucket, making sure he wasn't making any noise. One vial after another Abdullah proceeded determined that he would end 'The Program' on a rather 'high note.'

He proceeded like a heart surgeon scalping the capillaries with a scapular. At seventy vials Abdullah's hand started getting cold; part of the reason was that the vials were stored in a semi-frozen state, and the other part was that the vials were giving him the fear that accompanies any sort of act involving a need to cleanse one's soul for past sins. When he got to ninety vials the lights in the freezer went on. The alarm had been placed by Demetri as a last minute tool to safe guard the valued bounty. He had reasoned that one needed only two to three vials and that those had to be protected by some security system.

Abdullah hurried and quickly doomed three more vials. The alarm on the vial deck started flashing, ---- *security breach*.

The remaining seven vials started sinking downwards into self-lock mode. Abdullah hurriedly removed the three as they were half way deep into the security locking system. With four left Abdullah reached to grab another but the security vault shut and then he heard a voice from behind him.

"Abdullah what do you think you are doing? Get away from there!" Demetri shouted.

Abdullah did a 180 degree turn and said, "I had to."

Demetri looked at the bucket and the empty trays. He pulled out a 0.45 caliber and fired several shots into Abdullah. At which Abdullah fell hitting his head on the security sink, his body weight created a thumping sound.

"Sonnofagun," said Demetri. He reached for his cell phone and called Bob, who by now seemed to be an emperor in waiting.

*

"Bob we have a problem."

The voice on the other side - Bob's replied, "What is it now?"

"Abdullah has gone crazy, he destroyed the vials."

"What!"

"You are right, we have only four vials left!"

"But can we use four…"

"I think so, but now the probability of success has been greatly reduced. We might need those two clowns back."

"Oh no, it's too late for that, remember that the Troys have disengaged for return flights. So this was Ibrahim's way of getting to us."

"I think that is the message," said Demetri, looking at Abdullah, all splattered on the floor.

"The whys of this world don't matter, just how!" Bob said.

"I hear that." Demetri closed the cell phone and cleaned up Abdullah's mess.

He could not believe he was only down to four vials. He kicked Abdullah in the rib cage, "Sonnofagun, I tell you." Spoken with a Russian accent it had more bravado – everything sounds stronger in Russian, thought Demetri. He kicked Abdullah again.

CHAPTER SEVENTY TWO

The next morning Horace checked out of the motel *Al Mecca*. The hordes of men and women were already lining the front entrance giving the place the fluidity of Calcutta. He kept imagining the voice of Abdullah and the name, "Nola Gumelo."

Horace started to walk out of *Al Mecca*. Nola had also started walking to the lobby area and was paying close attention to the man in front of her who seemed light footed. She reached into her bag and unclipped the safety clip on her gun. Horace heard the gun unclick and knew Nola was around. He dashed out of the motel and turned to see who else would come out running.

From outside the motel, Horace observed a woman come out and look around. He paid close attention to what she looked like, 'Kinda cute.' He thought. Horace then headed northwards to find Zaniweri. He still had to relay the message of Rashid's whereabouts – something he did not particularly relish doing. There had been talk in the motel that Zaniweri was hiding as south as possible of Al Hambra, and that Horace should go to Morocco to find his archrival. Horace recalled that last night when he arrived on the Moroccan side, he saw lanterns at a distance. He did not make anything of them and thought of them as nothing but goat herders. Now he understood that the pattern of lanterns and shape only could have been Zaniweri. Little did he know that his guess was more accurate than he thought. The lanterns rose up in no particular military show.

Horace took the water taxi back to Morocco, for the second time. This time, the ferry was handled by an older man who seemed to be dozing off all the time. In no time Horace was back in Morocco. At midday, he spotted a camp and from a distance he saw Zaniweri himself, the big man in town, seated in the middle of close to twenty men eating and talking. Zaniweri had lost weight. But he still carried a musket and a machete!

Horace sat back into the bushes and contemplated some plan for moving forward. Although the lessons with Frank Perkins were only for two weeks he now processed information not on emotions but on strategic grounds.

In the camp Zaniweri was preparing to go scouting for Rashid yet again. In the past week, he had maintained close surveillance of the general but did not know his exact coordinates. He must have thought Allah had done a rush job on his prayers, because when he raised his eyes, in the distance he saw a figure coming into the camp.

"There is someone in the camp," Zaniweri said.

The small battalion of about fifty men scattered in the direction of Horace. A minute later, the men brought Horace to Zaniweri.

Zaniweri saw Horace's face and said, "Allah is good, really good." Zaniweri's men, led by Zahiri, forced Horace to his knees like a farmer forcing a cow in the right direction. In a primal show of masculinity, Horace quickly remembered he was for all purposes in Spain named, *Mustafa Al Mutaseed*.

"What brings you to my camp? We are close to finding your friend! Remember you helped him escape…dynamite they say. I should give you to the Spanish authorities. You are a wanted man Mustafa. I can get rich from your name."

"I never helped him, he did it on his own, you know Rashid."

"Really, now the two of you were close weren't you?"

"I am here to help you Zaniweri!"

"You punched my face in Toledo remember and then you ran…"

"Actually you tried to punch me first and I defended myself."

"Okay, so what do you want?"

"I will show you where Rashid is hiding and you can take him back to Spain!"

"And how do you know this…."

Horace looked away from Zaniweri and then back at him and said, "Trust me on this."

Zaniweri called Zahiri closer and the two men seemed to gossip a bit. Horace could hear Zahiri and Zaniweri talking. He overheard Zaniweri say, "No we kill him, he is a liar…"

The two men stopped talking and Zahiri did not look happy at all. Zaniweri leaned forward and held Horace's neck, "My dear lieutenant here says you are telling the truth. Who walks into his enemy's base camp?" Zaniweri whacked Horace with the butt of his musket and Horace fell to the ground. It seemed that with Frank's training Horace's ability to take pain had also increased.

"Tell us Mustafa, where can we find your friend ha?"

"At the high Atlas at Midlet. There is a small village thirty minutes east by mule from Midlet."

As soon as Horace finished Zaniweri said, "Zahiri take three men and go, you heard what he said."

"Yes commandante."

Horace watched the men disappear into the thick forest, their dirty boots pounding as they ran into the foliage. He vowed that he would never again sacrifice one person for the benefit of many. It was not an even exchange - one human life for seven billion. It was not a numbers game but every human life is as much a part of the whole…

Now Zaniweri instructed his other henchmen to tie Horace to a pole, and soon Horace was starting to show the signs of dehydration. From a distance he could hear Zaniweri reaffirming his position, "If he is lying, we will fix him."

CHAPTER SEVENTY THREE

At midday Horace saw from the corner of his eyes Zaniweri's men returning. Horace's eyes looked jaundiced and he was struggling to feel comfortable with the ropes holding his hands. Rashid was being pulled like an ox into the camp. Horace looked the other way and Rashid did not even see that it was his dear and long forgotten friend Mustafa Al Mutaseed tired to the termite eaten pole like a rotting piece of banana.

Zaniweri was not wasting time; from a distance Horace could see him slapping Rashid around. He pointed in the direction of the exit and the men started pulling Rashid out again. 'Heading for Spain,' thought Horace as he watched.

Horace had not eaten and now resembled an emaciated man on a spiritual fast. Little did he know that the small amount of food was helping him tighten and maintain perception and concentration. And like a quarter back he waited for the best moment when the rival team is relaxing.

Because the soldiers had not bothered to search him, Horace had managed to keep a knife on his right ankle. As night approached he remembered the knife as if the sole reason for the night was to act as camouflage. Horace remembered the words from Frank Pickens, *"There is good and bad on all sides in a fight."* Soon enough he had wrestled his hands from his back using a Japanese self-defense move designed to make one's hands escape from tight ropes ---- Houdini, imagined Horace. Again courtesy of Frank Perkins. Horace now pretended his hands were tied behind his back. He observed that the guards were on loop and at certain intervals the shift changed, at forty five minute intervals. At 8:45, Horace made his move.

The unfortunate recipient of Horace's plan for escape was a newly minted guard who still had the look of mommy's milk on his face. The young guard looked at Horace and then started his shift. He was the only moving guard while the rest were stationed in precise positions.

Horace waited patiently for his moment. The guard walked to the pole where Horace was tired and then to the gate. After every interval the guard was getting tired. On the fiftieth walk he started showing the signs of fatigue and that's when Horace struck like a cruise missile flashing through the sky. When the guard got to the pole, Horace was gone. The guard rubbed his eyes, "Impossible." Horace had timed his exit to coincide with the moment the guard leaves and under the guise of night had merely walked out of the gate pretending to be the guard going to use the bushes as his bathroom.

Outside Zaniweri's base camp, Horace lifted his leather satchel hidden in the bushes and located his electronic locator. The locator flashed: Troy forty five minutes away. Horace hit the ground running, all the conditioning from Frank now seemed to work and he felt a sense of respect for the former marine general. He ran so fast that he was now in what appeared to be a bath of sweat. A part of Horace still wanted to work with Frank. "Frank is the kind of brother, that once a brother, always a brother," Horace said to himself.

As for Troy, forty five minutes away from Horace, it noted an intruder. From Troy's central command the magnetic field was activated. Troy ran a body scan on the warm body and concluded it was a woman. Troy waited for the intruder to get closer and then when the intruder touched Troy it sent a jolt of electricity through their body sending the intruder nine feet away. It was Nola.

It took another forty minutes for Nola to recover from the jolt. This time Nola dug a hole four feet away from Troy and planted something in the ground. Troy concluded that what ever had been planted was of an explosive nature as it picked up nitroglycerine as the primary strand of its organic composition.

To avert the worse case scenario Troy started to flash and an alarm went off. Horace's locator also started flashing. Horace was five minutes away and he started running as fast as he could, his feet dug into the ground and the dust rattled off the hills like a farmer working overdrive trying to harvest every bit of corn in the field.

Horace turned the valley way and to his surprise was now facing the woman known as Nola Gumelo, the African. He reached for his gun. She did the same, but slower.

Now Horace had the upper hand and said, "Nola Gumelo, what do you think you are doing?"

Nola's gun was kicked out of her hand with a standard operations Kung Fu kick from Horace. He wasn't wasting any time with her, especially since he had the note from Abdullah.

"Horace." Nola said.

"Where did you put the explosives? I know all about you."

"And I know all about you!"

"Look, you ,....we have been set up." Horace shot back.

Just then Nola's watch indicated that Troy II was compromised. She looked at her watch and said to Horace.

"Someone has!"

"Destroyed your flight?"

"How do you know!"

"That was the plan, you and I are just collateral and are supposed to be trapped here in Spain, --- they cloned us Nola."

"Who is they!"

"It's a long story, and I need to turn off what ever you have planted, we need a ride back home."

"I have all the time. Talk!" Nola said.

Horace handed her the letter from Abdullah. "Read this!"

310

On the other side of the rock, the two heard a beeping sound. Nola's gun had accidentally triggered the remote device to the bomb.

"And that is obviously your handiwork!"

"Sorry!"

"How many minutes!"

"Four."

"We have no time. Show me at once…this is complicated. These cats followed me and lied to me, from my second year at Harvard and I can't explain how they have accomplished what they have in just two minutes."

At one minute counting, Horace started running towards Troy. He turned around and said, "Where are the explosives located?"

"On the left flank, under the wing, you won't miss it. Good luck Horace."

"Thanks, I think!"

Two minutes later, Horace dug out the explosives and started running with them in his hand. He threw it up in the air and it traveled for a good one hundred feet, tumbled downwards and exploded. The explosion turned Zaniweri's men around and pointed them in the correct direction – they had been trailing Horace since his escape and were heading in the wrong direction.

Soon Nola had arrived at Troy. She read the instructions on how to repair Troy; *she was good with instructions having realized that most people, especially men, can not follow simple directions.*

Horace opened the front deck and started looking for the disengaged stutter. The lazy Zinner, had merely pulled a plug, thinking that Horace would press enough wrong buttons to create a domino problem in Troy's mechanical set-up.

In the meantime Troy started doing a full diagnostic. Nola kept watch and said, "I see something moving."

Horace stopped and looked at the moving haze, four hundred yards way. "Zaniweri!" He said.

"…And who is Zaniweri? Do you make enemies whereever you go!"

Horace shrugged and continued looking for the dislocated stutter. Then his hand found a loose plug, something that was hanging out of place. Now all that's left was for Horace to plug it into the slot with the name 'Stutter Connect'. He did that. Troy ran a system's diagnostics and responded affirmatively, "all systems ready."

Horace said, "Thank God, thank him as my mother says."

Nola and Horace entered Troy and fastened their seat belts. They adjusted their screens and Horace turned the EMPS on; he negotiated the side stick and his favorite part – he loosened the stutter and Troy lifted up. From a distance Zaniweri started yelling and muttering something about evil and Mustafa going hand in hand. The heavy lift jet blasted into the lunar system and Horace kept an alert eye to see if anything was off. The colors, the sounds, anything…

He did not see any planetary changes and was ready to return to the world he knew. Soon he recognized the test site in Palm Springs California on screen. Troy indicated two live bodies in the flight tower. Horace responded by asking Troy.

"Do a full body identification."

"Timmy Teague and Demetri..." Horace just about laughed; Troy did not have a last name for Demetri and had put a dash sign.

Horace thought out a solution. He needed a different place to land. Horace turned away and then circled around and came back from behind, faster and sweeter, like sugar dripping from a Caribbean Plantation. He blasted the test tower. The two men were caught off guard. The explosion knocked Timmy out and Demetri managed to recover. The two men had been there trying to welcome Horace and pretend that all is well... *they needed more DNA sample*.

Troy returned a screen analysis that said: *one dead, one alive*.
Horace was finally relaxing and returning to the unmoved Horace Arthur Bates of the months past.

"How do we know that this world is correct – magnetic and systemic?" asked Nola as Troy circled away heading towards Frank's farm house in Yorba, Linda California.

Horace thought for a moment and said, "Take my cell phone and call Reuben Howard."
"The president!'
"If we did it right he is waiting for our call."

The phone rang in the oval office and carried through. "Seems like Mr. President is busy Mr. Horace." Nola said.
"Hold on!" and at that time Reuben picked up the phone, his beaming voice. "Someone has picked up the phone."
"Good evening sir, it's Horace..."
"Mr. Bates, so you made it."
"How did you know sir that all this would be in your favor sir!"

Reuben went on to explain to Horace that he had made a diary from the incident as a school teacher and kept this for himself through the process.

The man is not only smart enough to be president but also smart enough to cover his ass, Horace thought.
"Very well sir, you covered all bases."
"You could say that..."

Reuben, while running as president, had always known that there was another fight taking place in another dimension at which his destiny was being decided; somewhere in the shadows of time. The two men burst out laughing as Troy tailed and corned towards Frank's farmhouse.

"Is there anything I can give you for your service to this country and humanity, you know something private."

Horace did not miss a beat and said, "I need a bureau to monitor all this time travel business."
"You got it... like an FBI for time travel."
"Correct."
"I will be judge marshal." Horace declared.
"I like that, directly reporting to me."

"Yes…directly reporting to the president of the United States."

Reuben was ecstatic and said, "So where are you going to put Troy!"

"I know a man named Frank, a good man. He will help me."

The phone was dropped and Nola looked at Horace, "We good?"

"Ohh yes," said Horace, as he thought it through, "Tell me Nola, what are you going to do with yourself after all this. You know what they say, once you see the light, life is never the same."

"I don't know, go back to Sudan."

"We don't know who survived the blast, it's unsafe in Africa. Join me, I am starting an organization, the *Bureau of Time Travel Prevention*. I am dedicating my life to preventing the misuse of time travel. People will need licenses to time travel and for very specific reasons. I have a presidential mandate."

"Sounds like fun."

"I need you Nola."

Nola did not have a word to say and Horace pondered whether the silence meant a yes or a no.

"What will you call yourself?"

"The Bureau of Time Travel Prevention."

"I like it."

"What's your motto?"

Horace remembered Frank and said, "Veni, vici, vidi – I came, I saw, I conquered."

"Wise ass!"

"I get that from my namesake, Hoariotus, the poet."

"Silly!"

Horace had already thought about a mission statement for the organization. In developing countries, African ones especially, the fear of God is predominate. In developed countries sometimes the fear of a man surpasses the fear of God. He would avoid a situation where people feared him by making sure the organization was answerable to the whole of humanity. It belonged to everyone. At least that was the idea…

*

At the test site, the crimson setting sun shown on the face of Demetri. He was wounded, but alive. The suitcase had opened and three vials were now destroyed. By the time Demetri got to the suitcase there was one vial left and he saw the computerized freeze case registering life capability at one hundred percent. The vial was the only mix directly combining Horace and Nola's genes. It had the determined zeal to continue living through everything. The half burnt Demetri staggered away into his crown mercury and started away to Bob. As long as Bob was still alive, the program would continue…

"Better luck next time," thought Demetri, "but as long as there was still a vial capable of germination, there was hope." They would re-build the whole program - this time from the ground up.

In its seductive insistence, the skyline in California continued changing.

KEN SIBANDA, born Kissinger Nkosinathi Sibanda, is a South African born American writer and film director. A lawyer by training, he holds law degrees from the University of London (with Honors) and from Temple's Beasley School of Law in Philadelphia - LL.M (Trial Advocacy).

His most recent book is, *The Songs of Soweto: Poems from a Post-Apartheid South Africa* (Africa World Press).

In 1998 he attended the summer writing program at Columbia University in New York.

He lives in New Jersey with his family.

By Independent Research Team

$$E = h v. \qquad m = \frac{m_0}{\sqrt{1 - \frac{v^2}{c^2}}} \qquad E_K = m_0(\gamma - 1)c^2 = \frac{m_0 c^2}{\sqrt{1 - \frac{v^2}{c^2}}} - m_0 c^2$$

THE RETURN TO GIBRALTAR

*T*he law is life, and with that HORACE BATES begins a journey into a world of science and politics. Horace, a law student at Harvard, is soon at the center of a "PROGRAM" designed to enable time sequence ----- time travel.

In this rush for new science there are men like the mysterious DEMETRI IVANOVICH, who - *appears to have melted from the Russian cold war and right into the slash suburbs of America.* Men like TIMMY, the Texan, - *eager and ready for the next frontier.* HORACE must ultimately contend with who he is and what time-change does for the human heart.

KEN SIBANDA

Also the author of *The Songs of Soweto: Poems from a Post Apartheid South Africa* (Africa World Press), writing in his first novel, has penned a modern tale of origins and development, *a bildungsroman*, about HORACE BATES and how he became a man and of the consequences of modern science.

FROM THE PUBLISHER

In his first book since the publication of the *Songs of Soweto* ten years ago, Ken Sibanda's *The Return to Gibraltar* is a powerful epitaph to the invention of culture at Babel.

PRAISE FOR THE SONGS OF SOWETO

The Songs of Soweto enters the South African political dialogue with enough edge to swing the faces of old foes apart and demand to know- - when do we meet in truth?

James Burger
Columbia University

Return To Gibraltar

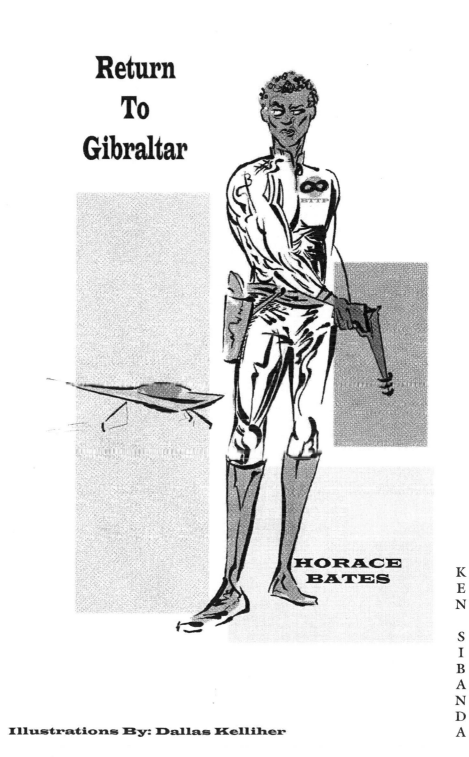

HORACE BATES

KEN SIBANDA

Illustrations By: Dallas Kelliher

CPSIA information can be obtained at www.ICGtesting.com
Printed in the USA
BVOW032334070612

292072BV00001B/4/P